THE
COLOR
OF
LIFE

A Novel

CLAUDETTE CARRIDA
JEFFREY

The Color of Life

a novel by

Claudette Carrida Jeffrey

Carrick Publishing

Copyright: Claudette Carrida Jeffrey, 2015

Print Edition 2015

ISBN 13: 978-1-77242-016-6

Also available in

Kindle Edition

e-Pub Edition

Cover Art by Joan Tillotson

Author photo by Tracey Upton

Formatted by Donna Carrick

Cover Finishing by Sara Carrick

The people, places and events in this story are entirely fictional.

Dedication

To my hometown
New Orleans
A city with a unique history
where strong women persevere

ACKNOWLEDGMENTS

My sincerest gratitude to: Julia Day, Nicole Biederman, Betty Boyle, the late Gerry DeMarco, Rita Iadarola, Jean Hamernick, Larry Jenkins, Mitzie Neisz, and all my many friends and neighbors for the motivation I received each time they asked, "How's book two coming? Almost finished?"

Many thanks to Shirley Oaks, Kimberly Payne, Matthew Iadarola and Ashley Sousa for reading and critiquing my manuscript . You spoke; I listened!

Thanks to Joan Tillotson for the beautiful front cover art.

Circumstances and situations do color life
but you have been given the mind
to choose what the color shall be.

~John Homer Miller
American Writer and Educator

PROLOGUE

1 August 1957

Dear Miss Claire Soublet,

I am sorry we were unable to meet before you left the city - my sincere apology. As Mr. Leonard Stern's business manager and executor of his will, I am sending you your great-aunt Seraphine Menard's memoir and the deed to the Esplanade house as stipulated in his will.

Mr. Stern's cousin, Joshua, was not truthful when he told you the manuscript was unsalvageable. And because Mr. Stern had reason to believe he couldn't trust his cousin, he asked that I keep the edited and retyped memoir at the office and to have it bound in leather. Joshua had no idea the copy he read and later burned was the rough draft.

After Joshua read your great-aunt's life story and learned his true identity – that he was not Mr. Stern's grandson - he unleashed a bitter tirade against

Mr. Stern. He called that elderly dying man such vile names – ones that I dare not repeat here. When Mr. Stern tried to apologize for having lied to him all those years, Joshua told him he didn't deserve to be forgiven. The next day Mr. Stern had me rewrite his will and find two witnesses and a notary. He died a week later.

In the new will, Mr. Stern left the Prytania house to Joshua, the businesses to me, and the Esplanade house to you. Joshua accused me of changing the will because he thought his cousin wasn't mentally competent to draft a new will. I showed him the signatures of two of Mr. Stern's real estate colleagues who were present when the will was changed and the notary's stamp.

Upon learning the businesses had been willed to me, Joshua was profoundly stunned. He expected to be the sole heir. He doesn't know that I saved those businesses during Mr. Stern's long illness and I've made them lucrative again. You might say…I earned them. I write this to you so that you do not think that through some kind of fraud and trickery I was able to dupe Mr. Stern into willing them to me.

Joshua told me since he no longer trusted me, he was putting the Prytania house in the hands of another agent to be sold. He said he had no need for the house as he would never return to New Orleans. When I asked him how I might get in touch with you, he refused to give me that information. After he flew back to New York, I asked the housekeeper to go through the wastebasket in his room and that is where she found it.

I'm sure by now you must have discovered what a wonderful and generous man Mr. Stern was and how he loved and cared for your great-aunt until the end of her days. And in taking care of Sera, he was also taking care of you. This is why he bequeathed the Esplanade house to you – he did not want you uprooted from your home and your life interrupted by her death. However close you had become to Sera, you had become just as close to Mr. Stern. He knew everything about you through her…because everything Sera Menard loved, Leonard Stern also loved.

The "For Sale" sign on the Esplanade property has been removed. Joshua put it there before he found out the house wasn't his to sell. Now that you've left the city, I need to know what you intend to do about the house. I have a suggestion that will allow you to keep it and have it maintained until you decide what you want to do with it.

I obtained your New York address from Josephine Gagnier when I attempted to deliver the deed and the memoir to her home the very day you left. I had my secretary wrap them and mail them along with this letter special delivery to you later on that same day. Please sign and date the enclosed document stating you received the items named in the will and mail it back to me.

I hope your great-aunt's life story satisfies your longing to know about your family – the generations that came before you – and that it answers many of the questions about her life for which you've sought answers or were curious about. Do not be disappointed about anything you read; accept it all gratefully and be thankful you get the privilege of having closure. Some of us never get that opportunity.

3

Claire, I wonder if you felt the only way to erase the hardships you encountered growing up was to leave New Orleans forever – much like running away from home. I do not say this to reprimand you for leaving...it is just to remind you that we take the past with us wherever we go. It is never left behind.

I suppose your leaving wouldn't trouble me as much if I didn't know your story. Mr. Stern was quite thorough in telling me about the way you grew up in the Seventh Ward. He told me how you were affected by first the loss of your mother, then your grandparents, and how your aunts and your uncle vanished from your life leaving you without a family – abandoned. And, of course, how Sera Menard took you in, cared for you, and helped to educate you.

I am sorry she did not find the courage, when she was alive, to tell you she was your great-aunt. It seems secrets are never uncovered in a timely or convenient manner. We are not always strong enough to handle the shock.

I was curious about what happened to you after Sera died and you found out who she was, so I took the liberty of asking Mrs. Gagnier if she knew. She told me the two of you had a mutual friend and she agreed to rent you a room after Mr. Stern's cousin asked you to vacate the Esplanade house and that you lived with her until you left for New York. She confessed to me how she hated to see you leave and how much she misses you. She loved to hear you call her Jo instead of Josephine. There were tears in her eyes.

Forgive me, please, for asking for information about your life. There was no other way to satisfy my curiosity.

4

Perhaps you'd like to know that the afternoon I went to Jo's home, she looked quite unwell. You may want to check on her. The strong, old people never complain. We must sense their pain and take care of them. They are our most valuable sources of wisdom.

I've enclosed my business card. Please call me as soon as you're settled so that we can discuss the disposition of the house.

I remain,

Edgar Souté
Attorney at Law

PART ONE

SERAPHINE MENARD
The French Quarter Dressmaker
IN HER OWN WORDS

Told to and Edited by
Leonard Stern

1

The 1878 yellow fever epidemic in New Orleans claimed my mother Cecile when she was only twenty-five leaving behind four children - my older sister Aurelia was nine, I was five, Philomene was three, and my brother Augustin wasn't yet two - and if the two babies born between Aurelia and I had lived, there would have been six of us left motherless.

Sanité, my father's mother, took care of us until she died three years later. My grandmother was a very kind and gentle person. She was a Choctaw Indian who never sat in a chair or slept in a bed. She spent most of her time sitting, squatting, or sleeping on the floor. The only time I saw her standing was when she was cooking, cleaning, or leaving the house to go to the market.

Even after the "Tignon Law" was abolished in 1843, Sanité still wore the madras kerchief to cover her head. She taught our mother how to wrap it to cover her hair and told her how the law came about as Aurelia and I watched and listened. The law was passed in 1786, she told us, and it forced free women of color to cover their heads with the same type of kerchiefs the slave women wore. The Governor was determined to tighten control over the non-Whites in the city to please the White women who felt threatened by the beautiful, free women of color who had relationships with White men.

Before the undertaker came to pick up my grandmother's body, my father removed the tignon; her waist-length, coal black hair came tumbling out. He wept as he tied a shoestring at the top of her long thick plait. He cut it off, touched it to his lips, then wrapped it with the kerchief in a pillowcase and tucked it away in a drawer. "There," he said as he pulled her now shoulder-length hair from behind her ears and gently combed through it with his fingers, "you will not be buried with your head covered." My father threw his body across his mother's and sobbed without shame. Aurelia, Philomene and I fell on top of him and cried just as hard.

I could not fully understand why my father showed how much he cared about his mother in death when he'd never treated her kindly when she was alive; I was left confused. I'd heard him tell her how ashamed he was of her – of her being Choctaw. He hated having inherited her tan skin and shiny black hair. His blue eyes came from his French father, Etienne Menard.

I think only Aurelia was old enough to appreciate that our grandmother was finally free from the hardship and prejudice she'd had to endure. She told me even though my father was crying because his mother was dead, he was also happy she was finally at peace. I, too, came to understand this many years later when I looked back on it.

My grandfather, a hunter and a trapper, spent most of his time in the swamps and the bayous. He often traded with the Indian tribes who lived where he hunted. He found Sanité among the Choctaw and brought her to New Orleans to live with him. She was already twenty-four and none of the men of her tribe wanted her for a wife. She was shunned and considered taboo by the men and the women because she had been born with a dime-size black mole in the center of her forehead. Only the children and the very old treated her with kindness.

New Orleans laws forbade Etienne to legally marry Sanité, but Father Guillard secretly heard their vows in the rectory at St. Louis Cathedral.

Etienne bought a small house in the Tremé section and had two children with Sanité. When Pauline was thirteen and my father Christophe ten, Etienne disappeared. Sanité and her children didn't know if he'd been killed or if he'd returned to France without telling them. Without a legal marriage, who could Sanité go to for help? For years they waited for him to come home, but they never heard from him again.

Etienne Menard did two decent things before he vanished. He legally left the house to his children and he taught them, as well as Sanité, to sew. He was a tailor in France before coming to America. He taught them how to make a man's suit from the collar to the hem of the pant legs. And this skill was their saving grace.

Pauline, who was blond and blue-eyed, became a *passablanc*. She was tall for her age and looked much older than her fifteen years. It took several weeks of walking around uptown in the business section of the city to find a place that was willing to trust her with piecework she could do at home. Stern Brothers, a men's store on Dryades Street, though reluctant, gave her a few trial pieces. When she returned the half dozen sets of coat sleeves, Mr. Stern was so impressed with the quality of the sewing that he gave her steady work. Pauline brought the pieces home and Sanité and Christophe helped her sew them together. At first they worked on only suit coats, then suit trousers, and eventually they were making whole suits. They survived more than four years on what they made from the piecework and from what

Sanité made at the French Market selling the herbs she grew in her garden.

For more than three years, Pauline lived in fear that one day the owner of the store would find out she was passing for White and fire her. She was beside herself when she learned that the owner's son had followed her home several times and knew her secret.

"Pauline, I'll never tell anyone about you," he told her as he tried to calm her down. "I promise you, your secret will be my secret because I love you and want to marry you."

"Why do you love me? You hardly know me. We laugh and talk sometimes, but is that enough for you...to make you a good wife? And why would you want to marry someone with a secret like mine?" Pauline refused to believe this man of means loved her and wanted to marry her. She didn't trust him no matter how pretty his words were or how sincere he sounded.

"I love everything about you. You're beautiful; you're smart; my parents think highly of you, so you're everything I want in a wife. Everyone has secrets. You're not unique in this."

"What will you tell your parents when they ask about my family?"

"I'll make up a story to tell them about where you come from and make sure they never find out the truth. How does that sound?"

"I don't know. I'm not in the habit of lying. Do you often lie to your parents?"

"Only when it's utterly important and I think my future wife's secret is that important. It doesn't matter that they're my parents, you will be my wife. So therefore, you will have my complete loyalty. Now will you marry me?"

"I must talk to my mother and my brother first." Pauline realized this opportunity would never come again.

"Pauline, there is only one thing you must do for me and, of course, for my parents. You must convert to the Jewish faith."

My aunt begged her mother and brother to understand and to forgive her when she told them she was going to marry Daniel Stern. They feared for her and wanted to know if she trusted Daniel to keep her identity secret. She assured them that she did. She also promised that she'd always be able to help them and she was true to her word. Several years after she was married, Daniel gave her the money to buy a small building for my father on Marais Street in Tremé, and then she helped him set up his own tailor shop. Pauline was in the process of converting to Judaism and Daniel was so pleased with his wife that he'd do anything to help her family.

There was only one thing he kept from her; that was what he'd told his parents about who she was and where she'd come from. Whenever she asked what he'd told them, he gave her the same answer. "You were created solely for me. I received you brand new, unscarred by hatred or abuse. I will always be thankful to God for sending you to me and indebted to your Choctaw mother who took such good care of you."

Grateful to his sister and her husband for all they were doing for him and his mother, Christophe promised them that whenever they'd need his help – no matter what they'd ask – he'd help them. At last he could see to it that his mother no longer sat on a blanket selling herbs at the foot of the French Market. Finally, he and his mother could put the market behind them.

My mother Cecile was the daughter of a Frenchman and a woman of color. When her mother died in childbirth, her father gave her to the Sisters of the Holy Family. The

Colored nuns ran a school, a church and an orphanage on Orleans Street.

My father was twelve when he first saw Cecile; she was nine. From then on, he watched her as she grew up. She came to the French Market with the nuns several times a week to buy vegetables. He hated sitting on the blanket with his mother selling herbs and had to be forced to go to the market until the day he saw Cecile. After that he went willingly. When she'd arrive, he'd quietly get up from the blanket and follow her through the stalls the whole length of the market and back again. Whenever she turned around, he'd duck and hide behind the long garlands of garlic or large chunks of meat hanging from the ceiling on hooks. He'd quickly pass the skinned rabbits and possums that were stacked one on top the other in large bins; sometimes their eyes would be open. Their smell and oozing blood always gave him the heaves. Huge tubs of live crawfish and stall after stall of freshly picked vegetables were his favorite hiding places. After Cecile left the market, he'd return to the blanket to sit once again beside his mother. He knew one day Cecile would be his wife. And so did his mother.

At fifteen, Cecile was a beauty. She had her mother's hazel eyes, her father's fair skin, and her hair hung around her shoulders in light brown ringlets – all that – and a sweet disposition, too. The nuns doted on her. They vowed to find her a suitable husband, one who would appreciate her beauty and her goodness. A few months later, before they could even begin their search, the husband they were hoping for came to them.

Christophe turned eighteen that year. He and his mother still lived in the cottage his father had left them. He was a young man with his own house and his own tailoring business; he knew he now had something to offer a wife. Christophe didn't want any wife; he wanted Cecile. Several days after his birthday, he went to the orphanage to ask the Holy Family nuns if they'd allow her to become his wife. Only after they'd met his mother, saw his house and his tailor shop did they give their consent. After they were married, Cecile confessed that she knew Christophe had followed her all those years in the market.

Cecile loved Sanité and they would often sneak off together with their heads wrapped in tignons to sell herbs at the market. My father with all his pride never knew they went or that this extra herb money kept them from going to the poor house. My mother, according to my sister Aurelia, was always pregnant and there were suddenly a lot of mouths to feed. If it hadn't been for the herbs and the handouts from Aunt Pauline, we would have surely been in a fix. My father always ignored our condition. As long as he had his tailor shop, he was happy. Of course when my mother died, he had to face reality.

Even though we existed on very little, my father managed to keep us in school. Several of the Creoles of color had small private schools in our area and somehow he scraped enough money together to pay for us to attend.

I was eleven when my father brought home a new wife, a widow. Her husband had died of tuberculosis that same year. She moved into our small cottage with her three children, not one of them over four years old. The day she arrived she told my sisters, my brother and me to call her Miss Delphine. "After all," she said, "I'm not your real mother." She changed everything about the way we lived. My father was never again the boss in his house. When we tried to complain to him about the way Delphine treated us, he turned a deaf ear.

I was immediately pulled out of school to help with the housework and the care of the younger children. Aurelia was two years away from entering teacher's college, so they allowed her to remain in school. My father said she was the brain in the family and when she became a teacher, the money she'd make would help us to have a better life. I resented my sister for a long time but tried not to show it. I didn't understand why I wasn't good enough to get an education. Why was I only good for being a nursemaid and a servant?

Aurelia tried to pacify me by telling me it wouldn't always be so hard. She promised me that as soon as she could she'd take me, Philomene and Augustin out of that house. She was loving and caring and would sneak us treats to eat late at night when we were having our lessons with her. She was constantly teaching the three of us. We four slept on the kitchen floor, and when everyone was asleep, we'd read and do arithmetic by candlelight for an hour or so or until we got sleepy. I realized later that what I learned from my sister allowed me to have a better life later on. Because of the things she taught me, I've not been foolish in my dealings in business or with people...all sorts of people. She taught me the good side of mankind; I learned the other side just getting through life.

I would have never known anything about my family had Aurelia not told me. My grandmother Sanité would talk to her and she would talk to me. When Philomene was a little older, I told her about our mother, father and grandparents. I am not sure if she passed the stories on to my brother.

For most of those years, Philomene and Augustin were too young to realize what was going on in our house. Nevertheless, they too became nursemaids as soon as they were strong enough to carry the babies. Only Aurelia was never expected to take care of the children. My father and my stepmother allowed her to finish her education without being used as a servant.

In their first two years of marriage, Delphine had three children with my father – a boy and a set of twin girls. All the children slept on pallets on the floor wherever there was space. We often woke up to find two-inch flying roaches crawling on us. The two bedrooms in the house were used by my father and Delphine. My father insisted on sleeping alone in one room because his wife was not only fat and took up most of the bed, but she wanted to talk and complain to him all night. Delphine didn't object when he left their bedroom. She now had a room and a bed all to herself and several of her cockled husband's children to relieve her of most of her household chores and motherly duties. She sat around all day watching the world roll by.

Philomene and I did all the washing, ironing, and we took care of the children. I did all the cooking. Oh, how we all hated Delphine! Even her own children loathed her. She was a fat, lazy cow and I often wondered how she'd managed to fool my father into thinking she'd be a good wife and a mother to his children. He found out almost immediately, but it was too late by then. We could only watch him as he grew more and more distant and sullen. He spent as much time as he could away from the house. And when he was at home, he was locked in his bedroom.

The twins died of whooping cough when they were eight months old. My stepmother blamed me for not taking better care of them and my father didn't defend me. I knew right then and there I'd have to get away from that house as soon as I could. But I wasn't yet sixteen. Where could I go? What could I do to support myself?

My Aunt Pauline didn't come as often now that my father had a new wife. She had been fond of my mother but disliked Delphine. She was often rude to her and most of the time would not come into the house to bring the hand-me-down clothes and the few dollars she gave our family. My aunt would send her carriage driver Jonas to the door. He'd knock, then hand the bundle to whomever answered it. My father didn't seem to care that his sister didn't come in to visit. His only interest was the envelope with money that was always in the package.

His business dwindled to a trickle, mostly inexpensive alterations. Aurelia and I used to occasionally help him in the shop, but after he married Delphine, he told us we were needed to help in the house and we never went again. Every day he cursed his sister for insisting the shop be located in Tremé instead of uptown where most of the wealthy Creoles of color had their businesses. Pauline had told him those properties were too expensive and she was only willing to buy something reasonably priced. "Take it or leave it," she'd told him. Later my father would tell Delphine he knew it wasn't the price. He knew his sister expected him to fail.

2

After the Civil War and Reconstruction, the Creoles of color were having a hard time existing under the new Jim Crow laws. The wealthy ones got out before the war started, many of them settling in France, Mexico and Cuba. Some of our neighbors and friends sold their houses and businesses and left New Orleans for parts unknown. The rest of us huddled together in one area hoping to be able to help each other survive, and above all else, we were determined to preserve our tradition, our language and our culture. I used to listen to what the old people said when they'd talk with my grandmother, and after she died, when they'd talk with my father.

We were now classified as "Negroes." All the Creoles of color were lumped in with the ex-slaves. We had always been a separate class – free people of color – neither Black nor White and never thrown together with freed slaves as we now were. My father was incensed with what was happening to us, and now that Sanité was dead, he would often talk to Aurelia. He'd tell her he needed someone to tell his troubles to because Delphine was just a country girl who wouldn't understand what he was talking about.

Watching my father try to support his family during those difficult times convinced me that when I left that house, I would not live as a Negro. I knew that I could easily pass for White because I was a combination of my mother and my father: creamy skin and light, honey-brown hair like my mother's and my father's blue eyes. Who would know what I was? Aunt Pauline got away with it and had even married a White man. I didn't want to get married, not after what I'd seen of married life. I wanted my independence, even at that early age.

My stepmother was pregnant again several months after the twins died. She gave birth to a sickly boy who needed to be rushed to Charity Hospital several times a month. He was born with respiratory problems and every time he had the slightest problem breathing, Delphine would make a beeline for the hospital. The carfare and the cost of the baby's medicine had my father frantic for money.

The next time Aunt Pauline's driver came, she wasn't waiting in the carriage for him. My father answered the door, and when he didn't see her, inquired about her. The driver told him her husband was ill and that my aunt stayed at his side to nurse him. My father sent her a note asking if there was anything he could do to help her. He couldn't resist telling her how difficult it was now that he had a sick child.

The following day my aunt came in person to respond to my father's note.

"Good evening, Christophe," Aunt Pauline said as she brushed past my father when he opened the door. She had become extremely large weighing well over three hundred pounds, so when she sat in the middle of the settee, no one else could sit on it with her. My father remained standing and as he nodded for me to excuse myself, Delphine breezed into the room and quickly slipped into the rocking chair. I didn't go far. My gut told me to hide and listen, so I stood in the dark dining room with my back against the front room wall.

"Why can't you take care of your family, Christophe?" Aunt Pauline snapped. "One sick child has not put you in dire straits. Aren't you making any money in your shop?"

When my father was slow in answering, my stepmother spoke up, "Pauline, my husband is a hard worker. Business is just slow right now. Our sick baby is God's way of testing us to see if we're strong enough to bear another cross. I know this is hard for you to understand because you're not able to have children and you're Jewish now. If you were still Catholic, I think you'd understand that this sick boy is God's will. And you being unable to have babies and all, that's also God's will. That's why I pray for you all the time asking G…"

"Be quiet, woman! I'm not interested in what you think or in your deceitful prayers. This is about money. My brother has not been able to stand on his own feet ever since he married you. You're killing this poor man with baby after baby. Shut down that baby factory of yours and take care of this house and the children you already have." My aunt took a deep loud breath while waiting for my stepmother to respond. But she said nothing. "You call yourself a wife and mother," Pauline continued, "while you give your stepchildren all of your responsibilities for the care of this home and your children. You should have ample time to help your husband any way you can."

I could hear my stepmother click her tongue against her teeth. I wished I could have seen her face, because when she got mad, it got as red as her thick, kinky hair. "Christophe, aren't you going to defend me. Say something on my behalf to your sister."

My father stayed mum.

"The twins are gone, Pauline. Christophe and I have only two children. And…I am not a baby factory!"

"Might I remind you when you came you brought three with you, you found four already here, and then you had four more. Are they not all your children?" my aunt quipped.

"Well, ah…"

"No need to answer, Delphine. My suggestion is that you try kicking Christophe out of your bed…that might help. Another way you might help your husband is by trying to earn a little money. Take in some washing and ironing; sell something on the street…like coffee or pralines. There are many good corners for you to stand on all over the *Vieux Carré*. You're not too proud are you? I'm sure you're capable of doing something to bring in a few dollars." I could hear my aunt take a deep breath. "Christophe, I am addressing you directly this time and I do not wish to be interrupted by your wife again. Put a muzzle on her!"

Delphine wasted no time leaving the front room and never saw me as she dashed through the dining room.

It was all I could do to stop myself from cheering. I began to have hope that my aunt would offer my father the kind of help that would change our lives for the better and I wouldn't have to run away. While I was busy thinking of all the things we could do if we had more money, I failed to listen to what my aunt was telling my father. Suddenly, I heard my father call me to come to the front room. He didn't raise his voice; it was as if he knew I was on the other side of the wall. I waited a short while before I made my entrance.

"Yes, Papa," I said as I stood next to him. He told me to sit in the rocking chair. We could hear the kids laughing and playing with Delphine in the back yard. There was not a hint of her having been upset only minutes before. She was laughing loudly and making animal sounds, probably chasing the children the way she always did.

"Seraphine," Papa started, "you know how hard times have been for us. And because of our problems, I've asked my sister if she would give us a little more help." Papa gave a nervous little laugh then continued. "But she's only willing to do it if I send you to live with her."

I stared at my father dumbfounded as a feeling of happiness spread like a grease fire through my body. Finally, I looked at my aunt with overwhelming gratitude in my eyes.

"No, no, no, child! I don't think you understand. My husband is ill and I need you to help me take care of him. Instead of hiring someone else, I'm going to give your father that money every month in exchange for your service in my home."

"I'm going to be a servant in your house?" The tears flooded my eyes and flowed uninterrupted down my cheeks.

She ignored my weeping. "You'll help in the house at times, but I need you mainly to help me nurse my husband. And please remember, I am not your aunt as long as you're in my home. No one can know you're related to me. My husband has always known about my family, so he is not a threat to my identity. Do I make myself clear?"

"She understands, Pauline." My father didn't allow me to answer. I averted my eyes and looked at the floor as the tears soaked the front of my dress.

"One more thing, Christophe. I think you should try to do something else. The tailoring business seems as if it's going to fail." Aunt Pauline stood up and headed for the door with my father in her wake.

"Pauline! Tailoring is the only thing I know how to do. If my shop was uptown…"

"Don't start that again. You're just not cut out to be a businessman. I think this is a good time to tell you about the shop."

"You're going to take it back?"

"I don't have to. The building wasn't bought in your name; it was bought in mine. Had you made the business pay off, I would have sold the place to you for almost nothing."

"Why haven't you told me this before now?" My father stepped in front of my aunt blocking the doorway, his face inches from hers.

Aunt Pauline was forced to back away from him. "Have you ever asked me about the deed? You've never given it a thought. As long as you are stocked with a sewing machine, cloth and thread, you don't care about anything else."

My father couldn't speak. His eyes were locked in place on my aunt; his self-respect lay trampled beneath her feet.

"You're a lazy man, Christophe. You spend most of your time in the doorway of the shop socializing with your neighbors. You know everyone who passes and no one gets away without *conte*. You must know everything that's going on in Tremé. When do you get anything done?"

"How do you know this?"

"What does it matter? If I walked past your shop or rode past it in my carriage, how would you know? You're too busy being a *mashuquette*, a gossipy woman. You don't see what's happening around you when your mouth is flapping, and when you're not in the doorway, you're sitting in your chair reading."

My father's humiliation was complete. He stepped away from the door and stared at me with watery eyes. I wondered if he expected me to come to his defense the way my stepmother had done earlier. I looked away.

"Seraphine," my aunt spoke directly to me, "I will be here next Sunday afternoon to fetch you. Please be ready when I arrive. Christophe," she nodded to my father and let herself out. My father did not reply.

With tears blinding me, I raced out to the back yard and hid between two dry sheets hanging on the clotheslines. I heard the wheels of my aunt's carriage roll over the cobblestones as it pulled away.

My stepmother summoned me from the back door, then roughly pulled me into the kitchen and slammed me down into a chair. My father had composed himself and he was already seated. He told Delphine about my aunt's proposition but not about the shop. She couldn't hide her pleasure.

"Seraphine, please," my father's tone was apologetic but firm, "I need you to go to my sister's house. I don't know how we'll survive if you don't."

"I don't want to go, Papa," I cried.

"Do you want those children, your brothers and sisters, to starve?" Delphine pointed toward the back yard with her chin where the children could be heard squabbling. I wondered if Philomene was still dancing around with the sickly baby in her arms. "You're supposed to help us. How can you be selfish at a time like this? Don't you know that God wants you to do it? And if you don't, He's going to punish you."

I couldn't hold my tongue any longer. "If you'd stop having babies, we wouldn't be so piss poor. Aunt Pauline told you the same thing. She called you a baby factory."

Delphine slapped me twice, first on one side of my face then the other. "You mean little wench; you were listening to us, and now you're trying to start some *comass* in this house." She raised her hand to hit me again but my father stopped her.

"Delphine, let me talk to Seraphine. I can make her understand," Papa told her.

I was surprised when she walked out the back door without so much as a word.

"You won't be there forever, Sera." My father hadn't called me that since my mother died. "Do you know how much it would mean to me to be able to put enough food on the table and to be able to send all the children to private school? Catholic school - where they wouldn't have to go to school with niggers."

"But Papa," I screamed, "you're sending me to be a nigger in your sister's house!"

"No, Sera, no. You're going to be like a nurse...helping your aunt take care of her husband, and at the same time you'll be helping your family have a better life." He spoke very softly in an effort to calm me down while trying to manipulate me. "When we're better off, we'll buy a bigger house and then you'll come home...that's if you're not married by then." Papa tried to laugh, but when he saw my expression hadn't changed, his laugh evaporated.

"You know I'll never come back to live with this family, Papa. You can't make any money at your tailoring shop; how are you ever going to buy a bigger house? And as for being married, who will I meet as long as I'm a nigger servant in my *passablanc* aunt's house? You're selling me like a slave, Papa, and I hate you for what you're doing to me!"

My father's nostrils flared and he raised his hand to strike me, but didn't.

Delphine came rushing in. "I heard you screaming at your papa. What have you said to upset him?"

I refused to answer. My father walked out of the room and straight out of the front door.

"Just because you've got *good hair* and blue-looking eyes doesn't make you better than everybody else. If it was up to me, I'd put your backside out on the street. You'd learn what it's like to really be hungry. But I know how you'd end up. You'd use that thing between your legs to make money and wind up a *boozan* woman in one of those one room shacks in the Vieux *Carré*." Delphine took her rosary out of her apron pocket and kissed the cross three times. Wasn't it silly, I thought? She wore the apron but I did the cooking.

Not wanting to hear another word, I jumped up and started to leave the kitchen but my stepmother grabbed me and pushed me back into the chair.

"God don't like ugly; the nuns taught me that; they taught me a lot of things. They taught me how to speak properly and how to dress and walk like a lady. I know your father thinks of me as a dumb country girl, but the nuns took the county right out of me. Seraphine, I know how hard life can be. My people were poor sharecroppers on a big farm near Baton Rouge. I hated that life, so when I was twelve one of my older brothers and I ran away. We found our way to New Orleans and that first night we slept under a wagon parked on the street. When I woke up the next morning, my brother was gone. I never saw him again. The nuns found me a few days later begging for food on the street. I…"

"The only difference in our lives is that the nuns got you for nothing," I said, "I'm being sold to Papa's sister. I work like a slave and my earnings go to you and my father."

"You've never had to live the way I had to live. Your father is a gentle man, not like my father who was always tired and mean. He found a reason to beat me every day. My mother never tried to stop him because when he started beating me, he stopped beating her. The only parts of my life that were decent were living with the nuns and the short time I was married. My husband was a good man, but when he died, I went back to a dirt poor life. There was no one around to help me until I met your father. He needed a wife; I needed a husband."

"But you're not a real wife. Philomene and I do all of your work. You…"

"Enough! God's watching you. I hope you don't think He's going to let you get away with the way you're treating your father and this family, do you? One day you're going to have to pay for what you're doing...for letting the devil tell you what to do instead of God." She held up her rosary and raised her eyes toward the ceiling. "Oh Jesus, my Savior, forgive this foolish child. Help her to see that she has to do Your bidding. Give her the courage, Lord, to do what's right. Amen."

"This is not the Lord's bidding, Miss Delphine. It's yours and Papa's."

My stepmother made her voice sweet and low, "All we're asking you to do is go to your aunt's and work there for a little while; that's all, Seraphine." When one of the children suddenly cried out as if in pain, Delphine groaned. She jumped up from her chair, shook her rosary in my face, and then rushed out to the yard.

As I sat in the kitchen hating everything and everyone, I tried to convince myself that going to Aunt Pauline's couldn't be any worse than living with Delphine and being her slave. Why, I wondered, hadn't my father hugged me or even touched me to show me that he cared about how I felt. But then, I remembered he hadn't touched any of us after my mother died. He seemed to stay away from all the children. Not once did I ever see him hold or talk to the babies he'd fathered with my stepmother.

All day I was consumed and at night I couldn't sleep wondering if there was any way I could escape my fate. I was constantly trying to think of what I might do to support myself if I ran away before my aunt came to fetch me. Like Sanité, my father and Pauline, the only thing I could do was sew. Sanité had taught Aurelia and Aurelia had taught Philomene and me not only to sew on the machine, but to make things hand-stitched. We also learned to crochet. Perhaps I could use these skills as my saving grace.

After that realization, I felt calm, resigned. Maybe I wouldn't get the chance to run away from my family's house, but I might be able to leave Aunt Pauline's. I washed and ironed my few pieces of clothing and I was ready to be picked up by Mrs. Stern as my aunt was to be called when I lived in her home.

3

When my aunt arrived on Sunday afternoon and it was time for me to go, all the children cried. The little ones clung to my legs as I walked toward the door. My stepmother told me to remember my aunt was no longer a Creole of color; she was an American Jew who lived in the Garden District. And as long as I did a good job for her, my family wouldn't suffer.

Aurelia wasn't at home to say goodbye and no one knew my father's whereabouts.

It had rained and the streets were muddy and full of water-filled holes that were hard to see. Jonas was driving very slowly on Mrs. Stern's orders. "Drive sensibly, Jonas," she had called to him, "I don't wish to have the carriage turn over and end up a casualty." There was no mention of her passenger. I guess I didn't count. Because of the carriage's slow pace, it took a long time to get to the house on Prytania Street. My aunt took advantage of this gift of time to enlighten me about what to expect at the Stern house and to lighten the mental load that seemed to burden her. She didn't stop talking until we pulled into the carriageway.

First she told me about how she ran her house.

"I am a very simple woman and I like things in simple ways. My house is not an oversized palace built for the neighbors or the curious to gawk at or to praise. It's my home, a comfortable place to live and just big enough for me to take care of the way a home should be cared for. I never have problems with my servants mainly because I don't allow them to live in my home. They all gossip and I won't have it."

"You mean I won't be living..." I wasn't allowed to finish my question.

"Don't interrupt. Before I'm done, I will have answered all of your questions. As I was saying, I don't have problems because there are only a few excuses I will accept and the servants understand that. They know I believe if you learn it the right way, you'll do it the right way. That way, there are no failures and no need for excuses." Aunt Pauline stared straight ahead never once looking at me. She hadn't mentioned her husband once. It was as if she lived alone.

Jonas hit an unavoidable hole and I bounced up several inches above the seat. My aunt grabbed me and pulled me down again. She wasn't light enough to bounce. "Jonas!" she shrieked. He mumbled something we couldn't understand.

"I have little education, Seraphine, only the elementary grades, but I read and studied after I married Mr. Stern. His father was headmaster at a boy's school in Germany before he came to America. He gladly tutored me, especially in math. He told me I needed a good knowledge of numbers in order to become a part of their business. I learned enough, but I'm still not that good with numbers.

"The Sterns were what's called Ashkenazic Jews from eastern Germany who came to America during the 1850s. Three brothers, their wives and their children arrived first in New York. One brother and his family stayed, but the other two came south with their families where they were told they'd find greater opportunities. Both men ended up peddling cloth from carts on the street. My husband's father, Isaac, buried his brother and his brother's family all having died from yellow fever right after the Civil War. The brother in New York prospered and sent Isaac a sufficient amount of money to help him open a small men's suit factory on Dryades Street, the factory that gave me a job when I was very young. Except for my husband's uncle and his family in New York, Mr. Stern has no other relatives."

I tried to interrupt again only to be told to be quiet. My aunt said I was just a listening post. She needed to talk; I needed to listen.

With her index finger an inch from the tip of my nose she warned, "I'm sure I don't have to tell you what will happen if you ever repeat any part of what I'm telling you."

She told me before her in-laws died, she and her husband lived with them in the Lower Garden District. Jonas and his wife Lizzie, who was the cook, lived in a two-room cabin in the back of the property where Jonas tended the horse and stored the carriage in a small stable next to the cabin. After the elder Sterns died, Daniel and Pauline bought the Prytania house and moved to the Garden District. They rented a larger stable with a small apartment over it out in the Gentilly area for Jonas and Lizzie.

"My house means everything to me," she said. "When I imagined what I wanted in a home, I told Mr. Stern and he went out and found it. Imagine that. I asked for a large front yard with a long brick walkway with shrubs and flowers and small trees surrounding it. I wanted large, full-grown trees all around the edge of the property that would grow larger for even more privacy. It had to have a wrap-around gallery on both floors and shutters throughout. It had to be a corner house because I wanted a carriage entrance paved with oyster shells on the side of the house, not in front. It not only looks lovely, it allows me to hear a carriage when it enters my property. I've been reading about something called a motor car being built in the near future. I hope to have one before I die so that I can get rid of that infernal horse and buggy."

Aunt Pauline continued to tell me about the house and its contents, especially the expensive mahogany pieces, all built by the premier furniture makers of New Orleans: Seignouret and Mallard.

"The man who built the house was a very progressive fellow," she said. "He also knew quality and it shows in the beauty of every piece: the beds, the armoires…every piece."

I wondered why she was telling me this. Was it her way of informing me that she expected me to keep her treasured house clean and her beautiful furniture polished? Okay, I thought, I get it. Now shut up! But she didn't. She prattled on with her unique way of dragging out most of the letters at the end of words, especially t, s, k, and ch. For a long time I fought the compulsion to put my hands over my ears. Later on I learned to filter out those sounds and just hear the gist of what she was talking about.

"Now, let's talk about you," she said. "You'll have a temporary cot set up in the upstairs study which is across the hall from my bedroom. Mr. Stern's room adjoins mine. The stairs are becoming too difficult for me to climb, so I'll be moving downstairs as soon as the additional rooms are built. I have a maid who comes in two mornings to clean, Tuesdays and Saturdays, and Jonas's wife, Lizzie, does all the cooking, washing and ironing. You'll eventually be responsible for at least one of Mr. Stern's meals." My aunt finally looked at me, and with a long drawn-out sigh she said, "We're getting close to the house, Seraphine. Do you understand what's expected of you?"

"Yes," That's all I said; that's all I wished to say.

"Look, look! This is the front of the house. Isn't it beautiful?" My aunt forgot herself and patted my arm. "It always takes my breath away." It was clear she was obsessed with her home.

"Yes, it's beautiful," I said. And it was. It was small compared to the houses around it, but it was as magnificent as any of the fine homes I'd seen in magazines. I was awestruck and wondered if my father had ever seen his sister's house.

The sound the carriage made as Jonas drove it over the oyster shells did not disappoint me. It was better than the wheels rolling over cobblestones. I will always remember not only how the shells sounded under the carriage wheels, but how their pearlized insides sparkled when the setting sun hit them. The beautiful house and the oyster shells gave me a better start at the Stern house than I had anticipated.

"Tomorrow after I deal with getting the work started on the room additions, I'll begin instructing you on how to care for Mr. Stern. Get a good night's rest, Seraphine; I'll see you bright and early in the morning." Aunt Pauline was back to barking orders and being in charge. "Jonas, help me down, and then get Seraphine settled in the upstairs study."

Early the next morning, a contractor and a group of his workers assembled in the back yard. Mrs. Stern sent me out to tell the contractor to come in because she was ready to speak with him. I brought him into the dining room. When my aunt arrived, she told me to wait in the kitchen while she talked to him.

I had developed into a consummate eavesdropper and couldn't resist learning something more about the stern Mrs. Stern. I looked for something to keep the door slightly ajar and found that a large spoon did the trick.

"Mr. Meister, do you think adding these extra rooms will compromise my house's floor plan?" My aunt started to sit and then changed her mind. Perhaps she didn't want to go through the horrors of getting out of the chair in front of the contractor. Her back was toward me and I was glad because there'd be less of a chance of her catching me in the act. But having her back to me deprived me of observing her as she spoke. She used her hands as if she were sculpting the words she was speaking and I delighted in watching her.

"It will change the overall look of the house, but certainly not compromise your floor plan. We're going to add a room on each side. The room we add next to the kitchen can serve as a maid's room, an extra pantry, or anything else you want it to be. But if you really need the space these rooms provide, it shouldn't matter." Mr. Meister took a long time before he continued. "This is a beautiful house, especially the exterior. It has such clean lines with none of those fancy brackets and ornaments all over it. I like the fact that it's a small house when you compare it to some of the other monstrosities around here. The builder did a first-rate job."

"Yes, I think so, too. When I first saw the house, I couldn't believe someone else had built it the way I would have. He must have read my thoughts from afar." Aunt Pauline gave a tight-lipped little guffaw.

"Who built this house, Mrs. Stern?" The contractor's eyes darted everywhere in the room and out of it. He seemed to be examining everything around him.

"The owner did, a Captain Leland Trinity. He was a builder and a merchant from the northeast, from Philadelphia. After the war he moved here to New Orleans. I bought the property from his widow. She wanted to return to Philadelphia to live with her children. Have you seen the house, Mr. Meister?"

"Just downstairs, ma'am. You showed it to me when I was here to give you an estimate last week."

"Oh, I'm getting forgetful. I'll have to show you the second floor. Do you have time now?"

"I have a few minutes. Do you live in this big house alone?"

"No. My husband is bedridden after having a stroke. I have a live-in nurse for him. He's been making great progress, though, with his rehabilitation. I'm hoping he'll recover completely in a few months. Now, tell me, what prompted you to ask if I live here alone? That was certainly inappropriate of you?" I couldn't see my aunt's face, but from the tone of her voice I knew she was perturbed.

"I apologize for being so forward, ma'am. I didn't mean to step out of place. I thought that if you were thinking about selling the house sometime in the near future, I'd be interested in buying it." Mr. Meister couldn't have sounded more contrite.

"You were too forward, but because you have such good references and your building reputation is spoken of so highly, I think I'll give you the benefit of the doubt, Mr. Meister. And...if ever I sell this house, I'll keep you in mind."

"Thank you, ma'am."

My aunt told the contractor to follow her just as the sound of the carriage entered the carriageway. "Please wait," she said, "I need to give my servant instructions."

I grabbed the spoon, quietly closed the door and jumped into a chair in the kitchen.

"Seraphine," my aunt called through the door, "help Jonas and Lizzie carry the marketing into the house. Then come upstairs and we'll get started. Right now, I'm going to show Mr. Meister the second floor."

4

"Seraphine."

I quickly put down the biscuit I was eating and hurried to the doorway of the dining room. Lizzie was standing behind my aunt's chair waiting to clear the breakfast dishes. Her face was expressionless. She resembled a wooden statue.

"Yes, Mrs. Stern."

"Come here, child." Aunt Pauline couldn't turn her body to look at me. She needed me to stand where she could see me without having to swivel her behind or her neck. She was a solid, immoveable, human mass once she was seated. Her neck disappeared into her shoulders; her upper arms appeared to be fused to the sides of her enormous breasts. Her lower arms and hands were the only parts of her body below her chin that moved easily.

"I've decided to go back to the store today and leave you on your own. You seem to understand what to do for Mr. Stern and he seems to be comfortable with me leaving him in your care. But I won't tolerate any mistakes, especially with his medicines. I must be able to leave this house and be gone the whole day without any worries. Do you think this is something you can handle? If not, tell me now." I heard the threat in my aunt's voice.

"I know what to do, Mrs. Stern."

"Is that all you have to say? I've been training you for almost six weeks. Aren't you more confident than that? Make me believe I can trust you with Mr. Stern's life, Seraphine!"

"I am very confident. Everything I need to know, I know," I snapped.

Lizzie's eyes opened wide as she stared at me. The look of disbelief on her face seemed to say, "If you talk to Mrs. Stern that way, there'll be consequences." I tried not to look at her as she tried to imprison me with her eyes. She slowly and deliberately shook her head from side to side sending me her nonverbal message. But to her surprise, Mrs. Stern paid no attention to my belligerence.

"By now it should be clear that living here is far better than where you were. I'm sure you don't wish to return, do you, Seraphine?" she asked me with a slight tremor in her voice.

"No, I don't want to go back," I answered. Without any doubt, I knew I wouldn't be going back to my father's that day or any other day in the future. And as for the situation I was in, I planned to do everything I could to make it temporary.

"We'll see whether or not you stay in this house. If you keep Mr. Stern clean, medicated, and as happy as he can be in his condition...you'll stay. If not, I'll have no use for you." Aunt Pauline looked at me for proof that I understood. I nodded.

"Yes ma'am would be the proper answer, not a shake of your head." She quickly motioned for Lizzie to remove the dishes from the table.

"Yes, Mrs. Stern." There'd be no "ma'am" coming from my lips even though I knew she was signaling me to be aware that another servant was present and observing my behavior.

As my aunt rose from her chair, I saw how difficult it was to pull herself up to a standing position. Her fierce grip on the end of the table made her knuckles white and her face bloody red.

She struggled to take those first three or four steps. It was the first time I realized what an effort it must have been for her to live with such a huge body. I knew that since her husband's illness, in order for my aunt to face her day to day life, getting out of the house to manage the business had to be what she desperately needed, physically and emotionally.

"Lizzie, after your work in the kitchen is done, you may go." My aunt told her the same thing every morning. Was it an order given daily so that her control was never questioned? There was no place for Lizzie to go until Jonas took her home.

"Yessum." Lizzie never seemed to look at my aunt. I asked myself if she'd learned to do that in order to peacefully exist in Mrs. Stern's house. No doubt she has to walk softly, be submissive and say as little as possible. I could do two of those...but be submissive...never!

"Seraphine will make Mr. Stern's lunch when I'm away, Lizzie. I don't need you here until six-o'clock to prepare dinner."

"Yessum."

"Tell Jonas I'm ready to leave. I'll be out directly."

"Yessum." Lizzie grabbed the dishes she had neatly stacked and ran to the kitchen.

"Are you nervous to be here all alone with Mr. Stern as your responsibility, Seraphine?"

"If Mr. Stern is satisfied with me, why should I be nervous? But isn't that the same question you already asked me? You changed the words, but you still want to know if I'm capable of taking care of your husband. I've already told you I am."

41

"You have a sharp, sassy tongue, my girl. I couldn't see Lizzie when you answered me earlier, but I know she must have been pop-eyed and shocked. You must be more careful in the way you speak to me or I'll have to put you in your place with a harsher tone. I know you're still angry because you have to be here, but as it is costing you, it is costing me, also. I need you and your family needs me. So...please, don't be difficult." Aunt Pauline had said please. Even though it had come out hesitantly, she'd said it. It was the second time that morning I'd felt a little respect for her, maybe even a little pity.

When I heard the carriage pull out of the carriageway, I returned to the kitchen to finish my biscuit. I found Lizzie drying her hands on her apron after washing the dishes. Nervously, she spoke to me.

"Ah ain't sposa talk to no otha maid, but Ah got to wawn you. You cain't talk to Miz Stern like you done jes na. She ain't gon have it." Lizzie was whispering to me while she seemed to be listening for the carriage to return, even though it had just left the yard. I think she was afraid Jonas would catch her talking to me.

"Mrs. Stern doesn't frighten me. Slavery's over. We just work for her; she doesn't own us," I told her.

"Who you is, anyway? You Colored or White? You talk like White folks. Where you come from?" Lizzie looked at me closely and then squeezed my hair between her fingers.

"Why do you want to know that?"

"Cuz Miz Stern say to me and Jonas she was gitting a colored gal to help nurse Mistah Stern. You sposa be Colored? Cuz if you is, then you jes as white-skinned as they is." Lizzie cackled a few times but quickly put her hand over her mouth. "Ah fagits, Mistah Stern might can hea me."

I laughed to put her at ease and she laughed again, but softly. "Lizzie, my daddy is a White man. That's why I look like this." I knew I could tell her anything. How would she know what was true and what wasn't?

"Fa Miz Stern to git you to take cara her husban, don make no kina sense to me."

"Why? What's wrong with me?"

Lizzie could tell she'd hurt my feelings. "No, I don mean you got somethin wrong wit you; I mean you too pretty."

"Oh! Then why did you say that?"

"Cuz Miz Stern know her husban like the ladies, so why she wanna temp him wit you? Lissen to me, you betta watch yoself round him. Cuz he gon be all ova you. He been having extra womens on Miz Stern from the start of they marriage. She know bout em, too."

"How do you know all that?" My aunt's words about not having servants living in her home suddenly jumped out of my memory bank. When she'd told me this in the carriage, I thought she was telling me she didn't want ex-slaves around because she was prejudiced and she may have feared one of them might find out about her. Now it's possible it could have been those things, but clearly the servants had her private information even when they didn't live in her house. I had to admit to myself, I would never allow them to live in my house, either.

I realized Lizzie hadn't answered me. I asked again, "How do you know about all that?"

Again, Lizzie didn't answer. She moved about the kitchen busily tidying things up and wouldn't look at me. I walked across the room and stood in front of her blocking her from moving away from me.

"If you want me to believe you when you warn me about Mr. Stern, you have to tell me where you got this information."

Lizzie was shaking when she finally spoke. "Ah'm the ony one…and Jonas…who know dis and if Mistah Stern fin out Ah tol you, we all gonna be gone from heah. You understan me?"

"He won't find out, Lizzie. I promise you."

"Okay, Ah ma hol you to yo werd. Um…befo Mistah Stern marry Miz Stern, he had his way with evy gal his mama and daddy got to clean da house. Two of em had babies fa him. Da ol folks give em some money and dey neva come back."

"You mean the old people let him get away with that more than once? Didn't they care that those babies were their grandchildren?"

"Dem ol people don care bout them half-Black babies. Mistah Stern sho didn't care bout them babies. He made dem churen, but he don care a pound what happen to dem."

"I guess you're right." I could tell Lizzie had more to say. "Is there more?"

"I ain't tol you da bad part, yet. Mistah Stern would lie to his folks sometime and say he sick and he don go to work at da sto with dem. Whateva gal was in da house, he chase her all day lon. He be neckid and come running thu my kitchen chasin afta her. He don care Ah seen him. He humped dem gals all ova da house like a dog. Don none a dem complain; dey musta liked it."

"Lizzie, did he ever do this in front of Jonas?' I asked.

"No, chil, he neva did. It be years fo Ah tol Jonas bout it. But he knowed da kin a stuff Mistah Stern do, cuz he knowed how many times he took him to dem hoe houses in da French Qwata." Lizzie voice trailed off. She seemed to be listening again for the carriage.

"Did Mr. Stern ever chase you or try to do something to you, Lizzie?"

"No, neva. Cuz a lon time ago, he tol me if Ah wasn't so black and ugly, he'd hump me, too. And Ah was some glad, too. He say he like nice-lookin mulatta gals. So…Ah think Mistah Stern gonna like you real fin. But he sick na and cain't move too much. Ah don think he can git neckid and chase you. So you safe na."

I wondered how safe I really was. Maybe because I was his wife's niece he wouldn't try to do anything to me. I thought I was strong enough to defend myself against a sick man.

The sound of the carriage pulling in stopped whatever Lizzie was about to say. She hurriedly whispered, "Please don tell Miz Stern what I tol you."

"I won't," I told her.

When Lizzie and Jonas had gone and the house was quiet, I sat at the bottom of the staircase and cried until my eyes rebelled and my chest refused to heave. It was the first time I had been alone in the house, alone that is with just Mr. Stern who was confined to his bed. I looked around me at all the beauty in the house in which I lived as a servant…this place owned by my flesh and blood who refused to acknowledge me as a member of her family. What did my aunt think every time she looked at me? Did she regret using me as a slave? She seemed to think she was giving me a better life than I'd had at my father's. But even though her treatment was a few degrees better than how Miss Delphine treated me, there was a big difference between being free and being a slave. The Civil War had been over for almost twenty-five years and I had been born free. Yet here I was in 1890 living as someone's chattel - my aunt's human possession working as an indentured servant to support my father and his family.

All of my smart talk to Lizzie was nothing but rubbish. I wanted to appear tough and unfazed by my aunt's authoritative manner and her threats. It was difficult to accept that my once-loving father had agreed to an arrangement to have his child work as an indentured servant. But I realized he needed the money I'd make more than he needed me.

Daniel Stern and my aunt inherited the store on Dryades St. when his parents died. Under Daniel's management, it had become a high-priced men's store and only New Orleans's elite could afford to shop there. A building next to the store housed the factory. Until Daniel's illness, he ran the store and Pauline ran the factory. Now she wore both hats.

Daniel's stroke paralyzed him on the left side of his body. My aunt had just purchased a wheelchair for him, but he refused to even sit in it. He'd angrily told his wife, "When I get out of this bed, I'll either be standing on my own two feet or leaving this house wrapped in a sheet." He hadn't stammered or hesitated between the words; his speech had improved dramatically since I'd been there.

My biggest fear was helping him to relieve himself, and after talking to Lizzie, I was more afraid than ever now. I pushed the things she'd told me to a holding place in my mind.

My aunt had taken care of all his personal needs when she was at home and had never discussed with me what she did to help him. How could she forget to give me those instructions? A chamber pot was kept under the bed, but I'd still have to help him to sit on it and then help him to get off. Even though there was a water closet built inside the room, he couldn't or wouldn't walk or use his new wheelchair to get to it. But maybe I was worrying needlessly. With his improved speech, I probably wouldn't have a difficult time understanding him. Why couldn't I just ask him to tell me what I needed to do? I threw that to the back of my mind.

I tip-toed upstairs to look in on Mr. Stern and found him sound asleep. I had never seen the house and the grounds in its entirety, so I decided to take a few minutes while everything was quiet and take a tour. I wanted to see the things my aunt talked about. Since I already knew a great deal about the house, it was time to see it.

5

The workmen had spent those weeks noisily sawing, hammering and painting and had just completed the rooms a few days earlier. I was eager to see the addition to the house, especially my aunt's room. That is where I started my tour.

Aunt Pauline's room was an exact replica of the master bedroom upstairs; the one Mr. Stern was in. I wondered when she'd moved to the bedroom next to his. Had they ever shared a bed? Maybe that's why they had no children. The armoire was only partially filled. It seemed my aunt wasn't interested in clothes. The dresses, skirts, blouses and coats she did have were very conservative and all in dark colors. They suited her personality.

The house was everything Pauline Stern had bragged about. Even though as a servant I wasn't able to enjoy my surroundings, I was aware that a profound change had taken place in my life. Instead of smelling the outhouse at my father's, I could inhale the many fragrances planted in every corner of the grounds. There were lemon and orange and magnolia trees; roses, lilies, jasmine and gardenia bushes; many colors of crepe myrtle, oleander and mimosas. And many plants and trees I had never seen. Lush green vines grew everywhere.

I thought about how I loved the smell of the books in the study where I'd slept. The cot hadn't been comfortable, but it was better than a pallet on the kitchen floor. I was excited to get up during the night when the Sterns were asleep to touch and sniff the leather bound books. I held them with the hem of my nightgown so that I wouldn't leave my fingerprints on them. I would look inside each one to see if I could read and understand anything that was written. That came to an end when Pauline moved downstairs and I moved into her old room.

My room had a bed and an armoire which were considerably smaller than the original pieces and made of pine not mahogany, but they were brand new. Mr. Stern's bed clothes, the linen for his bed, and the wheelchair were kept in my room, as well as his medicines, rubbing lotions and toiletries. There was an adjoining door to his room. An open stand with three shelves was next to the door. It held everything I needed to take care of him.

My aunt cautioned me not to think I was getting special treatment. She simply needed me to be close to Mr. Stern in case he needed me through the night as she was now on the first floor and unable to hear him should he need anything.

I had spent most of my time walking around the grounds smelling the air. I don't know how long I was there, but with the sudden realization that Mr. Stern might be awake and calling for me, I raced inside the house and bounded up the stairs.

"Good morning, Mr. Stern." I was completely out of breath as I stood in the doorway fighting to get air into my lungs, afraid to go into the room. To add shock to my already shaky state, Mr. Stern was sitting on the edge of the bed grinning at me.

"Look at me. I did it all by myself, but don't tell anyone, especially my wife," he snickered.

49

"Mr. Stern, I'm sorry I wasn't here. I won't tell Mrs. Stern on you, if you won't tell on me."

He started to laugh and I thought he'd never stop. "I haven't had a good laugh like that in a hundred years." Then he bent over chuckling and fell off the bed hitting the floor like a stone.

"Oh…oh my God!" I ran into the room and tried to help him up, but he was laughing so hard it was impossible. "Mr. Stern, stop laughing. I need you to help me get you back in bed."

He grabbed the bottom of my dress for support and managed to get up on his right knee. I put my arms under his armpits and lifted him the rest of the way. I didn't have as difficult a time as I had expected because although he was tall, he was thin and very lightweight. When I realized how wobbly he was, I let him lean against me for a few seconds before I gently put him back in bed. Finally, he stopped laughing.

"Are you hurt, Mr. Stern?" Please God, I silently prayed, let him say no.

"No, Seraphine, I just feel foolish. Where were you? I've been calling you for half an hour." I was surprised he wasn't angry. He was smiling up at me with large, clear blue eyes. His cheeks were a bit flushed and his hands were shaky from the fall, but I could tell it hadn't changed his mood which was always positive.

"I came up to check on you, and when I found you asleep, I went out to look at the flowers." I left out I had taken a tour of the house.

"Beautiful, aren't they? Mrs. Stern is very proud of her home and her trees and her plants." Mr. Stern was smiling with his mouth but not with his eyes. "My wife cares more about them, than she does about me. But I don't have to tell you, do I? You've watched her. She couldn't wait to train you to take care of me so she could get back to what she loves best, the business."

I was taken aback that he'd confide such a thing to me. I knew his wife was candid, now I realized so was he. I stepped away from the bed and stared down at Daniel Stern. Who was this strangely attractive man with the left side of his face slightly angled up toward his ear? His mouth was a little curled in that corner giving him a perpetual, devilish grin. His hair was thick and silky, and except for a few black strands scattered about, it was snow white. He had the most amazing widow's peak; many of the black strands of hair formed the point on his forehead.

How could my aunt not care about this man? There was something about him that seemed familiar to me, but I couldn't get my mind to think past why my aunt didn't think more of her husband. Deep inside, I knew even though he smiled beautifully and treated me with kindness and respect, he might be the monster Lizzie had described. Maybe he just hadn't shown me that side of himself. I decided to put off forming an opinion about Mr. Stern's character.

"It's time for your bath, Mr. Stern. I'll be right back. Oh, I forgot. Do you need to relieve yourself?" I tried sending him a subliminal message to say no in order to buy more time.

He nodded. "Get the wheelchair and wheel me across the room. That'll make it easier for you." He saw the stunned look on my face. "Haven't I the right to change my mind?"

There was just enough room in the water closet to put the chair in front of the toilet. Mr. Stern had enough strength in the right side of his body to stand, twist around and sit without my help. "I'll call you when I'm ready to come out," he said.

As I waited outside the door, I wondered how I'd gotten so lucky. I hadn't realized how many things he was actually capable of doing. Perhaps, I wouldn't have to clean him if he'd moved his bowels.

"I'm all finished," he called to me with a smile in his voice, "come and get me." When I opened the door, he was sitting in the wheelchair with a smug look on his face.

Mr. Stern couldn't stop grinning when I brought him back to his bed and got him resettled. He was a happy man. But he couldn't have been any happier than I was. My job had just gotten a lot easier. And he didn't have to tell me not to tell anyone that with minimal help he was able to use the privy and the wheelchair. My lips were sealed.

I went downstairs to fill the pitcher from his wash bowl with warm water, and then went to my room to get him a clean nightshirt, towels and his morning medications. When I returned to his room, I found he had already disrobed and had the top sheet thrown loosely over his body from his hips down. I shook off the initial shock and filled the wash bowl. I dipped the washcloth in the gelatin-like, liquid soap Lizzie made, then washed, rinsed and dried his face, his neck, his arms and his body down to his waist. When I turned away to rinse out the towel, Mr. Stern threw off the sheet.

"Does that mean I must wash your privates?" My mouth was so dry my tongue stuck to the roof of my mouth.

"Now, Seraphine, you can't just wash half of me. You're my nurse. You shouldn't be embarrassed." He found the whole thing very amusing because he was laughing again.

It took a little while for me to compose myself, then I asked, "Would Mrs. Stern approve of me doing it?"

"How will she know? Are you going to tell her?" He cocked his head to one side and looked at me from under his eyelids.

"No, I won't tell her. But what do I say if she asks me?" Maybe she didn't have too much love for her husband, but I didn't think she'd want my hands all over what she must consider her personal property.

"Tell her I did it myself. She'll be happy to hear I'm making that much progress. Oh, I'm beginning to feel chilled. Seraphine, get it done, please." He had visibly begun to shake.

I put the nightshirt he had taken off around his shoulders, then I grabbed a two-finger scoop of the jelly soap and flicked it on his abdomen. I knew it was cold. Mr. Stern groaned and shivered violently. "You're a she-devil, Sera." Then he deepened his voice and grunted while he slapped his chest like a gorilla with his good hand.

Sera...he'd called me Sera. Only my father called me that. And then...I realized why he looked familiar. He and my father looked alike, except my father's skin was brown. It was their hair and eyes that were almost identical. Daniel Stern constantly smiled and always seemed happy, the way my father used to be.

"Why did you call me Sera?" I asked. I had to know how he knew this. I didn't think he had ever met my father.

"It seemed the thing to do...call you a name I know you like...the name your father calls you. Pauline told me when she used to share everything with me. May I continue to call you Sera?"

"I can't tell you what to call me, now can I, Mr. Stern? But, if you want to call me Sera, you can." I knew that in front of his wife he would never call me Sera. And even though I knew the name would be clandestine, I liked to hear him say it. I could close my eyes and see my father and remember when he used to cradle me in his arms. Daniel Stern saying it was better than not hearing it at all.

I dipped the towel in the warm water, washed his penis and his testicles, then rolled him over on his side and washed his behind. Finally, I cleaned his legs and feet. Next I massaged him with rubbing alcohol from his shoulders to his toes and then patted him down with talcum powder. The whole time I was touching him he moaned and groaned. When Mrs. Stern did it, he never made a sound. I helped him put on a clean nightshirt and gave him a glass of water to take his medication.

"Was I too rough, Mr. Stern? I heard you groaning." I looked him straight in the eye when I asked the question and he looked right back at me.

"Not a bit. A massage is supposed to have pressure applied by the hands. That's what makes it feel good. Quite the contrary, Sera, you did a wonderful job. I enjoyed my bath and my rub down. I couldn't have asked for a better nurse."

"Thank you, Mr. Stern. And thank you for telling my au..., Mrs. Stern, you trusted me to take care of you on my own." I was talking but at the same time I was asking myself if it was normal to enjoy a bath and a massage the way I think Mr. Stern had done.

I'd heard horror stories from female ex-slaves and domestics who were my neighbors when I lived at my father's. They'd told us about what had happened to them at the hands of White men, and now with Lizzie's news, I realized this could happen to me. Suddenly, my heart started thumping in my chest; I heard the heartbeats inside my ears. My hands began to shake.

"What is it, Sera? Are you afraid of me?" Daniel reached for my hand but I stepped back.

"No...ah...I'm not."

"Then why are you shaking?"

"Maybe I am...a little." I thought it best not to lie. "You're too nice to me. That makes me nervous. I don't trust anyone anymore."

"Sit down, Sera."

When I sat on the edge of his bed, he took my hand and held it on his chest. "I heard you almost slip just now and refer to my wife as your aunt. Be careful. It's all right in front of me, but not anyone else. I'm sure I don't have to tell you what consequences that would have for your aunt and ultimately for me."

"I know, Mr. Stern. That's the first time I've done that since I've been here."

"That's the only thing I ask you to be careful about. Other than that, I want you to relax around me. I'm not going to hurt you. In fact, when I'm able, I'm going to help you to find a better life for yourself. I'm aware of what goes on in this house. My left side doesn't work well, but my ears and eyes do. I know how it must hurt to be here as a live-in maid or nurse as my wife calls you. You don't deserve to be treated this way. But I can't say that I'm sorry you're here because I'm not. You've made my life worth living again and I will repay you one day."

"You would do that for me? You'd help me get away from here...and away from my father's, too. I don't want to go back to that house, because there I'm my stepmother's nursemaid. I haven't been free since my father remarried. And, Mr. Stern, I don't mind taking care of you; you make it easy. I'll do it as long as you need me to." I tried hard to blink back the tears but they were obstinate. For the first time in all the previous weeks, I didn't regret coming to the Stern house.

Mr. Stern, able to reach his shaving mirror on the washstand, handed it to me. "Here," he told me, "look at yourself. Look at how beautiful you are without all the slop women put on their faces. You don't need all that; you're naturally pretty. Go on, don't be afraid to look."

I took a quick glance, but I didn't see the beauty he saw. I saw a servant, a slave, a trapped sixteen-year-old in a faded, potato-sack dress who didn't have a future. I wanted desperately for Daniel Stern to keep the promise he had just made to me. He had given me one little kernel of hope and I was going to hold onto it with all of my might.

"I need to straighten up your room and then go downstairs to fix your lunch, Mr. Stern, so pardon me." I began to tidy up the area around his bed. I rolled his washstand to the water closet and emptied his wash bowl into the toilet and flushed it. I returned to get the chamber pot under his bed but it had been emptied and washed out. That was curious, I thought.

I looked down at Mr. Stern and found him looking up at me with a silly grin on his face. "No, it didn't empty itself. Lizzie did it when she brought up my breakfast this morning. Sera, please don't rush to prepare my lunch. I had an enormous breakfast and I won't be hungry for a while. I'd like to sleep for an hour or so. Did anyone tell you what I usually eat for lunch?"

"No." And I realized I hadn't thought to ask.

"Nothing fancy. It's always cold, mostly boiled vegetables with a little olive oil and vinegar, a small piece of cheese and a piece of bread. I'll have something sweet with tea later in the afternoon." He smiled, "Thank you, Sera. Now go and have your lunch and relax for a bit." Then he closed his eyes and turned his head away from me.

Later that evening, when Jonas dropped Lizzie off before he picked up Mrs. Stern, I had the chance to ask her if there was anything else I needed to know about the Sterns. She must have told Jonas she'd warned me about Mr. Stern and he'd forbidden her to talk to me because all she said to me was, "Ah cain't talk to you no mo. Leave me be!"

6

For one full year, every day was like the one before it. My seventeenth birthday came and went unnoticed. I had not set foot outside of the yard. Most of my waking hours were spent with Mr. Stern, either in his room or in the study. I tried hating my isolation, but I enjoyed being with Daniel and felt lucky I wasn't wiping the snotty noses of Delphine's children.

During the year, my aunt gave me little news about my family. My sister Aurelia was less than one year away from receiving her teaching certificate from Straight University. She'd put my father on notice that as soon as she secured a teaching position, she was going to move out of his house and take my sister Philomene and my brother Augustin with her. My father's last child with Delphine, the sickly boy, had died. And to my aunt's delight, my stepmother wasn't pregnant.

As time passed, I had less and less longing for my father and my siblings. I rarely thought about them. After all, I'd never received a message of any kind from them. Eventually, my aunt's scraps of news seemed to be about people I didn't know.

Lizzie continued to prepare Mr. Stern's breakfast and dinner while I made his lunch and gave him his daily bath and medications. Life would have been boring had it not been for Daniel Stern's kindness and generosity. He constantly suggested activities we could do to relieve the monotony.

We also shared another huge secret.

Daniel began to get some movement in his left hand and foot. It took a great deal of concentration and effort before he could get his thumb, his index finger and his big toe to move. Even though he would get completely exhausted after each try, not a day went by that he didn't try at least ten times. His leg and thigh still had no feeling in them. He was overjoyed his speech came back to what it had been before the stroke, and because he liked to talk a lot, he said he would not have been the same man had he lost his ability to speak clearly.

We also used the wheelchair to transport Daniel to the study. He often read to me and told me stories about what he remembered about New York and Germany. We could only go to the study on the days the maid wasn't in the house to clean or Jonas wasn't roaming around looking for small things that needed to be repaired. I often wondered if my aunt was sending him to spy on me to see if I was doing my job.

My aunt never inquired about her husband's progress. Daniel said his wife was focused on the business – his progress was solely in his hands. But one day he planned to surprise her, but only when he was able to walk down the staircase unassisted.

I learned to play chess and often beat Daniel. He also taught me a variety of card games and how to gamble. Any money I won from him, he allowed me to keep. "Remember," he said, "make sure you hide these coins well. My wife is a good detective. She may claim to have a valid reason to search your room one day. So make sure you put them in a place you're sure she won't look."

I took his advice and wrapped them in a page I tore out of a magazine and then hid them in one of the dictionaries in the study.

Aunt Pauline decided to teach me to sew. I didn't tell her I had already been taught. She claimed to be tired of looking at my threadbare, homespun dresses. I was still wearing the two dresses and one shirtwaist and skirt I had brought with me from my father's house.

I no longer went to church, so I had no special outfit set aside for Sundays and holidays. In fact, I hadn't been to church since my grandmother's death. With all of Delphine's rants about God, heaven and hell, she never went to church and had never christened any of her children. I don't think she was religious at all; I think she used religion to bully the people around her, especially the children and my father.

My aunt turned the new room next to the kitchen into a sewing room. She purchased a new Singer machine and for two hours on Sunday mornings, she taught me to sew. She was so impressed with how quickly I learned, she said she wished she could have me work in her factory. Pauline professed to be thinking about my future. "You won't always have this job," she said. "Perhaps you're learning something you can fall back on when you're through here."

I allowed her to believe my sewing ability came solely from her teachings.

She'd said…job. Don't people get paid when they have a job? But in a sense she was right. I did have a job. I worked for her but she gave my wages to my father.

I let her comments pass. I wanted to learn as much about sewing as I could so that I would have that skill to make money when I left the house on Prytania Street. Whatever day an opportunity to leave presented itself, I wanted to be ready and able to take care of myself.

Pauline brought home a dozen different bolts of material. There were cottons, seersuckers, chambrays, gabardines and wools. She gave me permission to make anything I wished to make with the fabric. I was speechless at her generosity and thanked her profusely to which she replied, "I'm not doing this for you; I'm doing it for me. I won't have a shabby looking creature in my home. You've become an embarrassment to me with your cheap, thin clothing. Your clothes are not only threadbare; they're too small for you. You're bursting out at the seams." She was staring at my breasts.

I was insulted and couldn't hold my tongue. "Why are you embarrassed? Very few people come here. No one sees me."

"I see you and I'm the only one who matters." My aunt turned abruptly and left the sewing room. She grunted loudly as she made her way to the stairs where she'd lose her breath climbing to her husband's room. I could hear her grunting and panting with every step she took.

Except for Wednesday evenings, Sunday was the only other day Pauline attempted to climb to the second floor. She spent the entire day with Daniel, giving him a bath, a massage and a shave. She talked the whole time; he rarely said a word. She chattered on about the business, the employees, but mostly about all the new inventions...things she'd like to see installed in the house. With my ear to the door whenever I was in my room, I'd hear Aunt Pauline talking about how having the latest innovations would make their life easier to manage. As she prattled on, her husband mumbled something unintelligible the whole time to which she paid no attention.

My aunt subscribed to Good Housekeeping, Harper's Bazaar, Ladies Home Journal and some of the local directories. Every Sunday she mounted the stairs with an armload of newspapers and a magazine or two which she'd leave at the end of the day for her husband to go through during the week.

Lizzie brought up their lunch and dinner and snacks in between. She made bread pudding with a whiskey sauce every Sunday for dessert. It was Daniel's favorite. That was the only day Lizzie and Jonas spent the entire day at the house.

On Wednesday evenings, the plant and the store managers came to the house for a seven-o'clock meeting with Pauline and Daniel in Daniel's room to discuss the company's business and go over the books. In spite of Pauline's knowledge about the personnel, the raw material and the final products at the factory and the store, she wasn't very good at accounting. The books had always been her husband's forte.

Daniel loved those meetings. He said they gave him a chance to feel useful. He needed to feel current and not passé, and as much as he loved those working evenings, my aunt loathed them. She never let them run over two hours. Lizzie was ordered to serve tea and nothing else.

I wasn't allowed out of my room as long as the managers were in the house. Daniel told me he thought his wife insisted this be done because she didn't trust the men. She thought I'd distract them and she didn't want them to get out of place with me. But it wasn't what I thought. She didn't want to explain who I was, why my room was so close to Daniel's, and why she trusted me with her husband. I don't think she wanted rumors to start.

After eavesdropping on their meetings every week for half an hour or so, I used the rest of the time on those evenings to go to the sewing room. Besides making several plain dresses for myself, which pleased my aunt immensely, I taught myself to make miniature versions of some of the fashions I saw in the magazines. I hid those from her the way I did the coins. When I showed them to Daniel, he told me I was very talented and that sewing might be something I could use to become independent.

One Wednesday evening, the meeting was longer than usual and the talking louder than I'd ever heard it. It was Daniel's voice that rose above all the others. Pauline and the managers were quiet as they listened to his tirade. I couldn't understand everything, but it seemed there were discrepancies in the books and neither the managers nor my aunt knew why.

Several weeks later, my aunt informed me we were going to have one of Daniel's cousins living with us. He was an accountant from New York.

With her finger wagging in my face my aunt informed me, "He's just a few years older than you, Seraphine. To me, this means trouble. My husband doesn't think so, but there's no convincing me. So here is my warning to you: Do not engage in any sexual activity with this man or you will be turned out into the street. Don't get caught up in his advances…telling you how pretty you are or wanting a few touches here and there. Do not allow him to turn your head to mush with his sweet whisperings. Men are all the same. They want only one thing."

7

Leonard Stern arrived a month later. He was the opposite of Daniel: medium height, gray-green eyes and sandy blond hair. What he did have was Daniel's warm smile.

He was given the room directly across from Daniel's which made me uncomfortable, especially after the warning I'd received from Pauline. I was relieved, though, when I realized she'd put him to work immediately and that he would leave with her every morning to go to the factory and the store and wouldn't be around the house during the day except Sunday afternoons.

Sunday mornings Leonard went to church – the Catholic Church. Daniel was perturbed when he learned his cousin had converted to Catholicism while he was in college. It was easier, Leonard said, to be Catholic than Jewish. Many more doors were open to him and he liked doing things the easy way. And certainly, in New Orleans, being Catholic was going to make entering its society much less difficult than if he were a Jew.

I couldn't understand why Daniel was so upset. He and my aunt didn't practice their faith, as far as I could tell. I never heard any mention of a temple. No rabbi ever came to the house which was unusual because I thought most men of God always visited the sick. No holy days or holidays of any kind were ever celebrated. As for Sundays, they were considered days of rest. I wasn't unhappy with how I thought they viewed religion because after all the believing and praying I'd done, God had let me down. When I needed Him most, he'd abandoned me.

From then on, all the Wednesday meetings had only three participants: Daniel, Pauline and Leonard. According to Daniel, the business was back to normal in a matter of months. The managers had been replaced and the profits had begun to soar beyond their expectations. Leonard was a business genius, my aunt said. I had never seen her happier.

"Daniel, where did you find that nurse?" Leonard was dressed for work as he stood over his cousin's bed rolling his eyes and stroking his moustache. "That is what she's supposed to be, correct?" The smirk on his face said it all. He didn't believe I was only a nurse to his cousin.

"Keep your voice down, Leonard. Seraphine is on the other side of that door. I don't want her to hear that kind of talk." I was sure Daniel could see me peeking through the crack in the door. The moment I heard Leonard say Daniel's name, I flew to my usual spot to listen in. And although he had never confronted me about my eavesdropping, I was sure Daniel knew I did it all the time.

"Why are you being so protective of a servant? Could it be because she's beautiful? And succulent, I might add." Leonard closed his eyes and shivered while he rubbed his palms together. "Daniel, you're paralyzed! How, in God's name, can a lovely young thing like that be of any use to you?" He cackled like a mad man, then gave Daniel a hard smack on his thigh.

"Stop, Leonard! You're only amusing yourself. I appreciate everything you've done for the business...the way you cleaned it up and made the changes necessary for it to prosper. But please don't think that gives you the right to shit on me. I pay you a good wage and I give you room and board. I will not allow you to insult me in my own house. Is that clear?" Daniel's voice was shaking with rage.

"Oh, cousin, calm yourself. You don't want to have another stroke, do you?" The real concern in Leonard's voice surprised me.

"Don't patronize me, Leonard. I don't want you making nasty insinuations about my nurse. Do I make myself clear?"

"Yes, you do. But what is even clearer to me, my dear cousin, is that you're thin-skinned. You do not take my joshing very well."

"You were not joshing; you were insulting me. And I won't have it."

"Well then, please accept my apology, Daniel. It was not my intention to insult you. I was only trying to point out my surprise at seeing your nurse was not a Negro woman but a fair young damsel. I'm young, twenty-three years old. I appreciate beautiful women. Please don't hold that against me." Leonard breathed in deeply through his nose and then let it out loudly through his mouth in a show of exasperation. He ran his thumb and forefinger over the length of his moustache several times.

Daniel was quiet. I think he was trying to decide whether or not he wanted to accept Leonard's apology.

"Actually, I just stopped in to say good morning. We're leaving for the store in a few minutes." Leonard's voice was now softer and contrite. He moved closer to the bed. "May I return your breakfast tray to the kitchen?"

"No, thank you. Lizzie will come up for it as soon as she's finished serving breakfast to you and my wife." Daniel's voice was more controlled. "I'll see you tonight for our meeting."

I didn't go downstairs for my breakfast until everyone had gone. Lizzie had left me two biscuits and three pieces of crispy bacon. I gobbled them up and washed them down with water. I didn't take the time to heat coffee and milk for *café au lait*. I wanted to get upstairs as soon as I could.

When I got to his room, Daniel was quietly lying in bed staring up at the ceiling. He didn't say good morning to me and I took the cue to mean he wished to be left alone.

"Mr. Stern, do you want your bath now? If not, I'll come back later." I stood in the doorway and didn't enter the room.

"Come in, Sera, come in. I would like my bath, but I don't want to talk." He sat up suddenly and stuck his left arm in the air without much effort, and then moved all the fingers on that hand as he brought his arm down and rested it on his stomach. "I may not be twenty-three years old, but I'm not dead, yet."

"No, Mr. Stern, you're definitely not dead." I laughed when I said it and so did he. I was very comfortable talking to him. I felt I could tell him anything. He trusted me and I trusted him.

Daniel was quiet and lost in thought while I sponged his upper body. But when I put the liquid soap on his belly, he began to watch me. His eyes went from my face to my body, then to my hand. He followed my hand closely as I put the warm, wet cloth on him and began to wash his genital area. I felt him shudder. And as I began to wash his penis, it hardened and began to grow larger under the washcloth. I gasped and quickly pulled back my hand.

"No! Don't take away your hand, Sera." Daniel grabbed my hand and tried to put it back on the towel. I pulled my hand out of his grasp and backed up far enough away so that he couldn't reach me. I stood rigid, unable to say a word.

"Sera, look!" he screamed and snatched off the cloth. "Look at what's happened." And as fast as his organ had hardened and grown, it softened and shriveled.

I was dumbfounded and could only stare. Did I do that, I asked myself? Oh God, what have I done? I started to cry.

"No, Sera, no, don't cry. You didn't do anything wrong. You did something right...for me. You've given me back a very important part of my life." Daniel looked down at his penis. "Even though it didn't last long, I know I'll be able to do it again...we'll be able to do it again," he corrected himself.

I was still crying. Somehow I knew something else was going on inside me. It was guilt, my guilt. I had felt myself shudder when Daniel did and I was tempted to continue washing him when I felt him harden. I fought the urge to allow him to put my hand back on his penis. I didn't want to admit to myself that I felt excited. My heart was racing; I couldn't think clearly. Then suddenly my stepmother's voice rang out inside my head, "You're a slut, a whore, and a sinner." I wept even harder. I felt I needed to purge those nasty feelings from my mind and my body. How did they take hold of me and why? I had no experience in sexual matters.

"Come here, Sera. Sit down and stop crying." Daniel patted a spot on the edge of his bed.

Reluctantly, I sat.

Daniel pulled me against him wrapping both his arms around me. He held me close to him until I stopped crying. "Look," he said, "you've done it again." He had another erection. I tried to wriggle out of his arms but he held me fast. "No, stay here for a moment and let me enjoy it." He twisted me around and put his lips on mine. "Kiss me, Sera. Do you know how to kiss?"

"No, Mr. Stern." I could hardly breathe. "Please let me go. This is wrong. Your wife should be doing this with you. I don't know much about this sort of thing, but I know this isn't what we should be doing." I felt Daniel's arms loosen and I sprang up from the bed.

"My wife, you say, ask my wife. I can't ask my wife, Sera. She hasn't been a wife to me for almost ten years. What you did for me, you didn't do on purpose. It simply happened. Please don't blame yourself. You're a beautiful young woman; I wish I could make love to you. I wish you wanted to let me make love to you." Daniel hesitated as if he couldn't decide whether to continue talking. "I don't know what I'd do if I didn't see you everyday. I miss you on Sundays."

Daniel decided to finish washing his private area himself. "I don't need a massage today. Give me a clean nightshirt and just sprinkle some powder on me."

I did as Daniel asked, then cleaned up the area. "Should I get the book you were reading to me yesterday?" I asked but knew the answer before he spoke.

"Not today, Sera. I need to be alone to have some time to think. I'll call you if I need you before lunch. I hope I haven't frightened you and caused you to be afraid of me, have I?"

"No, Mr. Stern. I'm not afraid of you." And I wasn't. I was afraid of myself. Was I like the women who allowed him to treat them like dogs - to hump them whenever he wished?

I no longer went to church; I no longer had my older sister to confide in. I was no longer wrapped in the arms of God. But why wasn't I? Why was this problem being thrust upon me when I had done what Delphine told me God wanted me to do? Why couldn't He let me get through whatever my time was at the Sterns without changing how Daniel treated me? I did not want him to be like the men my ex-slave neighbors told me about or like the man Lizzie had witnessed. I certainly didn't want to be the object of his desires. I should not be made to feel guilty because I felt stirrings that may relate to me maturing. I felt ill with worry, but there was no one to counsel me. Where was God?

8

Month after month went by and Daniel remained withdrawn. Each morning I brought the water, but he insisted on giving himself a bath. He refused the massages and powdered himself. The wheelchair was now kept in his room and on the days I was with him, he wheeled himself to the water closet. Most days he'd send me away to find something else to do to amuse myself. I began to feel as if he no longer needed me. By seeing less of Daniel, I began to feel less guilty and I started to relax.

When I listened in on the Wednesday meetings, I could barely hear the little he had to contribute. My aunt and Leonard did most of the talking.

I was unaware of any other visits Leonard made to Daniel's room, except for their Wednesday meetings.

The factory was being renovated and the sewing staff was laid off during that period. That allowed Pauline and Leonard to spend their mornings at home and their evenings inspecting the work at the factory that was taking place around the clock. The store seemed to be well managed without them hovering over the person they'd put in charge.

Leonard used that time to expand his accounting business. He rented a small office in the business district and began to spend his mornings there. He said all sorts of business people sought his services - some mob bosses and a few of the madams who had houses in the French Quarter.

Pauline was upset he was spending less time taking care of Stern business, but Leonard assured her that everything was in order and he didn't need to spend more than a few hours a week going over the books and several hours a day checking the factory and the store. He told her she shouldn't worry. The factory manager knew Leonard had to sign off on any material orders before they were placed and he always had the papers ready for Leonard's signature whenever he was in the factory. His office was only minutes from the store and he could arrive in a timely manner if he was needed.

Pauline did not tell Daniel about Leonard's new business venture for several months after the renovations were done and the work schedule was back to normal. When she decided to tell him, Daniel was not as accepting as his wife. Pauline, afraid Leonard would leave altogether, tried to diffuse her husband's anger.

"I think we should wait and see if his business will interfere with what he has been doing for us." There was a hint of pleading, perhaps even a little fear in her voice. As I listened in on their Sunday conversation, I felt sorry for my aunt. She seemed afraid to let her husband dismiss his cousin and have the store and factory go into the red again.

"If Leonard is only giving us a few hours a week, we should pay him accordingly. And if he can afford an office, he should be able to afford a place to live and the food he eats. Why should we give him his original salary and room and board, too?" Daniel was using his low, rumbling voice, the one that always made his wife back down. He didn't use it often, but she seemed to understand that no amount of disagreeing with him made him change his mind.

"What do you want me to do, Daniel?"

"Ask him to find another place to live and let him know he will only be paid for work rendered. I will talk to him if you won't do it."

"No, I'll talk to him, but I want to wait until I feel comfortable with his reduced hours. You forget, you're still incapacitated and I'll be running both places alone...again. I don't want another disaster like the last time. When are you going to be able to walk again and resume your position at the store, Daniel? I need you; I can't do it alone anymore." She was nervous and all the consonants crackled when she spoke. She was speaking so fast, it was difficult to understand her. She sounded as if she was going to lose her breath.

"Why don't you talk to my limbs, Pauline? Perhaps they'll obey you. I can only recover as fast as my body allows me to. Do you think I've enjoyed being confined to this house for more than three years? I've forgotten what the first floor of our house looks like. You added on to it, but I have yet to see what you've done. Don't you think I'd like to sit at the dining room table and enjoy a meal? Do you think I'm having fun being paralyzed, Pauline?"

"Of course not, Daniel." My aunt was indignant. "How can you think that of me? It's just that you look so healthy. It seems as though you ought to be walking by now. Have you at least been trying?"

"I'll walk when I walk, Pauline. I can't tell you any more than that." Daniel was annoyed.

As I peeped through the cracked door, I could see his right arm flailing in the air as he talked. He kept his left arm at his side as if it were still paralyzed. His wife had no idea how much he had progressed. Perhaps even I wasn't privy to everything he was able to do.

Pauline changed the subject. She might have been a tyrant with others, but she knew when to back down with Daniel.

72

Everything changed on Prytania Street when Lizzie was killed. After preparing dinner for the Sterns one Friday evening, Lizzie and Jonas were returning to their apartment in Gentilly when the carriage hit a hole in the street. Lizzie was thrown from the driver's seat where she was seated next to Jonas. She landed under the wheels of a passing carriage.

Jonas was given the weekend off so that he could take his wife's body to Thibodaux to be buried on the farm where her family sharecropped. He wrapped her body in several blankets and tied it securely to the floorboard beneath the driver's seat.

Aunt Pauline cooked Saturday and Sunday while I served and cleaned up. It was the first Sunday she didn't climb the stairs to spend the day with her husband. I brought all his meals to him. Daniel said he felt sad for Jonas; he and Lizzie had been together a long time. My aunt showed no emotion at all. She didn't mention losing Lizzie until Monday morning.

"Seraphine, I have no time right now to find a cook and washerwoman to replace Lizzie. I must turn to you to fill in as our cook...our permanent cook. You'll also have to go to the market with Jonas to get what you need for your kitchen. I don't think you're needed as much anymore by Mr. Stern; he seems able to get along with less help these days. He still isn't ready to come downstairs, but at least he's trying to use his wheelchair now. As soon as he gets the complete use of that left arm, I think he'll be wheeling himself around the second floor. I'd like him to go out on the gallery and get a bit of sun. Do you ever take him out there?"

"No...uh...I've asked him if he'd like to go out, but...but he always refuses." I had trouble getting out my answer because I was still reeling from her pronouncement about my new job as the cook.

Aunt Pauline was seated at the dining room table and I was standing halfway between the table and the kitchen door. She was working on some sort of list and the only words I could read were: washing and ironing. Good Lord, I thought, don't tell me if she doesn't find someone to do the rest of Lizzie's chores, they'll fall on my shoulders. There was no doubt I had grown soft and no longer used to hard work ever since I'd been nursing Daniel. My stomach started to churn violently at the thought of having to market, cook, serve and then clean up the dishes and the kitchen in my new job, plus help Daniel.

The urge to scream out how much I hated my aunt for the way she had interrupted my life was overwhelming. I was beginning to believe I would never be able to leave that house unless I did something drastic to get out from under her. It was the first time I felt as if I could commit murder...or suicide.

"Do you understand your new duties, Seraphine?" My aunt didn't look at me. She was still busy jotting down things on her list.

"Yes," I replied angrily unable to hide the hate that had taken possession of me.

"Oh my, what a nasty attitude! But I have only myself to blame. I've allowed you too much leisure time. But, no more. You'll have much less freedom with the kitchen added to your responsibilities."

"Good morning." Leonard breezed into the dining room expecting his morning coffee. His smile dissolved when he noticed the empty table. He smiled again after Pauline explained to him what was going to take place.

"Are you a good cook, Seraphine?" He hadn't spoken to me since he and Daniel had words about me that morning months before. He would walk past me without acknowledging my presence. But as he'd pass, he'd slide his eyes down my frame from my head to my feet. I thought of him as a snake, uncoiled but still dangerous. I didn't want to ever be alone with him in the house. I was thankful Daniel was always there.

As I opened my mouth to answer, my aunt spoke for me. "She's one of the older girls in her family. She cooked to help her stepmother." Pauline gave me a look that told me she was telling the tale so I'd better remain silent.

"Good," Leonard said, "I look forward to having some wonderful dinners. Lizzie was a good cook, but all she knew was meat and potatoes. Do you know how to make…gumbos, jambalayas, étouffées…all those spicy Creole dishes? I've eaten them in restaurants, but I'm sure when they're homemade, they must be even better."

"Leonard," again my aunt doesn't allow me to answer, "those dishes are rarely cooked in this house. Daniel and I prefer plain food. The spices don't seem to agree with my stomach. Once in a while, Lizzie made a Creole dish, mainly for Daniel. I've instructed Seraphine to follow the same routine. I'm afraid you'll have to stick to restaurants that make high quality Creole food and frequent them."

Aunt Pauline had lied. She hadn't told me what she wanted me to cook. I got the impression I was at liberty to cook whatever I wished, since I would be going to the market to purchase what I needed for "my" kitchen.

Not only did she tell little white lies, she had failed to carry out her husband's instructions to tell Leonard about his pay cut and to ask him to move out. It was unlikely he would have requested special dishes if he knew he wouldn't be around to eat them. I didn't think my aunt wanted him to leave. It occurred to me she might enjoy having a partner again, even if he wasn't her spouse. She had breakfast with Leonard every morning and then they spent the whole day working together until he opened his office. But even then, they still rode home and had dinner together. The only thing they didn't do was sleep together.

"Seraphine, only Mr. Stern requires a full breakfast. Leonard and I have coffee and biscuits which is quite sufficient for us. What you'll do for dinner has already been discussed." My aunt rose slowly and painfully from her chair. Leonard rushed to assist her. "You're such a gentleman, Leonard," she gave him a big smile in spite of her pain.

"Why, thank you, ma'am," he answered with a phony southern accent as he bowed to her.

"There's no time for us to wait for you to prepare anything this morning, Seraphine. But we'll expect coffee and biscuits tomorrow morning. I'll have Jonas take us to Café du Monde for a quick bite." My aunt shook her head as she ran a gloved hand through the air, "It's such an inconvenience to stop before getting to the store, but I suppose a change of pace would be nice. Tell Jonas we're ready to leave."

9

My aunt's marketing system was unique. Even though she never had to do the shopping, she made it easy and money-free for Jonas and me the same way she'd made it for Jonas and Lizzie. Every merchant in the Poydras Market knew the Sterns, both generations of them.

Pauline asked that I wear a bonnet or a hat that covered all of my hair and told me to be sure I didn't chat with the men who owned the stalls. She said I should do what Jonas did – say as little as possible. Whatever we needed to buy, we picked it out, the vendor wrapped it up and that was that. Once a month, Jonas would take Pauline to the market to pay for our purchases. I wondered if any of them ever cheated her. It would have been so easy to doctor the bills. When I asked her why she trusted the merchants, she told me there were times when she believed in the honor system, but only when there was no other way of getting something done.

I was struck by how ironic it was that she was able to trust anyone when she was mean, calculating, unemotional and unforgiving. So, trusting Daniel, Leonard and me to live the way we lived without being crazed every second she wasn't around to observe us, meant she had no alternative. I concluded even though she was difficult to understand, the more I knew about her, the greater the chance I'd be able to walk away from her house instead of running away from it.

I'd wait for Jonas to go off to buy horse feed and whatever else he needed and I'd talk to all the merchants. I was flattered when I saw them fighting for my attention and I milked it for all it was worth. When Jonas returned, it was back to business and the men understood what they must do. They all gave *lagniappe* and were overly generous to me. I knew how to keep Jonas's mouth closed; I shared my loot with him. I sent him home with candy, fruit, bread, pastries and anything else the shopkeepers had given me as my "little something extra."

I always put those treats on Daniel's meal trays whenever my aunt or Leonard weren't at home. He enjoyed peppermints, horehound drops, French creams, éclairs and many different types of sweets I received as lagniappe. These were things he usually didn't get to eat because if Pauline didn't eat it, she didn't buy it. When she paid her monthly bill, the merchants gave her the receipts and she checked them to see what we'd bought. I guess the honor system did not apply to Jonas and me.

Jonas didn't wait long to replace his wife. One Sunday morning six months after he'd buried Lizzie, he brought Daisy, a young woman half his age, to meet Pauline. He asked my aunt if she'd give Daisy Lizzie's old job.

Pauline questioned Daisy about her knowledge of cooking, washing, ironing and some of the other tasks Lizzie had done. When she was satisfied with the information Daisy gave her, she told Jonas she'd think it over and let him know in a few days.

Just as the couple was about to leave, Leonard waltzed into the dining room on his way to church.

"Mornin, Mistah Leonard," Jonas greeted him as he entered the room.

"Good morning, Jonas," then he bowed to my aunt, "Mrs. Stern." He looked past Jonas and Daisy to where I was standing with my back against the kitchen door and simply nodded.

"And who is this?" he pointed to Daisy who had a mischievous smile on her face. She was wearing a tight-fitting chemise with her breasts begging to be freed. Her long, chestnut-brown arms were dangling at her sides. A thin wrap hung from one shoulder. Leonard took a long, hard look at her and she did not take her eyes off him.

"This here's, Daisy, ma new wife, suh," Jonas grinned with pride as Daisy giggled. "Miss Stern say she might give her a job. That sho would make it easy fa me if she work wit me." It was more than I'd ever heard Jonas say in any conversation.

"Congratulations, Jonas. Good luck to you and your new wife." Leonard looked at me and made a gesture of sipping with his cup. I read that to mean he'd like his coffee. I didn't budge; he'd get it when I'd decide to give it to him.

"Thank you, suh. We bes be gittin along." Jonas grabbed Daisy's hand and roughly pulled her along after him as they left the dining room. Daisy continued her flirty look at Leonard as she was being dragged away.

After I served my aunt and Leonard breakfast, I brought Daniel his tray. When they were at home, Daniel and I had a strict nurse-patient relationship. There was never any kind of relaxed conversation between us. When he seemed out of sorts, I usually brought his food and left his room immediately and went down to eat my own meal.

"Seraphine, come into the dining room. I want to talk to you." It seemed my aunt always knew when I was taking my last few bites to ask for something or want to talk to me.

"I'll be there in a moment. I need to dry my hands." I yelled to her knowing she'd be furious, but I was intent on finishing my breakfast. I wiped my mouth and my hands on my apron when I had finished, then I pulled the door open.

My aunt had managed to turn slightly to look toward the door and there she sat glaring at me with fire in her eyes.

"What is it, Mrs. Stern?" I asked nonchalantly. I was happy to see Leonard had gone.

"I think since Lizzie's gone and you've taken over the kitchen, you think you run this house now. Don't push me too far, Seraphine. I'll have to slap you back in your place and you won't like it one bit." She was out of breath when she finished.

"I made too many biscuits and I was trying to wrap them up to keep them soft. I thought someone might like them later on today," I lied. But how would she know? She couldn't move fast enough to ever catch me at anything. I was the hare; she was the turtle.

"Sit down," she said. "I have a few things to discuss with you. By the way, when you took up Mr. Stern's tray, did you tell him why I wasn't eating breakfast with him?"

"I told him Jonas was here and you'd be up later."

"You've a good head on your shoulders, Seraphine. You're a thinker; I like that. Uh, before you sit down, take off that soiled apron." Pauline patted the table in front of where she wanted me to sit.

I pulled off my apron, folded it neatly, and put it in my lap as I sat in the chair next to her.

It was the first time I'd ever sat at the dining room table. I could feel my cheeks become inflamed and wondered if it showed.

"Your father is ill," my aunt blurted out. "I don't know how bad it is."

"Where is he?" I asked.

"At home with Delphine. But there's no one there to help her. When Aurelia moved away with Philomene and Augustin, your father cursed them and told him he never wanted to see any of Cecile's children again while he was alive or dead."

"I don't think my father meant what he said. When did you find out he was ill?"

"Last week. I didn't want to tell you before I knew how sick he is and what's wrong with him. I found Aurelia listed in the City Directory and sent Jonas with a note informing her of your father's illness. She hasn't replied and I don't know if they've gone to see him."

"What should I do?" I asked. Surely my father hadn't disowned me. Even though I'm one of Cecile's children, he couldn't have meant me...not the one who's kept him and his family from starving the past few years.

"Nothing right now. I plan to have Jonas take me to the house tomorrow afternoon. If his sickness is not contagious, I'll go in to see him and find out what can be done for him." My aunt couldn't hide her sadness. Her eyes welled up with tears, but she fought them back. She seemed to refuse to allow them to fall because that would be a display of emotion.

I was numb. It was difficult being told my father had rejected me while he was still exploiting me. All I could feel was bitterness; there was not much left to feel for the man who was ill.

"How old is my father?" I don't know why I asked the question.

"Oh...let's see. He's three years younger than me." Aunt Pauline glanced all around as if someone might be listening to us, then lowered her voice to a whisper. "He was born in 1849 and this is 1893...that makes him...what?" She waited for me to do the arithmetic.

"Forty-four," I said, "he's not that old." That made my aunt forty-seven. She looked a lot older than her years. Her hair was a yellow-gray pulled tightly in a bun at the nape of her neck. The skin on her face wasn't wrinkled, but the lines and creases in her forehead and around her mouth told quite a bit about her life. I suppose in trying to hide her size, she completely covered herself from her neck to her toes. Nothing was exposed except her head and her hands. My father always talked about my aunt's beautiful eyes. They were the only things that hadn't changed.

They were as clear and sky blue as they must have been when she was a bright-eyed little girl.

"Seraphine...why do you stare at me as if you're seeing me for the first time? Pay attention to what I'm saying." My aunt was annoyed. She tapped her spoon loudly on her coffee cup as if to wake me up. I noticed she wore no rings on her fingers. Maybe her fingers had become too big and her rings no longer fit. Nothing about her suggested she was married.

"If I'm able to see your father tomorrow, I will tell him what I plan to do if he should die." Pauline was back to dollars and cents and there was never any emotion involved when she spoke of or handled money. "Delphine and her children will have to move. I plan to sell the house and the tailor shop."

When I had no comment she continued. "For your service to Mr. Stern and me and also because the money is partly Menard money, I'm going to give Leonard the entire sum to invest for you. It will be somewhat like a trust fund. Had your sisters and brother communicated with me, I would feel compelled to have them share in the money, but they chose to ignore me."

"I don't understand why they haven't gotten in touch with you. Don't they know I'm still here with you?"

"No, they don't and that's your father's doing. He was tired of them asking him when you were coming home, so he told them you'd run off from here with a White man."

"You knew he'd done that and you never told me!"

"What difference would it have made? This happened two years ago. I desperately needed you to take care of my husband and your father desperately needed the money. How could he ask me to give you back to him; how could I have done so?"

The tears ran down my face in rivulets. I took the apron from my lap and buried my face in it wiping away the hot, angry tears.

"Seraphine, it's too late to change what happened then. Listen to me. When your services are no longer needed here, Leonard will release the money to you unless something unforeseen happens that would cause me to change my mind."

"When do you think my services will no longer be needed, Mrs. Stern?" Even when she was trying to do something that made her seem human, she found a way to spoil the moment with a show of force and control. She offered you a handful of hope with a closed fist.

"A thank you would be appropriate." Her lips were tightly pursed.

"Thank you. Please answer my question." I wasn't going to let her ignore me. She'd told me not to fall apart and I didn't intend to.

"I don't have a crystal ball; I can't possibly know that. It really depends on Mr. Stern. If you're instrumental in speeding up his recovery and he's well enough to return to the store, I'll discharge you that day. Of course, if he dies, that will automatically release you."

Every synapse in my body seemed to be firing at the same time. It was hard for me to stay seated. "Do you really mean that? The day Mr. Stern returns to the store, I'm free to leave here." I stared into her eyes looking for truth.

"That is what I said. Have you ever known me to say anything I didn't mean?"

"No."

"Well then, get busy helping Mr. Stern get back on his feet and ready to start back to work. Now let's talk about Jonas and his new wife. What do you think of Daisy?"

She was asking my opinion – that was curious. Maybe she thought one slave ought to know about another one. Or maybe it's what people say: you lose your meanness when you're about to die. No, I thought, she's still too mean; must be some other reason.

When we heard Mr. Stern calling my aunt, she told me to think about Daisy and she'd find out what I thought later.

I would have said anything, done anything to get out of cooking when I first took over after Lizzie's death. But I had grown to enjoy getting out of the house to go marketing in the carriage. Even though I was told to sit next to Jonas on the driver's seat – Lizzie's death seat – I loved taking the ride because I had not ridden in the carriage since the day I arrived at the Prytania house. I had forgotten what the city looked like. The American sector where my aunt lived was so different from the Tremé section where I had lived. It was so much newer and everything was so much bigger.

10

I loved cooking in a fully-equipped mid-1890s kitchen. My aunt bragged about having one of the first gas-powered ranges. It had six burners and two ovens. I wasn't limited in how many things I could cook at one time. The kitchen had a place for everything and everything had to be in its place. Pauline occasionally cooked and she would raise the roof if the things she planned to use were not where she wanted them to be. I was amazed at the size of the pantry and the many tables, some of them with drawers to store the eating utensils. I admired the beautiful, blue tile that went halfway up the kitchen walls. Jonas washed the hardwood floor once a week. He'd throw buckets of water on it, scrub it with a straw broom, and then sweep the water out into the carriageway.

The Sterns seemed to enjoy all the dishes I prepared, Leonard in particular. It made me giddy to see him licking his fork. He no longer ignored me when he passed me in the house; he'd find something complimentary to say about something I had cooked.

"What about Daisy?" my aunt asked. She'd summoned me from the kitchen once again.

"Daisy...ah...I think she's a little too young for Jonas," I said. "She gave Leonard a few 'come and get it looks.' What are you thinking of hiring her to do?" I held my breath hoping my aunt wouldn't say to cook.

"I'd never allow that slutty thing in my house. And yes, I did see the way she was looking at Leonard. Jonas saw it, too. That's why he dragged her out of here as fast as he did. The only thing I'd hire her to do would be to wash and iron. She can do that where they live in Gentilly, the same way Lizzie used to do it. I've never wanted any washing and ironing done here. I'm sure Jonas will help her. The cleaning woman is doing the laundry right now, but she's a sloppy ironer. I have to find someone else." My aunt tapped the table with her fingernail, "Do you think Daisy would make a good washerwoman?"

"If she washes and irons as good as she flirts, she'll be fine." My aunt gave a small guffaw and nodded her head. There was no reason to say anything more because I was overjoyed I would retain my control over the kitchen and wouldn't have to worry about getting any more of Lizzie's chores dumped on me. I was feeling full of myself, but it only lasted a few seconds.

"I'll try her for a while, but I don't think she'll last. She's not the type to be a good, steady worker. She looks like a good-time woman and I don't think Jonas will ever control her. She's going to make him sorry he ever married her. I wouldn't be surprised if he didn't pick her up off the street like a stray dog."

"I don't think Jonas would pick up a woman on the street. He doesn't look like that type of man. He's so quiet." That was my opinion, but my aunt had known him a long time.

"Men do strange things when they're lonely. Besides, Jonas likes to fix things…take care of things. You can bet that hussy saw that right away. That kind of woman looks for a man like him to latch on to. She knew he was a good catch." My aunt grunted in disgust, "Uh, uh, uh…I hope those motor cars will be available soon. And when they are, I'm going to replace Jonas with one. Then I'll send him back to Lizzie's family in Thibodaux."

"Why?"

"Because the only family he knows is Lizzie's," she said.

I was tempted to ask Aunt Pauline how she knew what lonely men did.

It was ten o'clock the next night when my aunt's carriage pulled into the yard. I had been sitting in the kitchen for hours waiting for news about my father. I could tell whatever she had learned wasn't good because she didn't wait to get to the dining room to take off her coat, hat and gloves. She peeled them off and handed them to me as she made her way through the kitchen and into the dining room where she finally leaned against a chair out of breath.

"I'm afraid he's dead…your father is dead." She started to cry but forced back her tears. "Delphine took him to Charity Hospital. He di…died early this afternoon."

"What was wrong with him?" I asked with not as much sadness as I should have had. "Was Delphine with him when he died?" I wanted to know if he'd been left to die alone.

"No, she wasn't with him. I went to the house first where I found out she had taken him to the hospital yesterday and left him there. When I spoke to the nurse at the hospital who tended to him, she told me his heart just gave out and I didn't ask her any more questions. I went to Blandin Funeral Home to have them pick up his body. They've arranged the burial for Wednesday. I'm going to put him in the vault with your mother Cecile in St. Roch Cemetery. Don't you think he'd want to be there?"

"I don't know what he'd want. The man who died isn't the father I remember." I looked at the floor not wanting to see my aunt's face when I asked, "I would like to know something, though. Who did you tell the hospital you were in order to claim his body?"

"You don't fear me at all, do you? You say anything that comes into your head. I'm only going to answer your question because it's about your father and maybe you have a right to know." She paused and sighed heavily. I hadn't heard the whistling consonants in a long time, but when she began again, they were back with a vengeance. Now I knew for sure that when Pauline was extremely nervous or angry her speech was affected. "I told the hospital Christophe was an illegitimate son my father had with an Indian woman and that he was poor and unable to pay for his own burial. My explanation must have satisfied the hospital because I wasn't asked any other questions."

"Illegitimate!" I screamed, "Shame on you! How could you…"

"Quiet! I did what I had to do to make things less problematic. You'll understand that one day. You must do whatever it takes to get what you want done. Sometimes lying is necessary." My aunt hadn't sat down. She began to walk again, this time toward her bedroom. "Is Mr. Stern awake?" she asked.

"I don't know; I haven't been upstairs for a few hours."

"Why haven't you? I thought he liked your company." I detected a pinch of sarcasm.

Before I allowed myself to think I blurted out, "He hasn't wanted my company for a long time. He…" I almost said he didn't trust himself around me anymore. "Umm…I don't understand what's happening to Mr. Stern. He never seems to be in a good mood lately. So I only do for him what he asks me to do." I followed my aunt to her room. She stopped in front of her door.

"Mr. Stern is unhappy with me right now and maybe he's taking it out on you because I'm gone most of the time. Don't take it to heart; he'll get back to his old self again before too long. I'm very tired. Goodnight, Seraphine. Oh, has the young Mr. Stern come in?"

"No, he hasn't. Um...Mrs. Stern, who's going to my father's funeral?" I stepped in front of her and blocked the doorway.

"I don't know at this point. Now listen, it isn't going to be a funeral, just a burial. If you want to go, I'll have Jonas take you." Even though she was grieving her brother's death, she didn't intend to miss one day at her business to see him buried.

"Someone has to go. If you and the rest of my family aren't going, then I will go." I said.

"I'll arrange it." My aunt ignored my thorny statement. "I went to the house where your sisters and brother live to tell them about your father's burial. Jonas knocked, but when no one answered, he pushed the note I had given him between the front door shutter slats. He said he could see someone peeping at him through the lace curtains at the window. I suppose you'll see them at the cemetery should they decide to go."

"And what about his wife? Won't she be there?"

"I went back to your father's house after I left the funeral home and I confronted Delphine. She had no defense for leaving your father at the hospital to die alone and didn't seem interested in his burial. I asked her to be out of the house by the end of the month. That's all for tonight, Seraphine. Goodnight." Aunt Pauline pushed past me and closed the door behind her.

Wednesday was a dreary, rainy day. Leonard and my aunt were ready for the office a little earlier than usual so that Jonas could take them to the store before he took me to the cemetery. Since I didn't have to prepare breakfast for them, I was dressed and waiting to go to the cemetery when they walked through the kitchen.

My aunt's mouth dropped open in shock. She grabbed me and spun me around in order to see me from all sides. She patted my full skirt and touched the stand-up collar on my shirtwaist with mutton sleeves. She examined the way I'd made a piece of felt into a circle with the center cut out and then pushed it down on my head to fit like a crown. I sewed all the pieces of lace together to form a sash, put it over the felt crown, and then pulled it down the sides of my face to tie under my chin. I pinned three fresh gardenias on the left side of the hat above my ear.

"Did you make these out of the material I gave you?" Pauline didn't seem to want to believe it. She'd brought me a large piece of black, wool gabardine to make into a dress, a small square of thick, black felt and several, long pieces of black lace in which to fashion into a hat.

I was afraid to answer. Finally I managed to say, "Yes, I made them. What's wrong with them?"

"Not one thing as far as I can see." Leonard was eyeing me up and down; his face filled with approval.

My aunt shot him a look of disapproval, but it only lasted a second. "They're lovely, Seraphine. I see I've taught you well. We must talk later about this talent of yours. Come, Leonard, put your eyes back in their sockets. Jonas is waiting for us."

My father's casket had been left on the ground next to the wall of vaults early that morning. The rain was heavy at times and the umbrella my aunt let me use didn't do much to shield me. As much as we tried to avoid sinking up to our ankles in the mud, it was unavoidable. The sexton, who led us to the site, told us because of the rain we had only a few minutes to say prayers or conduct any other rites we wished to perform. He wanted to get the coffin into the vault as soon as possible. Besides the sexton, Jonas and I were the only other people in the cemetery. My father, no matter what he did or said, did not deserve the burial he was given on such a sad, soggy day.

I hoped he had received the last rites in the hospital because there was no priest to speak and no prayer book to read from to offer his body up to God. I recited all the prayers I could remember until we were told it was time to leave.

On our way back to the house, the rain came down in a deluge. My new dress and hat were soaked through and through. Jonas rolled over a rock and we almost catapulted out of the driver's seat. I was never so eager to see the Prytania house as I was that day.

Daniel didn't know his wife hadn't told Leonard about his pay cut or that he had to find another place to live. One Sunday when he asked her if it had been done, she told him she hadn't gotten around to it. Daniel was infuriated.

"You've let me believe this whole year that Leonard was out looking for a set of rooms or a house," he bellowed. "You sent yesterday's paper for me to read about how successful he's become. The article said he's so busy he's had to hire an assistant. He sure as hell no longer needs us. Why haven't you told him, Pauline?" Daniel was sitting in the wheelchair next to his bed. My aunt had just taken him out to sit a while on the gallery after breakfast.

"He's your family, Daniel. He's young and smart; he deserves his success. Besides, he's become like a son to me. I

91

enjoy his company and I hate the thought of not having him in the house with us."

"He should be looking for a wife at his age. Now that he's such a big businessman, it's time for him to have his own family. We gave him his start, Pauline, just as his grandfather gave my father his start. But that's all I intend to do for him. And the least he can do is to tell us he's giving us fewer hours, so that we pay him less. That's what an honorable man would do. But not my cousin, he's simply greedy."

"I don't think he's taking advantage of us, Daniel. He's just trying to establish himself and I don't mind helping him."

"Well, you may want to do that, but I don't. He shouldn't expect us to finance his accounting business." Daniel rolled his wheelchair around in circles as Pauline stared in disbelief.

"Why did you have me push you out on the gallery when you can roll yourself? And you have the nerve to call Leonard dishonorable. How much of your paralysis have you been faking, Daniel?" My aunt's eyes were wild with distrust.

"If you'd bring yourself up the stairs more often, you'd know how much I can do." Daniel's voice had risen to a shout. "Don't try to get me off the subject, Pauline, and the subject is Leonard. That same newspaper article said he's also interested in investments. Well, since he's dabbling in investments, and I'm expected to invest in him while he establishes himself, then I'd like to see dividends on my investment. So what I suggest, is that you tell him we're going to pay him only for hours worked, and tell him this afternoon or I will."

I couldn't see Pauline's face through the small crack in the door, but the anxiety in her voice told me she was angry and close to tears. "What do you want me to tell him about moving?"

"I'm willing to give him two or three months to find a place, but he needs to start looking. I hope you're happy now that you can have your imitation son a little while longer." Daniel stressed the word imitation. He rose from the wheelchair and fell face down on his bed. After he straightened himself in the bed he said, "I don't care to have any company today, Pauline. Find something else to do with your Sunday."

There was a short silence before my aunt began to sniff.

"Don't sniffle and snort. It annoys me and it doesn't become you. Remember, you're my unemotional wife." I had never heard Daniel speak so abrasively to his wife.

My aunt took a handkerchief out of the pocket of her skirt, wiped her eyes, then blew her nose. "I'm not going anywhere until you tell me what's wrong between you and Leonard. You don't talk about it and when I ask him, he tells me everything is fine. But I know there are bad feelings between you...I can feel it."

"There was a small problem, but it isn't anything for you to be concerned about. We hashed it out and it's over."

"It isn't over, Daniel. I can feel the tension in the room when you're together. But, never mind. I can see there's nothing I can do about it." Pauline grabbed the bed post and began pulling herself out of the chair. "I need to call down to Seraphine and tell her it's time to start lunch."

"Go down, Pauline, and tell her. Didn't I just tell you I didn't want any company today? Have you forgotten? Have Seraphine bring up my lunch in an hour."

Even though I scurried out of my room, I knew I didn't have to rush. Before my aunt could exit the room and get to the head of the stairs, I'd have made it to the kitchen and would be waiting to answer her call. I found being one step ahead of Aunt Pauline gave me great satisfaction.

11

"Good morning, Sera." Daniel was standing holding on to one of the posts at the foot of his bed. He looked steady on his feet. I hadn't seen him look so chipper since I'd become the full time cook.

"Good morning, Mr. Stern. It's nice to see you smiling again. Would you like me to change your bed while you eat your lunch? You didn't want breakfast, so I brought you some fruit in case you're extra hungry." I set the tray on the small table near the window. He had begun pulling his wheelchair up to the table to eat his meals.

"Not today, thank you. Sit down for a minute; I'd like to talk to you." When I didn't sit immediately, Daniel lunged toward me throwing me backward onto the bed. He sat next to me and placed his hand on my stomach preventing me from rising. "Stay where you are, Sera. Let me enjoy looking at you for a little while. I've been deprived of you for a long time and it seems like years to me. Let me soak you in with my eyes."

"No!" I struggled to get up but Daniel pushed me down harder. He was much stronger than he looked. "I want to get up, Mr. Stern. Please let me get up." My heart was pounding and I could feel the fear rising up and closing my throat. This was not the feeling of excitement I'd felt previously when I'd touched Daniel. When I tried to pry his hands off my belly, he jumped up and straddled me, sitting on my thighs.

"I'm hungry for a woman, but not any woman. I don't want to wait any longer, Sera; I've decided today is the day." Daniel tore open my bodice and ripped apart my chemise. He grabbed my breasts, squeezed and kneaded them as he groaned loudly. He pulled up his nightshirt and when he couldn't get it to stay up near his chest, he got up on his knees and took it off. Then he sat again, this time on my pelvic area with his hard penis resting on my stomach.

As he fondled my breasts he asked, "Don't you like this? Doesn't this feel good to you? You should be excited. What's wrong with you?" He was beginning to sound agitated. "Touch me, Sera, touch me." He grabbed my hands and tried to force me to touch his erection, but I stiffened my arms so rigidly he couldn't pull them up.

"I don't want to touch you, Mr. Stern. I want to get up. Please," I screamed, "please let me get up!" But no matter how much I screamed and writhed, Daniel continued his assault.

"I don't want you to scream, Sera." When I didn't stop, he leaned over and pulled out his handkerchief from under his pillow, the one he used to blow his nose and spit phlegm. He jammed it into my mouth. "When you stop screaming, I'll take it out."

I gagged and choked and tried to cough it out, but couldn't.

"I'm going to suckle you like a baby and you're going to feel it in here." He tried to shove his hands between my legs, but my skirt and undergarments were in his way. Like a savage, he clawed at my clothing until he tore every piece away from my body. He bit and sucked my neck and my breasts. My muffled screams did not deter him.

Daniel slapped me across my face; one of his fingers landed in the corner of my right eye. A sharp, hot pain shot through the eye causing my whole body to jerk. "Oh, you're giving me some movement. That's it, that's it! It's supposed to feel good to you. Now I'm going to make it feel even better." While forcing my legs apart, he slid down until he was able to forcefully enter me.

"Oh, Sera, I knew you would be wonderful. Don't cry, Sera, relax. If you relax, it won't hurt. Let yourself feel me. Oh, Sera, Sera…you're wonderful." Daniel groaned again and again as he pushed harder and deeper inside me.

I lost touch with reality. I had no screams or tears left. I lay beneath him as if I were dead.

"Sera, Sera," he repeated my name over and over again as he gyrated and violently thrashed about as he tunneled deeper into my body. "Sera, don't just lie there…help…help…" Daniel suddenly gurgled as he discharged his warm liquid and filled my insides. He continued to writhe and moan, "Sera, Sera…"

All of a sudden a shrill voice pierced the air. "Daniel! Daniel…stop! Oh God, oh God, oh God!"

I felt him freeze inside me when he heard his wife's voice. Slowly he rolled off me and sat up to face her. I was unable to move; my whole body felt like an exposed nerve.

My aunt rushed to the bed and threw the sheet over me, then pulled the handkerchief out of my mouth.

"Why, why?" she screamed. "Why did you do this, Daniel? Was it to hurt me? Look at this child. She'll never be the same. You've ruined her…you've ruined her."

Aunt Pauline helped me to sit up and she wrapped as much of what was left of my clothing around me. "Go to your room, Seraphine, and clean yourself." The moment I stood up, I realized Leonard was standing quietly in the doorway. The look on his face was a mix of horror and sympathy.

I was afraid to look at myself in the mirror. It was a small vanity mirror that didn't allow me to see all of my body at one time. First, I looked at my face, and then slowly I moved it from my face to my knees. Daniel's hand print took up the entire right side of my face and the bite marks on my neck and breasts had begun to turn purple. When I examined my body, I found bruises and scrapes made by my clothing as it was being torn away.

As I cleaned myself with soap and water, the caked blood on my thighs and the small amount around the nipples of my breasts seemed less important than what Daniel had done to me psychologically...to my trust. I had thought he and my father were the two people I could trust most in the world. But look at what my father had done to me. And now Daniel had made me believe he cared about what happened to me only to betray me. I never wanted to see his face again.

That day something broke inside me and I knew I'd never be able to repair it.

There was no need to eavesdrop on the conversation taking place in Daniel's room. All the voices involved were raised in anger.

"You're a rapist, Daniel, a wild animal who sickens me. You attacked my niece because you knew it would hurt me worse than if you'd attacked me." My aunt was shamelessly crying. "I hope you burn in hell!"

Daniel laughed. "Stop your sniveling; you're not so innocent. I haven't been able to touch you for more than ten years. After a while I gave up. I didn't have the strength to force myself upon you; there's too much blubber in the way. I finally resorted to frequenting a whorehouse until I had the stroke. But I do thank you for giving me your niece; she was better than I could have hoped for. Better, my darling wife, than you ever were."

"Daniel!" It was Leonard's voice. "Don't speak to your wife that way."

"This is no business of yours. Get out!" Daniel screamed. "You're a parasite. You're building your business on my back. You're jealous of what I have...I know...I know. And what I have that you really want is Seraphine. Don't look so shocked. I remember what you said to me about her. You've wanted to do to her what I just did, but I got to her first." He roared laughing.

"Leonard isn't going anywhere, but you are. You're going to return to the store tomorrow. If you have enough energy to overpower and sexually assault a strong young woman, you should be able to work. And if you don't, I'm going to have you committed to an asylum."

"What? You can't do that to me," Daniel's voice shook with rage.

"Yes I can. I will tell Dr. Schoenbaum what you've done and he will agree to help me commit you because no one in his right mind would do what you just did."

"He was my father's dearest friend. He would never agree to such a thing."

"Yes, he was your father's friend, but your father wasn't here these last times to help him pay his gambling debt. I helped him twice in the last couple of years. He was too ashamed to ask you. Leonard helped me hide the money I gave the doctor. I took it from the company accounts rather than from our personal assets. That was part of the discrepancy on the books that Leonard fixed. Dr. Schoenbaum was not only a friend to your parents, he was good to us. Because your father and I helped him, he has treated you free of charge since you had the stroke."

"My father helped him…you helped him…and I was kept in the dark. Why?"

"It doesn't matter now. That's all in the past; this is now. I want to know what you intend to do, Daniel?"

"What choice do I have when you threaten me? But tell me, my dear wife, how do you expect me to get down the stairs?"

"The same way you're able to move around in here and were able to climb on top of Seraphine; you should be able to figure out how to get to the bottom of the staircase. If you can't, Jonas and Leonard will carry you and your wheelchair down."

I refused to listen to any more of their shouting. I dressed myself and went down to the kitchen. Several minutes later, Leonard walked in.

"Seraphine, I'm sorry that happened to you. Is there anything I can do to help you?" Leonard cringed as he looked at my swollen face and the bruises on my neck.

"No, nothing. Is what Daniel said true? Do you want to do the same thing to me?"

"I admit to wanting you, but there is a difference between desire and rape. I would take you if you gave yourself to me, but I would never force myself upon you if you didn't want me." When Leonard saw the look on my face he added, "I know you don't believe me after what Daniel did to you, but I want to help you if you should need anything."

"The only help I need is getting away from here. Can you help me do that?"

My aunt's grunts could be heard as she made her way across the dining room and into the kitchen.

"Good," she said to Leonard, "you're with Seraphine. I thought you were so disgusted you'd left the house."

"I would never leave you and Seraphine in this kind of situation." Leonard took my aunt's arm and led her back into the dining room. He helped her to sit. I followed them and sat with them at the table.

For a long time no one spoke.

"I'm sorry." My aunt's voice trembled. She must have found it difficult to look at me because she either looked at Leonard or down at her hands she'd rested in her lap.

"Mrs. Stern," I couldn't wait a minute longer to tell her, "I can't ever go upstairs again. I cannot stay in that room next to Mr. Stern. I don't want to ever see him again. If you have no objection, I'll put a cot in the sewing room for the time being. I think it's time for me to go, for you to finally let me go."

"Not after what's happened to you, you're in no condition to be alone right now. Besides you have no place to go, Seraphine." Pauline flinched as she finally looked directly at me and saw my bruises. "Your eye, it's bloodshot. Does it hurt?"

"It burns," I told her.

"I think it's just bruised blood. It should clear up in a few days, Seraphine. Did Daniel deliberately hit you in your eye?" Leonard leaned in close to me to have a good look at it.

"His finger caught the corner of it when he slapped me in the face."

My aunt said, "You have a lot of healing to do; I'm not going to let you go anywhere."

"When Mr. Stern goes back to work tomorrow, I should be entitled to the money you gave Leonard to invest for me. It shouldn't take me too long to heal, and with that money, I can find a place to live on my own."

Leonard spoke up, "It will take me a little time to get the money, Seraphine. You'll have to stay here until then."

"All right, if I have to wait, I'll still do the cooking to earn my keep. But I can't serve the food. I won't come in contact with Mr. Stern. Someone else will have to do it. Maybe Jonas can do it for the time being."

Aunt Pauline didn't answer right away; she sat wringing her hands. I could tell she was wrestling with how best to handle the situation...and me.

"I don't trust Daniel right now, Leonard. He may try to harm Seraphine again or one of us. I don't think he's in his right mind." Pauline was quietly deliberating again. "There are two cots stored under the staircase. Seraphine will sleep in my room and if you don't mind, Leonard, I'd like you to sleep outside my door. Just for tonight; just until we can think more rationally." My aunt's eyes filled with tears as she spoke directly to me, "Who would ever think it would come to this. I'm so ashamed. I'm so sorry you've been hurt, child."

Leonard took both my hands in his. "Seraphine, I will be right outside your aunt's door all night. We're not going to let anything else happen to you. I'm so glad today is Good Friday and your aunt closed the factory and the store at noon. I don't know what would have happened had we not gotten here when we did. Oh, something just occurred to me. Did you forget, Mrs. Stern, that tomorrow is Holy Saturday? The store and the factory will be closed for the Easter holiday until Tuesday. That gives Daniel a three-day reprieve. Should I go up and tell him he doesn't have to get ready tomorrow morning?"

"No, let him stew all night, Leonard."

Leonard got up and stood behind Aunt Pauline's chair. He put his hands on her shoulders and reassured her about what he'd heard upstairs. "Mrs. Stern, I've suspected for a long time there was something strange about Seraphine's relationship to this household. I knew she wasn't just a nurse and a cook...that she was not an ordinary servant. Her beauty was my first clue. Please don't worry; your secret is safe with me."

My aunt covered her face with her hands and drew her shoulders up to her ears. When she finally spoke there was such pain and guilt in her voice. "At first I gave my brother money to make sure he stayed away from me so that I could keep my identity secret and I made him less of a man. Then I took his daughter and had her serve that ungrateful animal upstairs. And because of what I did, my niece was savagely raped by my husband. My husband raped my brother's child," my aunt repeated it in disbelief. "The gentle man I've known all these years did that horrible thing. I'm glad my brother is dead...that he's not here to know what happened to his daughter."

"How could you have known he was capable of such a thing, Mrs. Stern?" Leonard told her in an effort to comfort her.

"Do you know he tried to tell me Seraphine taunted him, tantalized him and revealed her body to him on many occasions? He said he was weak today; he didn't have the will power to resist temptation. If we had come home sooner, he told me, we would have caught her in the act of seducing him. We would have seen how determined Seraphine was to force him to want her. He said he feels betrayed that his wife would take the word of a servant over his." Aunt Pauline wiped away a few stray tears.

"Maybe he's not in touch with reality. Do you think he may have developed some mental problems from being shut in for so long?" Leonard asked my aunt.

"I suppose he could have suffered some kind of mental damage from the stroke. Dr. Schoenbaum told me he might. But frankly, I don't believe that caused his behavior. I saw the way he looked at me when I screamed at him to stop attacking Seraphine. The look was one of pure hate. If he's being anything, he's being cunning because he got caught. He simply did what he did to hurt me and I'll never forgive him.

I will remind him of it as long as we both draw breath." My aunt began to cough and couldn't seem to stop.

Leonard rushed to get her a cup of water. He suggested she lie down and rest until dinner. She quietly got up and padded off to her bedroom.

Somehow we made it through the rest of the afternoon and the evening. When my nerves had quieted down enough for me to stop shaking, I was able to cook a light, simple jambalaya for dinner. The three of us sat together in the dining room and ate – mostly in silence.

Daniel refused to open the door when Leonard took him a dinner tray. We could hear Leonard shouting to him through the door that he was leaving the tray in the event he got hungry later on.

While I cleaned the kitchen, Leonard and Aunt Pauline sat in the dining room and talked.

It was the first time I had no urge to listen in. I was physically and mentally exhausted. The only thing I wanted to do was sleep, but I knew that wasn't going to be possible given the sleeping arrangements that had been made.

When we'd all settled down for the night, my whole body was racked with pain. I could not find a comfortable position on that narrow cot in which to put myself to relieve enough of my distress and allow me to sleep. I lay in endless darkness seized by spasms of pain, attacked by ominous thoughts, and haunted by human monsters. The ugly, contorted faces of my father and Daniel Stern danced before my wide-open eyes. They threatened to harm me, and I was afraid if I closed my eyes and slept, they would make good on their threats. I lay terrified in the quiet blackness until the sun came up.

I had breakfast ready to be served when Jonas arrived shortly before eight o'clock. His curious eyes found my bruises the moment he entered the kitchen. When he asked what had happened to me, I told him I'd tripped on a soiled sheet I was carrying downstairs. His look said he didn't believe me.

Aunt Pauline sent Leonard upstairs to find out if Daniel had taken the dinner tray into his room. After a few seconds he called down from the top of the stairs, "Daniel isn't answering. The tray is still on the floor and the door is still locked. Oh wait, I forgot, I can go in through Sera's old room."

Moments later, Leonard cried out, "Pauline...Jonas, come quickly!" Jonas ran, then he stopped to help Pauline get up the stairs. Reluctantly, I followed.

Daniel was lying naked on his bed with his head propped up on his pillows. There was a white substance caked around his mouth and on his chin. The substance had run down the side of his face and formed a half-caked puddle on his chest just below his chin. Empty medicine bottles were strewn on the floor around his bed.

Pauline told Jonas to fetch the doctor who lived just half a mile away. Leonard told her not to touch Daniel even if he were still alive, to let the doctor decide what had to be done.

When Dr. Schoenbaum arrived, he pronounced Daniel dead. He said it appeared to be suicide. He told my aunt not to worry; he'd take care of everything related to registering the death. She needed to concentrate on Daniel's burial because according to Jewish custom he needed to be buried as soon as possible.

Even though Daniel hadn't belonged to nor had he attended services at a synagogue in many years, he had kept up his membership in the Harmony Club, a group of the city's elite Jews. Pauline got in touch with one of the club members who was a regular customer at Stern Brothers and he helped her to arrange the services with his rabbi and synagogue. Daniel was buried with his parents two days later in the Gates of Prayer Cemetery.

I stayed in my room whenever Pauline had guests unless she asked me to prepare and serve coffee or tea. I wanted no part in Daniel's burial. I tried not to feel responsible for his suicide, but I did. Maybe he sensed I had become curious the time I touched him, even a little excited. It was possible he thought I wanted him to entice me again and I'd finally give myself to him rather than have him force me. How could I have allowed him to throw me onto his bed? If I had steeled myself against his push, he wouldn't have been able to overpower me. I should have tried to hurt him. I could have grabbed his genitals and wrenched them which would have rendered him helpless and in severe pain. Then I could have run downstairs where he couldn't follow me. No, I thought, he could have followed me because he had been lying about his strength and the things he was able to do. Those kinds of thoughts haunted me and fortified my guilt.

I cried when no one was around. I refused to go upstairs for anything. Jonas and Leonard moved my furniture and belongings downstairs to the sewing room. And there, I felt free to cry myself to sleep every night. My body was healing but my spirit had been permanently damaged.

The short time that elapsed between Daniel's suicide and his burial made what had happened more bearable and I was grateful. My future looked bleak and it frightened me to think about it. I seemed headed for uncertainty and every ounce of my trust had been buried along with my rapist.

My aunt and Leonard made me a true part of the family. There wasn't anything I wasn't consulted about and they talked openly about everything in front of me. We ate all our meals together in the dining room. There was only one problem that was difficult to deal with: I refused to leave the house. I couldn't even go out to the yard to admire the flowers. Aunt Pauline consulted the doctor and he said it would pass with time.

Jonas was left to do the marketing on his own. I couldn't give him a list of what to get because he couldn't read. Eventually I realized I could send him with a list for each vendor and they could look through the group of lists until they found theirs. And it worked. Unfortunately, we missed lagniappe. The merchants gave it to me but would not give it to Jonas.

12

Five weeks after Daniel raped me, I began having bouts of nausea and lightheadedness.

My aunt was sitting with me in the dining room one day when she looked at me with her brow wrinkled and her eyes squeezed together expressing her sudden concern. "Your menses, you've had it lately, haven't you?"

"I don't remember when I had it. It's never been regular. Usually it's every five or six weeks. I think…ahh…," I got up and ran to the privy in my room. After vomiting for the fifth time that day, all I wanted to do was crawl into my bed and lie there until I died. I got into bed too weak to make it back to the dining room.

Several minutes later, Aunt Pauline was standing over me. "You're pregnant, Seraphine."

"No!" I screamed and started to slap my stomach as if that was the way to expel whatever was in there.

"Stop," my aunt took hold of my hands. "You're pregnant and you can't change that fact. Sit up, Seraphine," she was tender but firm. "Do you want to have a child…this child?"

"No, I'll hate it. I don't want anything to remind me of the monster who lived upstairs." I shivered and started to cry.

I could feel Daniel's body on top of mine and feel his teeth as they dug into my neck and my breasts.

"Stop the tears, Seraphine; this is your time to be strong. I was never able to have children, and you have one encounter with the same man and he makes you pregnant. And for me, that is difficult to swallow. But…if I were younger, I'd raise your child. Unfortunately, I'm too old and sick now. So…what will we do with this baby?" Aunt Pauline patted my stomach.

"What?" Leonard had come downstairs so quietly we hadn't heard him come into my room. "Did you say something about a baby?" When he realized my aunt's hand was on my belly, he said, "Seraphine, you're…" he couldn't finish his question.

"Yes," Aunt Pauline said. "We thought we had gotten through all those dark days, but it seems they're not over, Leonard."

"Are you going to keep the child?" Leonard looked first at me and then at my aunt as if he wasn't sure to whom he should direct his question.

It was Aunt Pauline who answered. "No, we've already discussed it. I think the best thing would be to give the child up for adoption. I trust Dr. Shoenbaum, so I'll get him to handle your confinement, and maybe, he can also be instrumental with the adoption."

"I'll try to help with finding a family for the child. I have quite a few clients now and I'll find a discreet way to ask them about a good family for the baby. I'm sure there are many childless couples who would be eager to have the child; it shouldn't be too difficult to find one." The way Leonard looked at me made me feel so ashamed that I turned away and hid my face in the pillow. Besides the nausea, the fact that I was pregnant erased the last vestiges of my self-esteem, and Leonard's look of disappointment made me want to stay in the bed and not get out until the baby was born and given away. My aunt had been right; I was ruined.

So while I was patiently waiting for Leonard to access the money my aunt had promised me - a new, unwanted life had been growing inside of me. I gave up at that point. There seemed no way out of the Prytania Street house. And to make matters worse, my aunt and Leonard seemed as if the baby news was wonderful. They seemed happy about it. They formed a cocoon around me, and because everything seemed hopeless, I let them. But as time passed, I realized for the first time in my life, I felt safe. Some of the trust I'd lost was trying to return.

Jonas was also a great help to me. He did everything he thought was too strenuous for me to do. It gave him something else to focus on besides the absence of his wife Daisy. She left him without a warning just as my aunt had predicted. The laundry was again without a laundress.

Jonas found a washerwoman at the Poydras Market. He delivered the laundry to her and picked it up several days later. My aunt was pleased with what he'd done. It saved her from having to give it back to the house maid. She gave him a sum of money each time he was scheduled to pick up the wash, and if it was too much, she allowed him to keep what was left. He was happier than I'd ever seen him.

I could tell he was curious about my pregnancy, but was too much a gentleman to ask me about it. I think by process of elimination he believed Leonard was the father. He smiled at Leonard constantly and once told him, "You a good man, Mistah Leonard, a real good man." I think Leonard understood what Jonas was hinting at and much to my surprise did not deny it.

On what would have been my father's forty-sixth birthday, I gave birth to a boy. And as I had requested, I was not shown the baby. Leonard, my aunt and Jonas had quietly taken care of getting the doctor, helping with the birthing, and getting the baby to his new parents. Leonard had found a couple he said desperately wanted a child and immediately after the baby's birth, he and the child left the house. He told us when he brought the blue-eyed, black-haired boy to the man and his wife, they cried.

No one ever mentioned the child again in my presence.

Pauline and Leonard worked all the time. Both businesses had expanded and required more of their time away from home. I was lonelier than I'd ever been. I began to think again about the money I'd been promised, but I didn't ask about it. I wanted to wait for what I thought would be the right time. I was feeling much stronger, emotionally and physically, and knew I would be able to take charge of my own life.

I had made one corner of my room into a sewing area. I used all of my alone time to sketch my creations, then make small samples of the dresses. Jonas fashioned pieces of wood into simple mannequins and I exhibited my dresses on them. I had enlarged them from the miniatures I'd first made and no longer had to hide them. Aunt Pauline admired everything I created and told me as soon as I thought I was ready to set up a business, she would be there to help me.

One afternoon, Leonard walked into the kitchen as I was preparing my lunch.

"Good day, Leonard. Where are Jonas and the carriage?" For the longest time I had not called him by any name. It was only after the rape that I'd begun to call him Leonard.

"I suppose he's at the stable. I never use the carriage during the day. I take the trolley and I walk quite a bit. That's how I get around to most of the clients who don't come to my office. I like the freedom. My office isn't too far away, so

I took the trolley here." He was eyeing the food and sniffing the air. "Do you mind if I share your lunch?"

I heated the vegetable soup, then made two ham sandwiches and a fresh pot of coffee. We ate as Leonard chatted about some of his notorious clients. It was clear he was impressed with handling their account books and their investments. And, he said, the best part was they paid him handsomely.

"But even with all my success, I'm thinking about returning to New York." Leonard shot the statement out into the air like a blast from a rifle.

I was stunned for a second and wasn't quite sure why. "Uh...does Mrs. Stern know? What will she do without you?"

"No, she doesn't know...yet. But you know what I wish? I wish you'd said you don't know what you'll do without me. Because...because...I've loved you from the moment I first saw you, Seraphine, and I don't care who you are or what you are." Leonard stopped for a moment. I think he was trying to read the expression on my face. "I love you and will always love you. Please, Seraphine, come with me to New York. We can get married there and live in peace. You can leave all the bad memories and who's Colored and who's White behind. You will be able to be free of all that rubbish."

"There isn't any place on earth where I'll be able to live in peace. My bad memories and who I choose to be, Colored or White, will follow me wherever I go. There's no point in going anywhere else. I do thank you for being so good to me through all the bad times and still wanting to take care of me. You'll never know how grateful I am. But, Leonard," I stood up abruptly and attempted to clear the dishes from the table. "I..."

Leonard stopped me. "I accept your gratitude, Seraphine, but a little of your love would be better," he said.

"There is no love inside me right now. I have nothing to give you. And I will not repeat my aunt's life as a Colored woman married to a White man and have to look over my shoulder my whole life. Whatever I choose, I'll live that kind of life alone. They'll be no one else to pay for my decisions except me. I'm sorry, Leonard, I can't marry you."

"You need a new start, Seraphine. Don't say no. Think about it for a while."

Twice a week Leonard came home to have lunch with me. I didn't know if my aunt knew and I decided I wouldn't be the one to tell her. Life was running smoothly and I wasn't going to be the one to stir up things.

Leonard never mentioned his love for me or marriage again for many years. I think for a long time he hoped I'd eventually love him and agree to marry him.

On one of Leonard's lunches with me, he mentioned that he had recently taken on three clients – madams from the newly established Storyville. They had three of the most profitable houses and he had visited them earlier that week to begin working on their books. Leonard was impressed with the way the women handled their businesses. During his visit, he said, he had even met Tom Anderson, the mayor of Storyville.

"I was thinking, Seraphine, if you're considering dressmaking, these women would be a good place to start. I think you could make a fortune outfitting them and their girls. I can take you to see them any time you like." Leonard was enthusiastic about anything pertaining to business and investments and he gave his advice freely to anyone who wanted it. He had single-handedly been responsible for the Stern Brothers recent expansion. They were now a full-line men's store, not just suits. They carried everything a man wore from his head to his feet.

I didn't even have to think about his proposition to give him a resounding no. I knew my aunt would object to it. At twenty-five years old, I had gone from being a servant to a member of the family, and only now did I realize how important her approval was to me – just as my father's and Daniel's had been.

Many times after that, I often wondered, if I had loved Leonard then and had gone to New York and married him, how would my life have been different? Would I still be seeking approval? Leonard's approval? When would I ever please myself?

One Sunday morning at breakfast, Aunt Pauline announced she was returning to the Catholic Church and if Leonard didn't mind, she'd like to attend Mass with him. He was delighted. Because Sunday was Jonas's day off, Leonard had to go out to rent a carriage. If my aunt had been able to walk or take the trolley that would not have been necessary. An hour later he returned with a rented carriage and off they went to Mass. Even though I would not have joined them, I wanted to be asked and wasn't.

It was the first time I felt left out. In all the time that had passed since Daniel's death, we entertained ourselves at home. We played cards; Leonard played the piano and we sang songs; we read newspapers and magazines, then shared or discussed the stories in them. Any activities that could be enjoyed at home, we did them – together. And even if my aunt and Leonard spent time with me out of guilt, I didn't care. The fact that they gave me the first feelings of love I'd had since I was a small child was the only thing that mattered.

While they were at church, I sat in the dining room mulling over where I was at that point in my life and what I should do to go forward. I knew it was the time to once again bring up the money my aunt had entrusted to Leonard for me. I needed to have a future. If I was as talented in designing and sewing as my aunt said I was, then why not open a dressmaking shop, one in the Vieux Carré. What a grandiose idea! Who did I think I was? But why not? I knew I was good at what I did and not as lazy or as disinterested in becoming a success as my father had been. So having a shop is what I knew I should do. I'd call it: DRESSMAKING by SERA.

Leonard loved my plan. He was eager to help. "That's an excellent idea. I think a shop in the French Quarter makes a lot of sense. It's accessible to both the Creole and the American sector. Although, I think the American women have more money, especially from this area, the Garden District. What will you call your shop?"

When I told him, he said, "I like Sera. I've wanted to ask you if you wanted to be called something other than Seraphine and now I know."

"Sera is what my father called me." I couldn't say Daniel also used it to make me feel I could trust him. "Mrs. Stern, what do you think? You've been too quiet." I still used her formal name as did Leonard. She didn't protest the formality and that made me think she probably enjoyed it because it gave her an air of superiority. Even though she'd changed and had become softer and more pleasant in her demeanor, she still needed to feel in control of whatever she was involved in. Calling her Mrs. Stern instead of Aunt Pauline did not diminish who I was and was of little concern to me.

"Hmm, I've been sitting here wondering if that isn't a big step for you, Seraphine. Do you think you're ready?" My aunt's voice was calm and her pronunciation was crisp but normal.

Since she'd become a widow, I rarely heard those hard consonant sounds again.

"I think I'm ready," I said then decided I needed to be more decisive. "I know I'm ready."

"Leonard, how quickly can you access that money? By the way, what did you invest it in?" Aunt Pauline asked.

"Cotton, what else is there?" He and my aunt laughed. How easily she laughed now. "Getting to the money is no problem," he said.

"What do you suggest we do first?" Aunt Pauline was beginning to show a little enthusiasm.

"Look for a shop to buy, then figure out how much it will take to get it outfitted with machines, material and other products Sera will need for her start-up."

"What about starting out with the things you have here in your sewing room, Seraphine? That sewing machine is practically new. We can take the fabric you already have and I will order more through the suppliers I use for the factory. You can start the shop that way until your clientele increases. Start small and then grow. What do you think about that idea?" When my aunt spoke, Leonard was always quiet.

"I like the idea because in the beginning I won't have any clients. I may not need any more machines or supplies for a long time. After all, I'll be the only dressmaker in the shop, so I only need one sewing machine." The feeling of happiness rose up from my stomach and overwhelmed me. I had never been nauseated from feeling happy. And of course, I started to cry.

When I looked at my aunt's and Leonard's worried faces, I quickly tried to reassure them. "I'm just feeling happy. I was afraid it wasn't going to be possible. I'd forgotten what it's like to feel someone cares and is willing to support me. My family…" I decided not to finish what I intended to say. Life was moving forward; I'd better follow it.

"Enough of those depressing thoughts. We've got a business to get started. What name have you chosen for your shop?" My aunt reached over and squeezed my hand.

"DRESSMAKING by SERA, is that the way you want your storefront painted?" Leonard was always a step ahead of everyone else when it came to planning. I could see why my aunt deferred to him on most things she wanted to do — business and other things, too.

Before I could answer, Aunt Pauline had thought of something else.

"There's something important we haven't discussed, Sera...phine." She couldn't bring herself to call me Sera. I wondered why. She was the one who had told Daniel that was what my father called me. Perhaps Daniel had called me Sera when he was speaking to her about me. There was something about the name that made her uncomfortable.

She hesitated a long time before she continued. "I...ah...know what I think you should do, but it is your decision." She waited again. "Colored or White?"

"White, I've already thought about it, Mrs. Stern. I'm going to be White. I've known that for a long time and I'm sure I told my sisters when I lived with them. Maybe that's why it was so easy for them to believe I'd run away with a White man. I've always known I could pass and how much better the world was on the other side. I'll never be Colored again...not ever!"

13

It didn't take Leonard long to find three shops that were available for rent. They were all situated in a good area of the Vieux Carré close to the river and the French Market. Aunt Pauline accompanied Leonard and me when we went to look at them.

The shop on St. Ann Street was the only one that had living quarters. My aunt found all sorts of things wrong with the place because she could tell I liked it. And because it had several rooms over the shop, she knew I'd surely leave Prytania St. Leonard, much to my aunt's displeasure, agreed with my choice. I did wonder why he supported me. Perhaps he thought I'd be more accessible to him if my aunt wasn't around which would give him time to try to change my feelings for him.

While Leonard worked on convincing the property owner to sell me the shop rather than rent it to me, I tried to bring my aunt around to accept that it was time for me to take charge of my own life. I told her how much I appreciated all she'd done for me and promised her that we'd see each other often after I moved.

It took almost a year and a half to complete the sale and have the shop and the living quarters cleaned and renovated. The property had been vacant for several years and needed extensive repairs.

The shop contained two extra-large rooms. I used the front room which opened onto the *banquette* as my reception room with a sitting area for my customers. The back room was the work and fitting areas.

As you stepped out of the back door of the shop, you walked onto a small, flagstone courtyard. Nothing was growing there, not even weeds. That was a job I gave to Jonas. He welcomed reviving the old fountain and replanting the flower beds. I made a storage room out of the small building at the end of the courtyard that had once been a kitchen and a laundry room.

My living quarters over the shop also had two super-sized rooms. I converted them into a front room, a bedroom, a kitchen, and a water closet like the ones on Prytania Street. I also put in a tin bathtub. My aunt insisted I allow her to hire the contractor who'd done her room additions and let her pay for the work as a gift to me. She refused to even listen to my objections.

There were two ways for me to enter my apartment: an interior staircase in the far corner of the work room and an exterior staircase in the courtyard that lead up to the gallery that ran along the right side and across the front of the building. I had the exterior staircase removed despite Leonard's protests. He insisted I needed at least two ways to exit the upstairs in the event of a fire. I refused to listen. I had never lived alone and I was afraid even though I never verbalized it. Leonard may have figured out why I wanted the staircase taken down because he suddenly relented saying he realized I was the one who had to live there and I needed to feel secure.

My aunt furnished the whole house with beautiful, expensive pieces. My rooms were half the size of the ones at

Prytania Street, so she didn't duplicate the massive, mahogany furniture that was in her home. She found a craftsman who made a smaller, lighter version of her pieces. The parlor was filled with velvet, damask and lace at the glass doors and on the sofa and chairs. My home was truly my palace. Many evenings after the shop was closed, I'd walk around my house touching everything, trying to accept that it was all really mine and that I no longer belonged to someone else. I was finally free.

I began to enjoy long, warm, scented baths in my new tin tub – a luxury I'd never known. At my father's and the Prytania house, I used a pitcher of warm water and a bowl to "clean myself." To have a water closet in my home instead of a chamber pot under my bed at my aunt's made me giddy. I wasn't allowed to use the privies in the house until after the rape. Needless to say, anything was far better than using the outhouse at my father's.

Aunt Pauline even purchased several chairs for my small, narrow gallery that over-hung the banquette. I imagined her and Leonard sitting with me during the Mardi Gras season watching the parades that passed on Decatur Street. I pictured us languishing on the gallery on hot, summer evenings with tall, cool glasses of lemonade. My aunt hated what she called "street galleries" and "sitting out in public." She found it to be a "vulgar habit." I knew either Leonard or I would have to convince her to join us.

One of the happiest days of my life was the day I went to the shop and watched the sign painter put the finishing touches on DRESSMAKING by SERA at the top of the storefront. I set up several displays of dresses, skirts and weskits around the reception room. Then Jonas helped me arrange my dressed, wooden mannequins on the glass shelves in the storefront windows. He put up a dozen of them, four on each shelf. I knew changing them every two or three weeks would attract the lady window-shoppers who might eventually become customers. I mixed a small bucket of vinegar and water and cleaned the outside of the windows until they sparkled.

Jonas was invaluable to me during that time and long before then. I couldn't have gotten through the pregnancy, after the birth, and the years that followed without him being there to help me. While the renovations were being done, he took me to the property every day to oversee the work as it progressed. He often pitched in and helped the men my aunt had hired to do the job. Jonas was an amazing man. He could do everything the workmen were doing and often told them a better way of doing whatever they were working on. A few of them resented an ex-slave giving them instructions, but most of the time they knew he was right and they did it his way. And if they refused to take his advice, I would insist they do it his way.

When all the work was completed, Jonas and one of his friends who owned a wagon and a mule moved my belongings, my sewing machine, assorted sewing paraphernalia, and the bolts of material from Prytania St. to my shop.

The next evening, Jonas brought my aunt and Leonard to my home for a celebration. They were loaded down with food, dessert, and several bottles of sherry. I felt sad when Jonas had to leave after all he had contributed to the finished product. Not only couldn't he leave the horse and carriage standing in front of the shop for too long, but to my aunt and Leonard it was unthinkable to have a Black man sitting at the table with us.

"Seraphine, I'm going to send Charlie Knight, my factory manager, to help you get the shop ready for your opening. I hope that's all right with you." Aunt Pauline was smiling and nodding as she looked around the shop taking everything in.

"I'm comfortable with that, Mrs. Stern; I need all the help I can get. Thank you. But shouldn't we have waited to celebrate...until the shop actually opens?" I was feeling frustrated and a little superstitious and didn't know how to handle a celebration, let alone a premature one.

"Oh, we'll just have to have a second party after you have your grand opening. Besides, the food I brought is incredibly delicious. I wanted you to taste it. Leonard found a new cook for us at one of his houses of ill-repute. She's too old to ply her trade, so she's resorted to cooking. I actually like the woman; she doesn't talk much." My aunt chuckled at her own observation. She gave a quick look around the shop then asked, "Where's Leonard?"

"I think he took the last of the food upstairs." As I said that, we heard him whistling in the kitchen.

"You go on up, Seraphine. It's going to take me a long time to get up there."

"No, I'll walk up with you," I told her.

Leonard had already set the table when I entered the kitchen. "I'm sorry I don't have a formal dining room." I don't know why I felt the urge to express my regret.

"Why are you apologizing, Sera?" Leonard asked. "A formal dining room wouldn't make the food taste any better; it's the people at the table that matter. Is Mrs. Stern on her way up?"

"Yes," my aunt called from the top of the stairs, "I've arrived. I needed a few moments to catch my breath."

Leonard looked content and comfortable getting dinner set up on the table. He fussed with the napkins, straightened the tablecloth several times, and moved the bowls of food around the center of the table until there was room for all of them.

My aunt's new cook was indeed extraordinary. Our meal consisted of filé gumbo, baked red snapper, a tomato-alligator pear salad with olive oil and vinegar and crispy French bread. The dessert was a bread pudding with butter and raw egg sauce so heavily spiked with whiskey, that along with the two glasses of sherry Aunt Pauline and I had had, we were a bit tipsy. It took two cups of strong coffee to get us back to feeling somewhat clear-headed again.

"Mrs. Stern, are you expecting me to fail the way my father did?" My tongue had indeed become loose.

"What possessed you to ask such a question, Seraphine?"

"I don't know. I guess I just have a need to know. Do you?"

It seemed to take her a while to find the wherewithal to answer. Finally my aunt asked through pursed lips, "Do you think you're like your father?"

"No."

"Then you already have the answer to your question. If I didn't expect you to succeed, do you think I would have invested as much as I have in you?"

"No, I don't suppose so. I think I'm nervous about what lies ahead and I'm going through a serious bout of doubting my ability to succeed. I know I'm much more ambitious than my father was and much more hardworking." I felt a sudden rush of strength flow through me and I knew I really didn't need to get confidence or approval from anyone outside myself.

"You've got both of us to help you, Sera. There is no way you're going to fail." Leonard looked at my aunt for her approval. She nodded. "So, when is opening day?" he asked.

"On Monday."

"Four days from now. Why not sooner?" Aunt Pauline asked. "Wouldn't the weekend be better? Saturday, maybe?"

"I thought Monday because the husbands would be back at work and their wives would have a longer time to window-shop and perhaps come in to have a look at the shop and meet the *modiste*."

"That's good thinking, Sera. You're a natural businesswoman." Leonard never missed an opportunity to give me a compliment. He knew just what to say to boost my ego. "Don't you think she's a natural, Mrs. Stern?"

"I most certainly do. You amaze me time after time, Seraphine. Don't you dare worry about your future! You have too much talent and intelligence to ever fail at anything." When my aunt struggled to get to her feet, Leonard leapt to his feet to assist her.

"It's already nine-thirty," Aunt Pauline said glancing at the clock on the mantle. "Leonard, is Jonas waiting with the carriage?"

Leonard opened one of the doors in the parlor and stepped out on the gallery. "Yes, he's there. Jonas," he called down to the street, "we'll be there in a few minutes."

I went down and walked out to the street with them. I handed Jonas the plate of food I'd saved for him.

"Thank you, Miss Sera. I sho preshiate dis. Ain't the cook's food some good?" Jonas's perfect white teeth were beautiful against his mahogany skin. His smile was spectacular.

"Everything was delicious, Jonas. If Mrs. Stern doesn't need you the whole weekend, will you be able to come and help me get ready for my shop's opening on Monday?"

Jonas didn't answer. Instead, he looked at my aunt.

"Of course Jonas will have time. I have a very light schedule this weekend. In fact, we'll all come to help on Saturday. Won't we, Leonard?"

Leonard nodded enthusiastically.

"I'll cook for us. The French Market is just a few blocks away and very convenient for getting everything I need."

"You'll do no such thing," my aunt shook her finger at me. "I'll have my cook make food for Saturday. You have enough to do for your opening. Now go in, Seraphine," my aunt commanded. "Make sure you lock up everything, especially your glass doors upstairs. Close and latch the shutters, too. I don't want you to wake up during the night and find a stranger standing over you."

"I will," I said. "Goodnight." I quickly slipped inside, latched the shutters, then locked and bolted the door. As I walked across the shop toward the staircase I said out loud, "Thanks, Aunt Pauline. Of all the things you could have said to say goodnight, you chose to say that."

The next day Leonard came to the shop on foot. He handed me a small package. "Open it," he said. "I'll explain after you see what it is."

It was heavy for such a small bundle. I put it down on one of the cutting tables to unwrap it. I was shocked when I saw it was a pearl-handled revolver and a velvet pouch of bullets.

"Why? Do you…"

Leonard didn't allow me to finish. "I saw the look on your face when Mrs. Stern made the remark about a stranger standing over you. I thought this might equalize the situation." He gave a mischievous little cackle. "Keep this somewhere close to you day and night. I'm sure people have already observed that you live here alone…the good ones and the bad ones."

"I don't know how to shoot a gun!" I was horrified.

"You don't have to. Put a bullet in it, point, and then pull the trigger. But make sure you're close enough to whoever you're shooting at because you may only get one shot. It's that simple."

"Nothing is simple."

"Pick it up, Sera, and get used to handling it. You're not afraid of it, are you?" Leonard picked up the gun and put a bullet into the chamber. He aimed at the mannequin closest to him and pretended to pull the trigger. Then he removed the bullet and handed me the gun. "Now you do what I just did."

I took the revolver. It was cold in my hands as I loaded it. I pointed it at the same mannequin and fired. The bullet lodged in the stomach area. "No, I guess I'm not afraid of it."

"Sera!" Leonard rushed to the front of the store and went out to stand on the banquette. He looked all around and then came back inside the shop. "I don't think anyone realized that sound was a gunshot." He looked at me in disbelief. "Why didn't you do as I asked?" Leonard grabbed the gun out of my hands. "This is not a toy," he growled.

I snatched it back. "I know it isn't. But it's mine now, so let me figure out how to use it."

Leonard gave a nervous little laugh. "Be careful, Sera; you're not Calamity Jane. If I had any doubts about your safety, they're gone now. That gun is your equalizer and you're a lady to be feared." Then he relaxed and laughed in earnest.

I laughed with him. "Don't tell my aunt you bought me a gun. She won't like it. And please don't mention I shot one of the mannequins she went through hell to get for me."

"I don't have to tell her," he crowed, "she's the one who suggested it. We both saw the look of fear on your face last night. As for the mannequin, she won't hear anything from me, but you're lucky it had a wooden form under that overlay of sawdust."

"Thank you. Did I really show I was afraid last night?"

"Yes, but the first hint of fear came when you had the exterior staircase removed." Leonard looked at his pocket watch. "Oh, I must be going. I have an appointment in half an hour. Are you comfortable with your new tool? Let's call it a protection tool."

"I am. And you're right, it isn't a toy. It's a tool. I can't match a man's strength, but with this," I patted the revolver, "I feel on equal footing with anyone. You called it an equalizer and that's exactly what I think it is. Too bad I didn't have it a few years ago when I was being attacked."

Leonard winced but made no comment. As he left the store, he looked back over his shoulder and asked, "Will Mrs. Stern and I be dining here regularly with you? Will you also grace our table at Prytania Street?"

"Yes, you will be my regular guests." I felt exalted to be able to say that knowing where I'd come from. "I have no desire to return to the Prytania house, however, for dinners or anything else."

Leonard turned to tip his hat and I saw the joy in his eyes, despite what I'd said about returning to my aunt's house. I knew I was being selfish to bask in his love when I couldn't return it. But I knew he'd redirect his love one day, and by then I'd be emotionally secure enough to let him go.

All of my dresses and skirts had deep pockets. I had made them to hold handkerchiefs, thread and bobbins, pieces of material and other things I'd often put in them. And they were big enough to hold my gun without showing a bulge.

I was never without it. I got used to its weight. Everyday I'd put it into my right pocket loaded with one bullet. Leonard had said I'd probably have only one shot, so I took him at his word. I never thought about the danger of walking around with a loaded gun, because I knew if I needed it in a hurry, I wouldn't have time to load it. At night, I'd put it under my pillow. Eventually I knew I'd buy another gun, one for my pocket and one for my pillow.

14

The shop opened that Monday as planned. More than two dozen ladies came to look around and inquire about prices, fabric, and the length of time it would take to give them a finished garment. At the end of the day, I hadn't made any sales nor had I gotten any promises for future ones. Something had happened. And it was only after the shop closed and I was sitting quietly reflecting on the day that I realized what had taken place. If Creole women were in the shop when American women entered, the Creoles left.

Even though I wanted to give more thought to my opening day, the burning pain in my hands took over my attention. That was the first evening I felt severe pain course through my fingers. I thought they were finally rebelling against how hard they'd had to work those past weeks. I held them in hot water until the pain subsided.

On Wednesday of my first week, two women from the American sector came in to order day dresses, nothing fancy, one plain cotton and one seersucker. My guess was that they wanted to start with something inexpensive in order to judge the quality of my work before they committed to evening dresses. The dresses were finished and ready to be fitted the next Wednesday.

Three Creole women had also come into the shop the first week and placed orders. On Friday of the following week when they came in for fittings, two American women, friends of my first American customers, also came in to order skirts and jackets. The Creoles began to huff and puff showing their displeasure, then they became hostile toward me.

"Sera," one said to me, "you're in the French Quarter...the Vieux Carré! Your clientele should be Creole, not American. Who will you sew for next...niggers?"

"I'm here to make clothes for everyone, madame. I don't choose my customers; they choose me. And I don't refuse to sew for someone because they're from the American sector. I don't care what side of Canal Street you live on. If you want me to make clothing for you, that's what I'm here for." I didn't dare address the "nigger" comment. My palms and my armpits were wet. I knew it was a speech that could cost me my livelihood.

"Very well then, wrap up our dresses. We'll take them without a fitting," the woman told me. "I'm sure you know we won't be back." She turned to the American women, "Why can't you stay in your little section of town. You invaded our city and you're trying to change our way of life. You're not welcome here. Go back across Canal Street, you heathens!"

The American women ignored her. They stood in the corner of the reception room as the Creoles paid me and I bundled up their dresses.

After that day, only American women patronized my shop. The Creoles never returned. They'd stop and look at the window mannequins and peer in to see who was in the store, but never came in. Leonard believed the Creoles were probably stealing my mannequin designs and taking them to whatever dressmakers made their clothes. My aunt and Leonard did everything in their power to keep my spirits high. They told me things would get better; the Creoles certainly wouldn't boycott me forever. They found all sorts of reasons for us to get together, especially for a meal. Sometimes my aunt would send her cook to prepare the food for us in my kitchen. Jonas would pick up the cook from the Prytania house about noon, and then return for her about 4:00. Other times, Aunt Pauline would bring the meal already prepared or she would help me to prepare it.

There were times Leonard did not join us and we were curious as to his whereabouts, but thought it improper to ask. He never apologized for his absences; all he ever offered was, "Sorry about last evening, ladies, but business comes first."

That first year, even though Aunt Pauline protested, Leonard and I convinced her to join us on my gallery to have dinner and watch some of the Mardi Gras parades as they passed a few yards away on Decatur Street. She came without complaint the years that followed.

It was unusually cold that year on Mardi Gras Day. We sat bundled up on the gallery waiting for the last parade of the season to pass. Leonard had made us hot toddies, and as we sat talking and enjoying our drinks, there was a sudden loud blast below. Leonard jumped up and looked at the banquette below.

"Oh, Sera, it's one of your windows," he shouted out as he leaned half his body over the railing to get a better look.

I ran through the house, down the stairs, and through the shop with Leonard on my heels. When I threw open the shutters, a drunken man dressed as one of the Knights of the Round Table was pacing back and forth in front of the window examining his handiwork.

"Look! Look what I did!" he shouted. "All it took was one little bottle and a damn good aim and...WHAM!" He laughed loudly as he drooled down the front of his satin shirt.

Leonard grabbed the man and held him against one of the shutter doors. "Is this your idea of having a good time…damaging other people's property?"

"This your property, mister?" the man asked.

"No, it's this lady's," Leonard told him pointing to me.

"I don't care whose property it is…this is Mardi Gras…what's done is done." He laughed again and tried to break free from Leonard's grip. As Leonard tried to hold him against the door, the man began to howl and throw punches. He started to kick wildly.

"Move away from him, Leonard," I said as I removed the gun from my pocket and pointed it at the drunken man. "Maybe he can't hold you against that door, but I can shoot you."

The man instantly quieted down as he stared in disbelief at the gun pointed at his chest. "Wait, please wait, don't shoot me! I can pay for your window, lady. Don't do anything crazy!" He struggled to open a suede pouch hanging from his belt. "Here take this…all of it. Let me go home, please, lady. I'm not a bad man; I'm just drunk."

I snatched the money out of his hand. "Sixty dollars," I said after counting it. "This should cover it. Now…go home! Get off the street before someone really does shoot you."

As the man walked away and weaved his way down the street, Leonard said to me, "I'll have Jonas take Mrs. Stern home and I'll stay the night. You can't be here alone with this broken window."

Aunt Pauline wanted me to go home with her and leave Leonard to guard the shop alone. When I declined, she was visibly upset. She tried desperately not to enjoy seeing the parade when it finally came, but she had a good time in spite of herself.

When Jonas arrived, my aunt told me I should go straight to bed and Leonard should make himself comfortable downstairs in the reception room. With an accusatory look on her face, she said to him, "I trust you. Do not do anything to erase my trust."

It was the first time I'd ever seen Leonard angry. "I am not Daniel, Mrs. Stern. I respect your niece...and you. You disappoint me. I thought you knew me. Goodnight." He turned abruptly and walked toward the back of the shop.

Aunt Pauline left with a parting shot for me. "A woman alone becomes a magnet for men with untoward intentions. This is not the place for you; you'll see."

I locked and bolted the front door and went to find Leonard. He was sitting in the corner of the workroom near the stairs. He looked hurt and dejected.

"Leonard, you know Mrs. Stern thinks of you as her son – she didn't mean to hurt you. She's afraid for me and she's lashing out at you because she knows I don't listen to her any more about moving the store to the Garden District. I like where I am; everything is convenient. I have made my own decision about that, and frankly, I will about everything else. Come upstairs, it's cold down here. Let's make some coffee, get something to munch on, and then get a few blankets to take down with us for the night. I'm not going to let you sit guard alone all night."

"No, Sera, go to bed. You need to..."

I cut him off, "I'm not a fragile creature, Leonard, and we will spend the night together in the reception room. Not another word. Come," I held out my hand to him, "let's get something warm to drink."

Leonard stoked the dying fire in the fireplace while I made the coffee. He didn't add any more wood since we'd be going downstairs shortly. He looked deep in thought.

"It's still early. Why don't we have cheese and bread before we go down," I told him. "Oh. Leonard, before we eat, would you go down and remove my small mannequins from the window shelves. I don't want to lose any of them."

"Sure, where should I put them?"

"On one of the work tables."

We sat on the floor in front of the fireplace as the last vestiges of warmth began to die out. We snacked on cheddar cheese and French bread with strong café au lait. Leonard talked briefly about Aunt Pauline not looking well lately. "Are you getting cold, Sera. Your lips are beginning to look a little blue."

"I am a little. I'll get a few more blankets for us. We should be getting downstairs."

"Not yet; wait a few minutes. Let's move closer to the fireplace." Leonard moved the plates off to the side and we moved as close as we could get. He found a way to sit touching me.

When I tried to move away, he said, "Don't move, Sera. Stay close to me. I'm cold, too." His voice was soft and caressing. I had never noticed until then how beautiful it was. I thought about how wonderful it would be if he read to me. "Leonard, if I get too warm and cozy, I'll fall asleep."

"Then go to sleep. I promise I'll stay awake with my ears perked up for any sound coming from downstairs. Go ahead, lean against me, relax and nod off for a little while." Listening to his soothing voice as I nestled against his warm chest invited me to close my eyes. I felt him wrap a blanket around us and in no time I nodded off.

"Sera," Leonard was whispering, "I think I should go downstairs now. You should go to bed. You're tired."

"No, no, I'm warm and comfortable; please don't make me move." As I snuggled closer, I realized he'd pulled me onto his lap and I was sleeping in his arms. The urge to pull away gripped me but my desire to stay warm and cradled in his arms was stronger.

Leonard laughed and held me a little tighter. I looked up at him with a look that invited him to kiss me. He did, tenderly. But then he said, "I told your aunt she could trust me. Don't make me break my word, Sera."

"She'll not hear it from me. May I have another kiss?" This time he kissed me hard and held me even tighter as he groaned. "I'm sorry; I know this is unfair of me. But I've never been kissed like this before...I've known only Daniel's savage kisses. I love your kisses; they're wonderful." I grabbed his face and planted kisses all over it. Then I felt Leonard's body respond and I knew I'd gone too far.

I jumped up. "Oh, Leonard, I'm sorry for my behavior. Please, please forgive me. I don't want you to think I did this to Daniel. I did not."

"Hush, Sera. I know you weren't responsible for what he did to you. I also know your kisses are everything I knew they'd be. I can still feel your soft lips on my eyes and everywhere you kissed me on my face. But...being trusted is important to me. Come, gather up the blankets; let's go downstairs."

15

The French Market offered everything I needed for the small amount of cooking I did. After the deliveries were made and the merchants restocked their stalls, the market opened just before dawn.

After first light, when the rush of people had cleared out, I regularly did my marketing on Tuesdays, Thursdays and Saturdays. I liked not having to wait while someone haggled with a merchant about the price of potatoes or some other fruit or vegetable. I could find everything I needed in half an hour.

One foggy Thursday, I returned to the shop with my basket full and several parcels in my arms. I opened the shutters, and as I fumbled in my purse for the key to the door, a disheveled man with his head down suddenly appeared out of the soupy atmosphere. He hurried past and once again was swallowed up by the mist.

Feeling apprehensive, I quickly found the key and opened the door. I pulled the chain on the ceiling light, then put my basket and parcels on the closest display pedestal. When I turned to go back and lock the door, the man had quietly slipped inside and was standing in front of the shutters. He was dirty and ragged and had no shoes. When he reached behind his back without looking and slid the shutter latch in place, I saw the handle of a knife resting against his belly.

"What do you want…money?" I asked. I wanted to distract him and not allow him to close and bolt the wooden door. Even though his menacing look frightened me, I was not going to let him overpower me the way Daniel had. I could not exhibit fear. "Do you need money for food?"

He didn't reply. Slowly he looked around him as he removed the knife from under his belt.

"Do you speak English?"

"No! You…no talk."

"Here," I threw him my purse. "I don't have much money. This is all of it." Had he come a few days earlier, I would have had a full cash box, but Jonas had taken me to the bank to deposit it.

The man grabbed the purse and tore it open exposing the few dollars. Never taking his eyes off me, he stuffed the money into his pocket and then threw the torn purse across the room. He glared at me from under his eyelids as he squeezed the handle of his knife. His swarthy face was heavily scarred and his thick, black hair and mustache were greasy and matted.

"I have no more money. Here, take some of this food; you must be hungry." I held out the basket toward him but he kicked it out of my hands. Potatoes, oranges and lemons rolled everywhere. The heavy cabbage, salt meat, and the sausage somehow stayed inside the basket.

"No talk!" he yelled. "No talk!" Then he began to unbutton the front of his trousers, but kept his eyes trained on me. As he moved toward me, he stepped on a lemon and temporarily lost his footing. When his eyes left me as he fought to regain his balance, I was able to pull my gun out of my skirt pocket. His near fall made him angrier and he plodded toward me again until he saw what I was holding. I steadied the gun and pointed it at a spot between his eyebrows.

Calmly, he flipped the knife and held the blade with his fingertips. As he was lifting his arm to throw it, I fired. He lurched backward crashing through the shutters and fell on his back on the banquette. When he hit the bricks, the knife flew out of his hand and landed at the feet of two ladies on their way to market.

The women's screams brought shopkeepers and passersby to their aid. Among them was Officer Kane making his morning walk-around. He saw me in the doorway with the gun still in my hand. He came inside in an effort to comfort me. When he saw I needed no comforting, he asked me to tell him what happened.

The policeman stayed with me until the man's body was removed. He speculated my robber and would-be rapist was a seaman who had jumped ship, and when he was hungry and unable to find work had become desperate. I found whatever reasons the man might have had for what he'd done were of no interest to me. When I shot him, his face had become Daniel's. His death had been my goal and I had no remorse. That's what I told myself over and over again in the hours after Officer Kane left.

Suddenly the pangs of contrition overwhelmed me. I felt cold and shaky. I couldn't concentrate on my sewing because everywhere I looked I saw the man's anguished face as the bullet struck him.

I closed the shop and went upstairs. I wrapped myself in a blanket and sat in silence until I heard Leonard banging on the shutters and calling my name.

I opened one of the parlor doors and stepped out onto the gallery. I called down to him and my aunt that I'd be right down. I saw them examining the blood on the bricks.

My aunt was visibly upset when I let them in. "Why are you closed in the middle of the day? Are you sick? Why is there blood on your banquette? Did…"

"Mrs. Stern! Mrs. Stern…give me a chance to speak, please." I looked to Leonard for help hoping he could get my aunt to calm down.

But all he said was, "Tell us, please!"

I explained what happened that morning. My aunt didn't wait for me to finish. She told me what she thought I needed to do.

"I've warned you about this location." She found a chair and sat. "Oh, my legs, they're starting to throb! Ahhh…Seraphine, please, you must listen to me. You're a woman and you're vulnerable."

"There are many women who own shops in the French Quarter, Mrs. Stern. This was just something random that happened to me and may never happen again. It's a rare occurrence."

"You'll never convince me of that. That cutthroat must have known you lived and worked here alone, that's why he followed you. Well…never mind. Here's my solution: sell this property and we'll find you another in the Garden District. Your clientele is already from the American sector, so you've nothing to lose."

"I can't have this conversation again. My head is bursting. I'm going upstairs to make some tea. Would you like a cup, Mrs. Stern? Leonard?"

Leonard finally spoke. "No, Sera, thank you. We only stopped to show you Mrs. Stern's new motorcar."

"Oh, I'm sorry. I didn't even notice it." I knew I'd seen something unusual when I'd looked down from the gallery, but I was too disturbed to comprehend what I saw.

I looked out of the window and saw my aunt's shiny, new Model T Ford. "It looks just like the ones in the magazines. Are you happy with it?"

"I am, Seraphine, but I'll like it more when I learn to drive it."

"Come and take a ride with us," Leonard chimed in.

Before I could answer my aunt said, "Seraphine, I think you should come and stay with us for the night. I don't want you here alone." She took my hand. "You were lucky today. You may think you can overcome what's happened here on your own, especially shooting that man, but I don't think you can. You're going to need us."

"I have to stay here tonight, Mrs. Stern. I have two fittings in the morning. There's some last minute sewing I must do – sewing I haven't been able to get done today."

"Very well then, I'm going to send Jonas to you this evening. He can clean up the blood and repair the latch on your shutters. I'll have him bring a cot so that he can sleep in your work room." Pauline was determined to solve all of my problems. "Seraphine? I'd like your consent."

"Yes, yes…but where will he put the horse and carriage for the night?"

"That's a problem I can solve," Leonard said. "Why don't I take you home, Mrs. Stern, and that way I can pick up a cot? Then I'll drive out to Gentilly to pick up Jonas." He waited for my aunt's approval.

"Go ahead; that's fine with me. How fortunate for us the automobile arrived today. Now I can finally get rid of that blasted horse and buggy." My aunt put out her hand signaling she needed assistance to get up. "Let's get started, Leonard."

One afternoon a few days after the shooting incident, I was unable to stop shaking. Jonas had left the shop and I needed someone to talk to who understood my anxiety mixed with remorse. Jonas had expressed his opinion to me, "Dat man was a bad one, Miss Sera. If you hadn't a kilt him, he'd a kilt you." He believed, along with the others, I'd done what I had to do given the circumstances. But I was unsettled and unable to think of anything else. I closed the shop a few minutes after noon and hurried across the cobblestone square to St. Louis Cathedral. I wasn't wearing a hat, so I took the shawl from around my shoulders and covered my head. I reluctantly entered the church.

I had spent the last two nights unable to sleep. The face of the man I'd shot appeared to me over and over again with blood dripping from a hole in his forehead. When I wasn't imagining the bloody face, I saw Leonard kissing me in front of the fireplace. I wondered why I repeatedly saw the same images. Was it God admonishing me for what I'd done in both instances? Was he telling me in order to find redemption I must return to the church? I knew I had to seek help and thought talking to a priest at the cathedral was what I needed to do.

The church was empty and the sound of my heels on the stone floor bounced off the walls. I darted into one of the pews in the back of the church to put an end to the noise. I also needed to gather my thoughts before I sought out the priest. I wanted to find the right questions to ask him. My heart was fluttering and my palms were moist. As I looked around me, my eyes came to rest first on the figures in the stained glass windows, then on the wooden figures on the Stations of the Cross, and finally on the statues around the altar. I saw them looking at me...pointing at me...condemning me. I tried to stand up. I had to get out of the church, but I couldn't move. I screamed as I felt my throat tighten and the light begin to close all around me.

As my eyes opened and I came out of my faint, I felt a cold compress on my forehead. I was lying on the wooden pew and a priest was bending over me. He quickly swabbed my face with a wet handkerchief and then stepped out into the aisle. I tried to sit up. "No, no, no, please lie there a while longer. You're still unsteady. I'm Father Adagio," he told me with a hint of an Italian accent. "I was in the sacristy when I heard you scream."

I obeyed because I still felt a bit woozy.

"Do you belong to this church, madame?" the priest asked.

"No, I don't."

"Are you Catholic?"

"Must I be Catholic to tell you why I'm troubled and ask you for advice?"

"No, but I might look upon you with different eyes and be more inclined to listen if you belong to my church," he chuckled. "It wouldn't hurt to be Catholic."

Perhaps he was joshing, but I wasn't amused.

"No matter how burdensome your troubles, you must first pray to God for help. Are you praying, madame?"

I sat up finally. The realization that the priest hadn't asked my name seemed an added insult to his "don't come to me, go to God" comment. He was content calling me madame. I decided I wouldn't give him my name even if he eventually wanted to know it.

Then he asked the same question in a different way. "Do you engage in deep, sincere prayer to the Lord whenever you're feeling overwhelmed as you seem to be now?"

"Well, Father Adagio, I came here to seek your help and to ask you questions about how to cope with the difficulties I can't seem to overcome on my own, not to be told to connect directly to God for help and answers. Isn't helping me, or anyone for that matter, through these kinds of periods in life what you became a priest to do?"

141

"No, madame, it is not why I became a priest. I became a priest to feel closer to God. I, too, have been burdened with sin. We're all sinners; we must all repent. When the end comes, we will all answer to God. So you must learn to go straight to Him now for your salvation in the end."

"Then what good are you? You serve no purpose. You just look pretty in your frock while your flock fend for themselves." I stood up and stepped into the aisle. "Good day, Father Adagio," I said as I made my way to exit the church.

"Good day, madame." The priest wasn't interested enough to defend himself.

I walked back to the shop feeling abandoned, not only by the church, but by God, again.

I knew the feeling would only add to my bitterness. I knew I must somehow find my own peace...my own forgiveness. I hoped that additional contention would toughen me even more and give me the courage to heal myself - to put the shooting behind me and to forget the taste of Leonard's kisses. There would be no one to help...not even God. In the past, I'd allowed my hostility to push me to a place where I felt estranged, alienated from everyone, but safe. Yes, I thought, I would settle for safety over redemption.

Jonas continued to spend nights sleeping in my work room. Leonard drove him back and forth until my aunt sold the horse and carriage and gave up the rented property in Gentilly. He brought his few possessions and put them in my storage building. Jonas spent from noon to sunset away from the shop. He was neat and clean, but I hadn't any idea where he bathed, washed his clothes or ate his meals.

I hated seeing him living in such horrible conditions. When I asked Aunt Pauline what we should do about a suitable place for him to live, she insisted he live permanently in the storage building. That way he'd be available for anything I'd need and he could be there if there was trouble again. She was convinced I wouldn't regret it.

"In that old building? It's cold and damp. That's no place to put an old man, Mrs. Stern."

"I've been thinking of sending Mr. Meister to put a small addition onto it, the way he did at my home. I'll have him put in a fireplace and a water closet with a wash basin and a toilet. I'll buy a bed for him, too. I need to do this. I simply can't tell Jonas I no longer need him. What would become of him, Seraphine? He's a part of this family and too old to go back to the country to sharecrop."

My aunt wouldn't have slaves or the help living under her roof, but she insisted on sending Jonas to live with me. Wasn't that cheeky! I thought it, but I didn't say it. He had done so much for me, how could I refuse.

Several months later, Jonas was permanently living in the storage building. It hadn't been necessary to add on because I was only using one-third of the building's space. The contractor walled off a section and created wonderful living quarters for Jonas. He was overwhelmed and cried. I didn't admit it right away, but I was glad to have him there.

16

I was making a decent living, but was nevertheless disappointed that my clientele hadn't grown as I thought it would. Not one Creole woman dared to break with the ban against me. I was thought to be money hungry – why else would I dare turn my back on my "own people" in order to serve the Americans who were known to have more money. This was the gossip that floated through the Vieux Carré and beyond. My aunt heard the tale from the seamstresses in her factory. She was disappointed when I didn't take her advice to sell the shop and open one in the Garden District.

After ten years of making myself content with a mediocre business, I gave in and asked Leonard if he would take me to meet a few of the madams in Storyville, the red light district.

Aunt Pauline was beside herself when I told her what I planned to do.

Sewing a full day was beginning to be more difficult. My hands grew more painful and my feet started to tingle. After sitting long periods of time, I was unable to climb the stairs until after I massaged the pins and needles out of my feet. I began doing all of the work upstairs that didn't require the sewing machine. Anything I needed, Jonas brought up for me. The days I worked downstairs in the work room, he was there at the end of the day to help me mount the stairs. I found with his help, I could complete most of my orders without too much difficulty.

My condition was our secret – I didn't have to make Jonas swear he wouldn't tell. I began to rely heavily upon him. I had no idea what a good cook he was. He told me he watched Lizzie all those years when she cooked for the Sterns, so when she died he found it easy to cook for himself. We reversed how we'd worked at the Sterns: I did the marketing and he did the cooking. We ate all our meals together at the kitchen table.

I knew at some point it would become impossible for me to walk to the market and then carry the heavy packages back. Jonas would not only have to cook, but he'd have to do the marketing as well. I decided to teach him to read and write.

He was an exceptional learner and gobbled up reading as well as arithmetic in a short time. I wished I were more learned so that I could have taught him more. I considered asking Leonard, but I knew what he thought about Colored people. He did not want them living at his level; they had a place in society and they needed to stay there. I was the only exception, and I was sure because he couldn't have me, Jonas didn't stand a chance of getting his help.

Leonard and my aunt had a standing invitation for dinner every Tuesday evening. Jonas and I cooked the meal together. He ate before they came so as not to incite their anger or make them privy to our living arrangement. We wanted to avoid making problems for ourselves.

After dinner one Tuesday, my aunt couldn't wait to confront me about considering the Storyville madams as possible clients.

"Do you know anything about that area, Seraphine?" she asked.

"I know the things I've read in the newspaper and the conversations I've heard between you and Leonard. There are about two thousand women of all different colors housed in multi-storied bordellos who ply their trade to White men for money. Does that sum up Storyville?"

"Not exactly," Leonard said. "The District was set up to cater to White men only, but it's common knowledge that as long as you can pass for White, no questions are asked."

"Is that area legal?" I asked.

"It depends on who you ask. I think it's regulated and controlled and it operates as a segregated area. Politicians and the police rarely interfere with how the District is run because they receive a handsome share of the enormous profits made from the houses, the restaurants, the bars and the dance halls. Gambling and drugs also pay them well."

When Leonard talked about the District, he spoke of it in glowing terms. I was sure it was because he was well paid for his accounting services, but I did wonder if he went to the brothels at night. He had told me that some of the profitable houses were run by Colored madams, even though they denied being Colored. I was Colored – yet he loved me. So it wasn't too hard for me to believe he might frequent those houses filled with quadroons. Why was I wondering what Leonard was doing with the women in those houses of ill-repute? Deep inside my memory and my heart, I had successfully buried the taste of his kisses and my desire to have more of them. We had never been in situations that put us that close to each other again. In fact, since we'd kissed, he avoided being alone in a room with me as much as possible. My encounter with Father Adagio made Leonard's avoidance easier to deal with. I had returned to my feelings of distrust for him…and for all men. The fact that he loved me didn't matter.

Lulu White and Willie Piazza were the two madams Leonard was most fond of. He often had lunch with them when he did their books and then spent hours talking to them because he said they were wise and he learned a great deal about life from them.

"Seraphine, can you really overlook how those people live their lives? You could not pay me a trunk full of money to make me look the other way. Those poor young women are not only mistreated by the madams who employ them, but by the men who violate their bodies. Men called pimps beat them and take their money. Diseases run rampant among those women. They spend countless hours in Charity Hospital and sometimes they don't come out. I wish you'd reconsider becoming a dressmaker for prostitutes." My aunt hadn't allowed Leonard to say anything else. Each time he tried to interrupt, she'd wag her finger at him and continue to talk.

"You're trying to scare me, Mrs. Stern. That won't work on me. I need more clients and I'm afraid I don't scare easily. Let's change the subject, shall we? How are you doing with your driving lessons?" As I finished speaking, I watched my aunt's mouth slowly fashion itself into a silly little grin.

"Ask Leonard how I'm doing," she replied.

"Poorly, she's doing poorly, Sera. She's afraid of the car! Lately, she's been too busy or too tired for lessons. I don't know how else to encourage her...I can't force her to learn." Leonard glanced at my aunt with pity in his eyes.

She was still smiling, but barely. "I doubt if I'll ever learn, Leonard. But I'm quite pleased you enjoy driving, so we both get something out of the automobile. I get driven where I want to go and you get a car. I'm going to sign it over to you."

Leonard's mouth hung open. He was too stunned to say anything.

One afternoon a week later, Officer Kane dropped in to check on me.

"Officer, did you learn who the man...I...I...I mean, did you learn who that stranger was?" In spite of my new-found courage and my attempts to forget about the man's death, it was hard not to have it come flooding back at the sight of Officer Kane and even more difficult to try to verbalize anything relating to the incident.

"Yes, Miss Menard, we certainly did find out who he was, and just as I suspected, he'd jumped ship...a Portuguese ship. He'd been seen hanging around the docks and the French Market for a few days. You were an easy target in that thick fog." The policeman moved closer to me as he spoke. I stepped away from him.

"Is there going to be some sort of inquiry into his death?" I asked. "Will I have to fill out papers or appear in court?" As I moved away again, the officer continued to move closer to me.

"There is nothing for you to do, lovely lady. I've taken care of everything. That fella was here without papers and he committed a crime. He was killed lawfully. We'll let that be the end of it. I made sure you'll be spared any further inquiries or problems."

Just as he was about to place his hand on my shoulder, Jonas walked into the shop leaving Officer Kane's hand dangling in the air. He quickly pointed to the mannequin display in the window, "Where'd you get those? They're well made." His voice shook a little from embarrassment and his hate-filled eyes followed Jonas as he walked toward the work room.

"Evenin, Miss Menard...Ofsa Kane." Jonas never looked up. He walked with his eyes looking down at the floor.

I pointed to Jonas, "This is the man who made my mannequins." The policeman was visibly upset when I called Jonas a man. He tried not to react, but his face was filled with loathing. "Good evening, Jonas," I said. "I must get back to work, Officer Kane. Thank you for making a difficult situation better then I'd hoped it would be. I'm in your debt."

"Yes, yes you are and I intend to collect." He looked directly at my bosom and then lowered his chin and raised his eyebrows as if to ask me if I understood what he meant.

"Yes, I do understand and you'll have my answer soon."

"What time are you here alone?"

"Come around noon tomorrow."

"I'll be here," he said with his eyes lewdly sweeping my body.

As soon as the policeman left, I sent Jonas to Leonard's office with a note asking him to come to the shop at eleven-thirty the next day - it was urgent that I see him.

Leonard was there promptly the next morning. I explained what had happened with Officer Kane the day before. He reassured me I needn't worry; he would handle it. We sat quietly in the workroom until we heard the door open, then together we walked into the reception room.

When Officer Kane saw Leonard walk out ahead of me, his face suddenly became flushed with blood from his neck to the rim of his cap. He looked like an over-ripe strawberry. He opened his mouth to speak but Leonard stopped him.

"Officer Kane, what would your superiors think of you if they knew you were attempting to extort sex from this woman who is the victim of a horrible crime? You tried to make her believe you and you alone have the authority to clear her of all responsibility for the death of that seaman. Your superiors made that decision, Officer Kane," Leonard's voice rose to a roar. "I'm a friend of the commissioner and the chief of police, and I know for a fact that you only delivered the news to her at their behest. I checked with them before I came here today. If you want to keep your job, I suggest you apologize to this lady and get back on your beat. And unless you must come to her aid in the event she is threatened again, I think it best you not return to this shop. Are we clear?"

"Yes, sir." The policeman was clearly unnerved. "I'm sorry, Miss Menard. I won't bother you again." He left the shop without another word.

I offered to make lunch for Leonard, but he declined and left immediately.

17

Every day before my scheduled visit to Storyville, I felt the urge to tell Leonard I'd changed my mind. But my aunt's condemnation of my father reverberated inside my head each time and I knew failure wasn't an option.

Lulu White was the first madam I met. I was astounded to see how lavishly she lived. Her house was a mansion called Mahogany Hall. Magnificent crystal chandeliers hung in both of her enormous parlors where she entertained her customers before they went upstairs with the girls of their choice.

Her furniture was the opposite of my aunt's. It was French Provincial – small, delicate and white. There were huge silver-framed mirrors everywhere on the walls. Everything sparkled including the madam. She dripped in diamonds which made her look weighted down.

Lulu was a hefty woman. She walked slowly switching her large hips. Her voice was deep and gravelly. But it was her full-throated laugh that told me a little about who she was. She never held it back. She'd throw her head back and let it fly through the air. I couldn't help but like her immediately.

"So…you sew." She gave a loud cackle and slapped her thigh impressed with her own pun. "You're a skinny one, girlie, nothing to hold on to." She grabbed my waist. "Look at this! You're all bones…no meat." Lulu's voice filled the room. She had a pretentious, arrogant way of speaking, as if she were performing on stage and everyone around her was her audience.

My face felt hot. I stared at Lulu trying hard not to give away how embarrassed I felt or how much she'd hurt my feelings. Maybe I'd judged her too quickly.

"Leonard's been telling me about you. Where is he, anyway?"

"He'll come back for me in an hour," I told her. "He thought I should conduct my own business."

"That Leonard's a good man. Sit down, honey." Lulu pointed to a purple, velvet ottoman with tassels hanging from all four corners.

I sat obediently.

She sat in a large tapestry-covered chair facing me. "I know you've got some troubles at your establishment…the Creole and American kind of shit."

"Yes, I do."

"Listen to me, honey. I'm not going to add to your troubles. You can do all your fittings right here. Bring your fabric samples for me and my girls to choose from and sew up our dresses in your shop. When you finish, bring them here for us to try on. That way, we won't come to your shop and run off those Americans."

I gave a deep sigh of relief. I had been wondering how I was going to ask Lulu if I could do exactly what she had just proposed to me so that I wouldn't lose the rest of my clients. I knew if she and her girls frequented the shop, my reputation would be further ruined and I could end up without any customers, Creole or American. But even though I was grateful to Lulu for being considerate, somehow I didn't think it was her idea. It sounded more like Leonard's thinking. He must have laid the groundwork for me.

Lulu loved champagne and always had a glass of it in her hand. She loved to hear the glass tinkle when she tapped her ring-filled fingers on the rim.

"C'mon, honey, I want you to meet Willie Piazza. Everybody calls her Countess. She's a couple of doors up the street." Lulu got up from her chair and handed her glass to a young woman who hovered around her like a handmaiden.

As we walked up Basin Street, Lulu spoke to everyone she saw. They all greeted her enthusiastically, even the beggar boys who formed the spasm bands and sat on the corners playing their special brand of music on homemade instruments. Lulu took a handful of coins out of a small lace purse attached to her waist and threw them in the middle of where the boys were sitting. They scrambled to grab as many as they could as they all hollered, "Thanks, Lulu."

"I love these raggedy-ass boys. One day a couple of them might be playing in my establishment." Lulu stopped to pat a few of them on the head.

Willie Piazza's house was not to be compared with Lulu's. She, too, loved mirrors, but her furnishings were much more conservative. She was fashionably dressed and walked with grace and elegance. I was most struck by the monocle she wore and the long ivory, gold and diamond cigarette holder she held between long, slim fingers. The only jewelry she wore was a diamond studded choker around her thin neck.

"Countess, this is the dressmaker, Sera, the one Leonard told us about." Lulu pushed me toward Willie Piazza.

Countess stepped back. She looked me up and down. "Your outfit is certainly well made. I want nothing but the best for myself and my boarders. Do you design and sew everything yourself?"

"Countess, a 'how do you do' would be nice." Lulu was looking at me apologetically.

"Sorry, I was impressed with what you're wearing. I forgot my manners." Countess switched her cigarette holder to her left hand and held out the right one for me to shake.

As Countess walked us around her parlors, Lulu told her about the trouble I was having with my shop and explained how we were going to work around it. Countess wasn't pleased she couldn't frequent the shop where she was expected to have her clothes made.

"I will have to think about whether or not I'm interested in such a business arrangement." She handed me her card which she took from a stack on the fireplace mantle. It had her name, her address and her telephone number. "Call me if the situation changes."

"Thank you for considering me. And I do design and sew everything." I finally had an opportunity to speak.

"That's good to know and it will figure in my decision. Now, if you'll excuse me, I have a client." She summoned a small Black man dressed as a doorman to show us out.

As we walked back to her place, Lulu tried to reassure me. "She's not as mean as she sounds. She's a very generous woman who's helped me out of quite a few jams I got myself into. Did you notice her clothes? She wears nothing but the best. Let me tell you something that all of New Orleans knows, girlie. When the Fair Grounds racetrack opens every year, all the high society broads come with their dressmakers so they can copy the outfits Countess and her girls wear."

I was smiling because I had read an article about them in the newspaper. "Lulu, I read about both of you going to the races. The article talked about your beautiful horses and carriages and how you drive through the streets as if you own them. It mentioned your fabulous gowns and fancy lace umbrellas."

"That's exactly what we do. Listen, Countess is a smart woman. She speaks six or seven languages, she's traveled everywhere and she's a good businesswoman. Ask Leonard about her." Lulu stopped and exchanged a few words with a man we were passing on the street.

"I noticed that big white piano when Countess walked us around her parlors. What a beautiful instrument!" I wondered if Countess had deliberately taken us around so that she could show off her house to me.

"That piano gets played by some of the most famous 'professors' in the District. That's what we call great piano players like Jelly Roll Morton and Tony Jackson," Lulu told me. "You ever hear of them?"

"No. But tell me, Lulu, doesn't Countess ever smile?"

"The tale goes like this, girlie: she had a face-lift in Europe and she thinks if she laughs, her face is gonna fall. I don't know if that's true because I never asked her and I never will." Lulu laughed for all the world to hear.

As we were mounting the stairs to Mahogany Hall, Leonard arrived to pick me up.

My association with Lulu worked out so well that Countess got jealous and agreed to the same terms, even though she protested every time she saw me. I was given so many orders for garments that I began to fall behind. When I confided this to Lulu, she told me she would try to help me find someone to assist me in the shop.

One of Lulu's girls had a sister who was not "in the life" and still lived at home with her parents. Florence Doyle came by streetcar from the Irish Channel to meet me and show me her skills. I liked her instantly and marveled at everything she could do with the sewing machine and by hand. I introduced her to Jonas to make sure she had no trouble with his constant presence.

The three of us worked well together and for the first time in a long time, I felt relaxed.

I never took Florence with me to Storyville. But I didn't need to tell her about the District because she corresponded by letter with her sister who told her things I didn't know and couldn't have seen in my short visits there. Every letter she received from her sister she'd bring to work with her the next day to share the District gossip with me. Her parents had disowned her sister and they refused to hear anything about her.

"My sister Edie says your clothes are the envy of all the houses. The girls want to wear your styles but the madams are jealous of Lulu and Countess, so they won't let the girls do business with you. And their pimps won't let the girls have the money to buy the clothes on their own."

"That's too bad; I'd welcome more business. I'd have to hire another seamstress, though." I wondered where I'd put another sewing machine.

"Listen to this!" Florence loved to read parts of Edie's letters to me. "One of Countess Piazza's girls – she calls them boarders – withheld money from her pimp. He tied her to her bedpost and burned her all over her body with cigarettes. She didn't tell anybody and tried to hide the burns, but they got infected. Now she's in Charity Hospital in really bad shape."

"How old is she, Florence?"

"I don't know; my sister didn't say. But let's see, what else. Oh, one of the madams got two new girls, twin sisters…eighteen-year-olds. Their father found out where they were. When he arrived at the house, the madam refused to let him take his daughters and the father shot her in her shoulder. The police came, but they didn't arrest him."

"How did he find the girls?"

"One of the sisters changed her mind about living that kind of life and managed to get a letter to her parents without the other one knowing."

"When I hear these kinds of stories, Florence, I'm ashamed I work for District madams. But…I've got to make a living and you need a job, right?"

"I do, Miss Sera. My ma and pa don't know Edie sends me a few dollars every time she writes. I give the money to them and tell them I worked extra time and you paid me extra."

"What a lovely thing to do. Edie sounds like a very caring, young woman. What made her choose that life?" Maybe Edie wasn't that different from Florence.

"Edie has a beautiful voice. She grew up singing. But when she told my pa she wanted to sing for a living, he went mad. He told her if she didn't keep her sewing job at Stern Brothers factory, he was going to throw her out. Edie didn't wait for him to do it – she left the next day when my pa went to work. My ma had no say; she only cried when my pa wasn't around."

"Where did she go?"

"She stayed with one of the girls from the factory and worked nights at a cabaret here in the French Quarter. Lulu White heard her and asked her if she wanted to work at Mahogany Hall. Now she sings three nights at Lulu's and three nights at Countess Piazza's."

"When did Edie work for Stern Brothers?" I wondered if my aunt had known her.

"She started right after she turned seventeen and she worked there for three years."

When Florence received a letter from her sister, work was suspended for at least an hour until all the news was digested. Jonas always left us to our tête-à-tête. He'd go out to the courtyard and tend the flowers.

157

"You know anybody at Stern Brothers, Miss Sera?"

"Yes, I know the owner." I felt Florence didn't need to know any more than that.

"I tried to get a job there," Florence said, "more than once. Every time I tried, they were never hiring. Everybody wants to work there because they pay good wages."

"Aren't you glad they weren't hiring. You wouldn't be here with me if they had snatched you up. I can't imagine you not being here." It sounded mushy, but I meant it.

"Oh, Miss Sera, thank you. I love hearing I'm worth something. Nobody tells me I am at home."

"Why, Florence Doyle, you deserve to be complimented. You're pretty with your green eyes and curly brown hair; you're intelligent; you have a wonderful personality and you're an outstanding seamstress. Now do you think you're worth something?"

"Oh, Miss Sera, thank you! That's more than I deserve."

"No, you deserve that and more."

Jonas came in and waited to see if we were all talked out. He had a look on his face that said, "End it…please."

After I went upstairs that evening, I thought again about Edie. It occurred to me that if she spent that much time singing at Mahogany Hall and at Countess's, maybe she wasn't engaged in prostitution. I fully intended to ask Lulu about her.

With only two of the madams and their girls, my income tripled. Leonard was ecstatic. He took most of it and invested it for me. He wanted me to buy a house and move out of the shop. He thought I could expand the business by using the shop's second floor as sewing rooms, and if I hired two more seamstresses, he would see to it that some of the other madams changed their minds and used my services. He predicted I'd see my business increase tenfold.

I was so busy I didn't feel the pain in my hands and feet. I didn't know whether the pain had left my body for good or if something had happened to me to make the pain go into hiding. Dr. Schoenbaum had died and I couldn't bring myself to see another doctor.

18

On my next visit to Lulu's a few days after my talk with Florence, I asked her if Edie was singing and turning tricks or just singing.

"Sorry, girlie. I don't give away company secrets. If Edie wanted you and her family to know, she'd tell you. It isn't my place to share her private life."

"You're right, but maybe if her parents knew she isn't living as a prostitute, they'd take her back into their family."

"Her father threw her out because she wanted to sing. I don't think…"

"Miss Lulu! Miss Lulu! Come with me quick. Two girls on the third floor are fighting." Matilda burst into the parlor out of breath.

"Who's fighting?" Lulu screamed at Matilda. "I don't like being interrupted."

"Sorry, Miss Lulu, I don't know whose fighting. I didn't see their faces. But you better come quick cuz they're breaking up a lot of things…and they're both bleeding. It's bad, Miss Lulu."

Lulu shook her head in disgust. She looked at me, "Excuse me, honey, I'm going upstairs to kick a couple of asses. They'd better be breaking up their things and not mine.

C'mon, Matilda, run ahead of me and tell those miserable whores I'm coming up and I'm fucking mad!"

Matilda dashed out of the parlor with Lulu as close behind her as she could get while carrying her chunky-body weight along with her pounds of diamonds.

Matilda was a young mulatto from Jamaica, West Indies. Lulu had adopted her on one of her trips to the island. Matilda was born partially blind and mentally impaired. Her mother neglected and abused her. After Lulu found the girl begging in a tourist area, she bought the child for a few hundred dollars from her mother. According to Lulu, she was able to smuggle the ten-year-old girl into this country, but would not tell me how she did it. She raised Matilda in the bordello and as Matilda grew up, the only thing that gave her pleasure was pleasing Lulu. She'd watch Lulu and anticipate her every need. That's what I saw the first time I went to Mahogany Hall. I thought she behaved like Lulu's handmaiden and that she was there to serve Lulu and only Lulu.

As I sat in the parlor musing about Matilda, I was suddenly aware someone else was in the room behind me. A middle-aged man walked around my chair and stood in front of me.

"Madame White, I'm Henri Labastier, Philippe Labastier's son." He extended his hand for me to shake.

As I shook his hand I said, "I'm not Lulu White, Mr. Labastier. She's upstairs and will be down shortly."

"Please excuse me, madame. I've never met Madame White. This is my first visit to Mahogany Hall. My father died several months ago and I'm taking his place traveling to our clients while my brother runs the factory."

"What do you manufacture, Mr. Labastier?

"Forgive me, shoes, madame, shoes." He opened his briefcase, removed several catalogues and handed them to me. "I did not catch your name, madame."

"It is my time to apologize. I'm Seraphine Menard. Call me Sera."

"Yes, yes, please, call me Henri or Henry. You are French, Sera?"

"Yes, I am...French Creole." I was tempted to tell him what I was actually mixed with: French, Choctaw and African. But...I had chosen to be White and White I'd stay.

"Do you live in this house, Sera?"

"No, oh no. I'm a dressmaker. I'm here to collect payment for the clothes I made for the girls in the house."

Just then, Lulu rushed into the room. It was obvious she had been tousling with someone. Her red wig was askew and she was busily straightening her shirtwaist when she realized Henri Labasteir was standing in the room. She looked from him to me suspiciously. "And who is this, girlie?"

Henri stepped toward Lulu, "I'm the son of Philippe Labastier. My father died recently and I'm replacing him in order to continue our business relationship with you. Henri Labastier, Madame White." He offered her his hand, but instead of taking it, Lulu held out the back of her hand for him to kiss. And he did.

"Call me, Lulu, Henry." She saw the catalogues in my hand and gestured for me to hand them to her which I did. "Can you leave several of these for my girls to go through, Henry?"

"Yes, yes, of course." Henri took three of each of the brochures and gave them to her. She must have expected Matilda to be behind her as she spun around to hand them to her. There was no Matilda.

"What a helluva day! I'll have to take these up to the girls myself and then I'll take you down the street to Willie Piazza's. I'll be right back, Henry."

While we waited for Lulu to return, Henri asked me if I had a shop. When I told him I did and the shop was on St. Ann Street in the French Quarter, he wanted to know if I sold shoes.

"No, I don't sell shoes, but I may consider it because I like many of your styles."

"I'm here from Montreal for a fortnight and I'll be glad to come to your shop to discuss my shoe line with you."

I gave him my address and he told me he'd come to the shop the next afternoon.

Lulu came back with one of her girls in tow. Myrna had collected the money from all the girls to pay me for the clothes and she handed me the envelope. I was curious to know what had happened on the third floor a little earlier but dare not ask. I knew, though, that Edie would certainly put the incident in her next letter to Florence.

"Is everything there, girlie?"

"Yes, Lulu, it's all here." I really had no idea if it was, but I had no intention of counting the money in front of Henri.

"All right," she told me, "I'll see you on your next visit. Come, Henry, I'll take you to Willie Piazza's." Lulu took his arm and led him out of the parlor.

Myrna and I watched Lulu as she walked switching her hips as she held on to Henri's arm. She looked even more ridiculous when she looked over her shoulder, rolled her eyes, and then licked her top lip at us. When we thought they were out of earshot, we burst out laughing. Our giggles quickly ceased when Matilda came running into the room, but when she didn't see Lulu, she ran out again. We hoped she hadn't thought we were laughing at her. If so, she would surely tell

Lulu. All of Lulu's girls feared Matilda – she was her adopted mother's second pair of eyes and ears. She'd often tell Lulu lies about girls she didn't like.

As I got up to leave, another young woman entered the parlor. She looked remarkably like Florence – the same green eyes and curly brown hair. Before I could inquire about her, Myrna spoke to her.

"Where are you off to, Edie?"

"I'm going to Countess's to sing with Tony Jackson. He's visiting from Chicago and he's only going to be here another week. He promised me I could sing some duets with him this afternoon. We're going to do some opera music. I'm excited and I'm really nervous, too. If I'm good enough, Tony said he's going to take me with him to Chicago. He said there are plenty of great places to sing. I have to go, Myrna; I don't want to be late."

It was obvious Edie didn't know who I was. I started to introduce myself, but thought better of it. After my conversation with Lulu about not discussing Edie's private life, I knew it was best I refrain from telling Edie who I was. I watched her dash out of the parlor on her way to Willie Piazza's and realized the dress she was wearing was one I'd made for Countess. She had a lovely figure and I wished I could design a few pieces for her.

I stood inside the front door to wait for Leonard to pick me up. It wasn't wise to wait outside for him. The gutters were filled with the contents of chamber pots and garbage cans. I had learned to walk carefully and to reduce my time outdoors as much as possible. Not many of the houses in the District had inside plumbing. Although the correlation between disease and sanitation was known since 1905, it took years before certain pockets of the city cleaned up their areas. My mother's death from yellow fever in 1878 was a direct result of this same kind of filth in which mosquitoes carried the germs from the gutters into every home and business in the city. I had come to realize how fortunate I was to have gone to the Prytania house to live where there was inside plumbing. I no longer had to contend with the outhouse and the chamber pots at my father's. I shivered when I felt the guilt of leaving the cleaning of those filthy things to my little sister, Philomene.

As I stood mulling over my good fortune to have gone to live at the Prytania house, a priest opened the front door and walked in. I recognized him. It was the priest from the cathedral. He stopped abruptly and stared at me.

"Why Father Adagio, what on earth are you doing in a place like this?" It was my turn to jest. "No wonder you called yourself a sinner. What are you doing here? "

"I must ask you the same question, madame" The priest blushed a bit but was calmer than I'd expected.

"I'm a dressmaker for the house," I replied. "My shop is on St. Ann just across the square from the cathedral."

"Oh, I see." I could see that the information surprised him. "I'm here at the request of one of the girls. I come often to counsel many of them."

"Do you! So…I was one sinner who was unworthy of your counsel. So Father, tell me, what does it take to be worthy of your counsel?"

The door swung open and Lulu rushed in. "You're early, Father! I don't think Henriette is ready for you. You should have phoned me. Come," Lulu put her arm through the priest's arm and turned him away from me. She pursed her mouth and gave me an admonishing glare. "Let's have a glass of champagne while you wait for her." She walked away with him.

There was no time to contemplate what I'd just witnessed. Leonard had arrived and was honking his horn.

19

The next afternoon, Henri Labastier arrived just as Leonard was leaving the shop. The two men exchanged greetings and then Henri greeted me by kissing my hand. Upon seeing this, Leonard didn't leave and it seemed he might be waiting around for a proper introduction.

"Oh, Leonard, before you leave, please meet Henri Labastier. Henri, this is my accountant, Leonard Stern." I watched Leonard's whole body stiffen and his eyes widen when I called him my accountant. The two men shook hands.

"Henri is from Montreal, Canada. He has a shoe manufacturing company. I'm thinking of carrying his line in my store."

"I think that's worth some thought, Sera." Leonard turned and looked at me. His nose and ears were bright red. He turned again to Henri. "I hope you're enjoying our wonderful city. At what hotel are you staying?"

"The Monteleone." Henri quickly removed several catalogues from his briefcase and handed them to me. I, in turn, handed them to Leonard.

"I can't look at them now, Sera. I've got a 3:00 appointment at my office. I'll have to look at them another time. I know you're comfortable at the Monteleone, Mr.

Labastier; it's one of our best hotels. Enjoy your stay." Leonard bowed his head and left.

"Is Mr. Stern opposed to your making decisions without his approval," Henri asked, "or is there something else between you?"

"No, there's nothing between us; we have been friends for many years. I think he was taken aback because I usually talk to him about whatever it is I'm planning beforehand and I didn't this time; that's all." I wondered to myself why it was necessary to lie to Henri and concluded that neither man deserved the complete truth. After all, I didn't belong to either of them.

I called to Jonas who was in the work room and asked him to make us a pot of tea. Florence had a toothache and had gone home early. When Jonas returned with the tea, I told him we were finished for the day and if he needed to go anywhere, he was free to go. He hesitated to leave and I realized, not only had I not introduced him to Henri, he was probably afraid to leave me alone with a stranger.

"Jonas, this is Mr. Labastier; he makes ladies shoes and I think I'm going to sell them in the shop. Henri, this is Jonas, my right arm. I could not operate this business without him." The two men politely bowed their heads to each other. Jonas left and I heard the back door close.

I poured us a cup of tea. "Now," I said, "let's have a look at your catalogues."

The shoes were exquisite, even the ones for day wear. Henri had several, miniature samples of his shoes to show his company's craftsmanship and the quality of the materials. The shoes were moderately priced which was unusual. Most of the salesmen who worked the District sold overpriced, inferior products, and this happened mainly because most of the girls never left the District to shop. They relied on the salesmen who brought their merchandise to their houses to sell or their catalogues from which the girls could order items and have them shipped.

"What are your thoughts about the shoes, Sera? Do they meet your approval for quality and workmanship?" Henri moved his chair closer to mine so that he could point out certain types of shoes.

"I think your shoes are quite well made and the materials are of high quality. I know fabric and leather and they certainly meet my approval. In fact, I've already decided to carry your shoes in my store. I have but a small business, so I don't know if my order will meet your minimum…that's if you have a minimum."

"There is no minimum for you. If you like my shoes, you will receive whatever you select in whatever quantity you want." Henri's shoulder touched mine as he leaned over to point to one of his best-selling styles. I surprised myself when I didn't move away. He looked at me for a moment, then continued to talk about the shoe.

Henri was medium-height with a thin, muscular body. His suit was made of lightweight, sand-colored cotton and was expertly tailored. The fit was perfect; there wasn't any wasted material. It looked very much like the work done at Stern Brothers. I suppose he would be considered average-looking as there were no outstanding features to speak of, but he had an appealing face: soft, intelligent eyes, ruddy, pink cheeks, and a warm smile that seemed to say, "You can trust me." Even in a suit at the end of hot, humid July, there wasn't a bead of perspiration on his brow.

We decided on several styles and an appropriate number of sizes for each. He gave me his card in case I needed to get in touch with him.

"Do you have a telephone, Sera?"

"No, not yet." I felt a bit embarrassed. Most of the madams and their girls had business cards with their addresses and telephone numbers on them, but I'd never given a thought to having a telephone. "Did you need to make a telephone call, Henri?"

"No, I thought perhaps I would call you tomorrow to ask for a convenient time to come for another cup of tea. Is that possible, Sera?"

"Yes, I'd like that very much. Why don't you come for lunch, about 1:00. I'll make a Creole dish I think you'll enjoy. Is that a convenient time for you?"

"My schedule is not so rigid that my appointments cannot be moved around to make time for such pleasantries," Henri said. "I accept your invitation."

Henri was my lunch guest for most of his fourteen days in New Orleans. On the days he came, we all ate together upstairs. He seemed to have no objection to Jonas joining us, and when he learned Jonas had cooked the meal, he showered him with praise. Florence was smitten with Henri and was quite giddy while we talked and ate.

Curiously, I saw nothing of Leonard or my aunt for those two weeks. I suspected Leonard may have come to the shop on one of the days Henri was there and may have seen us in the reception room before we went up for lunch. He often looked through my window to see if I had customers before he came in. I'm sure he told Aunt Pauline about the Canadian shoe manufacturer and exaggerated my relationship with Henri. That could only mean he was jealous. I must admit, it gave me a bit of pleasure to know he was probably seeing me in a different light, not as that passive, passionless spinster he'd been forced to accept against his will. Did he now see me as more than a lonely dressmaker content to live out the rest of her life without companionship?

During lunch on Henri's last day in the city, he told us how much he had enjoyed his visit to New Orleans. "The people here are so hospitable, especially at the Monteleone

Hotel. I have made many friends and have added many business contacts there. There is no doubt I will come back, for business and for pleasure."

"Henri, I hope I'm not being rude, but how is it you speak such perfect English with only a slight, French accent?"

"In Montreal," he told us, "we have many Americans who come to live for business and some permanently. Their children attend our schools. When I was a child, many of them became my friends. I learned English faster than they learned French, so we spoke English all the time." Henri looked around the table at everyone. "Thank you for making my visit so wonderful. I've been in a strange town, but I haven't felt like a stranger."

Florence's cheeks glowed like big, red Creole tomatoes. "Oh, thank you, Mr. Labastier."

She tried to control her giggles, but couldn't.

Jonas smiled at Henri and quickly got up to clear the table and make a pot of coffee.

"When are you leaving for Montreal, Henri?" I asked.

"Tomorrow morning. I think my train leaves at 8:45. I have several stops to make before returning to my home. There are many clients in Atlanta, Memphis and New York City. I will try to send you a note at each stop. That is, if I have your permission." Henri took one of my hands as he waited for my answer.

Florence started to giggle again and couldn't stop. Jonas beckoned to her to follow him downstairs. Henri seemed amused by her behavior. I wondered, though, if he was just being polite for my sake.

"Sera, may I write to you?"

"If you have time, I'd welcome hearing from you." I felt my face grow as red as Florence's.

"Did you ever meet my father, Sera?"

"No, you're the first salesman I've met in the District. I'm not there often, and when I am, it isn't for long. Why do you ask?"

Henri smiled as he touched my cheek with the back of his hand. "I didn't think you'd ever met Philippe Labastier because surely he would have told me about you." Slowly he took my face between his hands and kissed me softly on my lips. "Please forgive me, Sera," he begged, "I could not deprive myself of your sweet mouth."

"It was quite a big surprise, but I do forgive you." I smiled at the wording of his apology.

Henri looked at the clock on the mantel. "It's time for me to leave, Sera. I have one last stop to make at Madame Honoré's on Conti and Royal. Do you know Madame Honoré?"

"I've seen the shop, but I don't know the owner."

"She moved here from Montreal many years ago. She lived near us and has kept in touch with us over the years. She sells only slippers in her lingerie store." Henri paused for several seconds. "Oh, Sera, I'm making light chatter because I don't want to leave you." He kissed me again. "I'd better go…immediately!"

The second kiss startled me. It was longer and harder against my lips. I didn't kiss back, but the desire was there. I hoped he'd kiss me again, so that I could respond, but he didn't.

Henri picked up his briefcase and quickly headed toward the staircase. I followed him down the stairs. He said goodbye to Florence and Jonas and kissed my hand without saying anything. I knew he'd said everything that needed to be said upstairs.

20

After a two-week absence, Leonard and my aunt showed up for a visit the very evening of Henri's last lunch with me. As soon as they arrived, Jonas excused himself as if he anticipated trouble.

My God, I wondered, were they watching me? Did they know it was Henri's last afternoon? The only person who was in a position to know that and could have told them was Jonas. We had too many secrets between us; Jonas would never betray me. How, then, did they know?

They brought a light meal for dinner. Leonard insisted on serving us: baked eggplant with an alligator pear and cucumber salad. We had baked apples and heavy cream for dessert.

My aunt was unusually quiet; Leonard was noticeably anxious. We ate in silence until I got fed up with the situation.

"All right, tell me what the hell is on your minds. This silence is ridiculous." I slammed my fork so hard into my plate, they jumped and gasped.

Leonard put down his knife and fork. "What do you know about Henri Labastier, Sera? Why are you so familiar with him after knowing him for so short a time? He called you, Sera; you called him, Henri. Don't tell me you're going to settle for a salesman...a salesman who cheats those poor women in the District out of what little they have. How far has your relationship gone with this man?"

"Frankly, Leonard, I don't have to report my relationship with anyone to you. It isn't any of your business. Mr. Labastier is returning to Montreal tomorrow, but you probably already know that." I smiled when I said Henri's name. It softened Leonard's nasty diatribe.

"Tell me, Miss Menard, after two weeks with Henri Labastier, whatever will you do without him?" He looked at my aunt as she continued to eat. I think he was hoping to get her approval for the barb he'd just lobbed into my lap. Instead she pointed to the coffee pot as if she was without hearing or speech. I got up and made a pot of coffee.

In a calmer voice this time, Leonard asked, "Did you order any shoes, Sera?"

I replied just as calm. "I ordered several styles and a few sizes of each. I'll see how they sell before reordering." I found the catalogues and showed them to Aunt Pauline.

"These are lovely, Seraphine. Unfortunately, my feet are much too wide to wear any of them," she said.

I didn't like that my aunt was so lethargic and seemed unwilling to say any more than she needed to. She had contributed little to our evening. I felt she may have been ill and wasn't telling us.

"Aren't you feeling well, Mrs. Stern? I've never seen you so quiet."

"I'm just overworked, Seraphine. I think it's time to go, Leonard. Tomorrow is Saturday and I just may spend the whole day in bed. Shall we?" My aunt could no longer get up or down the stairs without assistance; Leonard sprang to his feet.

No one spoke again until we said goodnight at the door.

I waited like an excited young girl waits to receive a note from her beau – where was Henri's? He had been gone for weeks and he'd written not a word to me.

Jonas became overly attentive after Henri left. He looked at me as if he felt sorry for me. I was touched by his empathy, but not flattered by his seeming belief that I couldn't handle a little disappointment. He hovered around me until bedtime. I noticed how frail and bent he was becoming even though he continued to do all of the strenuous chores around the shop without complaint.

Florence's next letter did not come from the District. Edie had indeed gone to Chicago with Tony Jackson and with the blessings of Lulu and Countess. Florence hadn't brought the letter with her. She tearfully told me that when she attempted to read the letter to her parents, her father took the letter from her and tore it in pieces, then tossed it out of the house and into the rain. He gave her an ultimatum: she was never to receive or send letters to her sister, and if she did, she would also be thrown out of the house.

When Florence started to cry, I tried to comfort her.

"Somehow, Florence, I don't think Edie going to Chicago is a bad thing. I don't know if you know anything about Tony Jackson, but here is what I found out. He's a Black man and he's said to be a musical genius. They say he's a homosexual which means he isn't interested in Edie; he's attracted to men. That's why he went to Chicago. The people are supposed to be more open-minded there. He can probably live his life more openly. Tony's made quite a name for himself there. I'm sure he's acquired many influential friends in the music business who can give your sister the break she needs for a career."

"How do you know all that, Miss Sera?" Florence had stopped crying and looked a little more willing to accept Edie leaving New Orleans for Chicago.

"Between Lulu and Countess, I've learned quite a bit in recent months. They care a great deal about what happens to Edie and they know how talented she is. But they also know Tony Jackson. I'm sure with him looking out for her, good things will happen for Edie."

"But how will I keep in touch with her if I don't have her address?"

"I'll talk to Countess, Florence. I'm sure she'll know how to reach Tony and your sister."

"Miss Sera, I had read all of Edie's letter before I tried to read it to my ma and pa. She told me Countess gave her many of the clothes you'd made for her. They're the same height and they wear the same size. She bought Edie new undergarments and shoes. Before they left, Countess warned Tony that if anything happened to Edie while she was in his care, she'd go to Chicago and shoot him dead."

"I'm happy to hear that, Florence. It doesn't surprise me, though, that Countess did that. Lulu told me she's the most generous madam in the District."

"I'm afraid for my sister, Miss Sera. She doesn't know anybody in Chicago."

"Well," I chuckled, "she didn't know anyone in the District either when she went there with Lulu. So, stop worrying. I'll ask for news about her whenever I go to Countess's and I'll get her address so you can write to her and get letters from her here at the shop."

"Thank you, thank you, thank you, Miss Sera! What would I do without you?"

I looked at the clock on the work room mantel. "Florence, let's knock-off early today and walk over to Café du Monde for beignets and café au lait. You can go home from there."

The news I got from Countess about Edie was even better than expected. With Tony's connections and the determination that her voice was of operatic quality, she had been introduced to a Chicago socialite whose charity gave financial help to budding opera singers.

Edie was accepted to the Levine School of Music. She was given room and board, a vocal coach and comprehensive music classes which were fully paid for by the Opera Association of Chicago.

Florence couldn't wait to tell her parents Edie's good news. She told Sera her father couldn't possibly feel the same way about his daughter after he learned the wonderful things that were happening to her. Her mother welcomed her news about Edie, but her father was unmoved. As far as he was concerned, he told Florence, Edie had died the day she'd left his house.

After weeks and still no word or shoe shipment, I decided to ask Lulu if she'd received her orders. She had not. Finding that unusual for Labastier Shoes, Lulu tried to call the factory in Montreal, but that number was no longer in service. And because the orders were not prepaid, no one was particularly upset.

It took me a few days to get up enough courage to discuss it with Leonard. He immediately gave me a smug: I-told-you-so look.

"Maybe the company has money troubles and they've had to declare bankruptcy after the senior Labastier died."

Again...my suspicions were aroused. Had Leonard asked Lulu for information about Henri and his business? He could not have known about Henri's father's death unless he'd been told. I hadn't told him.

"Leonard, if the company was in trouble, why would Henri have traveled to his clients in all those states if he wasn't sure he could fill their orders?" It simply did not make sense to me.

"Sera, there could be a hundred reasons why the company is no longer in business. If you really want to sell shoes, there are many other shoe companies that will gladly welcome your business. Have some of them send you their catalogues. Is there some other reason you must have Labastier shoes?" Leonard didn't wait for my answer. "You don't have to answer. You weren't interested in my love, but you managed to fall for a broken-down shoe salesman. Didn't you feel anything about how I must feel to have groveled at your feet all these years and then watch you melt into that foreigner's arms? Shame on you!" he screamed at me.

"You...arrogant opportunist. What were you before you came to New Orleans? A bookkeeper...you were a bookkeeper!" I screamed back at him.

"I was an accountant."

"Bookkeeper...accountant, it's all the same. You dare to call Henri a broken-down salesman when you didn't even have a job in New York City. You were unemployed. That's why you were available when Daniel and Pauline sent for you and started you off in their business."

"You mean I came to New Orleans to save their business, which I did."

"Yes, you did, Leonard, while growing your business on their backs. You lived free ; you ate free. And you're still doing it. You're still living on my aunt...a half-breed. Please remember, Pauline is half-Choctaw and you're a bigot. You believe if you're White, you're superior. What is Aunt Pauline's money that you're enjoying – White or Choctaw? And Jonas, after all the years of service he's given the Stern family, he will never be anything but a slave in your eyes. I don't know what..." I couldn't continue. I realized I was verbally assaulting the man who had been by my side through it all for more than twenty-five years. But so had Jonas.

"I'm sorry it's come to this, Sera. My only reason for saying the things I did is mainly because I love you and can't understand why you'd throw away my love for someone unknown. I don't want you to get hurt. I did check with Lulu to get information about Henri and to find out when he was leaving New Orleans. I'm sorry for being unable to step back and give him free rein. I love you, Sera." Leonard abruptly stopped talking and rushed toward the door. "I'll be here to pick you up on Thursday for your fittings in the District."

"Leonard, wait! I'm sorry for the things I said to you. You didn't deserve that."

"No, Sera, I did. I'm ashamed to have treated you, the person I love most in the world, with such possessiveness. That is not love, it's ugliness."

"There's been no affair with Henri Labastier. We simply flirted and left the rest up to fate. I may never see or hear from him again."

We heard a rustling sound coming from the work room. I had forgotten Jonas was in there doing some cutting. Florence was upstairs making tea and scones. Realizing Jonas had heard our argument, we looked at each other filled with shame.

Jonas and Leonard were as close as any two people could be with Leonard's feelings about the separation of the races. They seemed to respect each other in spite of those feelings.

After Leonard left, I lingered in the reception room not knowing how I was going to face Jonas. When my courage returned, I walked right into the work room and said, "Jonas, did you hear what we said in there?"

"Yessum, Ah did. But it don botha me none, cuz I know Mistah Leonard don really mean it."

"Maybe he doesn't, Jonas. I hope not."

We heard Florence coming down the stairs with the tea and scones.

After our tea, I decided to walk over to Mrs. Honoré's lingerie shop to ask her if she knew what had happened to Henri's company. I did not want to ask directly about Henri, so I planned to confine my inquiry to the company and the non-shipment of the shoe orders.

"Good afternoon, are you, Mrs. Honoré? I asked the middle-aged woman sitting behind the counter.

"No, I'm Celeste, her daughter. You're Miss Menard, the dressmaker. You're well-known here in the Vieux Carré."

"Oh my! Yes, I'm Sera Menard." I had the feeling she really meant notorious.

"My mother is in Montreal attending the funerals of some of her dearest friends, the Labastiers."

I looked at her unable to speak.

"My mother is originally from Montreal. The Labastiers were her neighbors. They've remained friends all these years."

I was screaming inside my head, "Tell me who died, please!"

"Do you know what happened to the Labastier family, Sera?"

"No, Celeste, I don't."

"Some kind of flammable glue spilled and caught fire in the factory. The building was old and burned very quickly. All the workers got out, except Mrs. Labastier and her son, Armand. They were trapped in the office and burned to death."

"Oh...oh!" I felt faint. Celeste came around the counter and grabbed my arm and led me to a chair. She poured a glass of water for me from a decanter on the counter.

"Are you all right, Sera?"

"Yes, yes…thank you. That was such a shock." While I was saying that, I was thinking how grateful I was she hadn't said Henri's name.

"Only Henri, the youngest son, is left. He was on his way to Montreal when it happened. I don't know what will become of the company now. I doubt if Henri will rebuild it. He never handled the business and manufacturing ends of the company. He and his father were the sales division."

"I must get back to my shop, Celeste. When you speak or write to your mother. Please ask her to extend my condolences to Mr. Labastier."

21

The night before we were to celebrate my forty-fourth birthday, Aunt Pauline died in her sleep. I had never seen Leonard cry, but he had no shame the evening of her death when he sat in the dining room at the Prytania house, in front of Jonas and me, and wept until he was too weak to stand.

He loved my aunt as much as he loved his mother and he often told her so. In turn, my aunt told him how brilliant he was, and how much his being a savvy businessman had helped Stern Brothers. What meant the most to her, I think, was that he was loyal to her and did not abandon her after Daniel died. On many occasions, she'd tell me that only a special young man would spend so much of his time with an old woman.

Aunt Pauline had discussed her burial wishes with Leonard, but not her will. Just before her death, he confided to her where he'd been all those times he'd missed our gatherings. He had returned to school and had recently earned his law degree. She told him she was proud of him but she had already hired a lawyer to handle her will and she would not discuss its contents with him. This he confided to me the day she died.

Not wishing to be put next to Daniel, my aunt was buried in the Menard vault on top my father. And as with my father's burial, torrential rain came down the entire day. The priest from St. Ignatius, my aunt's church, joined Leonard, Jonas and me at the site. The understated burial suited my aunt; it was the way she had lived her life.

The lawyer came the afternoon of my aunt's interment. The will was straightforward and uncomplicated. The house on Prytania Street, the store, and the factory were all left to Leonard. When the businesses were sold, I was to be given twenty-five percent of the monies from the sale. All of her liquid money was to be divided between Leonard and me, except for $1,000 to be given to Jonas together with the promise of always having a home with the family until he died. Her jewelry was willed to me, except her wedding ring. That was Leonard's. None of my siblings were mentioned.

Leonard closed the store and the factory for two weeks, paid the employees for their time off and went to New York. In all the years he'd been in New Orleans, he had only gone to see his family twice. Many of them were now dead.

With Leonard out of sight and out of mind, I felt free to think about Henri. Celeste invited me to have tea with her whenever I had time and I found the time several times during the two weeks Leonard was away. Mrs. Honoré still hadn't returned and Celeste was lonely. She was overjoyed to have me visit her. I was happy to oblige knowing those visits were the only way I'd get any news about Henri.

"What news are you getting about the shoe company? Is Mr. Labastier planning to start it up again?" I felt safe asking this after Celeste and I talked about the current trend in fashion and about our aches and pains. We were about the same age and she was also having arthritis problems, so we had a great deal to commiserate about.

"My mother's last letter didn't mention Henri. The last she wrote about him was that he was having difficulty adjusting to his life without his mother and brother."

"It is difficult to be without a family when you're not married. I know about how that feels. It must be terrible for him."

"Henri isn't without a family. He has his wife and children. They've been helping him through his pain. He's a difficult fellow to get along with. His wife was on the verge of divorcing him when the tragedy happened. I don't know what she's going to do now."

This was no time to faint. I forced myself to remain composed. "I'm…I'm happy he has his family by his side. He…he never mentioned he had a family."

"That's Henri! As pretty as you are, he probably looked forward to another conquest."

"Celeste, are you saying Henri is some kind of Casanova?"

"Yes, Sera, I'm afraid that's exactly what I mean. I knew you had become infected with the Henri charm the first time you came here. You looked like me many years ago. You see, Sera, I was Henri's first wife. The woman he has now is his third. She is the only one who has been brave enough to give him children."

"Oh, Celeste, forgive me if I've been deceptive. I'm sorry to have brought back such bad memories to you. Henri was so convincing and I suppose I was vulnerable." I stood up to leave.

"No, Sera, please sit down. There is no need to apologize. That happened to me so long ago that it doesn't hurt anymore. Because the families have remained close, I've learned about all of his philandering. I'm so glad I saw who and what he was early in our marriage."

"Did your experience with Henri cause you to never want to remarry?"

"I don't think so, but perhaps it did. I believe, though, I just have not met anyone whom I've wanted to marry – here in New Orleans or in Montreal. What about you, Sera, have you ever been married?"

"No, never." I knew I had to stop talking. I had been so rattled by Henri's news, that I knew I couldn't reinvent myself in so short a time. In all the years I'd been living as a *passablanc*, I'd never been in a situation where I needed to talk about my life. Then I realized she'd only asked if I'd ever been married, not who I was and where I'd come from.

"How could a beautiful woman like you be unmarried? Why?"

I had found my composure again. "I suppose like you, I have never found anyone I wanted to marry."

"I hope what you learned today won't put an end to our friendship. I enjoy your visits, Sera, and I hope you'll continue to come. I won't tell my mother anything about you and Henri. She still adores him, in spite of what happened to me at his hands."

"Is helping Henri the reason your mother is spending so much time in Montreal?"

"Not entirely. Her brother has been very ill, so she's spending a few months helping him. He's a widower and lives alone. She feels it will be the last time she'll be able to spend time with him before he dies. He lives close to the Labastier's, so she gets to see Henri often."

"I must get back to work, Celeste. As shocked as I am to hear about Henri, I won't let that ruin our friendship. I recently buried my aunt and I miss her very much. We were more like friends than relatives. It's been a long time since I've had a friend my own age. It makes my aunt's absence tolerable. You'll have to come and have lunch with me soon. What about a day next week?"

"That would be lovely. I'll close the shop a little early next Wednesday and I'll be there about 1:00. Is that a good time for you, Sera?"

"Yes, it's perfect."

There was a sadness that hung in the air around the shop. Florence was very quiet while she worked. I don't think she knew what else to say to Jonas and me about losing Aunt Pauline, except to give us her condolences. With Leonard in New York, there was no one to lift us out of our grief. When he returned, he had a surprise for us. He brought home a wife!

That was the end of 1916, and by the end of the next year, I'd realized they were two of the most unusual and chaotic years of my life.

After Leonard returned to work, he brought over the papers that stipulated what my aunt had left me and gave me advice about what he thought I should do with the money. He wanted to invest it as he always did, and since I knew of no mistakes he'd made, I allowed him to do it.

"Leonard, will I ever meet your wife? I'd like to." I shocked him and he hesitated before he answered.

"I don't think it would be a good idea, Sera. She knows nothing about you and I think if she saw me in your presence, she'd know immediately that she's my second choice. I won't do that to her."

I was taken aback but knew he was right. "I want you to be happy, Leonard. And if that's the best way for you to have a good marriage, then that's what you need to do. Mrs. Stern must have known you were planning to marry. Is that why she left you her wedding ring?"

"I think so because she knew I was considering it. I had held out hope all these years that you'd marry me, but after

Henri Labastier came into the picture and then Mrs. Stern's death, I realized how alone I was and I had to do something about it. Rose and I met when I went back to New York a few years ago and we've corresponded ever since. Excuse me for a few minutes, Sera. I want to go downstairs and say hello to Jonas and tell him my news."

I was as happy for Leonard as I could be with the peculiar kind of love I felt for him. He had always been there when I needed him and I felt safe as long as I knew I could depend on him. I also knew had Daniel not changed my life the way he had, I would have been free to love and marry Leonard. But distrust and fear held me prisoner and I couldn't free myself. He belonged to someone else now - to someone he'd kept secretly waiting in the wings until he was tired of waiting for me. With Aunt Pauline gone and Leonard married, I wasn't sure how I'd manage to exist without them. They had directed more than half my life. Would I be able to think for myself now?

Why did Henri have to come into my life so late, and then not only disappear, but turn out to be a philanderer? How could I have been so gullible to think a man like that would have an interest in a mousy spinster? I hated that he'd left me wanting more than the small taste of affection he'd given me. It was the first time I'd ever admitted to myself that I wanted more than kisses, but perhaps it was too late.

"Sera," Leonard told me, "I have another surprise for you and it's a wonderful one. Mrs. Stern was planning to give this to you at your birthday celebration." Leonard pulled several papers from beneath the stack related to the inheritance money.

"No, no, no...I don't want any more surprises." I sprang up from the table and started to pace in the kitchen.

"Sera, sit down, please."

I sat and Leonard put the papers in front of me. They were the deed to a house on Esplanade Avenue.

"Leonard...a house? Why? I like my life here." My God! My aunt was controlling my life from the grave.

"How can you insist on living here after shooting a man who was either going to hurt you or kill you? Don't tell me you've forgotten that?" Now Leonard was up pacing.

"I'll never forget as long as I'm reminded it happened. Don't you think taking that man's life will be with me forever? I will always see his face and the stunned look in his eyes as that bullet left my gun. The one thing that allows me to forgive myself is that it was either him or me. Had he had time to throw his knife, there would be no me to have a memory." I was slow to anger, but I could feel it trying to erupt.

"Sera, the Vieux Carré is changing. This place has become a slum; look around you. Many of the Creoles have moved and the mob has moved in. This whole area is not what it used to be. Don't you ever look at the shopkeepers around here? Are they the same ones who were here when you first opened your shop?"

"I don't see what you see, Leonard. And as for the mob, they're here and in Storyville, too. Some of them are your clients. I've been making clothes for many of their wives for years. So why am I suddenly vulnerable?"

"Your aunt...and I...have been trying to get you out of here...to a better area. Having your business here is one thing, living here is another." It was the first time Leonard had referred to Pauline as my aunt.

"You have a wife now. I can't impose on your time the way I have in the past. I'm wondering this very moment how I'm going to get back and forth to the District."

"Do you think I'll desert you and not find a way for you to continue to get there? Why do you think so little of me, Sera? I will always take care of you and make sure you have what you need. But you know that don't you?"

When I didn't answer, he continued.

"I will drive you to Basin Street whenever you need to go. In the meantime, you need to purchase a car – nothing fancy – just something to take you to the places you need to go. And…I will teach you to drive it. You also need to put a telephone in here and one in your house."

It was the end of 1916 and things were changing – everywhere. I saw the changes but did not acknowledge them. Life was so much easier when I excluded whatever was unpleasant. However, I couldn't ignore the United States would be joining the war in Europe. President Wilson had asked Congress for a declaration of war against Germany. Men were being drafted into the armed forces. The newspapers and the people on the street were saying we were going to war. Oh, Aunt Pauline, I thought, you should be here to discuss what's happening in the world with me. I miss our chats. The times Leonard hadn't come to join us for dinner, my aunt and I would talk about politics, fashion, religion - anything and everything. It seemed she was trying to make up for lost time with me.

When Mrs. Honoré returned from Montreal, she informed Celeste she was selling the shop and they would be moving back to Canada. Celeste tearfully told me what her mother planned to do when she came for tea one afternoon.

"My uncle is hanging on to life and he needs my mother. She can't afford to leave me and the shop indefinitely. My uncle is willing his house to her. He has no children."

"Do you want to leave New Orleans, Celeste?"

"No, of course not. I hate the cold weather in Montreal. But, Sera, I have never had a job other than in our store. My mother has taken care of me all these years. I have nothing of my own. I have no money in which to stay in New Orleans if I refuse to leave with her."

"Stay here if you want. I will give you a job and a place to live. I recently received a house my aunt was planning to give me before she died. It's a large house and you're welcome to live there with me. You would not be imposing."

"Oh, Sera, you're a wonderful friend. I wish I could accept your kind offer."

"What's stopping you, Celeste?"

"I can't leave my mother after all she's done for me. She's only two years younger than her brother and I can see the physical changes happening to her, too. She'll need me in a few years the way my uncle needs her now."

"You're a wonderful daughter, Celeste. I understand what you must do. I'm sorry you'll be leaving New Orleans and me. I've truly enjoyed your friendship and wish things were different. I'll really miss you."

"Maybe you'll consider visiting me in Montreal one day."

"I doubt it, Celeste. My body is no longer fit for travel. When are you leaving?"

"In a few days. Everything in the shop and our living quarters will be sold. We're sending our clothes and personal items by rail as soon as they're packed. Mother has put the property in the hands of a realtor she's known for years. He'll take care of everything."

"So soon! Is this a goodbye visit?"

"I'm afraid it is." Celeste stood up and held out her arms to me. She embraced me. We couldn't help the tears that flowed down our faces. "Goodbye, Celeste, have a safe trip. Please write to me. We mustn't lose touch."

I purchased a used Model T Ford and Leonard taught me to drive it. Not many women were behind the wheel in the South, so I turned heads wherever I went. Even though the house on Esplanade had been renovated, there were problems no one anticipated. There was no bathroom in the downstairs servant's quarters where Jonas was going to live. But on the second floor there were two. Jonas and I already knew how to keep secrets, so I did what needed to be done. I gave him the use of one of the bathrooms. There was also no place to park the car on the premises. It had to be left on the street. Nothing could be done to solve that problem without destroying what looked to have been a beautiful garden at one time. I was more interested in restoring the garden than finding a place for the automobile.

The house had been sold to Pauline with most of the original furniture. All I needed to do was renovate the kitchen and convert the privies into real bathrooms. Mr. Meister had retired, but his son had taken over the business and his work was as exceptional as his father's.

Three months after my talk with Leonard, I moved into the house.

22

By September of 1917, everything was going along smoothly. One morning, I drove to the District with my car filled with garments. We had worked feverishly to get half a dozen dresses ready to take to Lulu's girls for fittings and another nine for Countess's boarders. I found Lulu nervously pacing on the banquette in front of Mahogany Hall. She told me she had gotten some inside information about the District.

"Sera, they're going to close us down and I'm not ready. They're going to close down the whole fucking District!"

"Who, Lulu?"

"They say the Department of the Navy."

"But why?"

"Because we're too close to military bases and there's going to be a war. They don't want those boys running loose in here before they send them to fight." It was obvious Lulu was well educated and well-spoken. Why couldn't she find a safe, legal occupation? I wanted desperately to say that to her, but I knew I'd better keep it to myself. I didn't think she needed to hear that when she was about to lose everything.

"How reliable is your source?" I asked

"As reliable as they come...the goddamn police chief himself."

"Did he tell you how soon it was going to happen?"

"Two or three months. He wasn't real sure."

"What did you mean when you said you're not ready, Lulu?"

"Sera, most of my money is gone. I made some bad investments Leonard told me not to make. I didn't listen to him. And thanks to Hollywood and George Killshaw, my man of more than twenty-five years, hundreds of thousands are gone. For twenty-five years that bastard lived on me enjoying my bread and my body. Countess told me not to put all my trust in that slick pimp, but did I listen? Hell no! I gave Killshaw hundreds of thousands to set me up in Hollywood to start a new career making movies and he disappeared with it. I've always had good instincts about men. How did I sleep next to him every night and not have suspected what he was going to do?" Lulu had no tears, but her voice cracked several times while she spoke.

"Have you told Countess about the closing?"

Lulu smiled. "That Countess...nothing surprises her. She's always got her shit together. She's already planning what she's going to do. She's been tired of this life for a long time. I think she's planning to go live in Europe. I know she's got a lot of money hidden away." She adjusted her wig which was partially pulled down over one ear. I'd never seen her look so disheveled.

"Sera, what will you do? Do you have enough business from those Americans to keep you going?"

"Lulu, don't worry about me. What will you do?"

"Not sure, but I always land on my feet just like a cat."

"Whatever happens, Lulu, if I can ever help you, please let me know."

"This is a crazy world, girlie. Right now, I'm trying to decide if I ought to tell my girls. They talk too much, though, so it might be bad for whatever business we've got left."

I thought about how timely it was for a number of my clients who had married "out of the life." Most of them had developed relationships with professional men who had frequented their houses. When a couple decided to marry, the young woman would often leave the brothel and go to a neighboring state. In about six months, she'd return with a new identity. She'd then walk into my shop as a new customer. Her fiancé or new husband would pay her bills.

Lulu was right about Countess. She asked to talk to me before she called her boarders down for their fittings. She beckoned me to follow her into the parlor with the white piano where she closed the door behind her.

"Did Lulu tell you what she heard?" Countess asked me.

"Yes, a few minutes ago," I answered.

"I expect to be ready when it happens, Sera. So I'd like you to make a new wardrobe for me: several travel outfits, a day and an evening coat, a light cape and a heavy one. I haven't yet decided on the other pieces. Come tomorrow, if you can, and bring as many sample materials as you can for me to make my selections."

I hesitated before asking Countess personal questions. I knew how she felt about being asked, but I was curious. "Where are you going?"

"France," she answered spontaneously. "I know the country; I speak the language. I'll be comfortable there."

"I envy you, Countess. I wish I could leave this place with all its bad memories and live somewhere where no one knows me." I couldn't believe I had allowed myself to not only voice those thoughts, but I'd also shared them with someone.

"Lulu and I know your story, Sera. It's our story. You're living a lie in order to have a better life. You haven't been found out, yet, but we have. Whenever we're arrested, our court papers list us as Negresses. That is not who I am in France."

Florence, Jonas and I worked at a furious pace to complete Countess's new wardrobe. Word of the closing had spread throughout the District. I had no more orders from the girls in Lulu's or Countess's houses.

In mid-October, the day after I delivered the clothes to Countess, our troops in France entered the fight. We were officially at war and Countess was unable to travel to France. The Department of the Navy ordered the madams and their girls to vacate the District by midnight on November 12.

Several weeks after the District closed, Florence received a letter from Edie. She wrote that Countess had taken a train to Chicago and was staying in a hotel in the city until she was able to travel to France.

Lulu closed Mahogany Hall and set about operating her saloon next to the mansion. She was arrested for selling liquor to a soldier and sent to a federal prison. Somehow she managed to receive a presidential pardon and was released. Leonard saw her only once after the District closed. She gave him a large diamond on a chain to give to me to cover her last bill which hadn't been paid. We never saw her again.

There wasn't an abundance of work after the District closed, but I was determined to keep Florence employed. Her family depended on her salary to keep them going. With the slowdown in our work schedule, I gave her Holy Thursday through Easter Sunday off with pay.

When she didn't return to work on Monday and again on Tuesday, Leonard went to her home on Wednesday to check on her. The house had a quarantine sign posted on the door. The next-door neighbor heard him knocking and came out to tell him Florence and her mother had died of influenza on Easter Saturday. She didn't know where Mr. Doyle had buried them, but he had done it in twenty-four hours. On Tuesday, when she saw him leaving the house with a small suitcase, she asked him where he was off to and he told her he didn't know. He just knew he'd never come back. Then he said goodbye and walked away from the house.

There were many deaths that year when the disease became a nationwide epidemic. I had only a touch of the sickness, but with Jonas's help I nursed myself back to health. During my illness, the pain in my hands and feet returned. I had enjoyed such a long period being pain-free that I had forgotten how punishing it could be.

With Leonard's help, I tried to get in touch with Edie to let her know what had happened to her family. Florence hadn't left any letters with Edie's return address at the shop, and now that the District was closed, there was no way to get that information. I remembered the name of the school where she was studying and we got in touch with the Levine School of Music in Chicago. We were told Edie had dropped out of her studies several months earlier and the school had no knowledge of her whereabouts.

Through one of Leonard's mob clients, Tony Jackson was located in Chicago. It seemed Jackson's life was in a downward spiral from alcoholism. It took several weeks to get the following information relayed to us: Edie left the school because she didn't want to sing opera; she wanted to sing popular music. Countess Piazza encouraged her to go with her to Europe – so that's probably what he thought she'd done. I hoped one day Edie would return to New Orleans and learn what happened to her family. Or perhaps, she'd write to Florence from Europe and that would give me the opportunity to get in touch with her. I needed closure, it seemed, as much as Edie.

Leonard was glad when the war was over so that he could get back to expanding his business. He worried about not acquiring what he needed to be comfortable in his old age which he felt was fast approaching. Stern Brothers took several years before it began to be profitable again and he decided this was the time to sell it. He said his law practice was demanding more of his time and Stern Brothers needed someone who could devote a full day between the factory and the store the way Pauline had done.

I saw less and less of him. Our relationship had changed after his marriage and when Henri came into my life. He occasionally came to the house on a Sunday for lunch. There were usually papers for me to sign or the name and telephone number of the wife of one of his clients who wanted a dressmaker. With his referrals my business started to pick up again. But with the condition of my hands, I didn't know how I'd manage with only Jonas's help.

Leonard found me another seamstress without me asking. He told me he knew how important Florence had been to me in completing my garments on time. Georgina Massimiamo was a young woman from the Stern factory. When it was put up for sale, she asked Leonard if he knew of any places she might apply for a job if she was let go. After Stern Brothers was sold and the new owner took control, he let half of the seamstresses go and Georgina was among them.

She could do anything by machine or by hand and she eventually took over designing the new clothes for the window mannequins. Weeks after she came to work for me, I learned her father, Graziano, worked for one of the Mafia bosses. Georgina was his only child. Her mother had died during the influenza epidemic the year before.

At first, Graziano came once or twice a week to visit Georgina. But pretty soon he was there almost every day with some kind of sweet treat for us. This caused me to wonder if it was his daughter he came to see or was he there to chat with me. I must tell you honestly, I didn't discourage him. He was not Henri, but he'd suffice...for conversation.

After I moved to the Esplanade house, I entertained Leonard's suggestion about expanding the business, but after the District closed I did not act upon it. I left the upstairs kitchen intact. Jonas often made meals for us and we enjoyed many lunches and on occasion some dinners. We enjoyed the gallery during Mardi Gras as I had with my aunt and Leonard. Sometimes we'd even relax there with a cool glass of lemonade when we got tired of sewing.

Jonas often made tea or coffee for us when Graziano brought sweets. I was particularly pleased with Georgina and her father when there seemed to be not a hint of prejudice against Jonas. They treated him the way I did.

When the final papers for the sale of Stern Brothers were ready to be signed, Leonard brought them to the shop for my signature. He looked sad that day. His eyes were red-rimmed and his face was grey. I tried to ignore how he looked but I couldn't.

"Leonard, is something wrong?" I asked. "I've never seen you look this way."

"Rose had another miscarriage. This is her second one. The doctor told us she will never be able to deliver a full-term baby." He put his hand over his eyes and then squeezed his forehead as if he was trying to make the pain go away.

"Oh, Leonard, I am sorry." I was shocked that he hadn't told me about the first one. In my heart I wanted to caress him or take his hand, but I could not force myself to touch him. "Have you sought other opinions to be sure the doctor knows what he's talking about. Maybe he's wrong. How old is Rose? Maybe her age is a factor."

"No, she's only thirty-eight. We've already consulted two specialists and they concur." He pointed to the papers. "Please sign these, Sera. I need to get back to my office."

It seemed he couldn't wait to leave. When he was exiting the door, he glanced over his shoulder and looked at me with hurt, angry eyes. I felt his angry pain shoot through my body. I wondered if he blamed me for his being childless. And if so, was it because I could conceive and had refused to marry him and the person he eventually chose was barren? I wanted to know, but I knew he'd never accuse me and I'd never confront him.

It was difficult to hide my worsening condition. Some of my fingers had begun to curl and develop knots. My toes cramped constantly. I was in misery every day.

On one of Leonard's Sunday visits, he brought along Dr. Reilly.

After he introduced me to the doctor, he wasted no time telling me why he'd brought him to see me. "Do you think I haven't noticed what's happening to you, Sera? You need medical attention and I brought it to you. Now I'll leave you two to consult. I'll be out in the garden with Jonas. Let me know when you're ready to leave, doctor."

I knew Dr. Reilly had to examine me, but each time his hands touched me, I flinched. I apologized each time and he simply nodded. I hated hands, other than my own, to touch me. Leonard's and Henri's hands had been the only exceptions.

"Miss Menard, I'm sorry for causing you pain with my examination," he told me. "How long have you been suffering like this?"

The doctor thought my recoiling was due to pain. I needed to let him know he was mistaken. "It was not pain that caused me to flinch, Dr. Reilly. I don't like being touched."

"Thank you for being honest, but if you're interested in having me treat you, I'll need to touch you now and again? How old are you, Miss Menard?"

"You are direct, aren't you? I'm fifty."

He looked startled. "I'm surprised," he told me. "Your face looks twenty-five and your body about forty, so I expected you to tell me you were about thirty-five. Mr. Stern tells me you're a dressmaker. Sitting all day doesn't help when you have arthritis...rheumatoid arthritis. It's going to get more difficult for you to do that kind of work."

"But there are times when I have no pain at all. That baffles me. Why does that happen?"

"Those times are called periods of remission. They won't occur as often as your disease progresses."

"What can you do for me, Dr. Reilly?"

"I'm sorry to tell you not much. Right now there are only two things I can give you for pain: aspirin and morphine. There are new therapies they're experimenting with that will help in the future, but right now there's nothing else."

"I can buy aspirin at the drugstore, so I'll see if that helps me. I'm certainly not interested in taking morphine. Well...thank you, doctor." I realized, except for the information about the pain medicines, there was nothing else to be done for me. I was glad I didn't have a husband or a family.

"What are you currently doing for pain? Aren't you taking aspirin?"

"No. I just do hot soaks and liniment at night."

"Would you like me to stop in and see you once a month, Miss Menard?" Dr. Reilly seemed concerned having given me such a dire diagnosis.

"I don't think that's necessary right now. I will call you if I need to consult with you, doctor." I stood up. "I'll tell Leonard you're ready to leave."

It was hard for me to accept that with all the advancements in medicine there was nothing that could be done to stop the progression of my disease. I felt full of anger and hopelessness and I didn't want Jonas to see me fall apart. So as soon as Leonard and the doctor left, I went upstairs to my room. I wanted to cry, to scream into my pillows, and maybe even throw a few things against the wall, but there were no tears or tantrums, only the same cold, shaky feeling I'd had after I shot the man in my shop. I think it was clear to me that no amount of tears or rage would change what had been done or what was to come.

23

For a fifty-year-old spinster, the 1920s had begun full of surprises. With the advent of the "flapper," my volume of business was more than Georgina and I could handle. Many of the pieces ordered had fringes, sequins or extensive beadwork which took many hours to complete.

Georgina had a friend who was interested in the job, but she had two small children and needed to work at home. I found no problem in accommodating her because our work space was limited. Georgina delivered the garments to her friend and then picked up the finished pieces.

Despite our spike in orders, we were now competing with department stores and the dress shops that had converted to selling ready-made garments. I wondered how long I'd be able to stay in business after my customers decided they didn't have to wait for a dress to be made; they could buy almost any style right off the rack.

My arthritis was once again in remission and I was able to pull my weight on the sewing machine and also do some of the hand sewing.

Jonas no longer came to the shop; he stayed at the Esplanade house all day. He had developed severe shortness of breath and weak spells which made him unable to lift things or to be on his feet for long periods of time. He kept the house in order and cooked dinner every evening. He was able to do a little at a time as long as he was able to sit for short periods between chores.

I had only one problem with Jonas being at another location during the day – I needed to check on him and the telephone was the easiest way. But Jonas refused to use the telephone. He called it an "evil machine" and knew God didn't approve of it. He couldn't explain to me why he felt that way. I tried to make him understand why it was important for me to be able to call him to check on how he was feeling, but he wouldn't budge. That forced me to leave Georgina alone to mind the shop while I went home at lunchtime to check on Jonas.

One day, I arrived to find a strange car parked in front of the house. I rushed in to find Henri Labastier sitting in my front room patiently waiting for me to arrive.

"Sera, it's wonderful to see you," he said as he sprang up from the sofa. "It's been a long time. Look at you! Not one ounce of your beauty has deserted you." Henri opened his arms to receive me.

I stepped back away from him and began to clap my hands. "Bravo! Bravo! Bravo! You're no Rudolph Valentino, but you're a very talented actor. I remember the character you played about eight years ago when you were here. You were magnificent! I believed you were really that man."

"I am that man. I couldn't offer you more then, but I can now. I know you know about me, Sera. Celeste told me she told you everything. Before we talk about us, I must tell you about her. She suffered a stroke the week she arrived in Montreal. She's been paralyzed on her right side all these years. I know you've been wondering why she never wrote to you as she'd promised. She couldn't."

"Why didn't you write to tell me what had happened to her? I did wonder why she didn't write because we had become good friends in the short time we knew each other."

"I didn't think you'd want to hear from me, Sera."

I thought I'd better get back to the "us" part of the conversation. "What are you really doing here, Henri?"

"I'm a divorced man, Sera. I'm free to love you now. These...last years...I don't know how many it has been, but they've been hell for me. Your face, your voice...everything about you has been haunting me. You must give me a chance to redeem myself. Let me..."

"No, Henri, you were a contemptible cheater long before you laid eyes on me. That is your true character. You use women the way you must use domesticated animals. They serve specific purposes, but beyond that they have no value."

"I can't let you think that about me, Sera."

"You have no choice, Henri. I've accepted who you are and want no part of you. If you came here thinking I'm easy prey, you'd better do some more thinking. A madam of one of the old whore houses in Storyville once told me that her lover of twenty-five years had eaten her bread and used her body all those years and the way he thanked her was disappearing with hundreds of thousands of dollars of her money. Oh, I forgot, you met her...Lulu White, the owner of Mahogany Hall. By the way, did you ever rebuild your shoe company?"

"No, I went in a different direction. I'm a furniture manufacturer now."

"Wonderful, but I have no interest in you and want nothing to do with you, Henri."

"Please don't tell me you want nothing to do with me. I can't and won't take no for an answer, Sera. You've consumed my thoughts all these years. I don't care if you're Colored. No one will know in Montreal."

"What are you talking about?" I said almost losing my breath.

"You know what I'm talking about, Sera. You're Colored. Lulu White told me when she took me to Countess Piazza's place the day I met you. Lulu is quite the talker. I confided to her that I wished to be more than your shoe supplier. She told me you were a Colored girl passing for White. She advised me to take you to my country where no one knows you and where Leonard Stern couldn't interfere in your life. Imagine my surprise hearing that. But it didn't deter me as you can see. I'm here to tell you I can take good care of you. We'll sell your properties here and then we'll go to Montreal to have a wonderful life." Henri rushed toward me and pulled me roughly into his arms. His lips found mine before I could protest.

My muffled scream brought Jonas to the front room with his chest heaving as he fought to get air into his lungs. He was clutching a large knife at his side.

Henri let me go and looked at me as if asking me to stop Jonas from killing him.

"Don't worry, you're going to live another day. Jonas was using the knife to prepare lunch. He isn't going to filet you." I wanted to laugh but fought hard not to. I turned to Jonas, "I'm all right. Mr. Labastier is leaving."

Jonas looked at Henri with cold, hard eyes. The distrust and disrespect were present upon a face that was usually warm and trusting. He was letting Henri know that he thought he was a miserable excuse for a man without saying a word. Slowly, Jonas walked out of the front room and returned to the kitchen.

"Has Jonas become your protector...your body guard, Sera? I think you've allowed him too many privileges. He wasn't using that knife in the kitchen; you made up that excuse for him. Admit it, Sera; he had come in here to harm me." Henri was visibly shaken and didn't try to hide it.

"I don't need to make excuses for him and I don't need him to protect me!" I pulled my gun out of my pocket and pointed it between his eyes. "I'm very capable of defending myself. I used it once to kill a man, Henri. He was going to throw a knife into my chest. My bullet was faster than his knife and it found a spot between his eyes. So you've got a choice to make. Either you leave my house quietly or I'll have a man I know take care of you...permanently."

Henri laughed. "You're desperately trying to change the subject away from who you really are. According to Lulu, you're a Negress as they call you in America, and you've lived most of your life passing for White. If you send me away unsatisfied, aren't you afraid I might expose your true color to the people who count in New Orleans? I can see the front page of the newspaper: *French Quarter Dressmaker's True Identity Uncovered*. At the very least, I think you should give me a taste of what you won't let me have permanently. Don't you want me to go away quietly? Leonard will never miss it. Come on. Don't waste your time threatening me with some phantom mobster."

"This man isn't just a gangster, Henri; he's the mid-level boss who oversees all of the mob's bootleg operations in the French Quarter. Here's how this will work: I'm going to blow a hole in your belly and while you lay bleeding on my floor, I'll call the man from Sicily. He'll arrive with his goons, they'll slice off that part between your legs, pack it in dry ice and then send it to whoever receives your mail in Montreal. They'll cut up the rest of your filthy carcass and throw your parts into the nearest bayou. Are you brave enough to bet your life that I'm playing make-believe?" I pointed the gun at his stomach. "I need an answer, Henri."

"Yes, yes, yes…I believe you!" Henri's voice had become shrill. "You're mentally unbalanced, Sera. Now I understand why you're unmarried." He had to remove the handkerchief from his breast pocket. He was sweating profusely.

"Get out of my house, Henri! I don't want your blood on my hands, too. Go back to Montreal where you belong." I walked out into the foyer and opened the front door. Henri walked through it without looking back.

My fairytale frog had not become a prince.

I rented the apartment in the storage building in exchange for the work Jonas had done. Emilio Frattoli was a cook evenings at Tujague's Restaurant at the corner of Decatur and Madison. It was a short walk from the shop and this allowed him to work mornings for me.

Georgina and Graziano were overjoyed when Emilio came to work with us. He was also from Sicily and they loved that they could speak Italian with him. They tried to teach me to speak it, but like Aunt Pauline with driving, I was difficult to teach.

After a short time, Emilio and Georgina fell in love and wanted to get married. At first Graziano hesitated to give them his blessing, but finally did after he found out his daughter was pregnant. Emilio asked me to rent them the upstairs apartment and I agreed.

They were married by a new, young priest in the sacristy of St. Louis Cathedral in October of 1923. Except for Graziano, neither of them had family in New Orleans, so they decided on a simple, quick wedding. Graziano and I were their witnesses.

Graziano was promoted in the organization when the mafia's business grew during prohibition. He became the banker for the entire bootleg operation, making a "pile of money," as he put it when he was bragging, and he'd become well-dressed and extremely arrogant.

Georgina was pregnant again three months after giving birth to her first child. Her father showered her with gifts and money to thank her for giving him grandchildren and a family again. Emilio was unhappy. He didn't like Graziano spoiling his wife.

One afternoon after we'd all had tea upstairs, I volunteered to wash the china. Graziano stayed behind while I washed and dried the teacups and saucers. He asked if he could speak to me before we went downstairs.

"Sera, I will never be able to thank you enough for what you've done for my daughter."

He had only a hint of an accent which I found strange.

"You've already thanked me, Graziano. I'm happy Georgina is here with me. She's become more than an employee." I was already feeling uncomfortable because I felt whatever he was going to tell me, I didn't want to hear. I asked a question to stall for time. "I'm curious, Graziano, about how well you speak English. How long have you been in America?"

"Fifteen years. My wife taught me English; she was American. We met in Italy and lived there before we came to America. We also lived in New York for a few years."

"That explains it."

"I'm glad my daughter is not just a worker to you. She may need your help one day because I don't like that husband of hers. He's not ambitious enough for me. He's going to spend his whole life cooking in somebody else's kitchen. I want her to have more." He was cracking his knuckles loudly and his left eye started to twitch. "I can find him a good-paying spot with my organization, but he'll have no part of my business. He's a ballsy little bastard to tell me that to my face, but I'm waiting for him to make one wrong step with

Georgina, and I'll hang him from a meat hook." He started pounding his fist into the palm of his other hand.

"Georgina loves Emilio, Graziano. She's happy being a cook's wife. Leave her alone. Let her decide if she has enough to be satisfied." I had never thought of him as a possessive father.

He had seemed happy to have Emilio marry her and give him grandchildren.

"Could you be satisfied with somebody like me, Sera? I have grown very fond of you and I'd like to be more than an acquaintance." He was inching closer to me as I was removing my apron. I put my hands up in front of me to stop him.

"Now, now, Sera, you're not a little girl anymore. You must know how I feel. Why do you think I come here as often as I do?" Graziano tried to put his arm around my waist but I quickly moved out of his reach.

"Graziano, we are acquaintances and that's all we'll ever be. I enjoy your visits and our conversations over tea, but I'm not interested in anything more. If you're not satisfied with this arrangement, then I suggest you don't come back." I watched his eyes grow cold and hard.

"I'm not in the habit of being told no, especially by a woman. Are you sure you want to talk to me that way." He narrowed his eyes at me, sucked in his bottom lip, and then stiffened his neck and head like a snake getting ready to strike.

I pulled the gun out of my pocket and pointed it at his groin. "Graziano, there is only one bullet, but that's all I need."

His eyes froze as my words sunk in. "You're either crazy or someone hurt you real bad," he said. "Take your finger off that trigger, Sera, before there's an accident. Please!"

"Don't worry, it won't be an accident. It will be deliberate because I don't like being threatened with looks or words."

"I'm sorry, Sera. Please don't hold this against me. I don't want Georgina to know what I've done. I want to be able to come here to see my family. Please, Sera!"

"All right, but go downstairs," I said as I slipped the gun back into my dress pocket. "I need a minute to collect myself." My insides were quivering. I folded my arms across my chest and squeezed hard in an effort to stop myself from shaking. When I pulled my gun on Graziano, I had no idea whether or not he would challenge me. I had no desire to shoot anyone else. But I knew if he had made the wrong move, I would have.

He stopped his afternoon social calls and visited Georgina and Emilio only after I left the shop for the evening.

On Christmas Eve of 1924, Graziano was gunned down by someone, it was said, in his own organization who wanted his job. Georgina was inconsolable. A month later she had a miscarriage. She decided America was not the place to raise her children and she wanted to return to Sicily. She thought they could save the money they would need for the trip in a year and that would also give me time to find replacements for them.

Emilio wasn't as eager to leave. He said he loved New Orleans and was making more money than he could ever hope to make in Sicily. They'd be poor again, he told Georgina, and she'd be sorry. And what did she remember about Sicily, anyway. She was very young when her family left and came to live in America. He asked her what happened to all the money her father made. He hadn't had time to spend it all. Where was it?

"I don't know," Georgina said. "He only gave me a few gifts of money, but it wasn't that much. He must have saved a lot of it. He didn't tell me what he did with it or where he was putting it. There was nothing in his house when I went through it. But he could have hidden it somewhere I didn't look and the landlord might have found it?"

"Georgina, when you lived with your father was there a place he used to put things that were important?" I asked her in an attempt to head off another major argument between her and her husband. They had regularly begun fighting about going back to Sicily and had no regard for my presence.

"I don't remember any special place. But we didn't have much money then, so he didn't have any to hide. We had only one piece of jewelry; this cross and chain." She pulled it out from beneath her blouse. "It was my mother's and I never take it off."

"Maybe your father bragged about making more money than he actually made. He wanted to look prosperous, especially in your eyes, Georgina." I was also thinking about how much he wanted to shame Emilio into wanting more for his wife and children.

When Emilio left that afternoon for work, Georgina asked me, "Did my father ever tell you he didn't like Emilio?"

"He told me Emilio wasn't ambitious enough for him. He wanted more for you."

"My father had decided to give Emilio another year and if he wasn't making more money or talking about wanting to own a restaurant, he was going to take us, the children and me, back to Sicily. He said he was saving his money to do that. I didn't want to say that in front of Emilio. You won't say anything to him, will you?"

"Of course I won't." If Georgina wasn't concerned about what had happened to her father's money, why should

I be? I never mentioned it again and in my presence Emilio never brought it up either.

One year turned into two and when Georgina got pregnant again, they were unable to predict when they'd be able to go back to Sicily. They made me an honorary grandmother. Gino, their three year old son, called me, *nonna*.

24

Leonard hadn't come to the shop in years. The last few times he came, Graziano was there having tea with us. He was visibly upset and left without telling me why he had come. The following Saturday he would come to the house to explain why he'd come to the shop. After Florence died, I closed the shop every other Saturday. I began to need two days to rest my body.

When I hired Georgina, I left the shop in her capable hands and I took off every Saturday.

One Saturday afternoon, Leonard arrived after lunch full of thought and wishing to talk. We sat in the dining room and Jonas brought us a pot of coffee and a small pitcher of boiled milk. Leonard had switched from black coffee and joined me in having café au lait.

"Jonas, you don't look well today," Leonard told him. "Are you getting enough rest?"

"Yessuh, Mistah Leonard. I's jes a ol man." Jonas smiled as wide as his energy would allow.

"That may be true, but you still have to take care of yourself."

"Yessuh." Jonas walked away slowly. He was barely able to lift up his feet.

"Have you had a doctor look at Jonas recently, Sera?"

"Of course. I drove him to Charity Hospital last week and I went in with him because I knew he wasn't telling the doctors everything they needed to know. The doctor told me Jonas's heart condition is so severe there's nothing that can be done for him. We have to help him live out the rest of his life being as comfortable as possible. He told me to make sure Jonas rests as much as possible and eats well, even if he doesn't want to."

"That must have been difficult for you to hear. I know how much you depend on him. That reminds me...your garden. It's going to ruin. I suppose Jonas isn't strong enough to work out there now, is he?" Leonard had reached the end of his empathy; it was time to be practical.

"No. He sits outside quite a bit, but he hasn't worked in the garden in months. It's time I look for someone else to do it."

"No, don't. I'll send my gardener and I'll pay him one sum monthly for both gardens. It's easier that way than to constantly draw funds from your accounts. That way, I'll only have to draw funds twice a year, or so. Is that all right with you?"

"No need to ask me; you're the man who knows money. I have no desire to handle any more money than I do now. So, do you still think I don't think much of you?"

"It's wonderful to hear you say it now and again." Leonard blushed for the first time in a long time. He rarely smiled or held light conversation with me since Aunt Pauline had died.

"Now I think we should talk about what was on your mind when you arrived. You were so full of anxiety; I didn't know what to think might be wrong." I knew he hadn't come to talk about Jonas or the garden. My God, had Jonas told him about Henri's visit? Maybe Leonard had come to the house when I wasn't here and talked to him. I trusted he would never tell Leonard anything unless I told him it was okay.

"Sera...uh, have you been paying attention to the newspapers and listening to the talk on the street? The talk is about inflation and people living too high on the hog, that's what I'm hearing. The old timers are the ones who seem most worried."

"I haven't any idea what you're talking about, Leonard. What do you mean?"

"It seems in the last few years a great many people have a great deal of money. Hasn't your business increased dramatically since the war ended?"

"Yes, but isn't that how business works? Some years are better than others. But listen, I'm not educated enough to really know or understand how business or anything else works."

"Stop it, Sera! Stop trying to paint yourself as a dunce...a dummy...you're neither. You are a very smart woman. If you weren't, do you think I would waste my time asking for your opinion? And frankly, I miss talking to you. I miss the times I spent with you and your aunt, especially our discussions on the gallery at your shop." Leonard started to grab my hand, but instead picked up his coffee cup.

"What has you so concerned?" I quickly asked hoping to turn the conversation away from the two of us. I didn't want him to bring up Henri again...how different it was before Henri.

"Our investments...I...I haven't told you about the money we lost. So now I think it best to tell you all of it. Most of the money from your father's house and his tailor shop was lost when the cotton market bottomed out. I had hoped it would rebound, but it hasn't. That makes me wonder if our other stocks will do the same in light of inflation and the glut of manufactured goods on the market.

If these things don't sell, the companies will have to stop producing and people will lose their jobs. I could never forgive myself if all of your inheritance from your aunt is lost. You'll need that money when you can no longer..."

"Leonard," I interrupted, "I've wanted to talk to you about something similar. I'm noticing how many shops are now selling ready to wear garments. These stores have racks and racks of dresses and other pieces they've ordered from New York manufacturers. I'm the last dressmaker in the area. Do you think it's time for me to sell ready-to-wear clothes?"

"Yes, you have to if you want to stay in business. Your job will get a lot easier if you do. I'm referring to not having to deal with ordering material and other products you use day to day or have the worry of it getting to you on time...and a host of other problems. Think about it. You'll really appreciate having that new kind of shop, especially when your body is not in remission. If you have a need to sew, do alterations on the garments you sell as a courtesy to your customers. Doing alterations could be a job exclusively for Georgina and receiving the shipments and getting the garments on the racks could certainly be a job for Emilio. You probably wouldn't need to go to the shop everyday."

"You make it sound so simple. Will you help me convert the shop, Leonard? I need your expertise. I know what you did for Stern Brothers; can you do that for me?" I couldn't wait to tell Georgina and Emilio on Monday hoping they'd be as enthusiastic as I was.

Leonard sighed, "What a question! Of course, I'll help you. I've not handled women's fashions, but I'm ready for a challenge. Besides, it will take my mind off worrying about the stock market. We stand to lose all or almost everything if it crashes." Leonard started to perspire. He took a handkerchief out of his inside breast pocket and dabbed at his forehead.

"I trust you and whatever you think you need to do, do it. I've been poor before, so I won't wither and die. What do you want to do, Leonard?"

"I want to start cashing in and buying different kinds of properties, but mostly houses and buildings I can rent. That's what my cousin in New York suggests."

"What about banks? Will anything happen to them? Should I take my money out of my bank?"

"Is all of your liquid money, the money I haven't invested for you, is it in the bank?"

"Yes, all of it."

"Then take it out, Sera, but not all of it at once. Later on we'll figure out what to do with it. In the meantime, find a safe place in the house to put it. I hope my instincts are right and I'm not making you nervous with unfounded fears. Some people may get frightened and start pulling their money out of the banks and that will cause the banks to crash. So, let's be on the safe side." The look in Leonard's eyes told me he was unsure whether or not I was beginning to understand why he was worried.

But I had started to understand and I began to feel apprehensive. I wouldn't mind being poor if I had good health, but that was impossible now. I didn't want to end up dying in Charity Hospital like my father.

"Leonard, I've believed in you for more than thirty years; why would I stop now? Everything around me has changed, but never have I stopped trusting you. You and Jonas are the two constant forces in my life."

"You will never know what you've done for me today. I came here to see you in a sorry state and you're sending me home a much calmer man. Thank you, Sera. Now I think I'll go out and tell Jonas about my gardener. I don't want him to be surprised when he finds someone else out there." Leonard had grown a bit more considerate in recent years. I wondered if his wife was responsible. The little he'd said about her alluded to her being a very gentle woman.

A few seconds later Leonard was calling me, "Sera! Sera!" I heard the panic in his voice and I rushed out to the yard. I found him standing in front of the banana trees.

Jonas was sitting on the ground with his back resting against one of the trees. His head hung down and his chin touched his chest as if he had fallen asleep. Both legs were stretched out in front of him and his hands were cupped in his lap.

"He's dead, Sera."

"No!"

"Yes, he has no pulse. His heart must have stopped working."

"Oh, Leonard...Leonard..." I couldn't untangle my thoughts to say anything else.

"Come, Sera...let's go inside. You don't have to say anything right now. I'll take care of everything for you. First, we'll have to decide where to bury him."

"I know so little about Jonas. He never shared his life with me. How can I decide?" I almost slipped and said he only talked to me when I taught him to read and write.

"I know a few tidbits but only because I asked Jonas a few questions now and then." Leonard looked a bit smug I thought. I wondered if he'd questioned him about Henri.

"He answered your questions...all of your questions?"

"Yes. He said he didn't know where he was born, but that he was about twelve when the Civil War ended. That makes him about seventy-five. He doesn't remember his parents, but he was cared for by a woman who could have been his mother. When he was about five or six, she left him with Lizzie's family in Thibodaux and never returned."

"He took Lizzie back to her family in Thibodaux when she died. Do you think we can locate them there? Maybe he'd like to be put next to his wife." I wanted him to finally be in a place where he could really rest in peace.

"No, Sera, we can't run around in circles looking for them. Besides, Lizzie was not his wife."

"What are you saying?" I was bewildered.

"Jonas told me this after your aunt died. Lizzie had been his sister ever since he was left with her family. They were only a year apart and they did everything together. They picked cotton in the fields of the plantation before they were freed. Then they helped Lizzie's family sharecrop until they felt the yearning to find out what the big city had to offer them. Daniel's parents hired them as a couple and that's the way it stayed. No one ever knew they lived as brother and sister. Jonas only knew a woman in the physical sense when he married Daisy."

"Again, I cannot speak," I said. I thought about Jonas and Lizzie keeping that secret for that long a time. But then, Jonas and I were old hands at keeping secrets. But why would he tell Leonard and not me?

Leonard smiled as he watched me try to digest that information. He said, "I think I have to make a few calls to find a Colored funeral home and perhaps they will be able to give us the name of a place he can be buried. What do you think?"

I would never allow Jonas to be buried in a potter's field. I wasn't sure if that was what Leonard was thinking and I was reluctant to accuse him of such. So I stated my wishes instead.

"Leonard, I'd like to have Jonas buried in the Menard vault with my family."

"Sera! You're not thinking clearly." He was incensed.

"Yes, I'm very clear in my thinking. He has been my hands, my feet and my legs for most of the last twenty years when my body hasn't been in remission. I feel as my aunt felt;

Jonas is a part of the Menard and the Stern families. If you'd rather not handle the arrangements, I'll do them myself." I felt disappointed in Leonard. How could I care for…love…this man who believed another human being was inferior to him? How did he reconcile that with God? I had grown away from the church; he clung to it.

"No, I'll take care of things. I don't like what you want to do, but I will do as you ask." Leonard tried to hide his annoyance, but the harshness of his voice betrayed him.

On Monday morning, Jonas was laid to rest. His coffin had been left in front of my family's vault, just as my father's had been left. I was the only one there to say goodbye. I will always remember how bright the sun was that May morning and wondered if it had any special significance.

What would I to do without Jonas? The house was empty. The silence in it terrified me. It was so much bigger than the apartment above the shop. I had been afraid in the apartment, but my fear was much greater in the house. Every sound made me shudder: the wind, the branches of the trees hitting the roof or the sides of the house, the squeaking of the floor as I walked from room to room. I bought a second gun. I kept it in the front room pushed down between the cushion and an arm of the sofa.

I left Jonas's room intact against Leonard's urgings. He wanted me to dispose of Jonas's belongings immediately. Not only couldn't I get rid of his things; I couldn't go into his room. I called Georgina to tell her I wouldn't be coming into the shop for a few days and that I also had some news about the future of the shop to discuss with her and Emilio.

"Sera, Emilio left me," Georgina said in a flat monotone voice. "When he didn't come home from work last night, I went to the restaurant to find out what happened to him. The other cook was there cleaning the kitchen. He told me Emilio asked the owner for whatever salary he had

219

coming because his family had to go out of town to my aunt's funeral. He had a small suitcase with him when he left the restaurant. He told the cook he was meeting me at the train station." Georgina was much too calm. I wondered how long it would take before she fell apart. "He took half of the money we were saving," she said.

"Did he leave you a letter or a note, Georgina?" I asked.

"No."

"Did you open the store this morning?"

"No."

"Don't open it. Put a sign in the window. Say…there's been a death in the family. Then pack a few things for you and Gino and I'll be there to pick you up in half an hour."

I brought Georgina and Gino home with me to spend a few days. I hoped it would help to ease some of Georgina's pain of being deserted. I wanted to give her a place to let her hurt surface without being questioned by nosy neighbors. And I'd be there to keep an eye on Gino while she regained her footing. She was only mildly enthusiastic about my plan to convert the shop. I had hoped she'd show more interest when I told her she'd pretty much be in charge of running the place and would be making more money. Even that didn't get much of a spark out of her.

25

Converting my shop to ready-to-wear clothing was a monumental task. We worked diligently to complete all of the garments in progress and those on order. As soon as everything was finished, I let the woman who did the handwork go. I had planned to give Georgina and me a vacation while the shop was being renovated.

But that was not to be. As Georgina and I sat having tea one afternoon, she informed me she was leaving New Orleans and going to live with her aunt in New York. She wasn't interested in discussing the particulars of why she had decided to leave. She told me she was already packed and that she and her son would be taking a train to New York in two days. That same day a man arrived at the shop to transport her trunks to the station to be shipped by Railway Express. Two days later, the same man returned to escort Georgina and Gino to catch their train.

After Georgina and her son left, I felt despondent. In less than ten years: Aunt Pauline, Florence and Jonas were dead; Lulu, Countess, Celeste and Georgina had all gone away; Henri had turned out to be a rotten apple. My world had not become smaller; it had disappeared.

For the first time since his marriage, I called Leonard at home. He answered and all I could utter was, "Leonard, please come. Please!"

He arrived in less than half an hour and found me watching for him through the window. He opened the door and silently held out his arms to me. I didn't hesitate. I ran into them and began to sob for all the years I'd held back my emotions. Through the tears I managed to tell Leonard what had happened.

"I think what hurts most is that Georgina didn't want to talk to me. She made me feel as if I had done something to drive her away. The only thing she said about leaving was that she had to get away from New Orleans. Gino said goodbye to me, but she didn't. I couldn't believe she was leaving forever and didn't even look back as she drove away. I don't even know how to get in touch with her...I don't know her aunt's name." The tears started falling again.

"Stop crying, Sera. Maybe Georgina couldn't say goodbye because she was too distraught over having to leave you. At least she thought enough of you to wait until all the work had been finished."

"I suppose. But Leonard, you didn't see her. She looked so cold and unfeeling. It was as if she no longer cared about anything. She just went through the motions...even with Gino. I watched Georgina ignore the child several times when he spoke to her, and when she grew impatient with him, she'd yell at him and raise her hand as if she was going to hit him. Gino would run away and hide. I felt sorry for him, Leonard, but I didn't interfere."

"I'm glad you didn't, Sera. I think Georgina needs time to get over being abandoned by her husband. She'll become the mother she used to be when she's not so angry."

"I asked her why she wouldn't wait until after her baby was born to take such a long train trip. She shrugged and told me she felt fine and wouldn't have any problems while she traveled."

"Georgina's gone, Sera, that's over and done with. It's time to close the shop. I'll have someone make a large sign for your window about the renovations. Then we can get to work on clearing out everything."

"Oh God, Leonard! What would I do without you?" I started to cry again.

"No, no no…no more weeping. You will rest while I take care of converting the shop. The fabric in the storage building has to be sold and I think I'll contact that new factory on Carondolet to see if they're interested in buying it. Maybe they'll want some of the things in your work room, too."

"There are a few things I want to keep."

"Make a list for me right now and I'll see that you get them this weekend."

"Leonard, I can't take up all your time. You don't have to have it done right away."

"Why not? I'm alone right now. Rose is in New York. Her mother had surgery last week. Her foot had to be amputated because of diabetes. It seems Rose is the only one available to take care of her mother." His tone was sarcastic.

"Where is her father?" I asked.

"He died several years ago." Leonard gave a small sigh of resignation. "I think Rose will be gone a few months, so I've got time. Tell me what you want and you'll have everything Saturday." He took a small, leather-bound note pad and a pencil out of his shirt pocket. "I'm ready, go ahead."

"I'd like the sewing machine my aunt gave me, the mannequin I put a bullet in," I chuckled and so did Leonard, "all of my window mannequins and their outfits, and a supply of items for sewing things for myself at home." I didn't need

223

to itemize them; Leonard knew what it took to make a garment.

"That's all! Are you sure?" He started looking around the reception room. "What about all those pieces on display?"

"Oh, I forgot those. Yes, I want them. I'd also like several bolts of summer fabric and a few of light wool and gabardine. I may want to duplicate some of the ready to wear pieces for my window mannequins. That way I can advertise some of the garments I have in the store."

"That's a splendid idea. What do you think about the apartment upstairs? Do you want to get rid of the furniture?"

"No, I think I should wait. Maybe I'll be lucky again and be able to hire someone who needs a job and an apartment."

"They're laying off again at Stern Brothers. Business is slow. Maybe I can find someone the same way I found Georgina." Leonard had convinced the new owner to keep the name Stern Brothers because the store was well known in the city.

"There's also Jonas's little apartment in the storage building. That could also bring in some money if I rented it."

"Yes, but enough thinking for the day." Leonard put away his notepad. "Go home, Sera, and get some rest. I'll see you on Saturday."

With Leonard at the helm, the change-over went smoothly. I didn't go to the shop until it was finished. My only job had been to order the merchandise. I decided to carry gloves, hats and stockings along with dresses, blouses, skirts and coats. There'd be no shoes!

After being home for a couple of months, I grew a bit lazy. The first week I reopened the shop was grueling. And not because there was an abundance of customers, I simply grew so tired after lunch that I could hardly make it the rest of the day. There were a few customers but not as many as

Leonard and I had anticipated. In fact, as time passed, there were so few, it was not financially wise to hire anyone to run the shop.

Rose did not return to New Orleans for five months and then had to immediately go back when her mother suffered a stroke. Leonard was visibly unhappy that the burden of her mother always fell on Rose when she had so many brothers and sisters.

After putting a sign in my shop window, I rented the room in the storage building to a merchant seaman for about a year. He only used it between his trips at sea. Noel Jacquet was pleasant enough when you encountered him, but that was not often. When in town, he must have spent most of his time sleeping because he rarely left his room. I don't know when he ate. Once when he was at sea, I checked his room and it was as neat and clean as the day I rented it to him.

I had all of the things from the shop that I wanted to keep put upstairs in one of the three unoccupied bedrooms when they were delivered. That way they were out of the way until I wanted to use them.

The shop made very little money the first year I reopened. I kept myself busy making new outfits for the window mannequins. I hoped that would entice some of the ladies who stared in the window to come in and at least look around. Unfortunately, my window display didn't seem to lure in many of them. There were all kinds of customers now. The Creole vs. American feud seemed to have vanished. I was unaware when the problem had solved itself.

My arthritis was threatening to return. The pain was so erratic I didn't know when to expect it or how intense it might be. I tried to live and to be as active as possible as if I didn't remember Dr. Reilly telling me the remissions would eventually cease.

Most of 1928 Rose spent in New York nursing her mother. Leonard spent many of his evenings with me at the Esplanade house. On a few occasions we invited Dr. Reilly to join us. He was a widower with no children and seemed grateful to be asked to join us for dinner, glasses of sherry and conversations that were boundless. Leonard and I had managed to duplicate the evenings we'd spent with Aunt Pauline.

One evening when there was only the two of us for dinner, Leonard told me, "I've been buying rental properties, Sera. They're mainly in Metarie, but a few in Marigny and two, so far, in the Tremé."

"You certainly don't waste time when you set your mind to something. That's what Aunt Pauline liked about you. What's happening with the investments?" I watched Leonard's face grow pale and his lips quiver as he opened them to answer.

"Not much. I'm trying to be cautious because of what I see in the business world. I've been pulling out a little at a time and using that money to buy the real estate. In fact, today I bought your first property – the store that closed three doors down from you. When your business picks up, you may need to branch out into a second store." Leonard looked pleased with himself.

"We still haven't done anything with the money I withdrew from the bank. With the shop making so little profit, having that money turned out to be a good thing. I've had to use some of it to pay the bills. Should I put the rest of it back in the bank?"

"No. When Rose's mother dies and she receives her part of the assets, they aren't going into the bank. We're going to keep it in cash." He now spoke openly and often about Rose. I think he was angry with her for abandoning him and grateful to me for being there to comfort him in his loneliness.

"Is Rose's mother near death, Leonard?"

"Well...not actually at the point of death at this moment, but her family's been told it's only a matter of time. But who knows? She's a very strong woman." I think he realized how insensitive his statement sounded. "Sorry, I didn't mean to sound so unfeeling."

"The running back and forth to New York must be hard on your wife," I said.

"Yes, it is. It's hard on both of us. Now, back to your money, Sera. Do you have it in a safe place?"

"Yes, it's almost in plain sight. I sewed it into the hem of the drapes. Can you tell it's there?" I pointed to the heavy damask drapes hanging at the dining room window.

"No, I can't tell. But aren't you afraid of fire?"

"Yes, but I think it's the safest place in the whole house."

"Okay, then I think you should leave it there. Maybe you can use it to buy another property. For now, just keep it safe." The worried look was back on Leonard's face. He shook it off and quickly said it was late and that the next day was going to be a busy one for him.

Rose returned to New Orleans several days later and once again Leonard's visits were Sundays only. Several months later when her mother died, he accompanied her to New York for the funeral and to help her settle her mother's affairs.

One Saturday night I was lying in bed in the dark unable to sleep. I had become use to Leonard being there most evenings and now that he was back to Sundays only, I missed him and the calm he brought to my life. When I was willing to admit it to myself, I knew I was carrying on an affair with him. Even though it was platonic – it was still a love affair – and I was disgusted with myself.

How had I allowed myself to become infatuated with Henri and hurt Leonard the way I knew I had? Henri was only a distant memory now. The incident that happened during his last visit had enabled me to let him go forever. There were no more dreams or fantasies about him. It made me appreciate Leonard so much more.

Leonard had always been the consummate gentleman, so when we touched I was usually the one who initiated it. Except for Daniel, I had never known a man in the sexual sense, but I had grown to feel physically attracted to Leonard. Oh, the many times I wanted to touch him, to kiss him, but I held myself in check. Those fireplace kisses had returned to haunt me.

Finally after several hours, I grew tired of thinking about a man I would never have. I went downstairs to Jonas's room. I hadn't set foot in it since his death and I knew the time had come for me to dispose of his belongings.

I removed the few pieces of clothing from his small dresser. He had a Catholic prayer book in the top drawer. That was curious. But then Jonas was a private man, so that should not have surprised me. Everything in the room seemed crisp and clean as if Jonas had just dusted and changed the bed linens. The quilt on his bed lay smooth without a wrinkle. I stripped the bed, folded the sheets and the pillowcases and stacked them on the mattress at the foot of the bed. When I attempted to fold the quilt, it felt heavy on one side. I squeezed several of the squares and felt something imbedded inside. I ripped open the stitching and pulled out everything inside three of the squares. The envelope containing Jonas's inheritance from Aunt Pauline and several wads of cash came tumbling out. On the envelope Jonas had written: *everything is for miss sera.*

The money my aunt left him was untouched and still in the original envelope. The cash totaled seven hundred dollars and was probably some of the money he'd earned over the years doing odd jobs for the shopkeepers near my store.

I sat on the bed wishing he were still alive. I thought about how many times we had come up with an identical solution to fix a problem. I smiled when I compared him sewing his money into the quilt to me sewing mine into the drapes. There weren't any tears because I had only wonderful memories of Jonas. He had become a part of me when he was alive and I knew I had grown to love him. And if guardian angels existed, then Jonas would sit beside me for the rest of my days.

Just before dawn, I sat on the floor in the dining room and added my inheritance from Jonas to the hem of the drapes.

As I climbed the stairs hoping I could finally get a few hours sleep, there was a loud knock on the door. It was Leonard.

"Sera, I need your help," he said. "Not for me, for one of my clients."

"Of course. What do you need?" I asked.

Leonard looked frightened and he was nervously looking toward the street as if he was waiting for something or someone to appear. Just then another car pulled up. In the partial light, I recognized Dr. Reilly and another man as they rushed up the walk toward the porch.

"Let's go inside," Leonard told the men. He led them straight back to Jonas's room.

"Miss Menard, I'm going to need some clean sheets and a basin full of boiling water." The order came from Dr. Reilly who was tearing the man's shirt sleeve in order to expose his left shoulder. When I'd given the doctor everything he'd requested, he closed the door to the room.

Leonard and I sat at the dining room table. I waited for him to speak – to tell me what kind of trouble he had brought to my door.

"Sera, forgive me. I didn't know where else to turn. One of my clients was in trouble and I couldn't turn my back on him." Leonard was sweating as he sat wringing his hands. He didn't offer anything else.

"What happened to that man…your client? Who is he?" I was not only curious about the man, but I wondered why Leonard had brought him to my house and not his own. Did he trust me more than he trusted Rose or was he simply keeping the wolf away from his door?

"Uh…he was shot. I don't know who shot him and neither does he. I'd rather you didn't know who he is. It's better if you don't. As soon as Doc Reilly patches him up and he has a chance to rest, I'll get him out of here. I'll come back this evening to get him and help him get out of town."

"Why did you bring him here? Am I in danger now?" I needed an answer.

"I wouldn't have come here if I thought I'd put you in danger. All my clients know where I live, so I couldn't go there. And no one knows you or would have any idea to look for Mar…my client here." Leonard had almost said his client's name.

He didn't have to tell me anything else. It was clear to me that I had a wounded member of the Mafia in my home. And it seemed Dr. Reilly had become the mob's doctor.

The house was eerily quiet. The doctor stayed behind the closed door with the wounded man. I cooked breakfast and lunch. Each time I announced the meal was ready, Dr. Reilly came out and took a plate of food for his patient and one for himself to eat in the room. I knew they'd have to go upstairs to use the bathroom, so I spent most of the day either in the front room or upstairs in my bedroom. I was sure the doctor avoided me because Leonard must have told him not to divulge any information to me.

Leonard returned right after it got dark and wasted no time taking his client away from the house. Dr. Reilly followed them in his car.

I never found out what had happened or to whom it had happened. Each time I asked, the only thing Leonard would say was, "Someone owes us…big!"

26

The stock market crash in October 1929 was the disaster Leonard had been expecting. He promptly suffered a heart attack. Against Dr. Reilly's orders, he was up and about in three weeks. He claimed the doctor told him he'd had only a mild attack.

As he had predicted, most of the money we had invested was lost – his losses much greater than mine. Fortunately, he had been able to buy more than a dozen rental properties, two of them in my name. I was thankful I had removed my money from the bank because many of them failed.

I now had three shops: my original one on St. Ann St., the second one several doors down the street, and the third one around the corner on Royal. One was open and two were closed.

Three weeks without seeing or being able to talk to Leonard filled me with anxiety. When he finally called to announce he'd be coming to lunch on Sunday, I was thrilled.

When I opened the door, I was stunned to find a man with a gaunt face and fifteen pounds lighter. Leonard had grown totally gray in twenty-one days.

I pulled him into the house and threw my arms around him without thinking twice about it. We held each other tightly for a few seconds and then I pulled away to take another look at him.

"Come," I told him, "lunch is ready. I hope you're hungry."

Leonard sniffed the air. "If it's baked mirliton, I'm ravenous. I haven't had it since you lived at the Prytania house." He may have looked a bit gangly and reduced from his former self, but he walked with a spring in his step. My anxiety started to ease.

As we talked over lunch, I realized he was not the same man he'd been weeks before. Even though there had been a tremendous loss of money, he seemed resigned to it. He didn't seem to be in a big hurry to get out and work hard to get it back. I thought it was a good time to tell him what I had been thinking. His illness had made me face my own mortality.

"Leonard, I have a special request."

"Uh oh...I don't like the sound of that, Sera. Can it wait for another time?"

"No! I have to tell you while I have the courage and it's fresh on my mind. Please listen to me."

"Go ahead." He sounded perturbed but he gave me his full attention.

"I think this will be the last place I live. With my disease, I can only think that I will live out the rest of my life here. I feel like an Egyptian pharaoh sealed in his tomb." I laughed but Leonard did not join me. From the look on his face, he apparently saw no humor in my words. His face had grown red and his lips trembled.

"Don't say anything more, please. Life is hard enough without you now, Sera. Do you know what it was like for me those three weeks? Why do you want to bring up your death now? That is what this is about, isn't it?"

Even though I wished I hadn't brought up the subject at that particular time, I knew I needed to continue. There was no one else.

"Leonard, aren't you the one who has always told me death is inevitable. Well, it is. All I'm asking of you is that when the time comes you have me cremated."

"And then what?" he asked.

"Throw my ashes into the Gulf of Mexico, Lake Pontchartrain or the Mississippi River, whichever is convenient," I said.

"My God, why?" he looked horrified.

"I've never traveled outside of this city. I've lived on this one little piece of land for fifty-six years with the rest of the world out there somewhere...and me...unable to see any of it. So when you throw my ashes into the water and that water moves and then mixes with the oceans, I'll be carried to all those places I never got to see when I was alive."

"Get up, Sera, get up!" Leonard commanded me.

We stood up at the same time. Leonard grabbed me and held me tightly in his arms and I didn't pull away. He kissed me over and over again and I returned his kisses. When I tried to pull away, he held me tighter. Those kisses surpassed the ones in front of the fireplace.

"Don't leave me, Sera. We've lost so many years. I don't care if we're old." His voice was so tender and loving, it made me cling to him even tighter.

"This is wrong, Leonard." I spoke to him with my head in the crook of his neck. I was ashamed to look at him. "When I should have given you the love I felt for you, I was unable to because of what Daniel had done to me and all the time that had passed. Then ..."

He cut me off. "You're saying you did love me, Sera?"

"Yes, I did love you, I still love you, and I always will love you. But now it's too late. You're married, I'm old and sick, and...and a hundred other reasons."

Leonard let me go suddenly and plopped down in a chair. It frightened me because I thought he was having another attack. When he assured me he was all right, I realized what I'd said to him had shaken his entire being.

For a long time neither of us spoke. Finally he said, "Now that I know you love me, I will always find a way to keep us together. Life is strange and it may open another door for us one day. I'll be ready, will you, Sera?"

My shop had minimal business during the Great Depression, and I think the worry about whether or not I'd run out of money before business picked up caused my arthritis to flare up again. The pain was brutal and I often had to close the shop early. Driving was becoming difficult. I had decided not to worry Leonard with my problems because he had enough of his own. Rose was diagnosed with diabetes and had become severely depressed. Leonard had to spend more time at home looking after her. Because his business was also slow, he worked from his home most of the time.

Late one morning, I was forced to close the store early and go home to rest. I was in such pain, I thought I might have to call Dr. Reilly. I wrapped my feet in a towel with a hot water bottle and then did the same to my hands. Then I took two aspirin and slept for two hours. When I awakened with less pain, I went to my sewing room to find something to occupy my time.

I looked at my bullet-holed mannequin and decided to put her in a new outfit. She hadn't been changed for over a year, before Georgina left. She had told me how much her father loved the story about how I shot the mannequin and that he'd always feel around the middle of it to find the spot where the bullet had entered and then stick his finger in and out of it. She said he'd made the hole much bigger by doing that, so she had asked him to stop.

I found the pieces I'd had on display in the shop before it was renovated and chose a blouse and a skirt. The skirt was the calf-length style worn before the knee length was made popular during the flapper period. When I removed the mannequin's old outfit, I saw that adhesive tape had been put over the hole. The tape was covering a hole the size of my fist.

I was incensed that a grown man would damage someone's property for his own amusement. There was a small amount of sawdust that had stuck to the tape when I pulled it off, but there was none at the opening of the hole. Without a logical reason, I stuck my hand inside and then I froze. I felt what I knew was money. I knew what I'd found belonged to Graziano. This was where he'd stashed the money he was saving to take his daughter and his grandson back to Sicily.

Most of the money was in two silk drawstring bags, except for the bundle I'd felt when I'd thrust my hand inside. The bags were jammed into the belly of the mannequin where the sawdust had been removed.

My arthritic hands were left shaking and throbbing after counting…fifty thousand dollars!

Why hadn't Graziano told Georgina it was there? Why hadn't the mob come looking for her after her father was killed? Where was she? I hadn't heard from her since she went to New York without giving me her aunt's name and address. This was her money…but how was I supposed to get it to her?

I could not solve this problem. It was too much for me to handle. I had to call Leonard for help. There was no answer at his office or his home.

When he called five days later, I learned Rose had to be hospitalized and then she'd been sent to a sanitarium for a short stay. She had threatened to harm herself if Leonard wasn't with her twenty-four hours. She would not allow a full-time nurse or anyone else to care for her.

Leonard looked haggard when he came to the shop. He said he felt guilty having put his wife in such a place, but with the economy and the loss of so much business, he had to work as much as he could to keep his head above water. And he couldn't do that when she wouldn't let him out of her sight.

I couldn't help but ask, "Does she suspect you of having an affair? Have you given her reason to distrust you?"

"No, she has no cause to think I've strayed from our marriage."

"Does she know about me?" I asked.

"What is there to know, Sera?" Leonard raised his voice in anger. "I loved you before I ever met her and I have never been unfaithful to her with you. She only knows you as one of my clients. Surely you don't think I'd ever tell her who you really are, do you?"

"Well...no. I only meant..."

"Maybe someone else told her something? I don't think so. Anyone who knew about us is dead! So, how could she know?" Leonard was short of breath when he finished talking.

I led him to a chair and gave him a cup of tea I had just made. I didn't say anything else giving him a chance to calm himself.

"There are just too many problems to deal with right now. I'm scuffling to keep my properties rented, my law practice going, and now I'll have to run to see Rose every day. But I guess that's better than worrying about her being at home alone. Sera, I think I'm getting close to the edge and if

I encounter another damn problem, I'll probably lose all my marbles and join Rose in the nut house."

"Leonard, you've got to force yourself to be calm." I forced myself to ignore what he'd said. "If you don't, you're going to have another heart attack. How can I help you right now?" I was at a loss as to what else to do for him. Maybe he could tell me what I could do.

"Take me home and give me a good meal and a few glasses of sherry...and a normal conversation."

"Is that all? Let me close the shop and I'll meet you at the house in fifteen minutes." I could feel my chest quivering as I anticipated spending the evening with him.

On the drive home I realized I had never gotten the opportunity to tell him about the money. And after what he'd said to me about "another damn problem," I didn't know when I'd tell him. I thought it best for the time being to let the money stay where I'd found it, and when Leonard could handle one more problem, I'd tell him about it.

27

I, Leonard Stern, must resort to telling you, from my perspective, what happened to Sera and me from the 1930s through the beginning of the Second World War. My hearing has deteriorated and much of what Sera dictated to me about that period I was unable to understand. It is also my feeling she glossed over those years with little or no detail, mainly because we were not married. I cannot let that happen. I cannot look upon that time superficially, when to this day, I relive it again and again. Yes, it is Sera's story, but a great deal of it is also mine.

It has been extremely difficult to hear and then write about what Sera thought of me in the beginning. Many things that happened I've wanted to write a different version than what was dictated to me, but I couldn't betray Sera, the woman I've loved all these years.

My wife Rose was quite a bit younger than me, but miscarriages, female disorders, and family obligations kept her indisposed much of our married life. We slept in separate rooms and rarely ate meals together. She tried to keep busy with her charities and church work and was amenable to my needs, but she was passionless.

Rose missed her large, Irish family and New York. She hated the oppressive humidity in New Orleans and the lack of a distinct changing of the seasons. She found the south barbaric and the Irish New Orleanians beneath her. She insisted on taking a trip to New York at least three times a year. Each trip lasted four to six weeks and after her mother's medical problems began, she was gone even longer.

After Rose began spending extended periods in the sanitarium, I was able to spend more time with Sera. I grew to depend on her as if she were my wife. I had most of my meals with her; she took care of my laundry; every evening she massaged my tired shoulders.

After dinner one evening, Sera and I knew that embraces and kisses were no longer enough. I followed her upstairs to her bedroom. That night we held each other for hours and talked. It was wonderful to touch her, to have her shudder when I held her body close to mine. I could not help but think how content I could have been for those forty years and how many children we could have created. I hated to leave her that night. Even though there had been no lovemaking, some of our hunger had been satiated.

Intimacy was difficult at first. Sera was self-conscious about her hands and feet. She was often in pain, especially now that her remissions had ceased. I didn't know how my heart would react to that kind of excitement and exertion. It had been years since Rose and I had sexual relations. Dr. Reilly advised me to take things slowly but not to be afraid.

The next time we found ourselves upstairs in bed, there was no hesitation. Sera amazed me when she took control of the situation. She told me I didn't have to treat her like something breakable; she wanted to feel my arms around her. She wanted to know firsthand that making love involved a total release of passion and not violence.

I think we tried to make up for lost time; we were both insatiable. It seemed Sera could forget her pain during those times. Of course, as the years passed that was no longer the case. At certain times, Sera could not be touched. I could not even hold her hands.

I wanted desperately to sleep all night with her cradled in my arms, but I needed to be where the sanitarium could reach me. In time, I was able to do that, too.

My life became rich with Sera. I knew time was no longer on our side, so we had to make the most of what was left. Because I was a married man, I could not put Sera on my arm and escort her around the city. She understood that. We enjoyed her home, her garden and her gazebo. Unfortunately, when the gazebo was damaged by hurricane winds, it could not be repaired. We had it removed but still used the area for picnics.

Rose's home visits stopped completely in 1935 when she reached a point where she didn't talk at all. Eventually, she became catatonic and seldom left her room at the facility. Rose's catatonia lessened Sera's guilt somewhat, but not mine. Everyday that I live, I will wonder if I had loved Sera less and my wife more – would the outcome have been different.

By 1937, my finances were at crisis stage. Because of my inability to make a decent living with my law firm, the investment business going belly-up, and Rose's sanitarium bills, I was drowning. The only money I could count on was the money from the rental properties. I had not confided this to Sera until one night when I realized I had to talk to someone.

"Why did you wait to tell me this, Leonard?"

"I didn't think you needed more stress. This problem is mine and I know you can't help me solve it. I just needed to get it off my chest." I was embarrassed and sorry I'd told her. What kind of man dumps his money problems on a woman?

"How do you know I can't help you? Let's go upstairs," she told me.

"Not right now, Sera. My mental state is not where it should be. You know what happens when my head doesn't work." I could feel my face grow red.

"I'm not inviting you into my bed. Come with me. Come on," she beckoned. "I have a surprise for you."

I followed her upstairs and into her sewing room. She began to undress the mannequin.

"What are you doing?" I asked.

"Patience!" she said loudly. I sat in a chair and watched her.

When the mannequin's clothes had been removed, Sera stepped aside and pointed to the patch of adhesive tape on its midsection. I started to laugh remembering the time she'd shot it.

"Don't laugh at this naked lady. She comes bearing gifts." With a flourish, Sera ripped off the tape and thrust her hand into the hole. She took out two bags, loosened their strings, and then dumped out a pile of money on the floor.

I was stupefied. "Whose money is that?"

"I'm sure it's Graziano's. I think he hid it there until he was ready to whisk Georgina and Gino out of the country and away from Emilio."

"How long have you known it was in there?" I asked her.

"Five or six years. I didn't tell you because you told me if you faced another damn problem, you'd lose your marbles. I know this is Georgina's now; it must be the savings she hunted for after her father's death…the money he made when he was the bootleg banker."

"Sera, did Georgina ever contact you after she went to New York?"

"No."

"Then you have no idea where to get in touch with her. You've held onto this money all these years without one clue as to how you'd get it to her. Even though I said I couldn't handle another problem, you should have told me, anyway. That's mob money, Sera! Maybe Graziano was skimming off the top and didn't actually earn all of it or any of it. Surely you don't expect me to try to return this money to his old mob boss, do you? Are you trying to get us killed?"

"That's the farthest thing from my mind. I think there was so much money flowing back then that this is a drop in the bucket compared to what they hauled in. And if they haven't come after Georgina in more than five years, they never will. You need money, Leonard. Here it is! I have had so few needs in the last few years that I haven't needed to tap into it. Tell me, Mr. Stern, if you had found this and I needed money, wouldn't you give it to me?"

"Yes, and I wouldn't hesitate. But it does not mitigate my fear. How would I live with myself if this money can somehow be traced back to us or to Georgina and her family? The Mafia is ruthless – there's no just saying you're sorry."

"Well, Leonard...take it or leave it. You can't turn your back on such an unusual gift, can you?"

"No, Sera, I guess I can't. I can only look upon this as some kind of miracle and wonder what I've done to deserve it...and you." I was embarrassed to have to accept this money from a woman who lived frugally without complaint and who had dedicated the last few years taking care of me while I took care of my wife. I started to cry.

"Leonard, don't you dare!" Sera ordered me. "I can see you feel humiliated, but you really have nothing to feel ashamed about. If it were not for the way you've loved me and taken care of me all these years, I have no idea what would have become of me."

She stood next to me and put my head against her bosom. She took a handkerchief out of her pocket and dried my eyes, then leaned over and kissed my forehead several times.

"There's fifty-thousand dollars here, Leonard. Will that help?"

"Fifty-thousand dollars! Oh, Sera!" I inhaled deeply in disbelief. My heart fluttered and scared me for a moment. "I've gone through all of the money Rose inherited from her mother and almost every dime of my savings. I am only a few months away from the poor house."

"Now you don't have to go," she said.

"Because of you." I put my arms around her waist and buried my face between her breasts.

While I was busy using the mob's miracle money to get out of my financial hole, Sera's ability to move around was being compromised. She could no longer shift her car without excruciating pain. Many days she couldn't leave the house to open the store.

Our sexual life had all but ceased. She asked me if it was difficult to love her now that her body was becoming deformed and she was untouchable most of the time. I tried to tell her she was still beautiful and there was not one thing in this world that would make me stop loving her. I don't think I ever convinced her.

Self-conscious about her appearance, Sera began wearing dresses that covered her from her neck to her ankles just as Pauline had done. She still had a beautiful figure and could wear any kind of fashion, but she packed away all the dresses and skirts that were either calf or knee length and cut below her collarbone. I wonder if she realized how like her aunt she had become.

I tried to get her to return to the church, but to no avail. She told me she had gone to the cathedral one day to talk to a priest after her aunt died and she'd shot that intruder. She was in desperate need of advice and guidance. She said instead of help she found a disinterested priest who gave her a lecture about finding forgiveness and redemption directly from God. She never returned to the church.

After much discussion and arm-twisting, I got her to agree to close the shop permanently and sell the car. She immediately slipped into a kind of depression that frightened me. She was able to walk and talk, eat and sleep, but it seemed she had lost most of her enthusiasm for living.

Was it happening again? Another woman in my life was unable to cope with things when they became difficult. I understood why Rose couldn't stand up under the pressures of her life after she married me. She was unprepared. Not only was she timid, she had been raised in a sheltered environment with indulgent parents. She thought the world outside her home was harsh. I don't think she decided to marry me; I think her parents thought it time she left the nest.

But Sera...she'd had a troubled life from the time she was a small child. I expected her to be tougher and to handle this phase of her life with the same kind of fortitude. I didn't know what the future held for us, but what I did know was that Sera would never want for anything as long as I had breath.

The relief programs set up by the Roosevelt Administration put many of the unemployed to work, especially the WPA. That allowed me to rent my houses in the Marigny and Tremé areas and keep them rented.

After it went bankrupt, I bought the Carondelet Street factory that had bought Sera's fabric inventory. I was also fortunate to pick up another factory on Baronne Street with what was left of the "mannequin money."

I rented all three of Sera's shops. Two were turned into restaurants and the other into a bakery. When I put the rents directly into her hands, she was finally able to see that despite having to close the dress shop, she was going to have an income and was not completely dependent upon me. This was a major turning point in her mental attitude and the easing and eventual disappearance of her depression.

With the onset of the Second World War and the ensuing war economy, it seemed everyone went to work. Many of my tenants got good paying jobs making PT boats at Higgins.

I bought more property and stopped practicing law and handling investments. Buying and renting property became my full time job.

In March 1942, Rose died leaving me free to marry Sera, but she refused to marry me. Nothing I told her convinced her we'd have a better life in New York now that we were getting older. Sera was estranged from her siblings in New Orleans and I had no kin in the city. We'd have a family to look after us in New York and the use of hospitals that were considered more modern and with the latest medical technologies. I believed the doctors there would have more advanced treatment for her disease and they could probably do a better job of alleviating her pain than Doc Reilly. It all fell on closed ears.

Sera's refusal was all I needed to push me over the edge. Several weeks later, I had a stroke followed by a massive heart attack. A cousin from New York came to take care of me until I regained my speech and some mobility. Then my housekeeper moved in to give me twenty-four hour care.

Eventually, Edgar Souté, a young lawyer I had mentored and whom I trusted, took over managing my finances and reopened the law firm. He hired another lawyer to handle most of the cases while he helped me deal with my rental property. I gave him instructions as to how Sera was to be cared for and he followed them to the letter. When I was able to speak with more clarity and had gained a bit more mobility, I advised Edgar on business matters.

I never saw Sera again. We were now both Pharaohs sealed in our tombs. The telephone, the mail, and messengers kept us connected. We began to write her memoir about 1947, when Claire came into her life. She learned right away who the young girl was. We spent many hours on the telephone discussing her life. I had the freedom to change the way she expressed herself in many instances, but there were parts she wanted written exactly the way she dictated them to me. Sera never had the courage to tell her great-niece who she was or why she lived as White. She told me that's why she was writing her life story; it would tell Claire all she needed to know.

When I could no longer hear much of her telephone dictation, Edgar would try to take some of it, but it was too time consuming. He also found it too personal when she talked about the deterioration of her body and the intensity of her pain. At that point, he asked her to wait until I recovered because the information was too intimate for him to be involved. Several times she sent me written parts of her story, but her penmanship was so illegible, I could not transcribe what she'd written.

I was pleased when Claire came into Sera's life and eventually lived with her in the Esplanade house. The circumstances under which she was left without a family and homeless when she was seventeen was a terrible tragedy. I believe caring for her great-niece and helping her to get the education she desperately wanted allowed Sera to feel less guilt in never having contacted her siblings after their father died.

Sera admitted how lonely she was now that I was unable to visit her. I wanted her to get a live-in housekeeper, but she refused. She said she didn't trust anyone and confessed that she had almost pushed Claire away permanently by lashing out at the child for asking why in her condition she didn't have a relative or someone else live with her. I advised her to waste no time in apologizing to Claire when she saw her again. I reminded her that the girl was her only link to the family she had not seen or spoken to in over seventy years. She took my advice.

Sera became a different person when Claire began the drugstore deliveries to her home. She would often order things she didn't need so that Claire would have several deliveries every week. Although she loved hearing about her sister Philomene, she didn't like her sister pressuring a teenage girl to think about marriage instead of getting an education. Sera remembered how she had been pulled out of school at a young age to take care of her father's home and a house full of children. She always resented being uneducated; she didn't want this for Claire.

That situation is what fueled her desire to have me write her memoir. She wanted Claire to read what life was like growing up, not only for her, but for Claire's grandmother Philomene.

Claire shared her life with Sera before and after they met and Sera shared all of it with me. One thing that saddened Sera was that she was unable to design and sew beautiful clothes for her niece, especially after she entered high school and no longer wore a uniform. She told me Claire was tall and thin and had the type body that was a dressmaker's dream. When I suggested she teach Claire to design and sew, she told me she had asked her if she'd like to learn and the girl told her she didn't, she preferred reading books. Claire admitted that her grandmother had tried to teach her to sew, but gave up when she showed no interest.

One of my greatest regrets is that I never got to meet Claire nor did I ever see a picture of her. Sera's dealings with me: getting money to her, paying her bills, taking care of the upkeep on the house were all done when Claire was not at home. Sera made sure of that and I don't understand why. I suppose it all ties into her not wanting Claire to know who she was.

Sera never liked taking pictures and apparently neither did her sister Philomene. Many times I asked Sera to buy a camera and to take a few pictures of herself and Claire and send them to me. She never did. She insisted on describing herself and the girl to me, especially after Claire grew out of what Sera called "her awkward stage."

One day during Claire's first year in college, I asked Sera to describe to me how Claire looked in her new Easter outfit that Sera had been raving about.

"Why are you always so interested in what my niece looks like?" Sera asked in a hostile voice that came like a blast from a rifle through the telephone and shocked me.

"Sera, don't we talk about Claire all the time? I look forward to it. I've gotten used to hearing about what she does and how she looks. You seem to love talking about her. What a curious thing to ask me in such an accusatory tone."

"No, it isn't accusatory. It suddenly occurred to me that you're different when it comes to Claire. You don't seem to think of her as a Negro, do you?"

I was too stunned to answer. It had been years since Sera had mentioned how I felt about non-Whites. I had changed over the years for many reasons, but I hadn't ever shared that with her.

"Hmm," Sera said, "no answer. I guess that means you accept two of us now – Claire and me. I suppose you can call that progress. I wish you'd…"

"Sera…stop, please. I don't want to have a heated discussion about this. Let's just say you've grown to love your niece and so have I. Listen to this: Several times recently I've caught my assistant eavesdropping when I'm talking to you on the telephone, so I decided to tell him all about Claire. Perhaps we're both infatuated with her now. I hope you don't mind, Sera."

"You're too old and Edgar is not her type, so no, I don't mind if you idiots are infatuated with someone out of your reach. But, Claire minding is a different story. She's extremely private and I wouldn't want her to find out I've been sharing her life with you."

"Well, the only way she'll find out is if you tell her," I chuckled, "we certainly won't." I knew she was furious and perhaps even a little jealous.

I knew that Sera needed Claire at that time in her life. She was no longer alone. I couldn't be with her, but there would be someone there when the end came.

Joshua, that wonderful boy…dear God, how I've disappointed him! He was visiting me when Sera died and insisted I allow him to go to the Esplanade house the next morning to meet with Claire. I was unable to go, so I felt fortunate he wanted to handle things for me. Ordinarily, Edgar would have taken my place, but I knew I had to let Joshua go because I needed Edgar to make Sera's final arrangements.

When Joshua returned that afternoon, he seemed ill-at-ease. He wasn't interested in telling me about his visit with Claire. Instead, he asked to read the manuscript. He said I'd told him all about Sera, but he wanted to read her life story himself. I instructed Edgar to give him the rough draft I kept in my study. The final copy was at my office being typed by my secretary. She is waiting for the last pages in order to have it bound in leather. Sera had planned to give it to Claire as soon as it was finished.

Joshua stormed into my bedroom hours later red-faced and filled with rage.

I tried to explain to him that life happens in strange ways no matter who we are or how much we try to avoid what happens to us. I hadn't wanted him to find out about his heritage that way, but he had and I was trying to put out the fire. He told me to be quiet.

Joshua tried to get Edgar and my housekeeper to leave my room, but they refused. It was the first time I was glad I couldn't hear because I could tell his voice had risen to a roar. Unfortunately, though, I had learned to read lips and I read every damnable word he uttered to me. He called me a nigger-loving bastard over and over again. He wanted to know how it felt to fuck a nigger woman. How could he ever tell his father? He had a bad heart and it would kill him to find out his mother was a nigger and his father a rapist.

Joshua walked to the edge of my bed, leaned toward me, and spit in my face.

Fearing I'd have another heart attack, my housekeeper pleaded with Joshua to stop his attack, but he continued until he was spent. Then he calmly left the room and went out to the garden where he walked for several hours muttering to himself.

Edgar and my housekeeper did not leave my room for fear Joshua would return to do harm to me. When they heard him drive away, we all relaxed. They took turns guarding me all night.

The next morning after breakfast, Joshua popped into my room. He was happy-go-lucky as if nothing had happened the previous day. He informed me he was going for a long drive to clear his head and that he didn't plan to return until late in the evening.

Edgar, at my urging, flew into action. He managed to assemble two of my real-estate colleagues and a notary by that afternoon. With their help, I rewrote my will.

I did not wish to end my relationship with Joshua on such a sour note. So I, too, tried to be jovial and pretend, as he was doing, that there had been no bad blood between us. After all, he has been kind and wonderful to me for many years. Someday I hope he realizes that I could not change the course of events – that Daniel, the rapist, is his biological grandfather, and Sera, the mixed-race woman, is his biological grandmother. Later in his life, perhaps Joshua will also come to know that I was thankful for all the time he spent with me and called me grandfather. I've only had that privilege because of him.

My last conversations with Sera were held with Edgar's help. He told her I was too weak to hold the telephone. He'd write out her words to me and then relay my reply to her.

Very little is left to tell. I apologize for the parts that are lost, but I do believe the most important events have been recorded here.

PART TWO

28

I awoke in a stupor as the noise coming from my door grew louder…pounding, pounding, pounding…causing the nerves in my head to pinch, the muscles in my body to tighten…making me want to scream, "Damnit, go away." But instead, I forced myself to ask, "Who is it?"

"Who do you think?"

I recognized the voice. "Just a minute," I yelled at the door realizing it was Frank. I had been asleep on the sofa in the clothes I had arrived in. My great-aunt's memoir was lying on my chest. I looked around to make sure I was really in my New York apartment.

When I opened the door, I found Frank standing with his arms folded across his chest and with a look of pure annoyance upon his face.

"That was damn rude of you not to return to our welcome party," he said through his teeth. "Obviously it was your aunt's life story," he said pointing to the book in my hand, "but really, that's no excuse, Claire. Before I forget, I'm in apartment 104."

I knew he was right; my receiving the book did not excuse my behavior. "I'm sorry, Frank. I should have come back after I finished reading it or at least come up and told you I was tired and needed to sleep for a bit. What time is it, anyway?"

"It's 8:30. The evening is just about gone now."

"Why didn't you come down earlier? I finished the book in one sitting…several hours ago. I was tired and after reading this," I held up the book, "I needed to sleep. I am sorry, Frank."

"Charlie and Luis wouldn't let me disturb you. I know what that memoir means to you, Claire, I'm not really angry. Go to bed for real this time. I'll see you in the morning."

"Thanks for understanding. goodnight." I'm not sure he forgave me, but he put on a good front.

I took a long deep breath as I gave the apartment an in-depth look this time. I was pleasantly surprised at how well-furnished and comfortable it was. The sofa turned into a double-bed with a firm mattress. The kitchen was fully-equipped. I was shocked when I opened the refrigerator and found eggs, bacon, milk, bread, butter, bagels, several oranges and apples. There was coffee and a coffee pot on the counter next to the stove; salt, pepper and sugar were there, too.

Frank Beauchamp…Doctor Frank Beauchamp. I had left New Orleans with him. He had invited himself to travel by train with me to New York City. We were going to rent apartments in a building owned by his friends and he was going to join their medical practice. I was going to look around New York to find out if I liked it well enough to stay, then I'd go to Paris for a short trip just for the pleasure of going. Yes, that's why I'm here in this apartment. I had awakened a bit wool-gathered, but now I knew who I was and why I had come.

A bath, I thought, as I realized, once again, I was still wearing the same clothes I was wearing when I left New Orleans. I drew a tub full of really warm water, peeled off my dirty clothes, pinned up my hair, and slowly eased down into the water. Sleep had interrupted my thoughts about not only the memoir, but our arrival at the brownstone. I had an urgent need to recreate them, especially meeting Charlie and Luis. There was something quirky, actually unsettling about them and the time we spent in their apartment before the memoir arrived. I closed my eyes and forced my mind to conjure up our arrival.

Frank and I had traveled light, each with only one suitcase, which allowed us to easily hop on the subway and travel to uptown Manhattan. It was only a short walk to the brownstone on Hamilton Terrace which was in a lovely area near City College. The doctors were waiting for us with a wine, cheese and cold cuts spread. Frank introduced us.

"Claire, these are my old buddies, Charles Knox and Luis Cantana. Boys, this is Claire Soublet."

"Frank, you old dog! You didn't lie when you told me she's gorgeous. Welcome, Claire. Call me Charlie, and the quiet-one over there," Charlie swung his head around to look at Luis, "he doesn't like nicknames, so just call him Luis or Dr. Cantana." Then he howled laughing.

Luis smiled at me...barely. He glared at Charlie. Hmm, I remember thinking, the doctor isn't too friendly. What's going on here? I watched Luis as he watched Frank.

We made polite conversation, mostly about the train trip from New Orleans as we ate and drank. Charlie asked me only a few questions about myself and I concluded Frank had already filled him in. Luis simply listened while he snacked without saying a word.

"Claire, Frank tells me you might be interested in staying in New York permanently," Charlie said. "Will you be looking for a job?"

I had concluded incorrectly.

"If I like New York, I'll stay. As for a job, I'll eventually have to get one, but for now I'm interested in getting my master's degree. And...there are one or two things I need to do before I make any

decisions." When I finished answering, I observed the glances that went back and forth among the men, especially between Charlie and Frank.

"You have no family left in New Orleans?" Charlie asked.

"No, but I have aunts in California. Oh, and an uncle, too. They've all been estranged from the family even before my grandparents died. I do have an elderly woman in New Orleans I've been close to since my great-aunt died."

"You poor little orphan! Fear not, sweetie, we'll take care of you," Charlie told me in an affected stage voice.

"Knock it off, Charlie. Stop your teasing. Claire is anything but a poor little orphan. She's a strong woman and doesn't need a man to take care of her," Frank told him as he looked at me apologetically.

There was a loud buzzing sound. It startled me and I jumped.

"It's just the downstairs buzzer; probably a package or a piece of mail," Luis announced. "I'll go down."

"I know you'd like to see your apartments, but there's too much wine and eats left. You'll have to stay a while and help us finish it off. Then you can crash for the night." Charlie wasn't asking, he was telling us what we had to do.

"Listen, Charlie, Claire is probably tired. I know I am. Maybe, we can rest for a bit and come back later on this evening. What do you think?"

Before Charlie could answer, Luis was back. He handed me a package. "It's for you, Claire."

"What! You haven't officially moved in and you're already getting mail." Charlie was teasing on the square. I knew I'd have to get used to his kidding if I intended to stay here.

"Do you mind if I go down to my apartment to open this? I know what it is. I've been waiting a long time for it. Please excuse me." I looked first at Frank and then at Charlie.

Luis asked Charlie for the key to my apartment. "I'll take her down, Charlie. You two stay and finish talking. I have an errand to run, so I'll see you in about half-an-hour."

He walked me downstairs, opened my apartment door and put my suitcase inside. "You take as long as it takes to read your mail. I'm sure the boys have a lot of catching up to do and won't even miss us." Luis handed me the key. "See you later, Claire."

There was another loud banging on the door interrupting my reverie. The water was no longer warm, so I hopped out of the tub, grabbed a towel and headed for the door.

"Who is it?"

"Claire," it was Frank again, "is everything okay? Just thought I'd check on you again."

I didn't open the door; I answered through it. "Everything is fine. I had one foot in the bathtub when you knocked. I'm going to get a good hot soaking and then I'm going to find out how comfortable that sofa bed is. Thanks for checking on me. I'll see you in the morning...late in the morning." I wished I didn't have to lie, but I needed some time to myself.

"Okay...sleep tight," Frank muttered as he left my door and then I heard his door slam shut.

I hadn't had time to think about what I'd read in my great-aunt's memoir. I hadn't enough energy left to even begin to think about what was in it. The only thing that continued to roll over again and again in my mind was that she'd died with her identity hidden. I also needed to respond to the lawyer's letter and sign and send him that paper regarding the will. But it won't be tonight, I thought. I had only the energy it took to put on a pair of pajamas and fall into bed.

29

It was almost 11:00 the next morning before I was fully awake and dressed. When I opened my door to go over to Frank's apartment to invite him for bagels and coffee, I found a note stuck in it.

Claire, I've gone to look at my new office. See you about 1:00. Let's go downtown for lunch and some sightseeing. Frank

I decided to use that time to write a response to the lawyer in New Orleans.

August 4, 1957

Dear Mr. Souté,

You cannot imagine the enormous joy I felt upon receiving my great-aunt's memoir. There will never be an adequate way to thank you. Thinking Joshua had destroyed it, I have been in the process of forcing myself to accept that I'd never learn about my ancestors or who Seraphine Menard really was. I thought she'd have to remain a mystery, and that the life story she'd promised to tell me about in her memoir, I'd probably never see. That made me sick with disappointment.

Sera's reasons for not telling me who she was when she was alive will continue to nag at me, but learning how she navigated through all of the indignities she faced in her lifetime makes forgiveness easy. Her love for me wasn't expressed in the form of a confession about who she'd chosen to become; she showed me in the way she treated and cared for me. I hope that in spite of my issues with trust, she was able to see through my defenses and know that I appreciated her generosity and that I returned her love. Perhaps, in some measure, she was able to thank Leonard Stern for what he did for me through her. I can only hope she did.

It's funny…shocking…even ironic when I remember as a young girl daydreaming about being the mistress of the Esplanade house. And now, now that I own it, I don't know what I'm going to do with it. This is a piece of irony I never thought I'd get to experience.

Even though I've not as yet digested all that I've read – I am not disappointed with what I've learned about my family. My grandparents told me little about who their parents were or how they grew up. I was overjoyed to find out about two generations in my grandmother's line.

Mr. Souté, I did not run away from home. Like many twenty-three-year-olds, I left home to see the world and to learn what else is in it. Surely you don't begrudge me that. And maybe, when I'm old, I'll come back home to die and be buried in my family's vault in St. Roch Cemetery.

There is nothing to forgive about you asking Jo for information about me. I, too, am filled with curiosity. I'm flattered that you found me interesting enough to want to know more about me.

I plan to call Jo in the next day or two to see how she's doing. I'm grateful to you for alerting me.

Thank you, Mr. Souté, for all you've done on my behalf. It may not be soon, but I'm sure I'll get to meet you one day and I look forward to it.

The signed document you requested is enclosed. I will contact you again as soon as I make a decision about the house.

Sincerely,

Claire Soublet

I had packed postage stamps in with my stationery, so I could mail the letter immediately. I remembered seeing a mailbox a few blocks from the brownstone when Frank and I had walked from the subway station the day before. As I started down the hill, the mailman was leaving the building next door. He graciously took my letter saying he'd save me a return walk uphill. I was pleasantly surprised because Frank had told me people were not very friendly in New York; they had no time for smiles or small talk.

At 12:55, Frank tapped on my door ready to set out and show me New York. He had never lived in the city, but he had visited many times and knew how to get around. While we were on the train going downtown, he briefly explained the subway system to me. We got off at 34th Street and then walked one block to 7th Avenue and 34th to one of Frank's favorite places in the city, the Automat. It was the most unique place to eat that I'd ever seen. Fresh out of New Orleans, it didn't take much to amaze me.

I still remember what I ate. Of all the wonderful foods I could have chosen, I was fascinated with a brown, oblong casserole dish with franks and beans. It was in a revolving tower with different compartments. After you put your money in the slot, you slid the door open and took out your food. Hot apple pie with vanilla sauce was my dessert of choice. I don't remember what Frank had, only that he laughed and called me a cheap date. After leaving the Automat, we walked along 34th Street looking into Macy's windows.

Frank shook my arm. "Look across the street at the arcade, Claire, that passageway. As you walk through it, there's all different kinds of small shops, and at the far end on the left side, there's a walk-up, hole-in-the-wall Chinese restaurant. It has the most fabulous food." He stopped walking momentarily, but started up again. "We'll go there when we come downtown again." He stopped again and pointed, "If you look all the way through to the next street, that's Gimbel's, Macy's rival store. Would you like to go inside Macy's to have a look around, Claire?"

"No thanks," I told him. "I'm enjoying our walking tour. Where are we going next, Mr. Tour Guide?"

"To the Empire State Building, and then if you're not too tired, maybe St. Patrick's Cathedral. I'm glad you're wearing sensible shoes and not three-inch heels." Frank looked down at my espadrilles and then grabbed my hand as we approached 6th Avenue and had the green light. I wanted to pull away, but I knew he'd done it to be a gentleman, so I resisted the urge.

"Are you afraid of heights, Claire?"

"No, but I'm claustrophobic. Why?"

"I'd like to take you up to the observation tower. Are you okay with that?"

"Sure, it's okay. Are we getting close?"

"This is 6th and 34th; it's on 5th and 34th. Look ahead and up."

"Holy moly! I'm not too sure now." I had to bend my head back until it rested on my cervical spine in order to see the top of the building.

"Oh, c'mon now. Don't chicken out on me, Claire."

"We'll see," I chuckled. "I think I'll be okay. I'm just glad I don't have nose bleeds like one of the girls in my high school drama club. Everything made her nose bleed." I was remembering how Felicia's nervousness caused her to bleed all over herself and me when we were competing in the city championship.

We did everything Frank had planned and then we headed back to the apartments. As we entered the building, we met Charlie and Luis on their way out to a dinner party.

"Sweetie, you look bedraggled. I'll bet Frank dragged you all over New York City this afternoon. Every time he's come to visit us, he's spent more time walking the city than here with us. Right, Luis?" It was obvious Charlie was trying to make Luis a part of the conversation because he had failed to do it the day before. He'd laughed at Luis and had spent most of his time talking to Frank.

"That he did," Luis smiled his usual scant smile. "I'll wait for you outside, Charlie."

"I didn't drag her, Charlie. Please defend me, Claire," Frank pleaded.

"No, Charlie, he really didn't. I was a willing participant. This city is beyond my expectations. I can't wait for my second outing. Tomorrow or Sunday, I hope."

Before Frank could answer, Charlie said, "Well, sweetie, I'm afraid that will have to wait a bit. Frank has to get his office and exam room set up; he has got to get his practice going. I'm sure you're going to help him with that, aren't you?" Charlie's steely dark eyes looked at Frank as Frank looked down at the floor as if afraid of what I would say. Charlie folded his long arms across his chest, blew out a long burst of air from his lungs, and then stared at his friend with complete exasperation. He shifted from one foot to the other waiting for me to answer.

"Oh, before I forget, Claire, thanks for the rent you slipped under my door this morning. Did Frank take you to see the offices today? They're only about a mile and a half from here on St. Nicholas Avenue."

"No, we went downtown to the Automat for lunch, to the Empire State Building, and then to St. Patrick's Cathedral. That church is breathtaking. I felt like a tiny little mouse when I lit a candle and then knelt at the altar." I looked at Frank as we stood in the entranceway. He was staring at me and noticeably uncomfortable.

"The Automat, huh, that figures. It's Frank's favorite place to eat in the entire world. All of the fabulous restaurants in New York City, he loves The Automat." Charlie turned to Frank, "Haven't you asked Claire to help you? When you want something, you have to ask for it. Too much pride? What then?"

"Actually, I haven't asked her." Frank gave Charlie a dirty look which threw Charlie into a fit of giggles with his hand clasped over his mouth. "But now that you've pre-empted me, I guess I'm forced to do it now."

"No, Frank, you don't have to ask, but remember I am going to Paris." I watched his face flood with embarrassment. "So...I'll help you Monday through Wednesday and then I'm going to check on the ships sailing to France. When I find one, I'll be leaving as soon as it sails." I was tempted to remind him of his eloquent speech about spending a week together in Paris before he opened his practice. I figured Charlie was pulling his strings, and since he was giving Frank the opportunity to join his and Luis's practice, Frank needed to get started when he was asked.

"Look, kids, I've got to run," Charlie told us. "I'm afraid I've got to leave you on your own to settle your problems. Ciao."

I don't believe Charlie knew or had ever been told he wasn't handsome. He moved through the world as if he looked like Billy Eckstine. He was over six-feet tall with a long, bony, angular face and large ears that were bent forward an inch away from his head. He wore horn-rimmed glasses which were always on the tip of his thin, sharp nose. The only features that saved him were his smile, his magnificent teeth, and he dressed impeccably. As I watched him walk away after lobbing a grenade between Frank and me, I knew he was going to be trouble... big time.

As we walked to my apartment, Frank said, "Claire, Charlie's an ass. Please don't let anything he says get to you. He's all bluster. I think he talks without thinking. May I come in for a while? We need to talk."

"Of course, but I'm going to be busy cooking bacon and eggs. I'm starving! Want some?"

"Sure, I never refuse a free meal. To be honest, I'm shocked. I didn't think you cooked. I'll do the talking while you cook." Frank took my key from me and opened my door.

I smiled while I was frying the bacon remembering the question Jo asked me when I told her I couldn't cook. "How you gonna feed a man, dawlin?"

"What else can you cook, Claire?"

"Oh, not too many things. Jo taught me how to cook mostly Creole dishes: shrimp étouffée, jambalaya, red beans and rice, and shrimp with okra and tomatoes. Let's see, I can also make po boys, pralines, and a decent bread pudding with whiskey sauce. But no gumbo and stuffed mirliton; they take too long to prepare and then cook. I'm not in love with the kitchen, so the faster I can make a dish, the better."

"Wait until I tell Charlie you cook Creole food," Frank said. "He's going to become one of your best friends."

"You can tell him, but I didn't come to New York to have a bunch of men, or even just one, expect me to cook for them. Do I look like Aunt Jemima to you?" I was pissed and Frank could tell. He quickly apologized.

"Sorry, Claire, that was a monumental lapse of judgment. I won't say anything. I'm sure you've noticed how pushy he is. He's cheeky enough to expect you to cook a few dishes whenever he asks."

"I pay rent, so he can't expect anything beyond that. Since we're talking about Charlie, tell me something. What makes him so arrogant and Luis so anti-social? And are they a couple?"

Frank didn't answer right away. He must have been searching for the right words.

"Frank, please, I'm from New Orleans, not some hinterland. I know about homosexuality."

"I know you're not uninformed, Claire. It's just that I wasn't happy when I learned they'd gotten together. Luis is a scary creature sometimes, but that seems the way Charlie likes it. Luis wants Charlie with him day and night and whoever gets too friendly, meets with Luis's wrath. I know you've seen the way he looks at me. He hates my guts." Frank saw that I had finished cooking, so he helped me put the food on the table and then buttered the toast. He even said grace.

"About Luis, Frank," I decided not to let that issue go unresolved, "I did see the way he watched you last night. Why does he hate you?"

"I guess hate is too a strong word, let's say he's not particularly fond of me because he isn't convinced Charlie has no romantic interest in me, and that's Charlie's fault. He gets enormous pleasure out of making Luis jealous or saying unflattering things about him to me. He flirts a lot with me, and even though I don't respond, Luis gets angry and pouts. And that makes Charlie laugh and poke fun at him."

"Guess I'd better ask you directly, Frank. Are you interested in men?"

"Really! C'mon, Claire! Look at me." Frank was the one pissed this time. "Do I look queer to you?"

"Looks can be deceiving. Luis looks like a great, big, Puerto Rican hunk. He's not particularly effeminate, if at all. Charlie is another story. No one would miss his orientation. I plan to stay away from Luis, the angry man. But you can't, you have to work with him."

"Believe it or not, Luis is different at the office. Plus, he's the business brain behind the medical group. He's very professional."

"You're awfully trusting…I wouldn't be able to handle that situation."

Suddenly I remembered the lawyer's letter containing information about Jo. I told Frank about it and also that I'd answered the letter and mailed it.

"You're certainly self-sufficient. I'm beginning to like you more each day." He cackled loudly.

I ignored his comment. "I'd like to call Jo, Frank, and find out how she's doing. Didn't you tell me you asked Charlie to have a phone put in your apartment before your arrival? Did he put it in? And if he did, may I use it to call Jo? I promise not to talk a long time."

"He did put the phone in and yes you may call Jo. I'll help you clean up and then we'll go over to my place. By the way, you haven't told me about your aunt's memoir. Was it what you expected?"

"I'm still digesting it. Actually, I was shaken by some of the things I read. My great-aunt was a helluva woman in more ways than one. In fact, there were a few larger-than-life people, some of them my relatives, who were really strange characters. The things they said and did stunned me. You can read it, if you'd like."

"I would, thanks. You've whetted my appetite now to read about those people. When I have some free time, I'll ask you for it."

Frank's apartment was identical to mine. It took me no more than a few seconds to determine he was an unmitigated slob. It didn't appear to be an embarrassment for him; he walked over everything in his way and cleared a spot on the sofa for us to sit. The phone was on a small table next to the couch. He handed it to me. I was hoping he'd at least go into the kitchen area while I made my call, but he continued to sit next to me.

Jo answered on the first ring.

"Jo, it's Claire," I said.

"Ah know, dawlin. Ah been prayin you would call me. Some man come by heah...wait Ah got his cawd... a Mista Edga Soot. He come heah the same day you lef. He look like a importan fella, so Ah gave him your address. Ah hope I done the right thin."

"You did do the right thing, Jo. He's already written to me. I got his letter and my aunt's life story yesterday, right after I arrived." I didn't tell her what he'd told me about her. "How are you feeling?"

"Oh, Ah been a little winded for a coupla days. Ah'm a ol woman, honey, so Ah know that what happen when you git ol. How you liking Nu Yawk?" I could hear Jo's labored breathing through the phone.

"I don't know if I like it, yet." That's all I wanted to say with Frank sitting a few inches away. "Jo, I hear your shortness of breath. Have you gone to see the doctor?"

"No, not yet, but Ah'm gonna go the nex week comin."

"Okay, I'm going to check on you next week and God help you if you haven't gone." She laughed at my threat through her rasping. "I'm not joking, Miss Lady! Listen, Jo, I've got to go. I'm on Dr. Beauchamp's phone so I can't talk long. He lives in an apartment right across the hall from me. I won't have a telephone until I know whether or not I intend to live here, so I'm going to give you the doctor's number in case you need to reach me in a hurry."

I waited for Jo to get a pencil and paper to write down Frank's phone number. "Take care of yourself," I told her, "I'll call you in a few days."

Frank had been listening. As soon as I hung up, he asked, "Do you think Jo was telling you the truth about her condition?"

"She didn't have to tell me. I could hear how hard it was for her to breathe. Now I'm really worried."

"Claire, Jo's in her eighties. She's probably experiencing congestive heart failure."

"There's that diagnosis again. It's the second time someone I needed in my life has been diagnosed with it. She's going to die soon, isn't she?"

"I have no way of knowing that without examining her. She needs to see her doctor. With proper treatment and rest, maybe she can live a few more years, perhaps even longer."

"Well that's good to know. I feel better knowing that. I'll call her again in a day or two. I hope you don't mind, Frank. We'll get the charges for my calls and I'll reimburse you. Will that be okay?"

"I'm not worried about how much the calls cost, Claire. Call Jo as often as you need to. You're going to help me get my office up and running; the least I can do is let you make a few phone calls."

"Thanks, Frank, Jo means a lot to me. If I decide to go back to New Orleans, I want her to be there when I get there."

"Listen, we've got to keep the worry monster away from you. So...I think seeing New York and helping me at the office might help to keep it at bay. I'll try to make sure you're too busy to think," Frank told me.

"Okay, but this evening I'm too tired to be concerned about the worry monster. Are we going downtown tomorrow despite Charlie's admonition?"

"Hell yes!"

"Glad to hear it. Thanks again for the use of the telephone. I'll see you in the morning." As I headed to the door, Frank put his hand on my shoulder and stopped me.

"I hope it's settled now, Claire," he said grinning, "that I'm all man. I hope that doesn't come up again."

"Yes, it's settled and it won't come up again. Your word is good enough." I said that, yet, I wasn't a hundred percent sure, so I kept on talking trying to convince myself. "It's not important, anyway. We're not in a relationship. And for your information, a guy in high school liked guys and we were the best of friends. Goodnight, Frank."

I was pretty tightly wound when I finally undressed and crawled into bed. In spite of how tired I was, I felt not a hint of sleep. My thoughts went from the trio of peculiar men and how I might deal with them in the future to Edgar Souté and what I needed to say to him to properly thank him for my great-aunt's life story. When I didn't receive it as she'd promised, I assumed it had been destroyed and that her secrets would remain hidden. But now that I had it, I was truly grateful to Edgar and wished I had found the time to think about the contents of the memoir before I'd written to the lawyer. It would have beeen helpful to touch upon parts of it in my letter to him. But finding that time had proven to be problematic. Not only did I want to see New York, Frank seemed to be trying to monopolize all of my time. I barely had time to think. Something about his intentions troubled me, but I couldn't quite put my finger on what it was. I put it to rest by telling myself that, after all, I had stated unequivocally to him that we were not in a relationship. He had to know not to expect anything beyond friendship from me.

30

As planned, the next morning Frank and I left about 11:00 for lunch at the Chinese restaurant in the Arcade across from Macy's. It was the best Chinese food I'd ever had. In fact, it was the only Chinese food I'd ever had. I realized at that moment that I was an authentic country bumpkin. I fell in love with egg rolls, fried rice and peppered beef.

When we left the restaurant, we walked up to Radio City Music Hall and waited in line for the matinee performance. I don't remember the movie we saw, but the organist and the Rockettes were spectacular. I knew if I stayed in New York, I would frequent that theater as often as I could. Several blocks away we found Rockefeller Center crowded with summer tourists. Everyone was disappointed there were no skaters. We learned the skating season was from November to April.

After walking around downtown for a while taking in the city's hustle and bustle, we found a small Italian restaurant and had a light meal before heading back to the brownstone.

With a full day of cavorting around New York City, I had no trouble falling asleep.

"Claire!" It sounded like Charlie. He was pounding on my door. "Claire, I have a telegram that was just delivered at this ungodly hour."

"Coming," I yelled. I jumped out of bed and quickly smoothed my hair and made sure my pajamas weren't twisted. Then I opened the door.

"I'm sorry you were disturbed, Charlie. Why did they deliver it to your apartment?"

"Because the idiot who sent it didn't put your apartment number on it. So when the dummy who delivered it didn't see one, he decided to push any buzzer. Here," Charlie handed me the telegram. "I hope I'm able to get back to sleep." He jammed his hands into the pockets of his black, silk robe and left before I could respond. When I glanced at my watch, it was 5:30 on a Sunday morning. No wonder Charlie was furious.

My hands were shaking badly when I opened the envelope flap. I remembered all the telegrams my grandparents and my aunts in California sent back and forth – they were all filled with bad news. Finally I pulled it out and unfolded it.

New Orleans La.
DLR Early A.M. 1830 Hamilton Terrace NYC
1957 August 5
Miss Claire Soublet,
Josephine needs to be hospitalized. Called me to draw up her will.
Come as soon as possible.
Edgar Souté
WESTERN UNION

I hadn't thought about the past since I boarded the train to come to New York. Frank had occupied all my time on the two-day train ride and with sightseeing after we arrived. Now I was confronted with having to go back to New Orleans to possibly live through another person's death. I jumped back in bed and put the telegram under my pillow. Maybe I could fall asleep again, I thought, and wake up with a clear head and know definitively what I should do.

As soon as I was dressed the next morning, I went over to Frank's and told him about the telegram. He didn't try to hide his anger and I was stunned. That feeling of "being taken care of" which translated to me as "being controlled" caused that sick, sinking feeling in my stomach again.

Frank was looking at me over his glasses. His face was filled with displeasure as if he were chastising a young girl. He had become unrecognizable.

"You just got here," he yelled as he flopped down on his couch. "Surely you're not thinking of going back now, are you?"

"I think I have to go back."

"You realize, don't you, that this situation will cancel all of our plans. You're supposed to be starting a new life. Why would you go back and face another situation that may mess up your head again? What about Paris?"

"Frank, stop it! I love Jo and she's probably dying. She doesn't have anyone else. So calm down, please. I know what I have to do. Besides, I'm very capable of making my own decisions. I'm able to judge whether or not this situation, as you insist on calling it, will cause me to melt down again. You're scolding me like I'm ten. That is not your place. You're a friend; you're not responsible for me or the mistakes I make."

"I can see you've already decided to go, haven't you?"

"Absolutely!"

"Why would you put yourself through that again, Claire?"

"I don't owe you an explanation, even though I've already given you one."

"Well, there's no talking you out of it, so when are you leaving? You can fly, you know."

"No, I can't; I'm afraid to fly. The Empire State Building was enough height for a while. I'll go back by train and leave on Tuesday."

"That soon!"

"Yes, but I haven't forgotten I promised to help you set up your office, Frank. We can start today and I can also help you all day tomorrow. Okay?"

Frank gave me a half-hearted, "Okay."

"I'd like to call the lawyer and tell him my plans. I also want him to try and get Jo to have her doctor admit her to the hospital. I'm afraid she's going to die before I get there."

Frank handed me his keys. "Charlie and Luis invited us for lunch today. I'll go upstairs now. So make your call and when you're done, lock up and come on up." His face was frozen in disappointment. He refused to look at me as he walked out of his apartment and slammed the door.

Charlie and Luis were having a fierce argument when I arrived.

"You should have gotten a pound of each: one pound of pastrami and one pound of corned beef." Charlie began slapping the pastrami on a small platter.

"Don't handle the food that way because you're pissed off. Have some respect for our guests." Luis's voice had risen two octaves. "Next time, get your ass out of bed and go to the damn deli yourself. That way, you'll get exactly what you want."

"Hey, guys, is this a bad time? Should I come back in a few minutes?" I asked. I noticed Frank, still with an unhappy look on his face, standing in front of the living room window listening to his friends argue.

"Don't be silly. We do this all the time," Charlie cackled. "I wanted corned beef but Luis got all pastrami. So, I'll just eat bread, cole slaw, mustard and pickles. Yum!"

He came over to me and put his arm around my shoulder, "So, my lovely, what was so important in that damn telegram that forced me to get up at 5:30 on a Sunday morning."

It was clear in the way Charlie asked the question that he already knew the answer. I was certain Frank had already told his friends before I arrived.

"The elderly woman I lived with before I came to New York is gravely ill. I'm leaving to go back on Tuesday."

"You just got here, Claire. Are you coming back?" It was Luis who asked, not Charlie. He sounded sincere.

"Of course I'm coming back. I've paid a month's rent and the deposit, so I should have the apartment until the first of September, right Charlie?"

"Certainly! But Claire, we're just getting used to having you around. It isn't fair of you to run away so soon." Charlie popped the cork on one of the wine bottles and began to pour it into the glasses. "What say you, Frank?"

"I'm the wrong one to ask," Frank replied. "Claire knows exactly how I feel."

"I guess what I said earlier bears repeating. I'm an adult capable of deciding what's best for me. I would never forgive myself if Jo died without me being there for her. She was there for me." That put a hush over the room.

When the table in the dining area was finally set up with the food and wine, buffet style, we served ourselves and then sat on the floor around the big, round coffee table in the living room to eat.

We got through lunch without any more altercations. Most of the conversation went on between Charlie and me about New Orleans. Frank and Luis listened without contributing. When Charlie saw me looking at the paintings in the room, he pulled me up and gave me a tour of his home.

The evening Frank and I arrived, I hadn't noticed anything in particular in the apartment. Charlie told me he and Luis both painted and worked in ceramics. They'd made all of the pottery and painted several of the pieces that hung throughout the house. Because they liked a lot of light, their furniture was modern, sleek and light-colored, as well as the carpeting. Shoes were removed at the front door – no exceptions.

"It's almost two o'clock, Claire," Frank announced. "If we leave now, we'll be able to get a lot done today."

"You're going in on Sunday?" Charlie asked Frank.

"Sure. I thought you were anxious for me to get started. Claire told me she'll help me tomorrow, too. So, I've got to take what I can get." Frank's words scorched the air.

After being made to feel I was leaving him in the lurch, I offered him this, "Aren't you going to hire a woman for your front office, Frank? If you do that before you open your practice, she'll be able to help you finish setting up."

"Or…," Charlie chimed in, "you can share our gal temporarily until you find the right person." Again that funny look was exchanged between him and Frank.

"I'll figure it out, guys, don't fret. I'm an adult doctor capable of setting up my own practice." The men howled. I didn't think it was funny. How in the hell was I supposed to get through the rest of the evening with Frank and his lousy attitude. He had the gall to be hostile because he couldn't control my life. Why was I surprised? I had seen the need to control surface the morning we left New Orleans. He'd given me my first feeling of discomfort then.

"Oh, shit," Charlie gave an exasperated sigh, "go, you two, get out of here. It's crazy to sit around here sniping at each other. Go and work off some of that anger, aggravation, sexual tension…or whatever the hell it is."

"Good idea!" I said. "I don't know what's going on here, but I don't think it really matters, not to me, anyway. Shall we go, Dr. Beauchamp?"

"Sure," he said without even parting his lips.

And then I don't know what possessed me, but as I got up to leave I said to Luis, "Since you're the food shopper, Luis, when I come back you must show me how and where to shop, promise?"

"I promise," he said.

31

On Tuesday afternoon, Frank refused to accompany me to the train station. He claimed he needed those hours if he was going to open his practice in a few days. Luis volunteered to go with me. There was only one appointment he needed to reschedule, he said, and it was not an imposition.

The subway train was almost empty at that time of day. Luis sat quietly at first, then suddenly he twisted around in his seat and looked directly into my eyes.

"Claire," he asked, "how well do you know Frank?"

"Hmm, that's an unexpected question."

"Yes, it is. What's the answer?" Luis didn't mince words. He seemed to like saying things that shocked you.

"Well, let's see. He's been my doctor for about a year or so. We had lunch once after an office visit, and then when I left New Orleans, he showed up unannounced to travel to New York with me."

"I knew it! He had Charlie and me believing you're more than friends. I know this sounds weird coming from a man, but you've got to be careful, Claire. Frank doesn't treat his women well."

"Good Lord, Luis, what the hell is that supposed to mean?"

"He uses women; that's what it means. When he finishes with them – he walks away. That's how Frank got through medical school in Switzerland. He received very little money from his grandparents, so he depended on his girlfriends to pick up the slack."

"His grandparents…what happened to his parents? He's never mentioned anything about his family to me."

"His mother was a single parent. She died of tuberculosis when he was a small child and his grandparents raised him and put him through university and helped with his expenses during med school. They died while he was doing his residency."

"Luis, didn't these women realize early-on that he was using them?"

"No, it usually took a few months for them to see that they were feeding him and letting him crash at their places whenever he wished. They even paid for their jaunts to Paris, Milan, or wherever he wished to go. He usually juggled two women at a time as well as his studies. He's really a bright guy. He never really had to study. He could read something once and retain all of it."

"Didn't you fellas hate his guts?"

"We did, but we envied him more. While he was pimping around, we were drinking coffee and swallowing drugs to stay awake and cram. Listen, Claire, I said all that to tell you that the last woman he walked away from was pregnant with his son."

"What?" You mean he has a son in Switzerland?"

"Yes, the boy must be about ten or eleven now. Claire, I know you think I'm gossiping like an old crone, but I don't want to see him take advantage of you."

"Does he talk to you and Charlie about me, Luis?"

"To Charlie mostly, then Charlie tells me. Frank says you're the marrying kind. He wants to keep you barefoot and pregnant so that you'll be too busy to be concerned about his comings and goings."

"So, Luis, I'm destined to be married to and pregnant for a man I don't really know. He's insane! Who in the hell is Frank Beauchamp, anyway?" Oh damn, I thought, I'd run into another man who had my life worked out for me without me being privy to the plans.

"Wait…you haven't heard all of it. First you'll help him with his practice…in the outer office. He's not planning to hire anyone, Claire. He's going to use you." Luis watched me close my eyes in disbelief. It took me a few seconds to get over the shock of his words.

"Listen, Luis, I didn't just fall off the turnip truck. If he thinks I'm a push-over, he's going to find out who I really am."

"No," he laughed, "there doesn't seem to be anything naive about you, but Frank is clever, Claire, and extremely persuasive."

Luis suddenly jumped up, "Hey, this is our stop." He grabbed my suitcase in one hand and me in the other and we sprinted out the doors before they closed. "You're too early to board the train, so let's find a coffee shop in the terminal and have something to drink. Have you food for the trip? If not, we can get a bunch of stuff at the coffee shop."

"I went to the deli this morning and got what I needed. I bought some hard salami, cheese, rye bread and a few pieces of pastry. I bought a few candy bars at the drugstore…cuz, baby, ain't no bag of fried chicken going back with me." Luis must have been savvy about the meaning of my statement because we both laughed out loud. "All of my goodies are here in this little case Charlie let me use." I held out the leather zippered case for him to see.

"Charlie let you use it, huh. He's got a nerve – it's mine." When Luis saw the corners of my mouth turn down, he said, "It's okay, Claire, I don't mind. I was just pointing out how cheeky Charlie can be."

We found a coffee shop in the station and sat at a small corner table away from everyone. Luis needed to continue his Frank Beauchamp exposé.

"He's a dog, Claire. If you can, stay in New Orleans for a while with your sick friend. Maybe Frank will have thought better about what he has planned for you by the time you return. I don't know how some men get away with using women, especially someone like you."

"Luis, do you really think I'd allow Frank to use me that way, or any man for that matter. I've done some things that I don't yet fully understand, but God, I hope I'm smarter than you're giving me credit for. He can't make me do anything I don't want to do. I don't care how clever and persuasive he is. He's a friend and that's all he'll ever be. Don't worry about me, I can take care of myself…and handle Frank. Anyway, why do you care so much?"

Luis smiled. It was the first genuine smile I'd ever seen on his face. He usually had a fake spreading of his lips that meant absolutely nothing.

"I wish I weren't queer, Claire. I could love someone like you in a second. But unfortunately, I chose that ugly bastard Charlie. He doesn't deserve me; I know it. I'm not afraid of Frank or any man stealing his affection away from me. What I hate is his shameless flirting. I'm sure I'm the only stupid sissy to want that s-o-b."

I was truly taken aback by his admissions. Finally I said, "Thank you, Luis. It helps me to know that you're looking out for me." I began to feel safe knowing I had someone in New York who had my back.

"I do and don't you forget that," he admonished me. "Now tell me about this woman called Jo. She must be mighty important to you for you to go back to New Orleans after just arriving in New York."

I told Luis all about how Jo had taken me in when my great-aunt died and how she had not judged me when I had an affair with the priest. Jean-Michel and I had met every Wednesday afternoon in her home. And despite her deep religious feelings, she never felt the need to condemn me. Jo had stitched me back together when my aunt died and Jean-Michel was sent away. She meant a great deal to me. As I talked, I watched Luis's face to see if I could tell whether or not he was shocked, but his face showed no emotion at all.

Before I could finish, he stopped me. "Enough, Claire. I've heard enough. Look at you. You're full of apprehension thinking I'm going to judge you. How would I dare judge you? By now you should know we all do what we have to do to survive, whether the church approves or not. Does Frank know about the priest?"

"Hell no! I'd never tell him about Jean-Michel."

Luis looked at his watch. "C'mon, they're probably boarding now. I'll walk you to your train."

I suddenly remembered I was "up North" and I could sit anywhere I pleased. But, when we'd get to Washington D.C., I'd have to move to the Jim Crow car...the first car after the engine. So, why not sit up there from the beginning and then I wouldn't have to move when we'd get to D.C. I'd just have to exercise my "inalienable rights" another time. We walked the length of the train until we reached the first railcar. Luis let me go up the steps before he handed me my suitcase.

"I hope things go well with Jo and she's better by the time you get there. Take care of yourself. Don't forget...stay as long as you need to." He blew me a quick kiss and started to walk away. But as the conductor shouted, "all aboard,"

Luis stopped and began to walk alongside the train as it started to pull out of the station.

I stood on the top step looking out at him. He quickly walked a few steps to keep up with the train so that we had a final glance at each other. And when I could no longer see him, he yelled to me, "Don't look back; find another road to travel. Don't come back, Claire. You…" The train picked up speed and his last words were lost to me.

I grabbed my suitcase and found a seat in the empty coach. As I stared out of the window the thought of going back to where I had just come overwhelmed me. I quickly closed my eyes hoping to stop the flood gates from opening and allowing the tears to wash over me, but I was too late.

I don't know how long I sobbed, but suddenly I heard a voice above my head say, "Ticket, please."

As I lifted my head and opened my tear-filled eyes, the conductor said, "Oh, sorry. I'll come back later to get your ticket."

PART THREE

32

Jo didn't know I was returning. I hadn't wanted to use Frank's telephone again after calling Edgar Souté to tell him I'd be there in a few days. Frank had little to say to me while we worked setting up his office. If he was too angry to speak to me, I certainly didn't want him to think I was taking advantage of his generosity.

When the cab arrived at Jo's, she was sitting on her front porch swing fanning herself. What was she doing outside, I wondered? She stood up as I alighted and strained to see who was getting out of the taxi. I took my suitcase from the driver and paid him, then I walked up to the stoop and stood there until she recognized me.

"Oh, you bad girl," Jo scolded me. "How come you don tell me you was comin? Come on up heah and give me a hug. You hongry? Ah got some stuff mirliton Ah jes made taday."

"You know me, Jo, I'm always hungry." I hugged her and she felt smaller than when I left. Her face was gray – she looked sick.

"How lon you heah fa?"

"As long as I need to be to see about you. You're not fooling me, Jo. I can tell you're not feeling well. I heard how hard it was for you to breathe when I called you last week."

"Ah'm a lot betta this week. You know nothin keep me down. You probly gotta see that lawyer that call me, don you?"

"Yes, I do. I have a paper he sent me to sign regarding the Esplanade house that Leonard Stern left me in his will," I hated having to lie. "We need to discuss the best thing to do with the house." I couldn't let on I knew she'd hired Edgar to draft her will or that he'd told me she needed to be hospitalized. "I'll call him in the morning, Jo."

"Mr. Edgar tol me bout the house and your aunt's story. Ah didn't tell him where you live in Nu Yawk til he tol me why he need your address."

There were no flowers on the dining room table. That told me everything I needed to know about her health.

As Jo headed toward the kitchen, I stopped her. "Sit down, Jo. Let me heat the mirliton."

"Okay. Ah got some lettice and tamada all cut up. You jes gotta put it on your plate and dress it." She tried to take my suitcase from me, but I wouldn't let her. I pointed to a dining room chair and she sat under protest.

"Jo, did you see your doctor as you promised?" I asked her from the kitchen.

"Ah sho did, honey. He say Ah got the ol people sickness. All ma body weak and plum woe out, specially ma hawt."

I could hear the strain in her voice as she tried to shout to me. I turned off the burner under the pot with the mirliton and went back into the dining room. I asked Jo to tell me exactly what the doctor had told her.

She was hesitant. Finally, she said, "He say I need to stop workin, stop drivin, and stop gardnin cuz they all cause me diffrent kinds of stress and strain. He tol me to consida havin somebody live with me or Ah'd have to go to the Colored ol folk home cuz I cain't live alone no mo."

"Well, it's settled! No more washing and ironing for you, Josephine Gagnier. You are retired! Call all your customers tomorrow and tell them."

"Ah cain't do that! Ah need that money, dawlin. Ah jes cain't be sick when I know them folk need they laundry. Ah got to wash and iron fa them; Ah need that money. Ah cain't take care of maself without that job." Jo started to cry.

"Jo, I have enough money to get us through a year or so. You've paid off your mortgage, so we don't have to worry about that expense. We'll do just fine. And when we start running out of money, I'll get a job. I don't want you to worry."

"Ah got to worry, dawlin, cuz you cain't stop your life to take care of me. I done had my time on this earth, now's your time. You stay fa a few days, then get yourself back to Nu Yawk."

I thought it best not to upset her any more than she was already. So I said, "Let's talk about all this tomorrow. Tell me what's been going on at Corpus Christi and with all your friends we used to visit on Sundays. But first, let me finish heating the mirliton and making my salad."

While I ate, Jo told me there was nothing new at Corpus Christi, but that two of her friends had died just in the few days I was gone, and that her friend's son, the one who had refurbished her car, had been shot and killed a few days ago by a man who tried to rob him in his repair shop. I found it hard to get through the rest of the meal.

I convinced Jo to get ready for bed while I went upstairs to take a quick bath and put on my pajamas. It was only 8:30, but to my surprise she didn't put up a fuss.

When I came downstairs, Jo was already in bed. I hopped into bed next to her and propped myself up on two pillows. We talked about New York and what I did in the four days I was there. I was telling her about the Automat when I remembered I'd brought a few souvenirs for her. I shot upstairs and retrieved them from my suitcase.

"This is a replica of the Empire State Building," I told her as I handed her an eight inch metal likeness of the famous building. "And these are some postcards of a few places I had a chance to see while I was there: Rockefeller Plaza and Radio City Music Hall. This one is Times Square. Look at this one, Jo; this is St. Patrick's Cathedral. Isn't it magnificent?"

Jo was most impressed with the cathedral, but she also marveled at the Empire State Building when I told her it had 103 stories and that I had gone up to the Observation Tower on the 86 Floor and looked out over New York City.

"Oh, I'm getting tired, Jo. I'd better finish telling you about the Automat. I wish you could see that place…" But somewhere around the franks and beans and the hot apple pie with vanilla sauce, I went to sleep. I felt Jo throw a sheet over me, but I was unable to respond.

I awakened at 6:00 the next morning when Jo's alarm clock went off. Once again bewildered upon awakening, I slowly looked around the room and then realized where I was.

Jo hadn't stirred.

Quietly, I climbed out of bed and tip-toed toward the bathroom and then I stopped. Hmm, I thought, the alarm hadn't awakened Jo…why? I turned around and rushed to her side of the bed. She looked as if she was peacefully asleep with the Empire State Building resting in the crook of her arm. I touched her arm to shake her lightly. She was cold – as cold as my grandmother had been when I found her dead on the kitchen floor. I knew Jo was dead, too.

I started to tremble and when it grew violent, I sat in a chair on my hands to keep them still. Who can I call? Who do I know to call? Oh, God, it was happening again! Had Jo waited for me to come back to die? Did she know the lawyer would tell me how ill she was and that he'd drafted her will? She must have sensed I'd come and tried to hang on and wait – that's why she wouldn't go to the hospital. She needed me here with her in her last moments.

Was I capable of being rational at that moment; perhaps not? Nevertheless, I believed what I was thinking. Jo had no one else except her friends who were as old as she was and not able to give her the help she needed at the end of her life. She must have known how close she was to the end when she said goodbye to me when I left to go to New York. Suddenly, I was ashamed of having left her.

Where do I get the courage to bury someone else I love, I wondered? I sat there without moving, paralyzed with grief and shame. "I know it's me," I said out loud, "it's got to be me. I'm a curse – a death curse sent by the devil through me." I knew I couldn't be a child of God!

Where was Jean-Michel? Where was Father O'Mara? Do I call the new priests at Corpus Christi Church? No, I told myself. They will tell me what Father O'Mara had told Jean-Michel when he asked for funds to help Jo repair her house, "She lives uptown, no longer in our parish, so she is not entitled to any of our services."

I knew of only one person who might help. I forced myself upstairs and found the business card the lawyer had sent me. It had both his office and his residence telephone numbers.

"Mr. Souté, I'm sorry to call so early, but…but Josephine died in her sleep last night. I'm here in New Orleans, at her home; I arrived last evening. Can you help, please?"

While I waited for Edgar Souté to arrive, I sat again in the chair and looked over at Jo. I was calmer and able to think more rationally. She didn't have a smile on her face, but there was calmness, a peacefulness that had stayed upon her countenance when she'd taken her last breath. The first day I met her she told me she knew she was going to heaven when she left this world. She had been kind to people; she'd helped them whenever she could and she'd obeyed the Ten Commandments. She knew God would not turn her away when she met him face-to-face.

Unlike when my great-aunt Sera Menard died, I didn't sit next to Jo and talk to her. I had grown up quite a bit since then and felt I had fulfilled the promise I'd made to myself that I wouldn't wait for anyone else to die without telling that person how much I cared while they lived. I knew Jo knew how much I loved her; I just wish I hadn't left her to live her last week alone.

My thoughts went to her burial. Had she given the lawyer instructions about what she wanted? Had she given him the necessary papers to carry out her wishes? I prayed he had them because I had no idea where she kept them.

Edgar Souté arrived thirty minutes after my call.

33

The lawyer handled everything. It was clear Jo had instructed him down to the last detail. She was buried in the vault with her husband in St. Roch Cemetery. A priest from Jo's parish church, St. Boniface, came to the gravesite. I was grateful she had provided Edgar with the deed to the vault and all the other papers he needed and grateful to Edgar for his professionalism. I went with him when he made the arrangements, but he never asked me to make any decisions. I was convinced then that Jo knew she was going to die and she'd put everything in his hands to spare me. I began to forgive myself a little for leaving her after Edgar told me she'd told him she wanted me to have the life she never had and that God had put us together at the right time.

I had been there for her and when I thought about her life, I began to think of her death the way my great-grandfather thought of his mother's – she was finally free of all of life's indignities.

When we returned from the cemetery, I prepared a light lunch for us: a green salad and a pot of hot tea even though it was mid-August. Edgar asked for the tea. He was always calm and I wondered how he'd managed to get everything done in three days without appearing rushed. He hadn't asked me to do anything to help him. I thought not getting in his way was the best way to help. After eating, we settled in the living room to discuss what I needed to do next.

"Claire, I didn't bring Jo's papers with me. They're all at my office. I've been in and out for the last three days and I forgot them," Edgar confessed.

"I understand, Edgar. You've given me all of your time taking care of Jo's burial. I don't know how I'll ever be able to adequately thank you. As for those papers, whatever is on them will not determine what I'm going to do after I leave here."

"I'm sure you plan to return to New York, but may I suggest you take a few days ...or more to decide what comes next. You have several important decisions to make before you leave. So, please, take your time and don't rush them."

"You're right, I do need time. And I will take as much as I need to sort everything out before I leave because I don't plan to come back in the foreseeable future." I could hear some of Luis's last words to me echoing inside my head 'stay as long as you need to.'

Edgar was staring at me. "Mr. Stern told me you were a lovely young woman. He was right. Your aunt must have given him a most accurate description of you...which he conveyed to me. Never having seen you in person, it is uncanny how perfectly he described you."

My cheeks felt hot. "Thank you, Edgar. You're not so bad yourself," I quipped.

"Thanks," he laughed at my discomfort as he sat on the sofa with his hands cupped behind his head.

In the short time I'd been with him, I hadn't looked closely at him as I was now. If I didn't know any better, I thought, I'd think Edgar was one of our White-looking Creole men. His eyes were blue-grey; he had handsome facial features and curly light-brown hair like some of the guys I'd gone to school with. He was tall and thin with one of the most beautiful smiles I'd ever seen. And that smile was the key to his charm.

"Are you going to paint my portrait, Claire? You don't want to forget any nuances of my features…or perhaps there's something you'd like to ask me? If so, ask."

"Did Mr. Stern know your parents, Edgar?"

"Why do you ask?" His furrowed brow told me he hadn't expected that sort of question.

And then my mouth took over before I had time to think, "Because I'm wondering if you're mixed and passing for White. I don't condemn you for that; I believe a person has to do whatever he has to do to have a good life." I wanted to take back every word, but they had tumbled out so fast, it was too late.

"I look mixed, do I? If I were passing, Claire, do you really expect me to admit it…to you or anyone else?"

"To me, yes. Why not? Who would I tell that would cause you harm." I was digging my hole deeper.

"Your aunt went to her grave with her secret. If I'm passing, why shouldn't I?"

"By the time she died, it was no longer a secret. Leonard Stern knew for many years, and after the memoir was written, Joshua, your secretary and you found out." I had begun to feel remorseful. "Look, Edgar, it was just a flippant question I asked because I was curious. You're entitled to your privacy, so you don't have to answer it. Let's change the subject. After everything you've done for me, I don't want you to dislike me. I'm sorry for being so insensitive. Please accept my apology."

"Apology accepted. And as far as disliking you, that's the farthest thing from my mind. I think I like you too much already." Edgar's face flushed as he was speaking.

His admission made me a bit uncomfortable, but I was pleased he hadn't been offended by my audacity. In fact, I had to admit to myself I was pleased that he liked me. Why this mattered when I was returning to New York was crazy even to me.

"Let's talk about the Esplanade house, Claire. In my letter, I told you I had a suggestion for you regarding it. I thought you might let me rent it while you decide whether or not you want to sell it."

"You want to rent that huge house, Edgar? Do you have a family?"

"No, I'm alone. But hear me out. My living there takes care of two important issues for you: you'd have someone living in the house so that it won't look abandoned and I could take care of getting the repairs you need done before you sell it. I thought rather than send you rent, I'd use that money to fix up the place. Interested?"

"Hmm...let me think about it for a few days. Sounds like a great offer, but I was hoping once I leave New Orleans this time, I wouldn't have any binding ties to draw me back."

"Claire, you do realize you've inherited this house, too, don't you?"

"I did think about it in the last day or so. I was hoping somehow it wasn't so. Now I have two houses to worry about. What the hell am I going to do?"

"You sound ungrateful, Claire. Surely that's not your intention, is it?"

The strange sound of Edgar's voice was similar to the tone of the words I'd read in his letter when he told me "to be grateful." I had finally found a way to leave New Orleans and it never occurred to me that having more than I'd ever had in my life would drag me back here and impede my return to New York.

"This is the first time in the past few days I've seen evidence of your immaturity. You're so afraid you'll be permanently stuck here that you're thinking like an eight-year-old child. You don't have to be here to dispose of these houses, Claire. I can handle it for you. I can rent out this house for you now. You might decide to keep it and use it as a vacation house when you want to get away from New York."

"Be serious, Edgar. I don't even have a job in New York; I'm planning to go back to school. There'll be no vacations for some time to come. And why would I come back here when all of those wonderful places in the world I've been waiting to see my whole life are beckoning to me? Don't rent the house, Edgar; sell it, please."

"Claire, you're making a rash decision. Take your time and think about this. You said you'd stay for a while." Edgar stood up, narrowed his eyes and curled his top lip. I gathered that was his expression of aggravation.

"I am staying…for another week," I said.

"A week! You're planning to get over your grief and settle everything in a week? Edgar closed his eyes and shook his head. "Suit yourself!" he snapped. "I was hoping to get to know you better, but you're making that impossible."

"Get to know me better, why? I'm going back to New York. I'm not interested in a long distance friend." I stood up then. "How long will it take to get the repairs done on the Esplanade house, Edgar? I have to try and set some new goals."

Edgar answered with his lips. He drew me quickly into his arms and kissed me. The kiss was passionate. I tried not to respond, but I felt myself give way…just a bit. He kissed me again.

"What, no slap?" he said when he let me go.

I simply shook my head.

"Good, because I want to do it again." And he did.

"Say something, Claire. That was just a couple of kisses. Why do you look so shocked? Please, say something! Don't crush my pride and humiliate me."

"Shocked, absolutely! Because after reading the letter you sent me, I pictured a short little man in a three-piece, seersucker suit with wire-framed glasses on the tip of his nose - a sour little runt with no personality, let alone passion. You...are not that man! Tell me, Edgar, are you attracted to the 'Negro' me? Does your whiteness see me as exotic? Perhaps you're like my old White boss who got a chance to hug and kiss me the day I quit to go to college. But after he did it, he had to look around the drugstore to make sure no one saw him."

"I kissed a woman – not a Negro woman – a woman. I don't know what Negro lips taste like, but I do know yours tasted sweet and soft, and I might add inviting. Why are you spoiling the moment, Claire? Just tell me you don't want me to touch you again and I'll do as you ask." Edgar turned toward the front door and then stopped, apparently waiting for my answer. "Well?"

"You are so arrogant. I can tell you were raised to think you can conquer the world and everyone in it. I'm trying hard not to dislike you."

"Duly noted. Now tell me to keep my hands and my lips to myself or I'll think you enjoyed my kisses."

"Stop, Edgar, don't be obnoxious! I'm trying to deal with Jo's death, decide what to do about the houses, and think about what's going on in...never mind that."

"Finish you statement. Did you mean 'what's going on in New York?' Is there something happening there that's troubling you?" Edgar sat again on the sofa and gestured to me that I sit.

"No thanks, I'll stand. There's nothing going on in New York that I can't handle. My real problems are here. I've got all that I own in the world upstairs and I've got to figure out what to do with it. I have a studio apartment in New York and there's no room for those things. I'd forgotten about them until now."

"If you box them, I'll store them in the Esplanade house until you're ready for them. That will solve one of your problems."

"You may be arrogant, but you're very resourceful." I laughed at my own back-handed compliment. Edgar didn't.

"I'm happy to know I possess at least one quality that pleases you," he said holding on to his sarcasm.

"I'll have them packed in a day or two."

"I have a question to ask you, Claire. I hope it doesn't embarrass you."

"Ask away." God, I prayed, don't let it be about New York.

"Are you afraid of the dark?"

"Well, not so much afraid anymore, but now I just don't like the night. I still believe nothing good happens when it gets dark. I'm sure Leonard Stern told you about that. What made you think of that now?"

"Like you, I'm curious. I'd like to know if you've outgrown that fear. You've spent the last three nights alone in this house. Weren't you afraid?"

"A little. Getting to sleep is the problem. I imagine I hear all sorts of noises. But I've been so tired mentally, once I go to sleep, I sleep through the night. Aw…were you worried about me, Edgar? That's sweet!" I threw his sarcasm back at him.

"No, you're not the type of woman men worry about. You're too self-sufficient, except when it comes to death. If you think you'll sleep better, I'll stay with you at night until you leave."

"You've got to be kidding! Geez, you're suddenly full of empathy and you're willing to put yourself out and stay nights with me until I leave. God, another man who thinks I just fell off the turnip truck."

"Get your mind out of the gutter, Claire. My offer is purely altruistic. I don't want you to be afraid at night, not if I can be of help to you."

"Look, Edgar, you don't have an empathetic or altruistic bone in your body. I know damn well you don't care a hoot about me and my fear of the dark. I'm not interested in having sex with you. The last few years have taken a toll on me. Love and death have had their way with me. I need a break. I don't want to get involved with you or any other man right now."

"Okay, I hear you quite clearly. I'll check with you in a couple of days about your decision regarding the houses. Don't forget to pack the things you want me to store for you. That is if you're going to rent the Esplanade house to me. Goodnight, Claire."

34

Months before, I'd stored the boxes I'd used to bring my belongings to Jo's in the outdoor laundry room. Now, I was retrieving them to repack the things Edgar would keep for me at the Esplanade house. I had a hard time deciding whether to store my family heirlooms or take them with me on the train. By the time I had everything except the heirlooms packed, I'd made a decision to take only the jewelry with me. I didn't want to be burdened with a large box as well as my suitcase.

Everything I didn't plan to store, I packed in a box to give to the Baptist Church a few blocks away. Jo and I had taken donations there earlier in the summer.

When my stomach began to pinch, I realized I hadn't eaten breakfast. I found a carton of Creole cream cheese in the refrigerator and I toasted two slices of bread to eat with it. It had been years since I'd enjoyed the cream cheese – before my grandmother died. After eating the whole carton, I was still hungry. I decided to get dressed and go out to buy groceries I'd need to last the rest of the time I planned to stay. There was very little food left in the refrigerator. I'm sure Jo wasn't well enough to shop for groceries. I wondered if she was eating before I came. Had she made those two mirliton just for me?

As I stepped out of the house onto the porch with the box for the church, I was stunned to see a large sign that had been placed in the middle of the lawn. A truck was driving away and the man driving it waved to me. The sign read: For Sale – Call Souté Real Estate. It had Edgar's office and home telephone numbers on it.

Edgar was just too damn efficient! I put the box on the swing and went back into the house to call him. He'd not said a word to me about when he planned to put up the sign. I knew not everyone would call him; there'd be people who'd knock on the door hoping to get an immediate answer to their questions – mainly how much the house is selling for and if the furniture comes with it? I didn't know the answer to either question. I was glad I was on my way out and now I knew I'd stay out most of the day.

There was no answer at Edgar's office or at his home. I'd have to hold on to my questions until he got in touch with me or I'd manage to reach him. When I pulled up in front of Grace Baptist Church, Reverend Giles was standing on the sidewalk in front of the church. After I got out of the car, he walked to meet me.

"Good morning, Reverend Giles. You probably don't remember me. I'm…"

"Yes, I remember you. You and Sister Gagnier brought us a donation a couple of months ago. I don't remember your name, though." The minister removed his hat.

"Claire Soublet. Do you know Mrs. Gagnier died last week?"

"Yes…yes, I know. Nothing around here happens without my knowledge," he grinned sheepishly. "Do you happen to know what's going to happen to her home? I know Sister Gagnier was a widow without children. I tried many times to get her to join my church, but she told me she was Catholic and would never belong to any other church."

Without telling him that I had inherited the house, I said, "Yes, the house is going to be sold. The sign was put up this morning."

"I ask because my congregation is considering buying the house for me to use as my residence. The apartment attached to the church is too small for my growing family. By any chance, do you happen to have the realtor's telephone number?"

"Yes, I do." I fished Edgar's card out of my handbag and handed it to him. "Would you please copy the numbers, it's the only card I have."

"Sure." The minister took a pen and a piece of paper out of the inside pocket of his suit coat. While he copied the numbers, I looked at how the man of the cloth was dressed: very expensive suit and shoes. He was a big man with a big mustache. His fingernails were manicured. I wondered where he came from because he had a "back-east accent." He sounded well-educated and appeared to be a gentleman.

"Here you are," he handed me the card. "Are you living in the house now?"

"Yes, but I'm leaving to return to New York next week. Why do you ask?"

"I thought maybe you wouldn't mind showing me the house today."

"Sorry, I'm going to be gone all day. I'm sure if you call the real estate office for an appointment, you'll be able to see the house in a day or so."

"Okay, thank you. I'll get that box out of your car. By the way, is the car also being sold?"

"Probably. The realtor is handling Mrs. Gagnier's estate. Ask him about it."

"Well, Claire, thanks for the donation and the information." Reverend Giles grabbed the box off the front seat. "If I don't get to see you before you leave, have a good trip."

The feeling was strange as I drove across town without Jo next to me. I felt tears try to invade my eyes, but I blinked them back. This was no time to get weepy, I told myself. If I had cried on my way to New Orleans for various and sundry reasons, then I guess I could save tears for Jo and release them on my way back to New York.

The first place I went was to Corpus Christi Church to light a candle and kneel at the altar to say a prayer. I was glad to see two women sitting and praying in one of the pews in the middle of the church because I knew I wouldn't have stayed if the church had been empty.

I was shaking when I walked out. The memories of Jean-Michel and Father O'Mara had washed over me like a movie without a plot. I wondered how they were, especially Jean-Michel. Was he still thinking of me "day and night" as he'd said in his letter? He was slowly beginning to fade from my memory as I'm sure I was fading from his.

I drove around the area as if I was in a state of confusion not knowing where I was. But I wasn't confused, I was trying to see all of the places that had been a part of my childhood. I went up one street, down the next, and then I'd double back to look at something on the other side of the street. I started at the Circle Theater, then went to the Autocrat Club, Corpus Christti Elementary School, Belfield's Drugstore, Liuzza's Bakery, the bar across the street from the bakery that sold the most delicious stuffed crab sandwiches, and finally to the St. Bernard Market.

There was no camera to capture their images, so I had to print them indelibly upon my memory. I didn't stop and go into any of those places – I just wanted to see them again because there was a possibility I wouldn't see them ever again, or at any rate, not see them for a long time. I wanted those last images to become a memorial kaleidoscope that I could instantly recall when I felt homesick. However, I had no desire to miss New Orleans, not after all the difficult years I'd spent there trying to grow up and get an education. Besides, hadn't I waited years to leave so that I could see the many places I'd read about or saw in movies? There were no more people-ties that bound me to the city now that Jo was gone. So I needed to rid myself of the houses, then I could leave quietly and never look back.

After riding around for more than an hour, I drove to Laharpe and Galvez to George DeBlanc's grocery store. Always after long bouts of sadness, anxiety or introspection, I felt famished. This store had everything I wanted or needed to soothe my nerves and fill my belly. I found everything I was hankering for. I got a pound and a half of boiled ham, five of the hogshead cheeses made in cups, three cartons of Creole cream cheese, two pounds of hot sausage, a pound of liver cheese, two packages of sliced bread and two loaves of French bread. I picked out two of each: pears oranges, apples, plums and three big Creole tomatoes, and then a head of lettuce, a dozen lemons and a small watermelon. When I paid for my groceries, none of the clerks recognized me and I didn't identify myself to them.

I fully intended to get Edgar to pick up the boxes for storage that evening. Then I planned to spend two days locked in the house listening to music and eating.

The smell of the spicy sausage and hogshead cheese came through their wrappings and the grocery bag and permeated the inside of the car. Well, there'd be no more riding around; my appetite was dictating the next move. I was homeward bound. I'd have to complete my look-around another day before I left. Too bad if the house hunters planned to disturb me, I would simply not answer the door. As I turned onto my street, I could see two men standing on the sidewalk in front of the house. Edgar's Cadillac was parked in the driveway – the one he had inherited from Leonard Stern. I pulled up to the house and parked on the street. Reverend Giles and Edgar walked up to the car and greeted me. Edgar looked inside the car and spied the packages. Both men grabbed a bag and carried it into the house.

Well, I thought, so much for not answering the door!

"Claire, Reverend Giles has been inquiring about the house. He told me he spoke to you a few hours ago. I offered to show him the house since he told me you'd be gone all day. I see you're home earlier than expected. I…"

"I was tired and hungry. Am I guilty of breaking a law?"

Edgar laughed, "Of course, you're not. Jo gave me her extra key the day I drew up her will." Edgar looked at me with his usual authoritative air, "I hope you don't mind."

"Not at all – you are the real estate agent."

"I think this house is already sold, Claire. You're a lucky lady."

"Wonderful! I'll leave you two to tour the house while I put away my groceries."

"Follow me, Reverend, we'll start upstairs." Edgar led the minister to the staircase just off the pantry. Reverend Giles hadn't spoken at all since we'd come into the house. He'd only smiled nervously and watched Edgar's interaction with me. What's wrong with him, I wondered?

Several minutes later, the men came in from the yard laughing.

"What a nice big yard! There's lots of room for my children to play. I don't allow them to play on the sidewalk. That's how trouble starts. I want to pick my children's' friends and keep them close as long as I can." The preacher looked at me as if for approval.

"I agree with you," I said. "If more parents did this, we'd have fewer kids in juvenile centers. I believe you must plan wisely for your children as they grow."

"Do you have children, Miss Soublet?" the preacher asked. I was no longer Claire. Edgar must have referred to me as Miss Soublet when the men were talking on the sidewalk.

"No, I don't. I'm not married."

"Claire, Reverend Giles's church is planning to buy this house for him. I thought 9,000 dollars would be a fair price, don't you?" Edgar seemed to have made the sale before he'd checked with the owner. How had he arrived at that "fair" price?

"How much is the house down the block selling for, Edgar?" I asked. "It's a camelback, identical to this one."

"I don't know," he answered.

"Well, before we offer this house to Grace Baptist Church, I think we should check the other house's selling price, don't you?"

I watched the light go out in the minister's eyes. Perhaps, he'd called Edgar because he'd rather not do business with me. Maybe he thought he'd have everything wrapped up before I had anything to say about the deal. Was he one of those men who thought a woman belonged in the kitchen and not in the board room?

"I'll get the real estate agent's telephone number off the sign when I leave and I'll give him a call this evening," Edgar said a bit miffed. "I'll call you tomorrow, Reverend Giles, and we'll talk more about the price."

"What about the car and the furniture, Mr. Souté?" the minister asked. He handed Edgar his card.

"I'll have an answer regarding the house, the furniture and the car tomorrow."

Reverend Giles walked to the door and opened it. "Good day, Miss Soublet. Good day, Mr. Souté. I'll wait to hear from you." He stepped out on the porch and closed the door behind him.

"Claire, I had no idea you were interested in negotiating the price of the house." Edgar said as he plopped down on the couch. "Do you know anything about real estate prices and what you have to do to make a quick sale?"

"No, but I don't want to give away the house. I'd also like to be involved in the decision-making." I tried not to sound irritated, but I couldn't hide it. "Right now, I'm going to make myself a ham sandwich. Interested?"

"Absolutely! I never refuse a free meal, especially a ham sandwich. It's my favorite."

"Everything on it?"

"Whatever you put on yours, put on mine."

"Wow, you trust me?"

"Make the sandwiches, Claire. I don't scare easily."

Eating at the dining room table was a different experience than the ones I had been used to with Jo. I missed the flowers and their fragrance that always graced the table, and I missed Jo and I talking while we ate. Edgar ate in silence.

It was an unusually hot and humid day. We were so thirsty that we drank the entire pitcher of lemonade and two cokes I found in the refrigerator.

"That was delicious, Claire. What dishes can you cook?" Edgar was licking his fingers and eating the crumbs left on his plate.

"Damn! I can't believe another man is asking me about my cooking skills. I can make a few dishes, but I won't be making them any time soon."

"Oh boy, I didn't expect the claws to come out. Is there a New York man causing you problems? Have you refused to cook for him? Is he too demanding?" Edgar was fishing for answers about my New York situation and he was having fun at my expense. "You don't have to go back. Stay here – you have two houses…and a car…and a good friend." He pounded his chest like a gorilla and grinned.

"I don't want to talk about New York, Edgar. Please don't bring it up again."

Edgar raised his hand, "Peace, Miss Soublet. It's obvious something is troubling you about New York, but if you'd rather not discuss it, I'll drop it. Let's clear the table. I'll wash and you'll dry. Okay?"

"Wow! Who trained you? Offer accepted."

"My mother and my …aunt…when I was at home. I spent most of my life in boarding schools."

"I'd really like to hear about your life, Edgar. That's if you want to tell me."

"We'll see. There needs to be an exchange here, Claire. You can't hold on to what's eating at you and expect me to spill my guts to you. But for right now, let's relax in the front room with the air conditioner on high. It's hot as hell in here!"

"Sure, go in and turn it up. I'll finish in here."

When I got to the front room, Edgar was sprawled out on the rug. He had removed his jacket, his tie, and his shoes and socks. He'd rolled up his shirt sleeves and had unbuttoned all the buttons down to his waist. "Forgive me," he said, "I'm hot and tired. Right now, I don't wish to be a gentleman."

"Go for it, Tarzan. Did you forget your loincloth?" I teased. "I feel for you. I don't know how you men walk around all day with layers of clothes on in ninety-degree heat."

"If you're in business, you don't have a choice. At the end of the day, I'm usually dehydrated."

"I think I'll get us a pitcher of ice water."

"Bless you, my child," Edgar chuckled.

311

When I returned with the ice water, I kicked off my sandals and joined him on the rug.

"Thank you for joining me. What a nice thing to do. I knew you weren't all bad."

I grabbed a pillow off the couch and smacked him in the head with it.

He laughed, and said, "Thank you…again."

"Can we get serious, Edgar?"

"Uh, oh!"

"No, stop it. I just want to ask you some questions about the memoir. Okay?"

"Sure," he said and sat up resting his back against the sofa. "Go ahead, ask away. No, wait! Before we talk about the memoir, I need to clear my conscience."

"Oh God…what now?" My heart started to race. I had the urge to get up and run out of the room. I didn't want to face another surprise.

"Claire, I conspired with Mrs. Gagnier to get you back to New Orleans. I didn't know she was so close to death. She must have held on as long as she could."

I yelled, "I knew it; I knew it! I kept ignoring the clues: the way you were so subtle in telling me about her in your letter; then 'wham' the telegram. Nice touch, Mr. Souté."

"Claire, she knew if I told you I was concerned about her, you'd come. And you did."

"After I got here, I wondered why she'd stuffed only two mirliton and why there was an unopened carton of Creole cream cheese and not much else in the refrigerator. This was not normal behavior for Jo…to have an empty refrigerator. Tell me, what did you get out of the conspiracy? She got me to come back so that she could die peacefully with me here; what did you get?" I didn't feel angry. I was simply baffled as to why he'd do that for Jo when he hardly knew her.

"I got you…I mean…I got to finally meet you and hopefully know you. I've wanted to meet you for a long time. Mr. Stern had talked so much about you; I knew I had no choice but to get you back here. If I hadn't, I may not have had another opportunity. For this, I ask your forgiveness."

I was rendered speechless. Then quietly, I said, "You're forgiven. Let's talk about the memoir, shall we? Did Mr. Stern ever talk to you about what happened to the cop who tried to abduct me on the street near the Esplanade house when I was in high school? Maybe I should first ask if Mr. Stern ever told you that happened to me."

"I had just started working to reopen the law firm after taking the Bar Exam. Mr. Stern was working from home; he could no longer come to the office. I went back and forth between the Prytania house and the office. He did not speak about the incident to me, but I heard many telephone calls he took from or placed to Sera regarding it."

"Did he ever talk about what happened to the policeman?"

"After putting together bits and pieces of their conversations, I concluded Mr. Stern had called in a few favors owed him. He knew all the people with power in the city – the ones on the right side of the law and the ones on the wrong side. Remember, he was an accountant, an investment and a real estate broker. Many of these people were his clients. I can only tell you what I think took place, Claire."

"I'll take it, Edgar, tell me."

"I think Mr. Stern told the police he had information that the policeman was a spy for the mob and then he told the mob the cop was being chummy with them to get information for the police department. He knew one side or the other would take care of him and apparently that's what happened."

"That's exactly what Sera told me happened, but she made me believe neither she nor Leonard had anything to do with it. She contended that all Leonard did was inform the police department they had an out of control cop. Did Leonard ever talk about the cop being found? Sera told me if the mob got him, they'd feed him to the alligators in one of the bayous and there would be nothing left but his bones."

"No, I never heard about him being found. Next question."

"Okay. I'm asking for your opinion now. Why do you think Sera held on to her lie about who she was until her death? Why didn't she tell me who she was when she was alive?"

"Claire," Edgar took a deep breath and then continued, "Sera lied to you and Leonard lied in the memoir. They both were liars and cowards."

Here was the second pronouncement to explode in my brain. "That's a rather harsh statement. Is it fact or assumption?"

"Fact! Where in the memoir did you read that Leonard Stern is my father? You didn't! He never acknowledged me as his son even when he was dying. I was Edgar Souté, the son of his housekeeper and his right hand in business, but never his son."

"You are Leonard Stern's son?"

"Yes, my mother was a quadroon who worked in Countess Piazza's house in the District. Close your mouth, Claire."

"This is stunning! I'm realizing now how intuitive Sera was. She had an idea Leonard not only serviced the madams' books, but that he might have serviced some of their beautiful girls, too. Do you remember that part in the story?"

"I do. I know he indulged because my mother told me and she knew she wasn't the only one. The last year the District was open, though, he visited my mother exclusively."

"Why didn't Lulu White know about your mother? She seems to have told secrets, especially Sera's."

"Countess knew Lulu well and she would never tell Lulu any of her secrets. Lulu never found out about my mother's liaison with Leonard or how she came to be one of Countess's, boarders, as Countess called her girls."

"Can you share your mother's story with me?" I asked.

Edgar nodded and said, "Yesterday there were only four people who knew my mother's story, now there'll be five. Are you sure you want to hear this? It's long and convoluted."

"I'm sure, Edgar."

"My grandmother started it all. She was a young, Irish widow without any skills who needed to support herself. She went to work for Josie Arlington, one of the wealthiest madams, when the District opened in 1897. She fell in love with one of the Colored Creole musicians and ran away with him to Chicago. When he learned she was pregnant, he deserted her. She found her way back to New Orleans and asked Josie to take her back. But when Josie saw she was pregnant, she refused. My grandmother had heard about how generous Countess Piazza was and went to her for help. Countess took her in. My grandmother cooked, sewed and cleaned to earn her keep until my mother was born. Countess was very good to my mother. When my grandmother went to work as one of Countess's boarders, Countess practically raised my mother.

"When she was fifteen, my mother became one of Countess's boarders. My grandmother had died of syphilis a few years before. Leonard bought a house in Marigny for my mother before the District closed in 1917. He had just married Rose and he convinced her they needed a full-time housekeeper. Rose agreed and they hired my mother. Isn't that priceless!"

"Your mother went to work as a maid in her lover's house? What a lousy bastard!"

"No, I'm the bastard...Leonard Stern's bastard. We have a lot in common, Claire."

"So you know I'm also born out of wedlock. Leonard certainly knew everything about me. Damn...he gossiped as much as Lulu."

"I used to hate you, Claire, because he talked about you constantly. But then I realized that it wasn't your fault. You didn't know he knew that much about you, did you?"

"No, I knew he knew I lived with Sera, but I had no idea she told him my life story. What's interesting to me, though, is that Sera lied to me but not to Leonard, except about teaching Jonas to read. Actually she didn't lie, she just didn't tell him. As for Leonard, he lied to Sera over and over again. I had such a good feeling about him after I read the memoir – now he's forever soiled. I'm so disappointed."

"You'll like him even less when I tell you the rest of my mother's story."

I decided to sit up and rest my back against the sofa. I poured us each a cold glass of water.

"With Rose going back and forth so often to New York, Leonard persuaded her to make my mother a live-in servant. He sold the house in Marigny and my mother moved into Sera's old room – the one she'd moved into after Daniel raped her. So when Rose was in New York, Leonard and my mother were the master and mistress of the house."

"My God, Edgar, hearing this makes me really angry. This is the period he stopped going to Sera's shop as often as he had been going. How could Sera not suspect that something was different about his home life?"

"How could she assume that? I'm sure Leonard didn't tell her every time his wife was out of town. Sera probably thought he was getting used to being married. Leonard was a consummate liar and I'm sure he told Sera only what he thought she needed to know. He wanted her to continue believing in him and to continue to see him as her gallant knight. But by that time, I think Sera was beginning to realize she loved him. She had relied on him for so long, and when Pauline died, she leaned on him even more. But his marriage made her back away. She saw a change in him and believed Rose had made a calmer and gentler man of him. Leonard did nothing to dissuade her, As long as Sera believed that, he felt he'd be able to handle the situation and be free to continue living his lie."

"How could you know what Sera and Leonard thought or believed?"

"Not me, my mother. She formed these opinions because Leonard confided in her about everything and he told her all about Sera. He admitted that he'd always love Sera and take care of her. I wondered how she could stand to hear this from the man who'd made her sacrifice so much for him – mainly her dignity and me. How could she sacrifice me? She has never been able to answer that question."

"Speaking of her dignity - how did she handle Leonard's staying overnight with Sera?"

"I don't really know, but he must have convinced her it was necessary and she bought it."

"But Edgar, you had me believing you held Leonard in the highest regard. Explain that."

"To the rest of the world I present one face; to my mother and now to you, I can show my true feelings."

"When did you find out Leonard was your father?"

"My mother told me after his death. Incidentally, she's still wearing black mourning clothes."

"For how long?" I asked.

"Until the first anniversary of Leonard's death."

"I didn't know women still did that. Do you see your mother now? Where is she living?"

"Leonard's been dead for four months and I haven't been able to force myself to go and see her. Before he died, Leonard bought her a house near Audubon Park. She lives downstairs and rents the upstairs. That way she has an income."

"How does she manage to live there? Isn't that an all-White area?"

"It is, but she looks White. No one would know, unless they're told she has Negro blood. And...Rose would never have allowed her to live in the house if she knew my mother was a Negro; she despised them. She never would have loved me...and she did. So you see, you were right when you suspected I was a *passablanc*."

"I'm sorry I did that. I had no idea of the circumstances. Edgar, let's take a break and have the dessert we forgot to eat. There are lots of different pieces of fruit and a watermelon. Which do you prefer?"

"Watermelon."

I found a large metal tray in the pantry; I cut the cool melon in half on the tray, got two knives, brought the tray into the front room and put it on the rug between us.

"Claire, you forgot napkins."

"Too bad, I'm not getting up again. You'll have to lick you fingers like you did after the ham sandwich."

"You're a lousy hostess."

"I know. Shut up and eat."

"Okay."

After we'd eaten and cleaned up our mess, Edgar asked, "Are you ready to hear the rest of my story, Claire?"

"Sure, if you're ready."

"I've tried to forgive my mother, but I'm not there, yet. She's still a beautiful woman and in very good health. Leonard's dead and she's alone now. She telephones me once a month and recently asked me to move in with her. I declined. She's lonely now and ready to be close to me. When she should have considered what she was doing to me, she was too busy pleasing Leonard and settling for his scraps. She loved him so much, that I was sent away so that she wouldn't have me underfoot. It's difficult to believe she was not only cruel to me, but that she had the audacity to be in Rose's home and be pregnant, have the child, and then allow Rose to love me and take care of me. No decent woman does this! And my so-called father hatched this plan."

"Remember, Leonard took Sera's baby away right after he was born and had her believe he gave the baby to a childless couple in New Orleans when he really gave the boy to his sister in New York. When were you sent away, Edgar?"

"Not immediately. My mother and Leonard planned it all when my mother found out she was pregnant. On one of Rose's five-month trips to New York, my mother supposedly got married and got pregnant right away. Her husband got drunk and beat my mother when he found out she was pregnant. Leonard put him out and forbid him to return. This was the story Rose was told upon her return. Leonard also told her he had planned to hire the husband to drive for the family, run errands and be an all-around handyman. That way my mother and her new husband would be able to live at the Prytania house as a family and they would be a great help to Rose, and maybe, she'd even enjoy having a child in the house."

I felt sick for Edgar. But I had to ask the question once again. "When were you sent away?"

"I was five, but before then, Rose took care of me and really loved me. She asked me to call her Auntie Rose. I was with her all the time when she wasn't in New York. My mother didn't care that someone else was raising me; she was too busy taking care of Leonard."

Edgar took a few sips of water and continued. "Leonard found a boarding school, a place called St. Francis Boy's Academy in Mobile, Alabama, a school that took five-year-olds. Rose took me by train to Mobile to enroll me. The Catholic school housed students from first to twelfth grade. After I was interviewed by the school administrators, they felt because I was not only tall for my age and I was smart, that I would do well in first grade. Auntie Rose cried when she left me at the school. She was the only one who came to visit me all the years I was there until she became ill and finally died in 1942.

"When she died, I was almost seventeen and in my last year at the academy. After graduation and upon my return to New Orleans, I found plans were already in place for me. With the help of Leonard's sister in New York, my acceptance into Yale University had already been secured. I was shipped off to Connecticut. I completed my studies in six years, including my law degree. I returned again to New Orleans and was given a gift of a large sum of money to take a "well-earned" vacation to Europe – I didn't even have time to take the Bar Exam.

"I lived mostly in France and Italy. That was just a few years after WWII had ended. There were many towns that had been bombed. Food was still scarce. It really wasn't a good time to take a vacation in Europe. But despite that, I made many wonderful lifelong friends and enjoyed staying in their homes. In return, I helped them rebuild some of the areas they lived in."

"How did you get the name, Souté? Was that your grandmother's name? Oh no, you said she was Irish."

"My grandmother was a Reilly and so was my mother. My mother's imaginary husband was given the name Souté. Auntie Rose was told he was a French Creole from New Orleans. My mother never changed her name – it's still Reilly."

"Oh my God, Edgar, I'm so sorry this happened to you. I can't get over all the lies; how have you been able to handle all that?"

"Who says I have?"

"Where do you live now?" I asked. I tried to stifle a yawn, but couldn't.

"I've been in the converted storage area attached to my office since 1949."

"Geez, you live behind your office. What a life you've had! Wow, I'm tired, Edgar, aren't you? Let's take a nap – here – right here. I'll get us some pillows." I took two pillows off Jo's bed and gave him one. He looked sad and depressed.

"Do you have any afternoon appointments?" He shook his head. "Good, take a long nap. We've talked you into a coma. I'm sorry." I put my pillow next to him on the rug. He flipped onto his side turning his back to me and I knew he was crying. I felt guilty and wished I could have taken back all of my probing questions.

As I lay there overwhelmed with guilt, Edgar suddenly turned toward me and threw his arm over my waist. "Thank you, Claire. I needed to tell someone; I'm glad it was you. May I hold you in my arms for a moment?"

I turned toward him and put my arms around his neck .When the kissing began, I knew I wasn't going to just surrender. I would give myself wholeheartedly to the lovemaking.

When it was over, we lay drenched in sweat and panting…exhausted from not only our impulsive physical encounter, but from the stifling heat. It seemed the air conditioner wasn't able to cool the intense heat we had created in the room.

Finally, I sat up and looked down at Edgar. He was fast asleep. I curled up into a ball and decided to do the same. As I drifted off, I wondered what would happen when we woke up.

35

We woke up simultaneously. In spite of the air conditioner being on full blast, we were drenched in perspiration. It had gotten dark outside. I tried not to think of what we'd done.

"What time is it?" I asked.

Edgar got up and turned on a lamp. After checking his watch, he answered. "8:30," he told me. "That was a long nap, indeed. We went to sleep about 3:30."

How did he know that? Had he checked his watch before he went to sleep? He, too, was ignoring what we'd done earlier. He was making small talk to avoid addressing it. Maybe it didn't need addressing because it didn't mean anything to either of us, but I needed to make sure.

"Edgar, you know we did the wrong thing, don't you? Do you think we can forgive each other because we were both in a bad place? We needed each other in those moments and we never need to talk about it. We'll make believe it didn't happen. It'll be easier once I return to New York." I spoke rapidly without taking a breath.

"It will be easier when you return to New York, you say. How unfeeling you are! Maybe I don't want to forget. Have you considered that it may mean something to me, Claire?"

"I'm leaving New Orleans, Edgar, so it doesn't matter what happened between us – I'm leaving! Please don't make it any harder than it already is."

"Okay, I suppose if you're capable of erasing what we experienced, then I certainly can…and I will."

"Well good! I need a bath and so do you. My dress is soaked through and through and stuck to my skin. Why don't you use the bathroom downstairs and I'll use the one upstairs. Oh, wait…you don't have a change of clothes."

"Yes, I do. I picked up my dry cleaning and my laundry this morning. They're in the car. I'm not able to do laundry or to cook in my place, so everything must be done off-premises."

"Things will be different when you move into the Esplanade house," I told him.

"Oh, really. That means you're letting me have the house. What made you decide? Was it our coupling…my sexual prowess?" Edgar tried to sound like he was kidding on the square, but he was unable to conceal his acid tone.

"Our loins have nothing to do with my decision. I want you to live there because I think it should belong to you. After all the blood-letting this afternoon, you deserve something positive to happen in your life. I'm truly sorry for all that's happened to you, Edgar."

"You have apologized a hundred times to me. There's no need for any more apologies for what happened in my life. That's all in the past. I'm in a different place now. I hope you didn't have sex with me because you felt sorry for me."

"Hell no! I had sex with you to satisfy my own need. I hope you did the same. I'm going upstairs. Go out and get your clothes. I'll see you in half an hour or so."

I sat on the edge of the bathtub and cried. I had reverted back to the old Claire – finding what I needed in a pair of arms. Now I had to find a way to ignore whatever I felt for Edgar and convince him to do the same. I couldn't let him interfere with my plans to leave New Orleans.

When I came downstairs, Edgar was still in the bathroom. I opened up all the doors to let some of the heat escape while the air conditioner was still running. I was hungry, but it was too hot to cook the hot sausage I'd bought. It would either be ham sandwiches again or hogshead cheese. I'd let Edgar decide. I started making a pitcher of lemonade.

Finally, Edgar waltzed into the kitchen.

"Wow, you look refreshed," I said. "You clean up pretty good, Mr. Lawyer." He looked relaxed in a pair of cotton pants and a loose fitting, short sleeve shirt."

"You're not too bad yourself. I like your hair in a ponytail. I like your shorts, too. They're a bit modest, but they still show off your great gams."

"Thanks, I didn't think you'd notice. By the way, they're called Bermuda shorts."

"Claire, I may be a little rattled from our talk this afternoon and our subsequent lovemaking, but I'm not dead. I still have eyes. How could I miss those long attractive legs? Not a chance!"

"Okay, stop! You're embarrassing me." I was grinning as wide as my mouth would stretch.

"It's too late to be embarrassed. We were together, remember. I not only felt your legs, but I felt every inch of you."

"Stop! Don't bring it up again. I mean it, Edgar! Let's change the subject before I lose it. Listen, it's too hot to cook the hot sausage I bought today. So it's either another ham sandwich or hogshead cheese with crackers or French bread."

"Ham sandwich, please. I hate hogshead cheese!"

"Okay. But we ate all the watermelon, so we'll have to have a piece of fruit for dessert."

We ate once again in silence. I think we were talked-out and each of us wondering how the evening would end. We had bonded and made love over the ills of the past. Where would that coming together take us? After the dishes were done, we sat outside on the front porch swing for a while still not saying much to each other.

The phone rang. I went inside to answer it. Edgar followed me in.

An irritated voice came through the telephone speaker assaulting my ear. "Claire, this is Frank. Why haven't you called me?"

"Frank, hi. No I haven't tried to call you. Jo died the night I arrived. We buried her yesterday."

"You couldn't call and tell me that," Frank said.

"No. I was a little busy helping to get things done. She left everything to me, so I won't get back to New York until I take care of all that has to be done."

"Claire, why can't you let the lawyer handle everything for you, so that you can return?"

"Because I don't want to do that, Frank. There's no reason I should rush back, I have no commitments in New York. I have the time to get everything done here."

"We need to talk, Claire," Frank said. "I need you to come back...now!" His intentions came through loud and clear.

"Well, I'm sorry. I have no idea when I'll get back. This situation may take weeks."

Frank hung up on me.

"Was that the New York man that's become your problem?" Edgar asked when I joined him in the front room.

"Yes, but he has the problem; I don't. I suppose you heard the conversation – my side of it, anyway."

"I did. Are you involved with that man, Claire?"

"I guess it's my turn to tell you what's eating at me." I told Edgar about Frank from the time he showed up unannounced on the train to New York to the day I left to come to New Orleans. And also about the talk I had with Luis.

"You don't need that guy in your life. I agree with Luis, except I don't think you should go back at all. Stay here...with me."

"With you! Edgar, we live in two different worlds. You're not going to want to give up your world for me and I sure as hell can't and won't live in yours. We simply don't work."

"We can be together, Claire. Maybe not here, but there are many other places we can go. We'll move and get married."

"Oh my God, Edgar, you're scaring me! You just met me last week. I know you feel close to me after all that happened this afternoon. I feel close to you, too. We've created a bond. But it's a friendship bond – not one of love."

"It is love. I fell deeply in love with you this afternoon."

"No, Edgar, you only think it's love. Your life has been empty for a long time and because you shared with me the secrets you'd never told anyone else and in turn I shared mine, you misread what was felt. We were together physically, seized with a sort of "grand mal" fit of passion and somehow you think this is love. But it isn't. You're misunderstanding what you feel." Oh God, what have I done? Edgar couldn't be right. What we'd experienced was instantaneous lust...not love. I remember wanting the feeling to stop, but I couldn't control it. It rolled over me like a giant ocean wave; I had to succumb to it. It had been a long time since I'd had the urge to go to confession, but now I needed to tell someone what I had done again to myself and to Edgar.

"Edgar, please. This is not love. You don't understand the difference between lust and love."

"No!" he shouted, "it's you who doesn't understand. I knew I'd fall in love with you when I conspired to get you here. But really I have loved you long before I ever saw you in the flesh. And now that I have seen you, touched you, and physically become a part of you, that love has been confirmed."

"Please don't do this, Edgar." I could hear myself pleading. "Let me enjoy the peace I have here before I go back to New York and have to move because I will not be controlled or harassed by someone who will never be anything more than a friend to me."

"I think I'll say goodnight, Claire. You're probably suffering from heat exhaustion. I'll get the clothes I left in the bathroom tomorrow and also those boxes you want stored. Tonight, I'll get that telephone number posted on the sign of the real estate agent selling the house down the block. I'll see you about noon tomorrow with the information. You can decide on a price then. Goodnight."

In an effort to get Edgar out of my head, I put my mind on the price of the house. I took an inventory of both floors of what Reverend Giles would be getting for a total sum of money. I determined he could not have all the contents of this house for 9,000 dollars. However, it did depend on the selling price of the house down the street. The minister and Edgar would see that I was neither an uninformed woman nor a push-over!

I locked up the house and because it was too hot upstairs and in Jo's bedroom, I slept on the floor in the front room where the air conditioner provided a modicum of cool air.

36

A cup of hot *café au lait* would really do the trick this morning, I thought. But there was no coffee in the house. Jo must have stopped drinking it. I'd have the same hot drink I'd had since I arrived – hot lemon water with sugar. Anything hot with a strong taste would do. The oppressive heat and humidity had zapped my energy. I was just getting up and I was already tired…at 10:00 in the morning.

The phone rang before I could get to the kitchen.

"Claire, this is Edgar." The phone did not disguise a voice that sounded depressed. "That house is selling for 10,500 dollars, unfurnished. It does not have a separate laundry room."

"Wow, I told you. You were giving this house away. Last night before I went to bed, I walked through the house looking at everything that might be included in one price. Do you realize that most of the furniture in the front room and the dining room are antiques? Lots of shops on Magazine Street and in the French Quarter would love to have those pieces. The curio cabinets have loads of porcelain figurines and other whatnots. The buffet, china cabinet, and the sideboard are full of expensive china – many different kinds. That's a fairly new television set in the front room. This house was renovated about three years ago. It was given a new roof, new appliances, new doors and the fence was replaced. Oh, and the car was reconditioned this summer."

"Claire, I didn't know. I didn't have that information. What do you want to do?"

"Let's price the house at 11,000, the car at 400, and the furniture, appliances, etc., at 2,600. That's 14,000 dollars for everything. They can take it or leave it."

"But, Claire, that's 5,000 dollars above what I told the minister yesterday."

"Yes, I know. Why do you think Reverend Giles was so eager to finalize things? He knew what he was getting for 9,000 dollars...you didn't. You hadn't bothered to check with me about the contents of the house. I'm sure the minister had members of his church who were friends of Jo's tell him what's in this house. Anyway, this furniture is not kid-friendly. He'll probably sell it for a bundle and refurnish those rooms. Edgar, he's getting all that I just told you for 14,000 dollars. That's far below what he'd pay anywhere else."

"Okay," Edgar said in a lifeless, monotone voice, "I'll call Reverend Giles and tell him. I'll get back to you."

While I waited for his return call, I wondered why Edgar had called when he'd said he'd be here about noon. Why? Was he pouting? Was he feeling rejected? Shit! Who falls in love in a few days? Why is God giving me this man who really needs his mother...needs a family? I don't fit his needs.

The phone rang again.

"Claire, the minister said the church committee will meet this afternoon and he'll contact me with their decision. Are you willing to come down at all on the price if they want to negotiate?" There was a hint of a pleading sound in Edgar's voice.

"No, I'm not willing. Give it more thought, would you, Edgar. Think about what I've said is in this house and the condition it's in. I think 14,000 dollars is far less than it is worth."

"Okay, I'll wait here for his call."

"Why didn't you give him my number? You said you'd be here at noon and that you would pick up my boxes that need to be stored at the Esplanade house. Are you coming or not?"

"I've decided to wait here, Claire," he said.

"Fine, but I'm getting out of here for a few hours. I'll be back around 4:00. Talk to you later, Edgar."

I was dressed in half an hour and on my way to complete my farewell look-around.

On my drive downtown, I wondered if Edgar had considered the commission he'd make from selling Jo's house. I thought he'd make at least 10% and maybe as much as 20%. I'd soon find out. And somehow thinking about this, lead me to think about the 50,000 dollars of mob money Sera gave Leonard to keep him afloat when she was pinching pennies. I'm sure Edgar didn't realize that money not only took care of Rose, but also his mother. And I'll bet it paid his tuition at the academy in Mobile. Leonard, the womanizer, juggled three women. Rose was unaware of the other two. Sera knew about Rose but not about Edgar's mother. Edgar's mother knew everything about Rose and Sera. I guess the only good thing I care to think about Leonard is what I've said before, he provided for Sera until the end of her life and at the same time, he was providing for me when I lived with her, and for this I'll always be grateful.

It occurred to me Edgar never used his mother's name; he always referred to her as "my mother." So be it, I thought, I didn't think much of her, anyway, especially what she'd done to her son…all in the name of love. I vowed then, that I'd never love anyone that deeply.

Before I knew it, I was at Esplanade and Claiborne. I turned on Esplanade and headed to my old house. Slowly, I drove through the block and as I was passing in front of the house, I looked in the rear-view mirror and saw someone come out of Neal's grandmother's gate. On closer observation, I realized it was Neal, my high school, drama class buddy. He looked a wee bit older, but really, he hadn't changed much.

I jammed on the brakes, put the car in reverse, and then stopped where Neal was collecting the empty garbage cans.

I rolled down the window and shouted, "Neal!" When he recognized me, he came running to the car. I jumped out and we hugged and kissed like long lost relatives who hadn't seen each other in a long time.

"What are you doing in New Orleans, Neal?"

"Same question, Claire. I heard you moved to New York where I live, but nobody knew where in New York."

"I came back because the lady I lived with before I left was seriously ill. She died last week. What about you?"

"Long story, okay. I lost my mother two years ago to diabetes and kidney failure. She wanted to come home to be buried here. So I came with her and she died in our old house. My father was still living in it. No one knew he had never stopped loving my mother until he went to pieces when he watched her die. I went back to New York and finished my degree. My father sold the house, moved in with my grandmother, and then he quit his job. When my grandmother died last year, he proceeded to drink himself to death. He died last month. And I'm the one left to clean up the place and sell the house. My two aunts in St. Louis didn't want anything to do with my grandmother or my father and it's my grandmother's fault. He was her pet; his sisters didn't get much attention from her. They didn't come to her funeral or my father's."

"Oh Neal, I'm really sorry. You know, I never met your mother, I met your dad once, and boy, did I know that grandmother of yours. You're in my world now – everyone is either dead or estranged."

"In two years, all three of them died! I'm an orphan now and my head is spinning."

"Good Lord, I think I've met my match for catastrophe! But I think you've topped me. When are you going back to New York?" I asked.

"Next week, I hope. The realtor has an interested buyer – the man wants to buy it and rent it. I'm really grateful to my father for keeping the place in fairly good shape. I haven't had a lot of hard cleaning to do. The kitchen is in great shape because he didn't do a lot of cooking. He watched television and drank the last year of his life."

"Neal, did your mother forgive him before she died?"

"She did. He apologized to her and to me. He was holding her when she took her last breath. It shocked me to see how much he loved her. He went to the Mass but not the cemetery. He didn't want to see her put in the vault. And last month, I came back to put him in there, too." Neal sniffed and the tears fell before he could force them back.

I thought we'd better steer the conversation away from the sadness. "Let's talk about something else. Are you working?"

"Yes, I'm on summer break right now. I teach at a Catholic school in St. Albans."

"Where is St. Albans?"

"On Long Island, near Jamaica."

I laughed. "Okay, I don't know where Jamaica is either. I was only in New York a few days before I had to come back here."

"When are you planning to return, Claire?"

"Hopefully, next week, too. Jo, the lady who died, had no family. She left everything to me. It's all being sold; I hope to only one buyer which will expedite things."

"It would be great if we could travel back together. I flew here, didn't you?"

"No, sorry, I took the train. I'm afraid to fly."

"What, I don't believe it! You were never afraid of anything. I think I might be able to cash in my return ticket. If so, I'll take the train with you."

"That's wonderful!" Let's exchange phone numbers so…"

"There's no phone in the house, Claire. My father had it disconnected after my grandmother died."

I wrote my number on the back of the grocery receipt from George DeBlanc's grocery store that I found in my purse. "You'll have to call me to let me know as soon as you can so we can purchase our tickets."

"Will do. Where are you going now?"

"Oh, I call it my farewell look-around. Actually, I just ride around, mostly in the Seventh Ward, looking at all the places I frequented growing up because I don't plan on coming back, if I can help it."

"Want company? I'm done here for the day."

"Hell yeah, I'd love it."

"Let me take in the cans and lock up the house. Give me five minutes, okay?"

"I promise not to leave without you," I chuckled.

After Neal and I rode around until there were no other places we wanted to see, we headed to Orleans Street to have lunch at Dooky Chase's. It was still early after we ate, so I coerced him into going home with me for a while and I promised I'd drive him back whenever he was ready.

When we got to the house, Edgar had also arrived and was parking – this time in front of the house. I pulled into the driveway. The three of us met on the porch.

"Hi, Edgar. This is Neal Fontenot, my friend from high school. We haven't seen each other for about six years. Neal, this is Edgar Souté, the lawyer handling my friend's estate."

The men shook hands.

"Let's go inside," I said. "I left the air conditioner on hoping to keep the front room cool." I was pleased to find it had stayed cool.

"I'll leave you two to chat while I make a pitcher of lemonade. "I could hear them talking and was curious to know what they were talking about, but there was no way I'd ask either of them to share. I knew we had to talk about the house; there was no getting around it. So after I took in the lemonade, I brought it up.

"Edgar, what happened with the church committee? Did they make a decision?"

"Yes, they did. I'm almost afraid to tell you what they're asking for."

"Go ahead, I'll listen. Whether they get it or not remains to be seen."

"They feel since they're paying cash, you should give them a discount."

"I must say, I didn't expect that. But it's not an unreasonable request. What do you think, Edgar? Neal, I'd like your opinion, too."

Neal was the first to answer. "I agree. It isn't unreasonable. It does depend, however, on how much of a discount they want."

"Good point," I said. "What about you, Edgar?"

"I agree with both of you. But Claire, you have to give them something. You went up 5,000 dollars from the price I quoted the minister."

"Aye!" Neal groaned. "You really did that, Claire?"

"I did, but here's why." I explained to him what had happened over the course of dealing with Reverend Giles and how I had arrived at the final price of 14,000 dollars. "Neal, take a look at these two rooms and then tell me I'm wrong."

He took a quick look around both floors and agreed with me raising the price if everything he saw was included.

"And...there's an outdoor laundry room and a big yard full of flowers and all sorts of trees," I added.

"Then I definitely agree with the 14,000 dollar selling price," Neal said.

"Okay, Edgar, here's what I'm willing to offer them: a 5% discount. That's 700 dollars. Are they waiting for a call back?"

"Yes."

"Well, call them."

Edgar went into the dining room and made the call. He spoke so softly, we couldn't hear what he was saying. When he returned, he said, "Claire, I'm going to quote them, 'We really want the house for our pastor, so we'll give her what she wants. We just wonder what Sister Gagnier would have done?' So, Claire, you'll get 13,300 dollars. Does that satisfy you?"

"Yes, it does. And...if Jo were alive and selling her house and I was advising her, she'd do exactly what I'm doing. Now, tell me why you sound so angry?"

"It doesn't matter now. Where are the boxes you want me to store for you?"

"Get them another day, will you. I thought about something I wanted to take with me and I don't remember what box I put it in. I'll have to go through all of them until I find it."

"All right. It should take about three days to get all of the paperwork drawn up. I'll see you Friday for the signing, Claire. Neal, it was nice meeting you. Goodnight, you two."

"Damn, please tell me what that was all about." Neal got up and poured himself some lemonade.

"I'm going to quote you, 'Long story, okay.'"

"Okay, spill it. I've got time."

"Neal, after you left school and disappeared with your mother, so many things happened in my life. My grandmother died during my senior year at Clark High and there was no one else in my family I could count on. I'm sure you remember the elderly White woman, Seraphine Menard, I used to talk about, well…"

"The one you used to make drugstore deliveries to on Esplanade?"

"Wow, you do remember. She asked me to live with her and I did. I finished high school and college with her help. She died this past April."

"Damn, I had no idea, Claire. We didn't correspond with anyone here after we left. My mother was afraid my father would find out where we were and come after us. I wish I could have been here for you."

"I know, thank you. After Miss Menard died, I received a large manila envelope from her with a note in it. It turned out she was my grandmother's long lost sister…my great-aunt. She had passed for White most of her life and didn't have the courage to tell me when she was alive."

"Oh, shit, what else was in that envelope?" Neal asked.

"An eighteen-inch, black braid belonging to my great-great-grandmother was wrapped in a kerchief and in a wad of cotton was a diamond on a gold chain. The diamond was in lieu of money to pay off a dressmaking bill – my great-aunt had a dressmaking shop in the French Quarter."

"Geez, the tale thickens," Neal cackled and rolled his eyes.

"You're a comedian! I don't remember you being this funny."

"I wasn't. I learned to lighten up after life kicked my ass a couple of times. Please, continue."

"Sera, that's what most people called my great-aunt, promised me her memoir, but after she died I was told it was unreadable. After I went to New York, I learned Edgar had kept it safe for me and he mailed it to me. I have it with me, of course, and I want you to read it...maybe on the train going back."

"I can't wait; I'm intrigued. But you still haven't told me about Edgar and his problem."

I told Neal what had transpired with Edgar from his correspondence to me in New York, his opening up to me about his life, and to the scene before he'd left the house earlier. I didn't tell him Edgar and I had been intimate the night before.

"He scares me, Neal. I can understand that what his father and mother put him through is unforgivable and that he has a difficult time putting it behind him. But he claims to be in love with me...after knowing me five days. That's insane!"

"No, I think you're wrong there. You're a wonderful, smart woman and you're easy to love. I think it's entirely possible he does love you. His kind of anger is sexual tension, honey."

Neal howled laughing while stomping his feet.

"You're not amusing, Mr. Fontenot." Even though my head was on fire and ready to explode, I still couldn't let myself tell Neal what I'd done.

"If I'm not, why are you smiling? Never mind, go on, my dear."

"Edgar's a *passablanc*, Neal. We're not of the same world. Let him find a White woman."

"She won't be you. Invite him to come to New York for a visit. He'll be anonymous there, so he can be anything he wants to be...white, black, purple or orange. Don't smack me, but I think you'd be interested in him if he didn't have the color problem. Right or wrong?"

"He is interesting and I could be interested, but he doesn't only have a color problem, he's messed up mentally because of who he turned out to be. I have my own past to deal with, and I think I'm handling that well. I don't want to be his woman, his mother and his shrink. I ran away from that a long time ago and I'm not going to take on that kind of situation now. This is one scenario and I've got another one in New York." I told Neal briefly about Frank.

"My Lord, girl, you have men all over the place in love with you. Okay, hoodoo woman, what are you putting in their...lemonade?"

"Oh, so you want to tease me, huh. Well, I don't feel like driving you back downtown tonight. And you never learned to drive, so I can't lend you the car. You're stuck! You'll just have to spend the night. How's that, smartass?"

Neal burst out laughing. "I thought you'd never ask. I'd love to stay over. It's cooler in this house than in mine."

"It's not that cool. I sleep here in the front room on the floor because the air conditioner is in this room. The rest of the house is hotter than hell."

"I don't mind sleeping on the floor. This rug looks pretty cushy. We'll have a pajama party, except I don't have any pajamas."

"You can use one of my bottoms. You're a little taller than me so they'll be floods, but I think they'll fit."

"They're not full of flowers, are they?"

"Hell, yeah, big pink ones! No, I'm just kidding; they're solid blue. You know what, I'm hungry, again."

"Claire, you had a seafood platter at Dookie Chase's for lunch. How can you be hungry already?"

"That was hours ago. Listen, it's too hot to cook in the house. There's a sandwich shop a few blocks from here. They have spectacular po boys. Let's walk over there and get one and some soft drinks. I'm tired of lemonade." I saw Neal start to laugh and I knew he was going to reference the hoodoo woman comment. "Don't you dare say it," I told him. "I don't have to drug anyone. It all happens naturally. Let's get out of here, you scoundrel."

We brought the sandwiches and the soft drinks back to the house to eat and stayed up talking well past midnight. The next morning we got up at 8:00 so that Neal could get back to his house by 9:00 to meet the prospective buyer.

Later that evening, I picked him up with his suitcase. We had decided the night before that he'd stay with me until we went back to New York. I didn't come right out and say it, but I think Neal knew he was my insurance against any other bad scenes with Edgar. But he had no way of knowing he'd also prevent me from having another sexual encounter I might be too weak to resist.

Instead of going back uptown, we went to a little juke-joint somewhere around St. Bernard and Claiborne to have a few drinks, listen to music and dance. It was a dark secluded place, inside and out; a good place for a rendezvous. Neal was so much fun and a helluva dancer.

Many decisions were made those nights in Jo's front room. There were never any conflicting ideas; we agreed on everything. The most important decision we made was that I would not go back to the apartment on Hamilton Terrace. I would live with Neal in Jamaica.

I hadn't left anything behind in the apartment – everything I arrived with, I brought back to New Orleans. I didn't know I'd meet Neal there, but I did have a feeling I'd have to stay for a while, maybe even years. I did take only one thing that didn't belong to me: Luis's leather zippered case. I was sure I'd see him again to return it. I'd get in touch with him without Charlie's and Frank's knowledge.

37

Neal learned that Thursday morning he'd sold the house and all the papers were to be signed Saturday or Sunday. We were able to cash in his airline ticket and then buy our train tickets. We planned to depart on Tuesday of the next week. The realtor had been a friend of Neal's father and Neal trusted him to take his commission and send the balance of the sale money to him in New York.

Another decision we'd made was that the boxes I'd planned to store at the Esplanade house, I would ship to Neal's by Railway Express. We repacked the boxes, leaving out almost all of my books. I was heartbroken, but they were too heavy and would cost a fortune to ship. I selected six I felt I couldn't part with and put the rest on the shelves in the upstairs study. It was too late to have the boxes picked up, so we took them to the station ourselves.

There had not been a call or a visit from Edgar for two days. Because of my lack of trust in him, the two final decisions would have to wait until the next day after the papers for Jo's house were signed and the money handed over to me. I was nervous after all the preparations we'd made to leave the next Tuesday...what if someone became a "hitch in our git-along?" Edgar could become that hitch. I didn't know what he was thinking about my relationship with

Neal, but I wanted him to think we were romantically involved. And, unless he had come to the conclusion on his own that Neal was homosexual, I wasn't going to tell him.

The temperature had cooled a little allowing us to cook the hot sausage we were dying to eat. I wanted to eat everything I'd bought at the grocery store so that I could clean out the refrigerator. The rest of the appliances were clean; I just needed to take out the rest of the food Jo had left and then defrost it. The pantry had lots of canned goods and some jars of fruits and vegetables Jo had either pickled or preserved. I'd let Reverend Giles and his family enjoy all of it.

Neal asked me if I wanted to drive to the French Quarter and get some beignets and café au lait.

"Hell no! I'm not standing in line to get beignets from that little window in the back of the building – the only place they serve Colored folks. My grandfather and grandmother never stood in that line; we never had those beignets. My grandmother made ours." I thought of asking Neal if he'd ever stood in that line, but decided not to. He may have and after what I'd just said, he'd be too embarrassed to admit it.

"Is there anything else you'd like to do this afternoon instead of sitting around here waiting for tomorrow to come? I can tell you're anxious."

"Hmm, I'd like to ride the ferry. I did that a lot when I was a kid. Being near water always quiets my nerves. I also like to take baths when I'm out of sorts."

"Okay, let's go to the Mississippi River and ride the ferry. You can get in the bathtub tonight." Neal pulled me out of the dining room chair. "Let's go, Nerveena, let's get you calm."

We drove down to the foot of Canal Street and parked. Then we rode the ferry back and forth for about an hour and a half. We talked mostly about Neal's life in New York.

"My mom was sick on and off the whole time she was in New York. She worked in the garment district as a seamstress and made really good money. She refused to stay home when she wasn't feeling well. I know it was all for me. She wanted me to get an education and not work as hard as she had done. She thought my being attracted to men would complicate my life. She didn't discourage me, but she didn't want that life for me. I didn't get involved with anyone until after my mom died. And that was a disaster. I think I'm embarrassed to be queer. Maybe it's my mother's voice I hear in my head constantly telling me to get a better life. I don't know what's right for me. Right now, I concentrate on other things, get involved in projects, and go to plays and movies. I keep busy with no time to think. Now I have a brand-new, all-consuming project...you!"

"The hell you do! I can take care of myself, Neal. When we get back to New York, I'm going to get a job and start earning some money. I think I know what my new goal is...I'm going to move to California. I've always wanted to live there, what about you?"

"Me, too! That's something we can plan for, Claire. Let's say in three years we'll be on our way to California. Oh wait, what about getting your master's degree? What about Paris?"

"It was too late to enter a program this year. And now with California plans, I wouldn't start it in New York. I can't plan that far into the future. I can only say - if it's to be, it will happen. As for Paris, I'll get there...sooner or later." I couldn't believe I was saying those things. Had my priorities changed that much? I didn't know, but I did know I felt happy saying them. I wanted to be free and relieved of mental burdens. It seemed this was my chance.

344

It was cool enough for us to sleep in beds. I slept in Jo's bed; Neal slept upstairs. I woke up Friday morning startled by the telephone. I jumped out of bed and ran to the dining room to answer it.

"Hello," I said in a hoarse, sleepy voice.

"Claire, this is Edgar. You sound funny. Are you feeling okay?"

"Yes, I just have a frog in my throat this morning. What time is it, anyway?"

"It's 8:00, Claire."

"Gee, Edgar, why call so early?"

"I thought you'd be happy to know everything has gone well. I have all the necessary papers for you to sign this morning. I'll deliver the signed ones to the church this afternoon and pick up the check. Do you have any idea how lucky you are to have had this go so smoothly? It went off without a hitch."

"Without a hitch, you say." I had to laugh. There was that word again.

"Why is what I said funny?"

"It's just a word I used recently. It really isn't important, Edgar."

"When did you use that word, Claire?" The suspicion was ripe in his voice.

"You've got to be joking. I said it wasn't important; let it go. What time do you plan to be here with those papers?"

"I can come now."

"Edgar, it's 8:00 in the morning! I'm still waking up. Let's make it…10:30, okay?"

"I'll be there." He slammed down the phone so hard, bells rang inside my head.

I heard footsteps on the stairs. "Claire, who's calling this time of morning?" Neal walked into the dining room rubbing his eyes.

"Edgar! He wanted to bring over the papers. I asked him to come at 10:30."

"How did he sound to you?"

"He was pleasant until I told him it was too early to bring the papers here. But he did sound as if he were in a better place than he was Tuesday."

"Good, get dressed. Let's go out for breakfast and then get back here before he arrives."

"Okay, but it can't look like you've spent the night here. He's volatile; I don't trust him. Let's get the papers signed and the check in hand before I tell him what I've decided. I don't know why he wouldn't agree to it, but who knows how he'll react. He has a key, Neal. Jo gave it to him in case she didn't answer the door when he came to check on her. He thinks I'm here alone, so he'll come early. If I don't answer the door, he'll let himself in. Come on, hurry and get dressed. Make your bed and put away your clothes and your suitcase. Uh…the bed is high; shove your stuff under it."

We were out of the house in twenty-five minutes. We drove downtown to a little café on St. Bernard Ave. I knew served breakfast. It was a few blocks away from Corpus Christi Church. Jo and I ate there many times after Sunday Mass. We lingered over breakfast and stopped for a morning paper to make sure we were deliberately late. It was 10:45 when we pulled into the driveway.

Edgar was sitting on the porch in the swing.

"Sorry." I yelled to him. "Neal called and invited me to breakfast. We got back as soon as we could."

Edgar didn't acknowledge I'd spoken to him. The men exchanged greetings and we all went into the house and settled in the dining room.

"Claire, I arrived a little early, and on a whim, I went to the church and was surprised to find the committee having coffee. They were happy to sign all the papers and handed me the check." Edgar took it out of his briefcase and put it on the table. Then he took out the papers and he told me which ones to sign and where to sign them. "I'll see that you get copies of these."

Neal had busied himself reading the paper trying not to seem too interested in what was going on between Edgar and me.

"Now that this house is sold, Edgar, let's talk about the Esplanade house."

"The Esplanade house! You're going to sell it after you promised to rent it to me." He slammed his hand on the table startling Neal and me.

"Edgar," I said his name quietly, "that's not what I want to tell you. You were given so little by your father and mother – there was no love or nurturing, not even a place you could say was your home. You deserved to have those things. By the time Leonard died, he was once again faltering financially. Joshua Stern told me he was close to being bankrupt. I must believe that what he willed to you, the businesses, aren't worth very much, if anything. I would like to give you the Esplanade house. I'd like you to have something that isn't mortgaged. There are no strings attached. Please accept this from me. Bring the papers for me to sign it over to you."

Edgar was so taken aback that he closed his eyes and held on to the arms of his chair, and when he opened them, he just stared at me for a long time. Neal and I sat quietly watching him and waiting for him to speak. Finally, he said, "Do you mean what you just said, Claire?"

"Of course, I mean it. I think you're a great guy and you'll find someone here in New Orleans to live with you in your world. You shouldn't have to give up who you are in order to love and make a life with the person you choose.

Now you'll have a house, so go and find a wife and have a big family."

"You do mean it. I accept, Claire. Thank you." Edgar wanted to cry, but because Neal was there, I watched him silently command his tears to stay put. "I do love you, Claire, but I understand now that you don't love me and I'm going to be okay with that. One day I'll get over you because I can see you'll be happy with Neal."

The truth about Neal almost escaped my lips. But I couldn't trust the situation just yet. "Edgar, I've got another announcement. I'm not going back to the apartment on Hamilton Terrace. I'm putting Frank and his cronies in the past. I'm going to live with Neal."

"I'm happy for you, Claire. You don't need Frank in your life. But I've already told you that, haven't I?"

I nodded and then picked up the check and held it out to him. "How much commission do you get out of this?"

"Not a dime. How can I take any money from you when you've given me a house worth three or four times what this house is worth?"

"Really, you don't want your commission?" It was my time to be shocked.

"No, I don't want any money from the sale of this house. You're planning to go back to school for your master's. With that check, you may be able to get through without working." Edgar put the papers in his briefcase and then stood up. "I'll come on Sunday afternoon with the papers for the Esplanade house. When are you returning to New York? I'd like to let Reverend Giles know when the house and the car will be available."

"Neal and I are going back by train Tuesday. I'll leave the car key here on the table."

"Oh, do you still want me to store those boxes for you?"

"It isn't necessary now that I'm going to live with Neal. We shipped the boxes yesterday by Railway Express."

"Then I'll leave you two to get things wrapped up in New Orleans. I'll see you on Sunday."

The next two days flew by. We stripped all the beds and washed all the linen. It had gotten hot again and we were once again sleeping on the rug in the front room.

Edgar came on Sunday with the papers for me to sign over the Esplanade house to him. I had almost forgotten about the utility bills. When I asked about them, he told me he'd call the companies on Tuesday and have the services put in the buyer's name. He'd have the closing bills sent directly to me in New York. I gave him Neal's address and telephone number.

Edgar handed me a large manila envelope. "These are the things Mrs. Gagnier wanted you to have. She didn't believe in banks. She already paid me for the drafting of her will and for helping you plan and manage her funeral."

The fact that it was a large manila envelope unnerved me. I immediately wondered if it contained the same kind of jarring news I'd received in the last one. I took a long deep breath before opening it. I poured the contents out on the table. It was Jo's prayer book, her rosary, her gold cross and chain, and 1,800 dollars.

"Edgar, how could she have this much money? She worked for next to nothing taking in washing and ironing. Are you sure she paid you for the services you provided us?"

"Yes, Claire, she paid me. If I didn't collect for my services rendered, I'd go to the poor house fast. Jo didn't have many needs; she saved most of her money. Well, you two, I'm going to say goodbye. I won't see you again before you leave. Neal, take care of this special lady."

"You know I will, Edgar. She means a lot to me." Neal shook hands with him. "I'm going out on the porch for a bit. I'll let you two say a private goodbye."

After Neal closed the front door, I went over to Edgar and we hugged and kissed each other passionately. We held onto to each other until he broke away and walked slowly out of the house. I felt something happen to my heart, but I chose to ignore it.

On Monday, I left Neal at home to clean and defrost the refrigerator. I went downtown to my bank to withdraw the balance of my savings I'd left there when I went to New York. I had them add the money Jo left me and give me a cashier's check for the total amount. Next I went back uptown to the church's bank to cash their check. They refused to give me the money until Reverend Giles came to the bank to personally identify me. They also issued me a cashier's check. My last errand was finding the food for our train trip. I bought potted ham, canned tuna, crackers, cheese, raw carrots and celery, some pastries, fruit, and some candy bars. I planned to take a can opener and two knives and forks from the house. There'd be no soft drinks because they'd be too hot to drink. We'd have to drink the train's fountain water.

When I got back to the house, I decided what I was going to wear for the train trip: a cotton, short sleeve blouse and a long full skirt with pockets. It reminded me of Sera and where she hid her gun. I folded the checks and put them in one of the pockets and stitched it closed.

Early Tuesday morning, we were up and dressed before 7:00. We packed our non-perishable food for the train in Luis's leather bag. I grabbed a handful of paper napkins and shoved them into the bag. The memory of finding Jo's linen napkin that contained a ten dollar bill and a note on my trip to New York made my heart heavy.

The driver of the cab I'd called suddenly blew the horn. Neal picked up our suitcases to take them out to the taxi. "Don't forget to bring the bag with the food," he said to me over his shoulder.

It was the first time I'd allowed myself to cry for Jo. "Goodbye, Jo. Thank you for being so good to me when you were here and even now that you're gone. I put your Empire State Building in the crook of your arm when you were in your casket - the way you had it when I found you that morning. I thought you might want to take it with you to show your friends. I'm going to start that new life we talked about, Jo. Wish me luck. I'll be seeing…"

"Claire," Neal yelled, "c'mon. We have to go."

I closed and locked the door. I put the key under the flower pot near the swing.

About the Author

Claudette Carrida Jeffrey, a native New Orleanian, is a retired teacher who lives in Northern California. *The Color of Life* is her second book in a four book series. Book one, *A Brown Paper Bag and A Fine Tooth Comb* (2012), begins the coming of age story of, Claire Soublet, a young Creole of Color growing up in 1940s and 50s New Orleans.